· EPOCA ·

THE TREE OF ECROF

EPOCA

THE TREE OF ECROF

CREATED BY

KOBE BRYANT

WRITTEN BY

IVY CLAIRE

GRANITY STUDIOS

COSTA MESA, CALIFORNIA

For Vanessa. Thank you for always being the Realist to my Dreamer.

—Kobe Bryant

For Rakey Drammeh

—Ivy Claire

1

PRETIA

THE FLAME

PRETIA PAUSED ON THE GRAND STAIRCASE OF Castle Airim and looked over at the bowl of the Athletos Stadium, where the Epic Games opening ceremonies were held every four years. Earlier this summer the stadium had been filled with the best athletes from all over the land, from the Rhodan Islands to the distant Sandlands. But now it was empty. Towering Corinthian columns shaded her and threw long shadows from the colonnade down the steps while statues of her ancestors looked on from their pedestals. From where she stood she had a perfect view of the white marble seats that rose high into the air, the carved thrones for her parents, the black cinder track, and the winners' podium. It was her favorite view in the entire world—the best view of the most impressive stadium in the land. Pretia's dream wasn't to sit in the royal thrones and look down on the games as her parents had done, but to be on the field as a competitor.

The white marble looked even more brilliant than usual in the late-afternoon sun. The air was clean and dry, with a summer breeze that carried the salty ocean scent from the harbor up to the castle grounds.

Today the stadium had not been used for its intended purpose—

sports. Instead, it had been converted into the site of an elaborate feast for Pretia's tenth birthday. The party had been lavish, dozens of courses of the finest foods from the farthest corners of Epoca—Cretian honeycakes, figs from Phoenis, Berberian pistachios and persimmons. There had been towers of blue grapes, pyramids of juicy oranges, trays of sizzling meats, and steaming baskets of breads. For the adults, there had been fountains of the best Megaran wine, and for the children, Spirit Water from the Delphic Springs that cascaded down into cups from a waterfall built for the occasion.

There had been troupes of singers and dancers from the exotic outlands. There had been trained animals and acrobats. But one thing had been missing: fun.

Because Pretia's birthday was never just Pretia's birthday. It was a state occasion of the highest importance. Pretia Praxis-Onera was Princess of Epoca, heir to the Crown of Dreams and the Throne of Fears. And Pretia wasn't just any old princess. She was the first noble-born child to have parents from both royal houses in Epoca. Her father, King Airos, a Dreamer, was head of House Somni, and her mother, Queen Helena, a Realist, ruled House Reila.

The king and queen's marriage had been a scandal that had reached from the tip-top of Mount Oly in the East to the Rhodan Islands in the western sea and even to the distant outlands of Phoenis and Alkebulan. Marriage between the two houses was unheard of, especially among the highest ranks of Epocan nobility. But Airos and Helena ignored the gossip that said their union was improper and shameful. And when Pretia was born—many, many years later, after much worry and anxiety that the supposedly unnatural marriage would not produce an heir—the royal family named her the Child of Hope and declared that she was going to bring a new era of peace to Epoca.

Thinking of this now, looking out at the remnants of the gala left on the field, Pretia rolled her eyes. Child of Hope, indeed. She didn't care about any of that, especially not on her birthday. She just wanted a normal party, like a normal kid. But the truth was, she was rarely, if ever, treated as normal.

Pretia's birthday was the only time each year the royal houses Reila and Somni came together in their entirety. And not even the supposed Child of Hope could make it a relaxed occasion. Pretia's whole extended family had been in attendance, all her royal aunts, uncles, and second cousins on both her mother's and father's sides. Hundreds of people she'd never met before, or if she had, she'd forgotten. Hundreds of people, Pretia had begun to understand, who resented her parents' marriage: the union between the artistic, creative, and sometimes distracted Dreamers and the practical, determined, and often overly competitive Realists.

That morning, as she'd stood in her room, forced into her fancy party dress, her mother had once more reminded her of exactly how important she was to the country. How everyone was expecting great things of her. How she was going to be the most important queen ever to rule Epoca. And of course this meant that at the party, she had to behave. She couldn't twitch or scratch her nose or look bored or play with her food or laugh or whisper. Not that she had anyone to play, laugh, or whisper with. Which was why Pretia so vehemently disliked her birthday, year after boring year. It felt more like a state dinner than a celebration.

She'd overheard from eavesdropping on the castle workers' kids that at real birthday parties, there were games and songs and adventures instead of dull speeches and a formal procession of relatives paying their respects, kissing Pretia's cheeks with their old-people lips or limply shaking her hand.

Of course, there had been presents, *so many presents*, lavish tributes from the lands under her parents' rule. There were silks from the Sandlands and sea crystals from the Rhodan Islands. There were dresses made by the blind weavers on top of Mount Oly and bracelets from the silver mines of Chaldis. But no one could give her what she actually wanted for her birthday—grana. And not just any grana, but the highest level of godly given talent that would allow her to be an Epic Athlete. Now her tenth birthday had come and gone and she still had no grana at all, not even an inkling.

She ducked behind a column, closing her eyes and taking stock of her body—her toes, her legs, her stomach, her arms, wrists, fingers, neck, and head. All of it felt the same. All of it felt like it always did—normal, unchanged. And in this case, there was nothing good about being normal.

For a year she'd been hearing the castle kids whisper about how their grana had come, which filled her with jealousy and anxiety. She'd listened to them discuss their heightened senses—their tingling fingers, their twitching noses, and new exciting ways of seeing and interacting with the world. But nothing had happened to Pretia. Was it because she was half Dreamer, half Realist that she didn't have grana? Was her birth really as unholy as the dark gossip said? She was starting to worry. Was this the reason she hadn't yet received her invitation to attend the prestigious Ecrof Academy the next year, something that nearly every heir to the throne of Epoca before her had done?

Although Pretia had no idea what having grana felt like, she could easily identify it in others, especially the talented Epic Athletes she'd watched during the games in the stadium right outside the castle. It was what allowed the best basketball players to hang motionless in the air, as if the laws of gravity didn't apply to them, as they dunked the ball. It was what made the best gymnasts easily execute twisting backflips on a four-inch beam as if they were standing on a floor exercise mat. It was how in football, running backs could detect a path through the defensive line and run through it as if they were on a wide-open field. Or how amazing tennis players carved impossible angles with the ball so that their shots clipped the smallest millimeter of the line time and time again.

Pretia understood what grana was and she understood she didn't have it. She took one last look at the stadium now from her perch on the stairs, trying to imagine what it felt like to sprint around it, run, jump, and race as if your body were propelled by some magical energy, and then headed into the castle.

She passed through the towering Grand Atrium and up the stairs to the Hall of the Gods of Granity, the longest room in Castle Airim. Pretia guessed it was twice the length of a basketball court and half as narrow. She could kick a soccer ball just over halfway down the hall before it rolled and throw a tennis ball less than a quarter of the distance of the room. Not that she ever would. Gods forbid. At the far end of the hall, closest to the Atrium, the Granity Flame burned in a copper bowl, casting creepy shadows along the hall's rounded ceiling.

There were eight pedestals in the hall, four along either wall. On each of the pedestals sat a bust of one of the Gods of Granity. Seven of these stared out at passersby. But one remained shrouded, a black cloth draped over it. This was the pedestal of Hurell, the God of Suffering, who had warred with the other gods and ushered in the dark ages in Epoca.

Like most modern citizens of Epoca, Pretia didn't actually believe in the gods. They were myths, stories from long ago, a way to explain the culture of the land. If she hadn't grown up in the castle, where they were obliged to keep the old traditions alive, she wouldn't have thought about them at all.

Usually Pretia sprinted through the hall, but today she moved more slowly, looking at each bust in turn. Maybe, just maybe, if she prayed to the Gods of Granity, her grana would come. She approached the large copper bowl that held the Granity Flame—the eternal fire that the people of Epoca had sworn they would never let die. It was from this flame that the Epic Torch was lit every fourth year to signal the start of the Epic Games.

Pretia took a thin willow twig from a wooden box and held it to the flame until it ignited. Then she walked down the hall, lighting the fragrant oil in the ceremonial holder that was carved into the pedestal in front of the bust of each god. She whispered their names in turn as she went: Cora, Metus, Somni, Reva, Menti, Prosi, Dominu—Love, Fear, Dreams, Reality, Mind, Process, and Ego.

Each time the oil in front of one of the gods sprang to life with an orange flame, Pretia uttered the same prayer. It was a version of a prayer she'd overheard some of the Epic Athletes saying before their competition: "In exchange for this flame, grant me the grace of grana so that I might serve my country and uphold the Epic tradition." Seven times she uttered this prayer until she reached the end of the hall.

Still holding the burning willow twig, Pretia looked back at the seven small flames lighting up the marble busts and making shadows dance on the walls. Only Hurell's shrouded column was dark. Without a second thought she found herself walking back down the hall and dipping the burning willow into the brass bowl in front of Hurell's covered statue. Praying to Hurell had been forbidden since the end of the Dark Age of Suffering and the start of the Age of Grana. But no one really prayed to any of the gods anymore. So what did it really matter?

Pretia held her breath and lowered the flaming willow. In an instant a ghostly silver flame sprang to life. She jumped back as the flame climbed high, illuminating the black cloth draped over the marble head of Hurell. "Hurell," she whispered, "God of Suffering. In exchange for this flame, grant me the grace of grana so that I might serve my country and uphold the Epic tradition."

Pretia stared at the leaping flame, fascinated and a little frightened by what she had done. As she watched the silvery flame lick the walls of its holder, she heard footsteps approaching from the Grand Atrium. Panicked, Pretia looked for a way to extinguish the fire in the ceremonial bowl—some water or a cloth. But she saw none. Even though people didn't really believe all the old stuff about the gods anymore, it was still strictly forbidden to pray to Hurell. It was one of the gravest crimes in Epoca.

The footsteps were getting closer now. With no other option, Pretia sprinted away as fast as she could before someone caught her at her mischief—up two flights of marble stairs, down a colonnade, and into her bedroom, where the light winds were blowing her white linen curtains inward like billowing ghosts.

Pretia tore off her party dress, kicked off her fancy sandals, found her favorite shorts and shirt, then flung herself down on her bed, out of breath.

Someone had already piled her gifts in her sitting room. But she only squeezed her eyes shut, focusing all her energy on the burning flames she had lit. Maybe, just maybe, the gods would grant her wish.

There was a tapping on the door to her bedroom. "Pretia?"

Pretia heard the door open before the large curtain that divided her bedroom from her sitting room was pulled back. Anara—her nurse, her babysitter, and her closest confidante—stood at the foot of her bed, her arms crossed over her chest in mock anger. Anara's long blond hair, now with the first threads of gray streaking away from her temples, was braided and wound around her head like a crown. She wore a simple dark blue dress—the color of House Reila, Queen Helena's house. Anara's movements were gentle and slow, and Pretia often thought that she looked like she had come from another planet entirely, so different was she from the rest of the inhabitants of Epoca, who were devoted to the world of competitive sports. She was like a fairy in a world of dragons.

"Are you worn out from your birthday celebrations?" Anara asked, sitting at the edge of Pretia's bed.

Pretia opened her mouth to explain—but how could she? How could she tell Anara, without coming across as a spoiled princess, that she wasn't worn out, but rather disappointed. And a little bit bored.

"It's okay," Anara said, stroking Pretia's hair. "I understand."

That was one of the things Pretia liked best about Anara. She often didn't have to explain anything to her. Her nurse just knew what she was thinking, kind of like magic. Sometimes, Pretia thought there actually was something a little bit mystical about Anara. In addition to being her nurse, Anara was a Flamekeeper, which meant she had sworn an oath to keep the old ways of the Gods of Granity alive. Pretia often wondered if this gave Anara a closer connection to a world that hovered just out of sight.

"Were you wondering why I hadn't given you a gift?" Anara asked.

Pretia glanced over at the towering pile of presents guiltily. She hadn't noticed. But before she could apologize, Anara pulled out a box from behind her back. "Happy birthday, Pretia."

Pretia took the package. It was wrapped in old foil paper and tied with blue and purple ribbons—the color of each of her parents' houses. Although Anara was a Realist, she always respected Pretia's mixed heritage, even if most other people didn't. Pretia carefully untied the ribbons and pulled away the paper. Inside, she found a box. She opened the top. Her eyes widened in delight.

She was holding in her hands the most beautiful pair of golden sneakers she had ever seen—a pair of Grana Gleams. "Anara," she cried, flinging her arms around her nurse. "Thank you!"

"Aren't you going to put them on?"

Pretia slipped on the golden shoes. They fit like they had been made for her, which they probably had.

"Many centuries ago, not long after the gods granted us grana, a merchant traveling to the country of Tanis in the continent of Alkebulan returned with a barrel of their most sacred rubber," Anara explained. "The soles of these shoes are made from the last rubber left from that barrel. Only twenty pairs were produced."

The shoes felt cool like quicksilver, and the golden leather sparkled in the late-afternoon sun. Pretia sat back down on her bed.

"So what are you waiting for?" Anara asked.

"They're beautiful," Pretia said. "They're the most beautiful shoes in the world. But—"

"But what?"

"What's the point of running shoes if I don't have grana?" Pretia asked.

Anara stroked Pretia's hair again. "Pretia, your grana will come."

"That's what everybody keeps telling me," Pretia said.

And it was true—everyone was concerned with Pretia's grana, from the members of the high council to the Epic Priests down to her own parents. Because if she didn't have grana, she couldn't rule Epoca. This law had been written ages ago in the Scrolls of Epoca—the contract between the gods and men signed in exchange for peace in the land. But Pretia cared less about that than she did about one other thing—no grana meant no sports, because without grana she stood no chance against anyone, not least of all against an Epic Athlete. Without grana, she'd never be able to compete.

"Don't you want to try them out?" Anara asked.

"Of course," Pretia said. But here was another problem. Who could she play sports with? No one. Her life was filled with dull tutored lessons on Epoca Law and the History of the Age of Grana. Most of her days, she was left to roam the castle alone, inventing all sorts of games to amuse herself.

Pretia was about to explain this to Anara. But she stopped herself when she saw the eager look on her nurse's face.

"Come on, get going," Anara said.

"Okay!" Pretia said, leaping off the bed. She smiled over her shoulder at her nurse, then sprinted out of her room, down a large marble staircase and into the Hall of the Gods, where the flame in front of Hurell's shrouded bust was still burning. Pretia didn't stop to put it out. The shoes felt too good on her feet for that.

She raced through the Atrium, down the Grand Staircase. She

gave a quick wave to the marble statues of her ancestors. Then sprinted down the steps onto the castle grounds. She took a deep breath of the fresh air. The sky was a perfect lapis blue—the same hue as the sea. The sunbaked earth was the color of golden clay, and the crystal and limestone embedded in the ground glinted.

It was like magic, the way she took off from the bottom step and sprinted around the edge of the stadium. It was almost as if the shoes were enchanted. It was as if they were moving her feet for her.

She darted past the castle gates and into a thick grove of fig trees. Normally she would stop to pluck a few of the ripe, dusky purple fruits and spit the stems as she ran. But not this time.

She wanted to keep moving. She needed to keep moving. The wind blew her black hair behind her. Her arms kept time with her feet, everything urging her on, on, on. Pretia looked down to see the dazzling blur of the golden running shoes speeding across dusty clay earth, moving faster than she had ever thought possible. It was as if her feet didn't belong to her at all.

What had Anara done to these golden shoes? What magical spring had she dipped them in? Who had she asked to bless them? It was as if they had given Pretia superpowers. It was as if they had given her grana.

Pretia skidded to a stop, tripped over a tree root, and went head over heels until she came to rest, her knees streaked with reddish dust.

What if it wasn't the shoes? What if it *was* grana? Finally, after all this time.

Pretia lay on her back and looked up at the sun through the craggy branches of an olive tree. For the second time that afternoon she began to take stock of her body. Her fingers were tingling. Her muscles were twitching. She could smell different things in the air—the scent of the figs, the warm earth, the seawater hundreds of feet below the cliffs. And she could hear, too, the sound of individual waves crashing, the individual songs of dozens of different birds, the underground river that fed the castle's lakes and reservoir.

Pretia clapped a hand over her mouth. It was finally happening!

Her grana had arrived.

She could rule Epoca. But even better, she might become an Epic Athlete after all. And now, most certainly, her invitation to Ecrof would come!

She leaped to her feet. And once more, she was off. Faster this time. Faster and faster and faster. And then the strangest thing happened—it was almost as if she were *watching* herself run. It was as if she were standing back and another Pretia was sprinting on ahead, doing all the work, feeling all the pain that should have been in her legs and chest after so much exercise.

But before Pretia could figure out what was happening, a chorus of kids' voices rose over the woods. She stopped running—the illusion of being two people ceased. Then she tucked herself behind a tree at the end of the Royal Woods and peered into a clearing along the edge of one of the towering cliffs that dropped down to the sea. A group of castle workers' kids were chasing one another around the grass and laughing.

Suddenly one of them caught sight of Pretia and stopped running. Soon the entire group was staring at her.

"I'm sorry," Pretia said. "I didn't mean to interrupt."

The kids all looked at her, unsure about how to address the princess.

"You can keep playing," Pretia said.

The kids exchanged glances. Finally, one of them—Dinara, the Games Trainer's daughter—spoke. "You're not going to tell, are you?"

"Tell what?" Pretia asked.

"We're supposed to be helping after the, er, your birthday party. Not playing around."

Pretia's heart sank. She would always be the princess, treated differently because of her royal birth. "I'm sure there are enough adults to handle that," she said. "Anyway, if they want to throw boring parties, they can do all the cleanup."

The kids looked at each other, unsure whether to laugh.

"I mean, you guys probably don't have to sit around and listen to speeches about the tradition of our great land on *your* birthdays."

"Absolutely not! I'd rather jump in the sea," Davos, the son of the Royal Cook, exclaimed. "On my birthday, my father cooks everything I could possibly imagine eating and invites all of my friends over and we stuff our faces until we are sick and then stay up all night."

Pretia shuffled from foot to foot. She was itching to keep moving and to test her grana. "What are you guys doing?" she finally asked.

Once more the kids exchanged curious glances. Finally, Davos spoke. "Playing tag."

"Oh," Pretia said, feeling incredibly stupid. Of course that's what they were doing. Only someone who had never played tag before would ask such a dumb question. Only someone like Pretia.

"Do you want to play?" Dinara asked.

At ten years old, Pretia had never played with other kids before—at least not normal games like tag. First the golden sneakers, then her grana, and now a chance to play tag. Her birthday was certainly turning around.

"Sure," she said, stepping into the clearing.

The kids surrounded her. "Okay," Davos said, tapping Pretia on the shoulder. "You're It."

Immediately the kids scattered. Pretia stayed put. She swiveled her head, looking at the group spread out across the clearing.

"Don't you know the rules?" Dinara said. "Chase us!"

"I was just—" Pretia began. But instead of inventing excuses for why she hadn't moved, she began to run. The first person she caught was Christos, the son of the Royal Gardener. He screamed when she tapped his shoulder. He whispered to Pretia, "You're supposed to say 'You're It' when you tag someone," then sprinted away after the twin daughters of the Keeper of the Scrolls, who were near the edge of the forest.

The game whirled around and around the clearing. Pretia mostly avoided getting tagged. Occasionally someone got her, but in no time she had tagged someone else. After a while, Pretia grew distracted, paying more attention to the new sensations summoned by her grana than to the game of tag itself. Everything from the earth beneath her feet to the smell of the salty sea air felt heightened. When she tagged another player, she could feel a transmission of energy in her fingers. From what she'd overheard from her distant cousins, these sensations would settle as her grana developed and as Pretia learned to control them. But for now, they were pinging around in her head, coursing through her arms and legs, making her run faster and jump higher.

Dinara was It again and quickly tagged Pretia, who had momentarily stopped running, listening to the leaves rustling in the Royal Woods behind her. *Do the leaves always make this sort of noise?* she wondered. Would they always sound like an orchestra being played by the wind?

"You're It!" Dinara cried. "Princess Pretia, come on!"

It took Pretia a moment to snap back to reality. "You don't need to call me Princess," Pretia said. But by then the other kids had spread out across the field except for Davos, who stood smack in the center, challenging her. "Come and get me," he said, laughing. He was dancing from side to side, smiling. "Pretia, come and get me."

Pretia stood at the edge of the woods as the sounds of the forest and sea and grasses crashed in her ears, as her fingers tingled, her legs twitched, her heart raced, and her lungs filled with delicious air. She felt invincible. Of course she could catch Davos. That was nothing. She could do that and a whole lot more.

Then it happened again. She was standing by the trees at the edge of the Royal Woods as she saw herself take off and sprint in Davos's direction. This second self was a blur, an arrow flying at an extraordinary pace, speeding toward Davos.

Davos hesitated and Pretia watched herself—*watched herself*—race toward him at an amazingly fast pace, faster than she could even imagine running. She watched herself tag him, but not simply tag him. She tagged him with such force that she pushed him toward the edge of the cliff. From where she was standing at the edge of the woods, she watched Davos stumble and watched herself stumbling after him, almost tackling him. "You're It," she heard herself shout. But it was too late. Pretia watched herself watch Davos fall over the cliff and disappear from sight.

A cry from all the kids at once brought Pretia back to herself. She was no longer standing by the trees, but at the edge of the cliff, back in her own body.

What had she done? What had just happened? Where was Davos? Had she killed him? Had her grana killed him? What was she capable of?

Holding her breath, not wanting to look but knowing she absolutely had to, she crept to the edge and looked down, expecting to see a sheer drop to the sea below. Instead, what she saw was a more gradual hill with a ledge on which Davos was lying, moaning and clutching his left arm. "It's broken," he cried.

The kids all peered over Pretia's shoulder as she knelt down to help Davos up. But before she could, Dinara elbowed her out of the way. "We'll help him," she said.

Suddenly all the kids had crowded in front of Pretia.

"It—It was an accident," she stammered. "It was." Because of course it was—she hadn't meant to tag Davos so hard. She hadn't meant to push him off the cliff. But she had. She had stood back and *watched* as she had done it. Her grana had made her do it. Her grana was uncontrollable.

Pretia stepped back from the group and the kids closed ranks, leaving her out. She watched them lift Davos back up to the clearing. Dinara flung his good arm over her shoulder as she prepared to help him walk back to the castle.

Pretia wanted to tell them she'd make sure he got the best medical care. She wanted to tell them that she would make sure he got everything he needed to help him heal—the royal treatment. But she didn't dare speak. She was too horrified by what she had done.

She raced back to the castle. For once, what she wanted more than anything was to be alone. She sprinted up the steps, where she imagined her ancestors were staring at her in horror, through the Atrium and up into the Hall of the Gods. Most of the flames had died out. Only those in front of Cora, Somni, and Hurell still burned. *Hurell.* Pretia skidded to a stop. Her stomach flipped. Her heart felt like a cold stone. Had Hurell granted her wish? Had the Fallen God granted her grana?

She could feel the panic starting to rise in her throat. She clutched her stomach. She'd lit his flame and her grana had come. And not just any grana. But a grana that seemed evil. A grana that had helped her injure another kid.

Taking a deep breath, Pretia blew on the flame in Hurell's ceremonial bowl. Once, twice, three times she blew, but it only made the oil burn stronger. There was no choice but to let it go out on its own like the others around it had. There was no reversing what she had done.

Her grana had come from Hurell. Her grana was cursed.

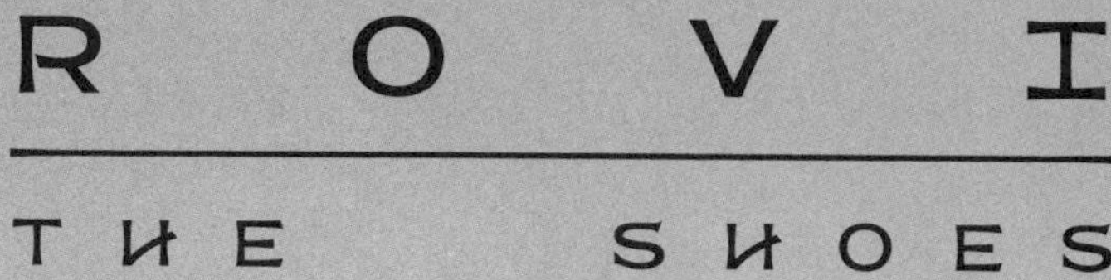

2 ROVI
THE SHOES

ROVI COVERED HIS EARS AS THE SORNA HORN blasted across the Upper City of Phoenis. Overhead, on the bridge that spanned the river Durna, he could hear the first carts rolling toward the Alexandrine Market. He sat up, his back stiff as usual from sleeping on the hard ground. It was market day. There was no time to waste.

Market days were the best days for stealing, everyone knew that. Which was why merchants tried to hire Star Stealers to be lookouts, paying them with a measly piece of fruit for a whole day's work. Rovi would never do that. Six hours of standing in one spot in order to get a peach was not good business. And it was boring.

He preferred to steal.

Not a lot, and never from the vendors who couldn't afford it. He stole only what he needed for a few days. Honeycakes from the baker with the line down the street. A bag of plums from the fruit seller whose stand was so overstocked that he didn't care when a pile of oranges or figs tumbled to the ground.

But Rovi knew he had to be cautious and keep an eye out. Not just because of the merchants and their lookouts and the red-turbaned Phoenician guards—members of a severe military order—

who patrolled the marketplace, but also because of the other gangs of Star Stealers who might either rat him out to the authorities or steal from the best stalls before he got there. Everyone wanted to catch Swiftfoot, as he was known. Luckily, no one had.

Rovi had been on his own ever since his father had died. His mother had died many years earlier, when he was only two years old, and he had barely any memory of her at all.

His father, once one of the brightest minds in Epoca, had wound up a beggar on the streets of Phoenis, the capital city of the Sandlands region. And once his father was gone, Rovi had become just another lost boy, a Star Stealer, neither Dreamer nor Realist. A missing soul.

It didn't take long for him to become famous in Phoenis, or rather infamous. From the head of the Phoenician guards to the common street criminals, everyone had heard of Swiftfoot. He had stolen an entire side of beef on its way to the head magistrate. He had stolen a wedding cake made for a visiting Realist princess. He had stolen a crate of fish freshly arrived from the Rhodan Islands. He had stolen a plum right out of the hand of the head of the guards himself and eaten it while running backward to avoid capture.

But today, Rovi wasn't out to steal food. There was something else he needed—running shoes. His last pair, hand-me-downs from Issa, had worn thin. There was a hole in the sole of one shoe, and the rubber on the other had come unglued and flapped loudly when Rovi ran. And the last thing a good thief needed was to make additional noise.

He rolled up his bedding and stashed it in the archway under the Draman Bridge where he and the rest of Issa's gang slept. He could hear the carts rumbling overheard as merchants flooded into Phoenis. He gnawed a day-old crust of bread and took a swallow from a canteen someone had filled from a public fountain. For the last time, he hoped, he laced up his battered running shoes.

Today was the final market day of the month—the largest one—when vendors from all over the Sandlands and even from some of the other regions of Epoca traveled to Phoenis. This was the day that the best goods would be available, not just the local crafts, but ones perfected in distant lands. This was the day that the Alkebulan rubber merchant would arrive with his stall of bold and brilliant running sneakers. And Rovi could think of nothing better than a pair of those sleek, gleaming shoes—not a three-course meal, not a roof over his head, not even a bag full of gold coins. He wanted a pair of gold Grana Gleams. And he was going to get them.

It was early, but the sun was already strong. The first merchants and customers had wound their scarves around their heads to protect themselves from the bright glare. A light wind was blowing, enough to kick up some sand from the streets, but nothing like the sandstorms that could shut down the market for hours, driving everyone away from the stalls, choking the air with yellow grit that flew up your nose and into your eyes. Rovi did his best work during the sandstorms, using the sandy tornado as cover to dodge from vendor to vendor, taking what he wanted and slipping away literally unseen.

But there would be no such luck today. The weather was not on Rovi's side.

He crossed the bridge, darting among carts filled with silky shorts and shirts, handcrafted sandals, woven bags, and hammered bronze replicas of Epic Medals. When he reached the Alexandrine Plaza, Rovi's nostrils were filled with hundreds of tantalizing smells at once—caramelizing meats, exotic spices, buttery breads, sweet fruits ripening in the sun. His stomach growled. But he couldn't be careless. If he drew attention to himself too soon, he'd risk being banned from the market for good.

Rovi glanced up at the blue and purple onion-domed turrets overhead just in time to see the sorna player step out onto a balcony. Immediately the next blast of the sorna filled the air, telling the people of Phoenis that the market was open for business.

Rovi ducked into an archway at the eastern side of the plaza.

From his lookout he could keep an eye on the Alkebulan merchant setting up the stand. He had to get everything perfect. It wasn't just taking the shoes; it was taking the right size. And this meant doing something that might expose him—scouting the stand up close.

After an hour, the market had filled up so customers were shoulder to shoulder, bumping and jostling one another. Rovi hoped they wouldn't notice a kid in their midst, and not just any kid, but one who wore the telltale rags and had the unwashed face of a notorious Star Stealer. A boy who wore neither purple nor blue, who was clearly neither Dreamer nor Realist.

Rovi darted into the crowd and approached the Alkebulan rubber merchant's stall. There on the front row, just at his head height, were the gold Grana Gleams. They were the most beautiful shoes Rovi had ever seen—delicate mesh that looked like mercury, thick gold soles, and metallic laces that he knew would look like shooting stars as he raced through the streets.

Once, twice, three times he passed by the stall until he spotted his size—the fourth box in the stack. It would be a difficult grab, impossible without knocking the other boxes over. And that would mean drawing attention to himself, causing a commotion. But there would be no other way. He'd have to reveal himself, and then he'd have to run like everything in his world depended on it . . . which it did. To be caught would mean to be taken away to one of the dreaded workschools where he would spend the next eight years packing sand into bricks for the master builders.

After a final pass by the stand, Rovi was satisfied that he knew exactly which box to take. He headed back to the archway to plan his escape route. He passed a stand where a young woman was grilling skewers of golden beef from the sacred pastures. The smell was too much and he stopped, knocking into a man in front of him.

The man turned and looked Rovi right in the eye. He was short and bald and had the paler complexion of someone from Hydros or

Helios, the major cities on mainland Epoca. Rovi froze, the horror of discovery running through him. He'd tried to be invisible, a ghost, someone who slipped through the market unseen. And now this man was staring right at him.

"Are you hungry?" the man asked.

It took all of Rovi's willpower not to tell him the truth. He was starving.

"I bet if I asked nicely, this young woman might add an extra skewer onto my order for you."

Rovi bit his lip and shook his head. He clamped his hand over his stomach to silence its growling. "No, thank you," he muttered.

"Are you—" But before the man could finish talking, Rovi had darted away, back to the shelter of the arch. On any other day, he would have taken the stranger's offer in an instant. But today was not any other day. Today was the day he was getting his Grana Gleams.

From the shadows, Rovi kept an eye on the market. He watched the man eat his skewers then vanish into the crowd. Rovi darted through the covered archways that bordered the market on all sides. He leaped over musicians and beggars and all sorts of peddlers who were confined to the edges of the action. He made three circles, keeping an eye on the market, searching for the mysterious bald man—the one person who might identify him. Satisfied he was no longer in the plaza, Rovi returned to his spot across from the Alkebulan rubber merchant to wait for his window.

He didn't have to wait long. A large group of girls swarmed the stand and began examining the Gleams. They crowded the stall, passing boxes around as they sought the right sizes and colors. Soon the stand was in chaos with shoes and boxes all over the place. The merchant was flustered, turning around and around to search his inventory for different sizes and styles for his customers.

This was Rovi's chance. He knew it. He bolted from the archway, down the line of stalls that led to the rubber merchant's. There was a hand on his shoulder. He turned and was once again face-to-face with the strange bald man. There was a friendly twinkle in his green eyes. "Rovi," he said. Or perhaps Rovi had imagined it.

But Rovi was in the zone now. Nothing was going to distract him from his task, not even a stranger from the mainland who seemed to know his name. This was what Rovi was born to do. He had imagined it so many times, it was as if it had already happened. He could already see himself doing it—see himself taking the shoes, tucking them under his arm. He could see the path that he would take between the stalls. He wouldn't have to think as he darted between customers and vendors. It would be like a dance. His feet would lead him. They always did.

Without skipping a beat, he shook off the man's hand and kept moving toward the rubber merchant. Some of the girls had squatted down on the ground to try on sneakers. Boxes were piled all around them. Others were shouting sizes, styles, and colors at the merchant even as he handed over more and more boxes.

Rovi took a deep breath. Without looking, he already knew where all the Phoenician guards were stationed. He knew the best escape route—a small gate behind the archway at the northwestern corner of the market that led to a narrow flight of stairs, which would take him to the maze of the Lower City where he could lose himself in the tangled streets. And from there back to the bridge and down to the river where he could finally put on his Grana Gleams.

Now. Now, Rovi. His inner voice was speaking, telling him the time was right. His inner voice was never wrong. It knew.

Rovi leaped through the clusters of girls and grabbed the shoebox. "Sorry," he blurted as he knocked the boxes over and sent the girls tumbling into one another. Then he turned and ran. As he expected, his feet led him, finding the perfect path between two stalls, the best way to jump over a giant basket of melons. Behind him he could hear the Alkebulan merchant ringing his bell, crying, "THIEF! THIEF!"

Out of the corner of his eye, Rovi could see the guards leaving their posts. Their red turbans always gave them away, allowing Rovi to track them from a distance. Today was no exception. Except that there were more of them—ten as opposed to five turbans closing in on him from different corners of the market. He would need to alter his course.

So instead of heading straight for the covered walkway, he ran deeper into the market, into the thick, chaotic center where the vendors were jammed together so close it was sometimes impossible to tell one stand from another. Even in the crowd and commotion, Rovi's feet never faltered, always finding the narrowest passage through which he could move.

Still, the turbaned guards were closing in. But they didn't have the skill of a ten-year-old boy for disappearing. He could see one of them ahead of him signaling to one out of sight that they had him cornered. Rovi glanced from side to side. There was a low tent under which a tanned, creased old man from the Rhodan Islands was smoking fish over low coals. In an instant, Rovi was in that tent, trying not to choke on the fishy smoke. He could see the guards' red boots passing back and forth outside. He couldn't stay in the tent much longer. Either the guards or the fish vendor would find him.

So before that happened—he bolted again. Out the back of the tent, away from the center of the market, moving quickly, but more haphazardly than usual, knocking over baskets and barrels as he went, drawing more notice than it would be possible to outrun. Suddenly everyone was on the lookout for Swiftfoot.

Rovi gripped the shoebox to his side and took a deep breath. He was special. He knew that. He could do this. He wasn't sure why, but he knew. He just had to make it out of the plaza.

He could hear merchants calling out to one another to stop him. He could hear his nickname being shouted across the marketplace. *Swiftfoot.* But somehow he stayed ahead of his pursuers. He could see the archway. He was almost there. Just a few more steps. He was going to do this. He was going to make it.

He stepped out of the plaza into the archway, kicking a drum that an old Sandlander woman was banging for spare change. He leaped over a snake charmer. He jostled a juggler. *Finally!* He'd reached the gate to the stairs.

And there was the bald stranger blocking his path. Rovi skidded to a stop, his heart in his mouth, his stomach sinking to his feet. He was caught. He dropped the shoes.

The man stooped, picked up the box, and handed it back to Rovi. "Go," he said. "Quickly. Don't look back." The short bald man with the twinkling green eyes opened the gate. And Rovi raced down the stairs, clutching his Grana Gleams, into the maze of the Lower City where no one would ever find him. He didn't look back.

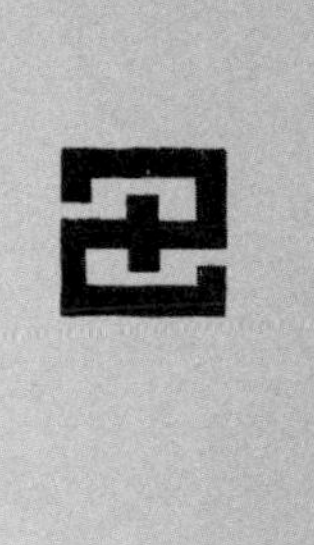

3

PRETIA

THE BOOK

PRETIA TURNED OVER A GOLDEN ENVELOPE with her name written on it in green lettering. This was easily the thousandth time she'd stared at this piece of paper—her admission to Ecrof Academy, the best sports school in Epoca. It had arrived the day after her birthday, a present even better than her Grana Gleams.

Admission to Ecrof was a mystery. Each year, the academy's Trainers opened the school's ancient scrolls to discover the names of the incoming class of recruits—students who were said to have the most powerful grana in the land. This year there were seventeen names. Pretia's was one of them. She was the first royal-born child in the land, the heir to both the Dreamers' and Realists' houses. Naturally, her name had appeared on the scrolls.

She knew what her classmates would say, that she was admitted for her heritage and not her talent. But she was accustomed to being treated differently by everyone. Ecrof would be no exception. Except now she had a secret: her bad grana. She wasn't so sure about Ecrof anymore.

Pretia looked at the pile of suitcases and duffel bags stacked in her sitting room. Anara had spent the weeks since her birthday in an endless flurry of packing, so much packing that Pretia had begun to worry that Anara had ordered even more clothes for her just to put them in bags. Now had come the time for final preparations.

"It's only for nine months," Pretia moaned as her nurse dug through her wardrobe one last time, adding just one more ceremonial dress, just one more backup pair of sneakers, just one more pair of pajamas.

"But I won't even need a ceremonial dress," Pretia complained, flopping back on the bed.

"It's not every day that my favorite person goes off to school," Anara said, putting a stop to her packing for one moment to kiss Pretia on her head.

"Yeah," Pretia said. "I'm going to school, not on an around-the-world voyage."

"Pretia—you do know that Ecrof Academy is on an island, right? If you forget something, it will take ages to get it to you."

Of course Pretia knew that Ecrof was on an island. There wasn't a single thing she didn't know about Ecrof. It was not simply the best school in Epoca, on the most sacred island in Epoca—the former home to the Gods of Granity—but it had produced the highest number of Epic Athletes of any academy in the land. And what's more, its Head Trainer was Janos Praxis, the most decorated athlete ever to compete in the Epic Games . . . and Pretia's favorite uncle.

Ever since Pretia could remember, she'd wanted to go to Ecrof and train on the sacred fields, play on the same courts, and use the same equipment as the most famous Epic Athletes. And tomorrow she was going.

There was only one problem. Ever since she had lit Hurell's flame and then accidentally pushed Davos off the cliff, Pretia had been unwilling to use her grana. She knew it was cursed. It was evil. And she was terrified of what would happen next. There was something dark and uncontrollable in her. She could step outside of herself. Half of her was bad. She was capable of horrible things. What terrible thing would she do next? Whenever she felt a wave of tingling in her limbs or her senses heightened, she remembered Davos disappearing from sight. Why had she lit the flame to the Fallen God? Why?

She saw the way the castle kids now kept their distance from her, giving her a wide berth every time she passed by. She'd looked for Davos, hoping to apologize again, but every time he saw her, he hightailed it in the other direction, as if she was going to push him again. She knew they wouldn't dare tell on her directly, but there was always a chance that gossip would spread. What would happen when people learned what Pretia was capable of?

Whenever she was tempted to put on her golden shoes, she distracted herself with something dreary—a dull book on the history of Epoca or a pamphlet on ceremonial attire for state dinners. Anything that made her forget how badly she wanted to run, play, compete. Anything that made her forget her cursed grana.

Her parents and Anara thought her moodiness had to do with her missing grana and Pretia didn't correct them. She could never let them know what she was capable of, what she had done. She couldn't let them know that Hurell might have granted her wish.

She would go to Ecrof as planned, as she'd always dreamed. But she wouldn't use her grana. Not now. Not ever. And she wouldn't be an Epic Athlete. Deep down she knew that giving up on that goal was a small price to pay for never, ever harming someone again as she had harmed Davos. But still, it hurt.

Anara zipped up the final bag for the final time. "That should do it," she said.

"I hope so," Pretia said.

"You'll thank me when you get there."

A bell clanged through the castle corridors. Anara's eyes widened in alarm. "Pretia, you're not dressed!"

"Dressed?" Pretia said. She was dressed, in shorts and a T-shirt.

"We've lost track of time," Anara said, opening one of the bags and tearing through it. "The Ceremony of the Book."

Pretia rolled her eyes. She'd secretly hoped that Anara and everyone else had forgotten. Another ceremony. Another important function at which she was going to be told how important she was to the nation of Epoca. Another lecture on how she was the Child of Hope—the child for the future. Well, Pretia had grown certain over the last few weeks that all of that was nonsense. The Child of Hope did not push other children off cliffs! The Child of Hope did not accidentally pray to Hurell.

"Can't they just hand me my book like a normal kid?" Pretia said as Anara began pulling a blue-and-purple ceremonial dress over her head.

"You are not a normal kid," Anara said.

"How did you get your book? Was there a big boring ceremony with all sorts of people staring at you?"

"My mother gave it to me. And that was that."

"See—" Pretia began to object.

Anara was now tugging at her hair, trying to flatten and braid it. "Pretia—every child in Epoca receives his or her Book of Grana in a personal way unique to them. If yours is meant to be a ceremony with all sorts of people staring at you, then that's what the gods have willed."

"But—" Pretia tried again.

Another bell rang. If Pretia didn't hurry, soon she'd hear her father's voice booming through the phonopipes.

"Now get going," Anara said, pulling her toward the door. "It's one last ceremony, and then tomorrow you'll go to school. *Then* you can be a normal kid."

One last ceremony—Pretia liked the sound of that. She opened the door and dashed into the hall.

"Wait," Anara called, "your shoes."

Pretia looked down. She was wearing her Grana Gleams.

“I can’t hurry if I can’t run,” Pretia said, “and these are my best running shoes.” She smiled over her shoulder at her nurse, then picked up the pace and sprinted through the Hall of the Gods of Granity, which led to the Atrium, where her parents were waiting. This time she held her breath as she passed Hurell’s shrouded statue.

At the far end, Pretia skidded to a stop. She smoothed her dress and patted her hair so it didn’t look like a rat’s nest. A glance down showed that the laces on her left shoe were untied.

“Pretia!”

Her father’s deep, melodious voice echoed from the Atrium below. “How many times have I told you not to run through the Hall of the Gods?”

There was no time to tie her sneaker. Pretia started down the final flight of stairs. “I wasn’t—” she tried. But she knew it was pointless. She could never lie to her father, and he could never stay mad at her.

“Sorry,” she said. The room was semicircular with great columns on all sides that let out onto a balcony that overlooked the Campos Field, where the Epic Games ceremony was held.

King Airos and Queen Helena stood together underneath the high-domed roof. They were dressed, as always, in the colors of their houses—the king in purple and the queen in blue.

Pretia was always struck by the sight of her parents standing side by side, especially by their height, but also by the fact that she didn’t look much like either of them. Some people acknowledged she bore a slight resemblance to her mother. They had the same black hair and the same green eyes. That’s where the similarities ended. While Helena’s pale skin darkened only after much exposure to Epoca’s constant sunshine, Pretia was naturally tan, the color of the people of the Sandlands.

Unlike her parents, who were both tall and sturdily built, Pretia was fine-boned and narrow, more like a long-distance runner than a formidable basketball player or soccer star. And she was short, shorter than her only first cousin, Castor, as well as all the castle workers' children. But she was only ten, her parents told her, and they assured her that height and strength would come.

The king was large and athletic, with reddish-blond hair that, like his wife's, was now streaked with silver. His features were round and had grown more so as he aged. Pretia knew the rumor that her father had been one of the most promising athletes in Epoca but had chosen the art of statesmanship over sports when he'd been selected by his father to lead House Somni. So now his stomach was a little larger than it used to be, and his face a little softer. Deep creases ran away from his eyes, the result, Pretia liked to imagine, of years of laughter.

Pretia understood that her parents had been much older than was considered normal when she was born. She had been born late, after much difficulty and sadness. She didn't quite understand the nature of this sadness, but she could see it written on her mother's face in the downward turn of her mouth and the distant look that crept into her eyes from time to time. While the king made his presence known at every moment with his rolling laugh and loud, jovial voice, there were times that Queen Helena seemed to retreat so far into herself that she became nearly invisible.

Pretia also knew that people, from the cooks to her royal relatives, whispered that her looks were due to the unusual—some would say unnatural—marriage between her parents. Until the king and queen married, there had been no royal union between Dreamers and Realists. The houses kept to themselves and only competed against each other once every four years in the Epic Games for control of Epoca.

But Pretia's parents' marriage had changed everything so that no matter whether the Dreamers or the Realists emerged from the Epic Games victorious, Helena and Airos would still hold power—together. And when it was Pretia's turn to take control of Epoca, the

Epic Games would be even less meaningful, since she would remain in control of the country regardless of the outcome.

"Are you ready?" King Airos said, looping his arm through Pretia's.

Pretia looked into her father's eyes. Was he crying? "Are you okay?" she asked.

"It's a big day for you, Pretia, receiving your Grana Book."

"Oh, come on, Papa," Pretia said. "It's just a book."

The king placed his hand on Pretia's shoulder. "No, Pretia, it's not just a book. It's the key to the rest of your life."

Grana Books were a tradition unique in Epoca. Every child had one made for them on the hidden island of Docen by the Guardians of the Book. No one had ever visited this island. But once a child's birth was registered, his or her parents would report the birth to the Guardians and a book would be crafted using craft known only to those on Docen. Some said that the books were inspired by a child's parental history. Others said their contents were conjured through prophecy. When the books were ready, they were sent to the new parents to be handed down on a child's tenth birthday. The books were made to guide children through life, to offer answers when parents could not, and then long into adulthood. They were a mixture of nature and nurture—half tailored to the child's projected personality and half reflecting the parents' worldview.

Pretia had heard rumors of outcast or orphaned children unlucky enough not to have Grana Books, who passed through life lost and without guidance. And there were even stories of families who had passed down the wrong Grana Book to a child, which made the child's work of interpreting the book much more difficult.

Now the queen looped her arm through Pretia's free one. "Sweetheart," she said. "You must never dismiss the importance of your book. Now, let's go. The Speaker of Grace and the rest of our family are waiting under the Gods' Eye." And together, Pretia and her parents proceeded to the very top of Castle Airim.

The top floor of the castle was off-limits to most of the castle staff and inhabitants. Only the immediate members of the royal family and their chosen advisers were permitted to ascend into the domed chamber.

Pretia and her parents climbed the increasingly steep and narrow stairs and emerged in the cool, domed room. The Speaker of Grace—a Realist in a somber blue cloak—stood in the center of the room surrounded by six esteemed Granics from House Somni and House Reila. Everyone was dressed according to the colors of their houses in high ceremonial robes with long bell-shaped sleeves and gold corded belts.

A small group of Pretia's closest blood relatives stood to one side. Her father's aunt Chryssia, an elderly lady who shook when she talked and smelled of myrtle tea; her mother's brother, Janos, Head Trainer of Ecrof; and his son, Castor. Chryssia was dressed in her ancient purple Dreamer robes with dozens of golden rings and necklaces, while Janos and Castor wore Realist blue dress uniforms. Janos's wife, Thalia, was not permitted into the Gods' Eye chamber because she was not related to the royal family by blood. She would gain access only in the unlikely event that Castor became king instead of Pretia becoming queen. Next to Janos was an empty spot where his and Queen Helena's oldest sister, Syspara, should have stood. But Syspara had been lost to the family many years ago—Pretia had never met her. Although the queen insisted that place always be held for her sister at royal events, Pretia had heard it whispered through the castle that her aunt was dead.

Janos always reminded Pretia of one of the sturdy and ornate columns that supported the Atrium at Castle Airim. He towered over both his sister and the king. He was the same age as King Airos, but unlike Pretia's father, he still looked as if he could defeat the youngest, fittest, and most promising athletes in the Epic Games. On the left lapel of his ceremonial uniform were seventeen gold bars representing his seventeen Epic Games gold medals. And around his neck was a heavy wooden whistle he never took off. His arms were like tree trunks, his fists tough like marble, and his jaw square and strong. Despite the stern look on his face, Pretia could see the delight in his deep-set green eyes that were shaded by a prominent brow that cast his face into permanent shadow.

"Hi, Uncle Janos," Pretia whispered.

Janos winked. But Castor, standing at his father's side, just rolled his eyes at Pretia.

Castor was a miniature version of his father—compact and muscular with a heavy brow. Pretia knew that the last place Castor wanted to be was in this room watching her, of all people, receive another blessing. Yet there he was as always, forced to watch as people made a big deal about Pretia—the Child of Hope. Pretia understood Castor's exasperation. Even she wanted to roll her eyes at the stupid nickname the kingdom had bestowed on her.

If Castor hadn't been so obnoxious, Pretia would have been tempted to pity him, the next in line to the throne after her, always forced to observe from the sidelines on the very small chance that he would rule Epoca one day. But Castor was extremely obnoxious, often whispering behind her back to anyone who would listen that she *was* no better than a Star Stealer because of her mixed heritage—that she didn't have two house affiliations, but none. He'd gotten even worse as they grew older. Like everyone else in the royal inner circle, Castor knew, or thought he knew, that Pretia hadn't received her grana.

The only light on the top floor came in from a single round hole at the peak of the dome called the Gods' Eye. Right now, with the sun nearly at the top of its climb, a massive shaft of sunlight beamed directly into the center of the room, lighting up the entire perimeter of the wall on which was painted a 360-degree mural showing the fall of Hurell and the departure of the remaining gods from the island of Corae to Mount Aoin.

The Gods' Eye was designed so that as the sun moved across the sky, Hurell would be cast into darkness, while the remaining gods, who were shown on their final day on earth before they retired to Mount Aoin, remained illuminated until nightfall.

The seven remaining gods had been painted on the eastern wall. They stood in a line that stretched from the shore of Corae to a towering gate, beyond which a boat was waiting to take them to the holy mountain in a secret corner of the realm. The first six gods were looking at the narrow boat that had been pulled up onto the beach, with its two elegant white sails trimmed in gold. But the goddess Cora, after whom the island was named, was looking back over her shoulder at a cave carved into the towering cliffs that rose from the beach toward a green plateau that touched the sky. Pretia knew that just before the sun left the room in darkness, it would alight on Cora's eyes for a final quarter of an hour, illuminating her longing backward glance.

Every time Pretia stood under the Gods' Eye, she wondered what Cora was looking at—what she was brokenhearted to be abandoning. She'd even climbed up a ladder an artisan had left behind when cleaning the mural to get a better look inside the cave. But she couldn't figure it out. Besides the rocky coastline and asphodel bushes, all she could see was a single tree root that burst through the roof of the cave.

Pretia felt her father's hand on the small of her back urging her toward the Speaker of Grace. Pretia stumbled as she approached—tripping over her untied shoelace.

She stood before the Speaker of Grace, the same man who had blessed her entry into the world, who had said her birthday devotion each year, who had made her suffer through weekly classes in the history of the gods. He was the oldest person Pretia had ever seen, with watery blue eyes and pale skin that sagged from his cheekbones. It had been decided at birth that Pretia's religious education would come from her mother's family and her academic learning from her father's, something that clearly did not sit well with the three high Dreamer Granics looking on under the Gods' Eye.

Because this was going to be a Realist-dominated ceremony, Pretia knew it would be short and straightforward, a transmission of information without a lot of poetic language. That was a relief, at least. There would be facts instead of mystic statements she'd have to try and interpret later, which was what happened when Dreamers took charge.

"Come with grace, my child," the Speaker of Grace said, putting two shaking hands on Pretia's shoulders. He wore an enormous blue ring that, over the years, had grown too large for his brittle finger and swung loosely as he talked.

The room was so silent, Pretia could hear each Granic breathing in and out.

"Today you enter into a new phase in your life," the Speaker of Grace said. "Today you no longer rely only on adults to guide you, but also on yourself. For today is the day that you receive your Grana Book."

Pretia stole a quick glance around to see exactly where her Grana Book might be. She'd only ever seen the Grana Books belonging to her parents. Her mother's was a thick volume, the size of a small painting, whose cover was embroidered with blue and gold. Her father's book was as wide as her hand and looked incredibly heavy. The binding was made out of bronze that had tarnished to a browned green color at the corners.

"As you know, every child in Epoca receives one of these books after his or her tenth birthday. They are the story of your life in pictures. They are your destiny, your soul, your spirit, and your inspiration. But they do not tell the future. They do not provide clear answers. Your life's work will be to learn how to interpret yours."

"How—" Pretia started to ask before her mother gave a polite cough, letting her know to keep quiet.

"Some people never bother to learn to use their books," the Speaker of Grace said. "Some people devote their entire lives to understanding them. Some people understand immediately what is depicted on the pages, and some force understandings that aren't there. How you use your book will be up to you. Your grana will guide you."

Pretia saw her parents exchange a brief look.

"Your book is a special one, I'm sure you understand," the Speaker of Grace continued, blinking his watery eyes. "It is the first book ever made for a Dreamer and a Realist child. And that means there is no one to help you interpret it—no Granics to guide your way forward. This is a path you are going to have to tread alone, Pretia. Your book has no rules and no guidelines. Everyone's book is unique to them. But yours is something that has never been seen before."

Butterflies rose in Pretia's stomach. Why did everything have to be different for her? Why did her book have to be unlike anyone else's?

Now King Airos stepped forward, cleared his throat, and addressed Pretia in the regal tone reserved for state occasions. "Until the gods gifted grana to the land of Epoca, we were a country at war with itself. On this day—the day you are to receive your book—I remind you of this story. During the dark ages, the god Hurell turned the houses against each other, forging war and stirring up retribution and hatred between House Somni and House Reila, the Dreamers and the Realists. For hundreds of years Epoca was thrown into darkness, until the houses came together and turned to the remaining Gods of Granity, begging for peace. And this peace was granted in the form of grana."

Pretia tried to stifle a yawn and stay focused. How many times had she heard this before? She'd lost count. Too many—she was sure of that. Her eyes wandered to the mural, landing, as usual, on the goddess Cora. What *was* she looking at? And, for a moment, it seemed to Pretia that Cora's backward glance was not longing, but fear. Then she caught herself. That was silly—gods had nothing to fear, especially not on earth.

Pretia was snapped back to attention by her father's voice. "Grana is a breath of inspiration from the gods. It's in all of us. It's what allows each of us to be the best at what we do. It's what allows us to be rulers, athletes, artists, writers, doctors, or whatever it is we want to be. And we use our Grana Books to guide us. Because at the end of the day, Pretia, only we can answer our own questions and set our own destinies." Pretia strained onto her tiptoes, ready to kiss her father, but to her dismay, he hadn't finished speaking. "When I learned to interpret my book as a young man, I saw the most extraordinary thing. I was to raise a child who was both Dreamer and Realist—a child of hope. That is who you are, Pretia. I can only imagine what wonders *your* book has in store for you."

Now the queen stepped forward. She was holding a small package wrapped in blue cloth, which she presented to Pretia. "On this day, grace is yours," she said.

Pretia could feel everyone's eyes on her as she took the package from her mother. It didn't feel special, just like an ordinary book. Still, she didn't want to open the blue cloth. Her cursed grana might betray her. She worried that her book would start talking or burst into flames or leap from her hands.

The Granics from both houses approached her. The ones from House Reila came first and offered the Realist Prayer, ending with "*Guided by fear, led by thought, steered by confidence, may you never go astray.*"

Then came the three Dreamer Granics from House Somni, whose prayer ended with the words: "*May your inspiration fly freely, toward a boundless sky and a sea of ideas, and lead you to wonders that never cease.*"

Then all six Granics knelt before Pretia. "To the future of Epoca," the kneeling priests said.

Pretia shifted from foot to foot uncomfortably. She didn't want these grown men and women at her feet. But they remained there, heads bowed, waiting—waiting for what? Pretia heard Castor muffle a snort.

"Your hand," King Airos whispered behind her.

And for the first time, just like she'd seen her parents do thousands of times before, Pretia placed her palm on each of the Granics' heads in turn, giving them her blessing. One by one they rose, then disappeared into the shadows of the Gods' Eye.

Janos approached, an imposing presence. He placed both hands on Pretia's shoulders and stooped down so they were eye to eye. "Congratulations, favorite niece," he said. "If your grana is as powerful as your parents', that book will be one of the most important and interesting ever to be bound in Epoca." He kissed her forehead. Then he looked at each of Pretia's parents in turn. "And I thank you both for entrusting Pretia to my care. Tomorrow she will be more than the Princess of Epoca. Tomorrow she'll be one of my recruits." With a strong hand, he ruffled her hair. "But I hope you understand that you won't be getting any special treatment," he added with a wink.

Pretia's heart soared. She forgot about the book in her hands. *Ecrof*—that was the most important thing.

Now Castor approached and stiffly shook Pretia's hand. He leaned in to whisper in her ear. "You heard what my father said, no special treatment for you. Which means no more dumb ceremonies for me to sit through." He squeezed Pretia's hand painfully. "When we get to Ecrof, no more special Pretia." They locked eyes and Castor raised his voice. "See you on the ship tomorrow, Cousin," he said.

It was like a balloon inside Pretia had popped—she had forgotten that Castor was also going to Ecrof. Of course he was.

When Pretia and her parents were alone, Queen Helena glanced at the package in Pretia's hands. "Aren't you going to open it?"

"I thought I'd wait," Pretia said. She couldn't admit to her mother that she was as afraid of her book as she was afraid of her grana. What horrible future might be contained in its pages?

But Pretia knew her parents wouldn't let her alone until she unwrapped the book. She slowly opened the blue cloth and took the book out. At first glance there didn't seem to be anything extraordinary about it. It was about the size of an average book, perhaps slightly heavier, bound in thick pebbled leather. The front and back covers were marbled blue and purple, and the binding was gold. She opened it. The glossy pages felt heavy. There were no words, only images—detailed paintings in dreamy, gauzy colors that spread across both pages. She flipped through the book. It made no sense: imaginary lands, still-life depictions of strange objects—clocks, feathers, a glass of milk. One page seemed to be different flowers painted close-up. Another something that was either a maze or tree roots. She saw pages that could be the sea, or perhaps the sky, or something else entirely.

She exhaled, relieved that nothing sinister seemed to jump out from the book. "It's just a book."

"The magic happens when you learn how to use your book," her mother said. "Until then, you're right, it's just a book. In time, your grana will guide you."

At the mention of her grana, Pretia's stomach clenched, and for the hundredth, no, the thousandth time, the memory of Hurell's blue flame and Davos flying off the cliff flashed before her eyes.

The king drew Pretia toward him. "There's something your mother and I would like to talk to you about before you leave for Ecrof. Something important."

What now? Pretia's heart sank. Surely it was possible to have a life without everything being so important, so stately, so political.

They led her to the edge of the room, to a small wooden chair, something a toddler might sit in. She sat, trying to make herself comfortable.

"Pretia," Queen Helena said, squatting down so she could look her in the eye. "Your father and I are wondering about your grana. You've never mentioned it. Has it really not come?"

Pretia bit her lip. What should she say? If she told them the truth, that her grana had come, there would be endless questions about when it had started, how she felt, and why she'd hidden it. Pretia was sure the whole story about Davos and Dinara and the disastrous and nearly deadly game of tag in the clearing would come out. And once she admitted that, she'd have to mention what she had done in the Hall of the Gods of Granity. And she was never, ever telling anyone that she'd lit the flame of the Fallen God.

There was no way for her to tell her parents that her grana was cursed, especially after the Ceremony of the Book. Everyone expected so much of her. She knew she'd disappoint them all.

"We love you no matter what," the king said.

"But . . . ?" Pretia asked. She knew from the tone of her father's voice that there was more to the story.

"When the gods granted grana to the people, it was so we could rule ourselves with kindness and wisdom. We lead with our grana. Which means that in order to rule, a king or queen must have grana."

"So if you don't—" the queen said.

"I can't rule." Pretia finished the statement for her. She knew. She'd heard this hundreds of times in passing. But she'd never heard it directly from her parents' mouths. She knew there were outcasts from society who'd lost or repressed their grana through various addictions—sweet wine and Somnium potions. She had also heard that every once in a while, someone was born without grana and was relegated to the lowest class of society. But she'd never dreamed she'd be categorized with these sorts of people.

"So, please, Pretia, tell us the truth. Have you felt anything at all? Any change?" Pretia had never seen anything like the look in her mother's eyes, desperate, pleading. "You are the Child of Hope. You must—"

Pretia stood up. "I don't even know what that means. I'm *Pretia*. That's who I am. I'm not the child of anything. Stop forcing that name on me." She began to run toward the stairs. But before she reached them, she whirled around and faced her parents. There were tears in her eyes. "And I don't have grana."

Her kind of grana wasn't what they wanted. Her grana was deadly, dangerous. It was cursed. And there was no way she was ever going to let anyone see it again. So what if she couldn't rule? So what if she wasn't everything her parents and the kingdom wanted her to be? She was going to Ecrof and when she was there she could figure out what to do about her cursed grana without having to worry about all this future queen of Epoca nonsense.

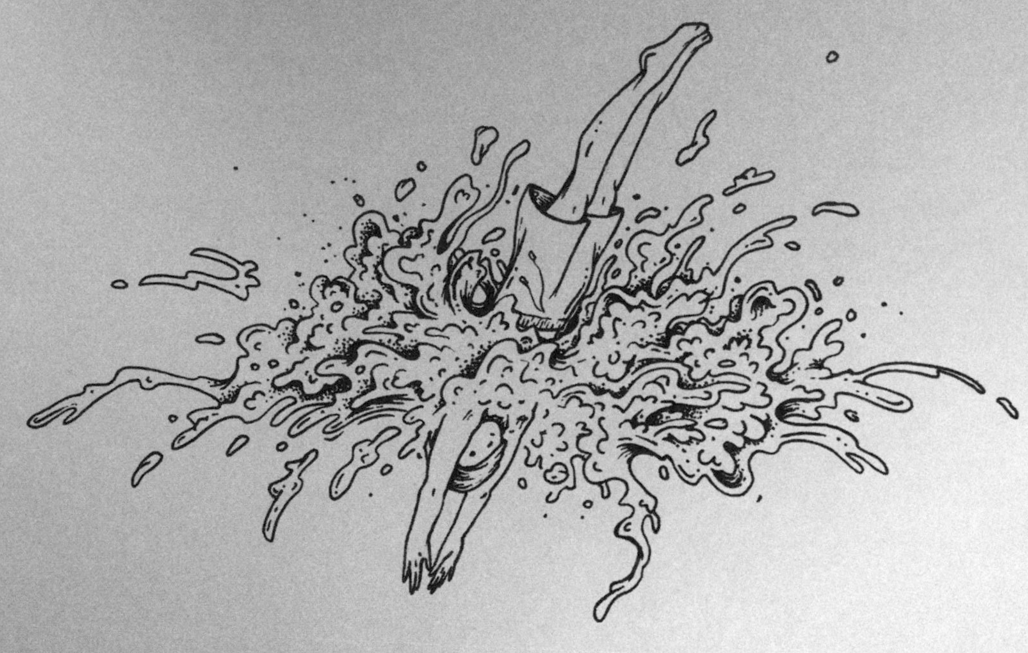

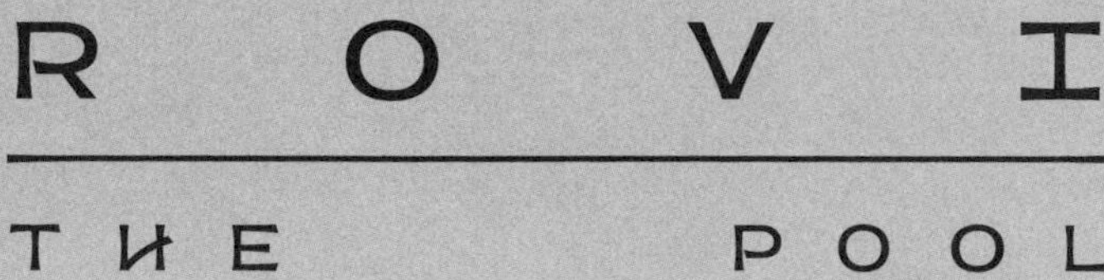

4

ROVI

THE POOL

OF THE TWELVE MEMBERS OF ISSA'S GANG, Rovi was the youngest. He was also the only one who hadn't grown up in the Sandlands. He'd grown up on Corae Island, home to the formidable Ecrof Academy, where his father had been the Visualization Trainer. But that had been a lifetime ago.

Rovi remembered Ecrof but tried not to think about it. It was too painful, too sad. It was where his mother had died, when he was almost too young to remember. And where his father had been labeled insane and then fired. He'd wound up a Somnium addict on the foreign streets of the Sandlands, with Rovi trying to put food in both their mouths at the age of seven.

But sometimes the memories came. Rovi couldn't help them. Especially around the time of his birthday. He remembered the beautiful campus on a high plateau on Corae Island—the bleached-white cliffs, the perfect blue sea below. He remembered the impressive stadium that opened to the cliffs, that looked as if it were balancing on the edge of the world. He remembered the famous Tree of Ecrof, the school's proud emblem and one of the Four Marvels of Epoca, that grew in the center of the stadium. He remembered the happy shouts of the students as they played sports and learned to master their grana. He remembered the few times he'd been allowed into his father's classroom and watched the famous Pallas Myrios show his class how to bring their imaginations to life, how to project images of themselves performing extraordinary things so that they might actually be able to do them one day. He remembered his last birthday before he'd left Ecrof—his seventh, when his father had promised him that he would join the ranks of the best athletes in Epoca, that he was destined for Epic greatness.

Now all of that was a laughable impossibility. Rovi, a street kid in the distant Sandlands, was never going to be anything but a thief and a beggar.

This year the lead-up to his birthday had been worse than usual. Because this year, Rovi turned ten. And that meant that he was supposed to receive his Grana Book. But with no adult in his life, there was no book. There had been one once, of course. Every Dreamer or Realist had one made for him or her at birth. But Rovi hadn't been able to find his in his father's possessions when Pallas died, so he assumed that it had been lost somewhere in his father's exile from Ecrof. So, no book meant no destiny. Like all other Star Stealers, Rovi had no future.

These were the thoughts that were consuming Rovi several mornings after his birthday—which had been an unexceptional day of stealing a few measly pieces of fruit and a loaf of bread, and then throwing rocks into the river Durna. Rovi woke up hot and hungry, which wasn't unusual. A heat wave was sweeping the Sandlands, making Issa's gang cranky and irritable. A few of the older girls had tried to steal buckets of fruit ice from a store in the Upper City the day before and had been caught by the guards and taken away to the sandlots to make bricks for a month.

The remaining members of the gang were at each other's throats from the moment they opened their eyes. Amrav, one of the older boys, kneed Rovi in the side. "Go steal us something good," he said. "Make yourself useful."

“Do it yourself,” Rovi said. It didn’t seem fair to have to share what he stole with some of the other boys, who spent their days playing pranks on the rich kids on the way to their fancy academies.

Amrav kicked Rovi hard. Rovi bolted up from the reed mat he used as a bed. He was already wearing his Grana Gleams—he never took them off. He couldn’t trust anyone, not even the members of his own crew. He snatched Amrav’s woven satchel and darted out of their encampment under the bridge. Amrav tried to grab Rovi, but he was too slow, and in no time Rovi was on top of the bridge, dangling the satchel down toward the muddy river Durna.

Below him on the bank, he could hear Amrav shouting furiously. He even picked up a rock and hurled it at Rovi. But what good would that do? If he hit Rovi, Rovi might drop the bag accidentally. Rovi leaned out over the railing and dangled the bag even farther. So what if he dropped it? How much worse could his life be? He had no future. When you were a Star Stealer, you had no house, no official family, no Grana Book.

He felt a hand on his shoulder and glanced around to see Issa standing behind him, his large black eyes filled with the only kindness Rovi saw these days. Issa had been born and raised on the streets of Phoenis. Sleeping outside and stealing was the only life he’d ever known.

“You don’t actually want to drop that, now do you, Swiftfoot?”

Rovi did and he didn’t.

Issa pulled a stale honeycake from his own satchel. “Here,” he said, “it’s not much.”

Rovi felt guilty taking the cake from Issa when he could have so easily stolen one himself.

“I know you’re disappointed about your birthday,” Issa said.

Rovi nodded. But he wasn’t sure Issa truly understood. When you’ve never had parents, when you’ve never had the promise of a Grana Book and a future dangled in front of you, you can’t actually be sure what you are missing.

"I know you wanted a Grana Book. Unfortunately, that's the one thing we can't steal," Issa said, his lips arching into a half smile. Even the underclass of petty thieves, street vagabonds, and common criminals obeyed the prohibition against touching someone else's Grana Book.

"It's no big deal," Rovi said, trying to blink away his tears.

"Exactly," Issa said. "Why would you want your life to be determined by a silly book? Me, I make my own destiny. I can do whatever I want without having to worry about whether or not I'm following the instructions in a book my parents made for me when I was born. Who wants to follow those sorts of rules, right?"

Rovi didn't correct him. He knew that Issa's free-spirited gang looked down on anything that came from the traditional world. They didn't follow any rules. They weren't Dreamers or Realists. They didn't wear the colors of either house—which made Star Stealers easily identifiable. They didn't follow the Epic Games. And they didn't care about things like Grana Books. He also knew Grana Books didn't offer instruction, they offered guidance. At least that's what his father had told him before his death—they offered guidance as to how you might unlock your most powerful grana.

Issa helped Rovi back from the ledge and looped a long, lanky arm around Rovi's bony shoulder. "I have an idea," Issa said. "How about today we sneak into the Royal Baths?"

"But there are so many guards," Rovi said.

"There's also a heat wave. Which means there will be such a crush of swimmers, there's a good chance no one will notice." Issa held out his hand. "But first, I think you have something to return to Amrav."

Rovi hesitated, taking one last look at the muddy water below, before handing the bag over to Issa.

Rovi had hoped that it would only be him and Issa on this adventure, but of course the whole gang wanted to go. Together they emerged from below the bridge and crossed into the Upper City. They spread out as they walked, not wanting to attract attention. They took an indirect route, through back alleys and narrow walkways, until they emerged in front of a large circular building with a copper-plated onion-domed roof.

Affluent Dreamers and Realists were coming and going through the front door. The ones exiting the building looked refreshed and glowing. Some of them carried sparkling bottles of Spirit Water, others still had wet hair from their swim.

"The pool is in a large underground cavern," Issa explained. "It's fed by a secret river that runs to Phoenis from the distant mountains of Quip."

"And of course, only people from the Upper City can use it. Just like everything else that's nice in Phoenis," Amrav said.

"Not today," Issa said, beckoning the crew around back.

There was a small alley between the far side of the building and one of the city walls, just wide enough for underfed street kids to squeeze through. Issa shinnied down, then got on his knees to fumble with a grate attached at the foot of the building. After a few minutes, he wrestled it free. "Rovi, you first."

Rovi inched past the rest of the crew and slipped down the open grate. He was in a cool, dark room. He could smell water and something else—eucalyptus, the same scent that rose from the Thera-Center at Ecrof. One by one, Issa and the rest of the gang alighted in the room behind him.

"This way," Issa said, leading them into a curved hallway where robes were hung on hooks. He pulled a robe off the wall and slipped it over his clothes, instructing his gang to do the same.

The robe was enormous on Rovi, trailing behind him like a cloak. But the cotton was plush and soft, and, like so many other things that day, dragged him back to Ecrof and the luxurious linens and towels that had been provided to the students and teachers alike.

Dozens of doors led off the hall and into the pool. Issa told the gang to spread out so they didn't all enter at once. "And," he said, "whatever you do, don't attract attention. Enjoy the water, but don't show off."

Rovi barely heard him. He had already stepped through a door to the pool. The pool was the most incredible thing he had seen since the impressive sports facilities at Ecrof. He guessed it was the size of two basketball courts. On one end was a wading pool for soaking or lounging, and on the other was a set of diving boards. In the center of the pool, hundreds of swimmers were floating on blue rafts staring up at the ceiling, which was painted with the constellations of the eastern sky.

Rovi dropped his robe. He tore off his T-shirt. He kicked off his prized Grana Gleams. He took a running start, threading past bathers on their way in and out of the water. At the edge of the pool, he pushed off, arced into the air, and dove into the cool, clean, fresh water. Down, down, down he sank. Deeper into the perfect blue. He swam through a tangle of feet, darting between other swimmers like a minnow. And just before his lungs gave out, he came up for air. He flopped onto his back and stared up at the blue ceiling with its golden stars. And without the help of a raft, he floated.

Rovi could feel the dirt and sweat wash off him. He did somersaults underwater, handstands in the shallows, and a few running cannonballs from the low diving board. He hadn't been swimming since he'd left Ecrof. His father had taught him there, in the secret pool deep in a cave hidden in the mountains, where they would sneak off to when his father didn't have to teach.

For once he didn't care that everyone else around him had money for Spirit Water and bright, juicy platters of fruit. He was swimming. He was moving quickly without being chased.

Every once in a while, he passed a member of Issa's gang. They acknowledged each other with a quick hello, but kept to themselves.

No one, not even Amrav, wanted to risk being hauled out of the pool by the guards, who might notice they hadn't paid their entry fee.

After a while, Rovi pulled himself out of the water and sat on the edge of the pool, his legs dangling into the deep end. There was a kid about his age, a Realist, judging by the blue color of his swim trunks, up on the high diving board. Rovi watched as the boy executed an impressive double-flip into the water to the polite applause of a group of adults gathered below.

Over and over again, the boy flipped off the diving board. Each time, the adults applauded and clapped him on the back. The boy had a self-satisfied look on his face that was starting to annoy Rovi. Six more times, the boy did his double-flip, each time growing prouder and prouder of himself.

Rovi stood up and hurried to the diving board, cutting in front of the boy before he could climb up again. "Let someone else have a go," Rovi said.

Rovi scampered up the ladder and hurried to the edge of the board. He hadn't counted on it being so high. Suddenly he couldn't imagine jumping into the water below.

"Scared?" he heard the voice of the boy call up from below.

The water seemed impossibly far away.

"You're scaaaaaaared," the boy taunted.

Rovi was about to reply when his foot slipped off the board and he went plunging down to the water in a graceless belly flop. As he hauled himself out of the pool, he came face-to-face with the boy. "Have you ever even been on a diving board before?" the boy asked.

"Of course," Rovi lied.

"Doesn't look like it."

From across the pool, Rovi could see Issa's eyes on him, pleading with him not to get into a fight with the young Realist.

"What's your name anyway?" the boy asked. "And why are your shorts ripped?"

"None of your business," Rovi said. His voice was a little louder than he'd intended. A few people looked up from their rafts and lounge chairs.

The boy stared at him. It was clear to Rovi that he wasn't used to being spoken to like that.

"Are you a Star Stealer?"

"I said mind your own business."

"Where are your house colors?" the boy demanded.

"I said, mind your own business," Rovi repeated. "Now excuse me, I have another dive to do, unless you plan on hogging the board some more."

"Dive?" The boy snickered. "That was the worst dive I've ever seen. If it was even supposed to be a dive. To me it looked like you just fell off the board." Now the boy was talking animatedly and gesturing to get everyone's attention.

Rovi tried to hide the flush in his cheeks. "You'll see," he said, once more pushing past the boy to the diving board. This time it was the boy who lost his footing and slipped on the wet pool deck. He hit the ground with a cry that echoed across the pool. But Rovi was already climbing the ladder.

He took his time walking to the edge of the diving board. He could sense some commotion below as people rushed to comfort the boy, who was sitting on the ground looking stunned.

Rovi bounced on the end of the board. He would dive. He would. It didn't have to be complicated. Just a simple swan dive into the water.

But what was going on at the edges of the pool? People were moving and pointing. They were pointing up at him. From his towering vantage point, he could see several of Issa's gang making for the exits as the pool guards began circling.

The boy's comments had alerted them, of course, to the suspected Star Stealer who'd snuck into the pool. Rovi bounced once more on the board as he scanned the pool deck. The only member of the gang left was Issa. Issa was waiting for him. Issa was risking being caught to make sure Rovi was okay.

Rovi's inner voice was already cooking up a plan. *Dive down as deep as you can, swim as far as you can underwater—the entire length of the pool, if possible—all the way to the side where you entered. Get out, grab your sneakers, sprint down the hall, up through the grate. Go fast. Don't look back.*

The pool guards were closing in. He had no choice but to dive now. It would be difficult—but it was his only chance of escape. *One. Two. Three.* Rovi sprang as high as he could on the board, reached his arms over his head, then dove down. He barreled toward the water, then plunged deep, until he nearly reached the bottom. Then he began to swim. He parted the water with his arms, pulling himself toward the shallow end, hoping he was swimming so deep that the guards couldn't track him. His lungs were bursting. He could see the far end. He was almost there. He touched the wall. He hauled himself out and, crouching on the pool deck, looked around. Now all he needed was his sneakers.

He shook water from his eyes. He could see his robe and dirty T-shirt where he'd left them. But his Gleams were gone.

From both sides, he could see the guards approaching. What was the penalty for sneaking into a pool? Surely it wouldn't be that bad. But when they figured out they had the notorious Swiftfoot, Rovi would be sent to make sand bricks for sure.

He had to run. He had to forget his Gleams. He had no choice.

And then suddenly there they were—his Grana Gleams, right in front of his face.

"I believe these belong to you."

Rovi stood. He was face-to-face with the short, bald man with the twinkling green eyes who'd let him escape from the market a few weeks ago.

"You weren't going to leave without them, were you?"

Rovi shook his head and took the sneakers.

The guards had closed in. Across the pool, Rovi could feel Issa's eyes on him.

"Excuse me," one of the guards said to the green-eyed man with a sneer. "That boy is a Star Stealer who snuck into the pool without paying."

"This boy?" The man, laughing, put a hand on Rovi's shoulder. "This is Rovi Myrios of House Somni from the island of Corae. He's no Star Stealer."

The guard narrowed his eyes at the bald man.

"You are sure?" the guard said, looking Rovi over from top to toe and clearly not liking what he saw.

The bald man cocked his head to one side. "Are you questioning my judgment or my sanity?"

The guard quailed. "I . . . I must be mistaken," he said. And with a final curious glance at Rovi, he left them.

"Who are you?" Rovi asked when the guard was out of earshot.

"You don't recognize me? I'm Satis Dario, a scout from Ecrof."

Rovi shook his head once, wondering if there was water in his ears. He couldn't believe what he was hearing. "Ecrof?"

"And I believe I have something that belongs to you. Your father left it behind when he was asked to leave the school."

Satis reached into a bag he had looped over his shoulder and pulled out a book, which he placed in Rovi's hands. "I found it after you left Ecrof."

Rovi held the book. "Is this—is this—?" he stammered.

"Yes," Satis said. "It's your Grana Book."

Rovi pressed the small, worn book to his face. It looked like one of the battered and dog-eared books at the antique bookseller's stall at the market. But Rovi didn't care. It was the most beautiful thing he had ever seen—ever held—in his life.

“Now put on your shoes,” Satis said. “We have a long voyage ahead of us.”

“A voyage?”

“Yes, my boy. Your name appeared on this year’s Scrolls of Ecrof.”

Rovi’s jaw hung open. Was he hearing correctly?

Satis smiled at Rovi’s bewilderment. “You are going to Ecrof. You are going home.”

“But my father—my father was fired,” Rovi said.

“Well, Rovi. We can’t let a dispute like that get in the way of one of the finest athletes in the land being recruited to our school, can we? After all, what’s written on the scrolls is law. Whosever name appears, that person must attend. I’m afraid those are the rules. Do you have a problem with that?”

Rovi shook his head vigorously.

“Good. I must admit, I was delighted to see your name. Although it took me a few weeks to locate you. You are a hard boy to find.”

“Sorry,” Rovi said.

“It’s I who should be sorry,” Satis said. “It wasn’t until I arrived in Phoenis that I learned about your father’s death. He was a terrific man. And a smart one. A very smart one, as I’m sure you know.”

Rovi felt tears sting his eyes. He looked down at the book in his hand. Finally, something positive to remember his father by. Finally, a destiny.

He opened his mouth to speak, but no words came out. He had a Grana Book. He was going to Ecrof. Suddenly he was a Dreamer again, no longer a Star Stealer. And at the very moment he realized this, he glanced across the pool in time to see Issa slipping away into the shadows.

5

PRETIA

THE SHIP

THE SKY WAS TINTED WITH THE FIRST PINK rays of dawn when Pretia opened her eyes. She hadn't been able to sleep all night, torn between excitement about going to Ecrof and anxiety about her cursed grana.

She heard someone enter her bedroom and pulled back the curtains that surrounded her bed to see Anara's kindly face peeking in at her.

"Trouble sleeping?" her nurse asked.

She knew. As always, she knew.

Anara sat on the edge of the bed by Pretia's pillow. "What's wrong?" she asked, stroking Pretia's cheek.

Was it so obvious that something was wrong? Pretia opened her mouth to reply. The whole story was on the tip of her tongue—the flame, her cursed grana, Davos and the cliff. But she couldn't. Not now. Not yet. If they knew her grana came from Hurell, would she even be allowed at Ecrof?

"Are you worried about leaving?" Anara asked.

Pretia nodded. It was an easier answer. "Nine months away without hearing from my family," she said. "That seems like forever."

"It will fly by," Anara said. "And before you know it, you'll be back here, sitting on your bed, bursting with stories about the island."

"And the school," Pretia added.

"Yes, the school, too." Anara closed her eyes. "But Corae Island is a magical place where magical things will happen. Ecrof Academy is only one aspect of it. The rest of the island is deserted. I imagine many wonders lie there."

Pretia rolled onto her side and looked up at her nurse. She knew what was coming—one of Anara's many stories about the gods and the time before grana.

"There are people who say that Corae Island is the most sacred place in Epoca." Anara twisted a lock of Pretia's hair around her fingers. "And not because of a sports academy. It was the last earthly home of the gods—the last place they wandered before they departed for their eternal home on Mount Aoin. As a Flamekeeper, I wish to visit that place most. But unfortunately, that's not possible. Our modern age has determined that only recruited athletes whose names appear in the Scrolls of Ecrof can visit Corae's sacred shores and see the temples built by the gods' own grana." There was a sad, wistful quality to Anara's voice that was unfamiliar to Pretia, a true longing. "You see, Pretia, the Age of Grana brought about many important, positive changes for the people of Epoca, but too many of our old sacred traditions were left behind. Both good and evil."

"Evil?" Pretia asked, sitting up.

"It is always good to remember that there was once evil in this world, so that our past mistakes can never be repeated. When the seven blessed gods sought refuge in their holy temples on Corae Island during the time of Hurell, they had nowhere else to go. They had built these impressive buildings for themselves with their own grana, a grace they had yet to give to the people." Anara closed her eyes. Pretia imagined that she was trying to summon the vision of these masterful buildings that she would never see. "The gods were being forgotten by the people of Epoca, and because of this, their strength was diminished and they were weakened." Anara paused and stared at Pretia with her calm gray eyes. "It was there they came together and used all of their different strengths to forge a new spirit of grana, one that they could give to the people of Epoca in exchange for turning away from Hurell once and for all. You see," Anara continued, "grana is the godlike quality in all of us."

Pretia tried to hide the shudder that tore through her body when her nurse uttered the Fallen God's name. If there was any so-called godlike quality in her, that god was most certainly Hurell. The thought made her sick.

"And as we all know," Anara continued, "the people of Epoca, who had lived in a dark age dominated by the God of Suffering, accepted this gift from the seven gods. Hurell was furious. He raged across the sea to the island. Now it was he who was weak. He beseeched his brother and sister gods to forgive him. And when they didn't, he hid in his temple. It wasn't long before grana took hold of the land. The people no longer had use for the gods. They were making their own destinies and had discovered their own godly talents. So there was no need for the gods to remain on earth anymore. Which is why they departed for their eternal home before they could be forgotten." Anara lowered her voice. "When a god is ignored by all people and all earthly trace of him or her is removed, that god loses all power in this world. That's why I'm a Flamekeeper," Anara said. "It's my duty, and the duty of my fellow keepers, to preserve the memory of the gods."

"So because praying to Hurell is forbidden, he lost all power in Epoca?" Pretia asked.

"Exactly," Anara said. "You've seen for yourself, in the mural under the Gods' Eye, that a swift ship with golden-trimmed sails came for the gods to take them away. Of course, Hurell was not welcome to join them on Mount Aoin. Before the ship departed, he emerged from his temple and bellowed out across the sea to the people of Epoca, demanding their loyalty. There was no answer. Once, twice, three times he cried. But he was only met by silence. Then, with all his remaining strength, he drove his Staff of Suffering into the ground, furious at his brother and sister gods, and furious at the offering of grana that had made the people turn away from him. His anger was so powerful that when he hit the ground with his staff, he split the earth, and his temple collapsed. He cried to his fellow gods for help as his temple was falling, but they didn't listen. It was too late. And the upheaval of the earth that he'd caused tossed him off the towering cliffs of Epoca into the churning sea below."

Pretia was wide awake now. "So there's no temple to Hurell on Corae?"

"That's what the stories say," Anara said. "Someone would need an impressive reserve of grana to rebuild it—a godly reserve. But Hurell has no need for a temple. Because as long as no one prays to him, he cannot return. And since praying to him is forbidden, he will remain apart from our world." Now Anara smiled sadly. "So few people pray to the remaining gods anymore these days. But that doesn't mean they aren't still with us. Remember that."

Before Pretia could ask any more questions, she heard her father's voice bellowing down the phonopipes, summoning her to the Grand Atrium.

Quickly Anara pulled her out of bed. "Hurry, Pretia," she said. "We've spent too much time on the myths and legends. You don't want to miss the ship to Corae."

The sun was already over the cliffs when Pretia and her parents arrived at the gates to Castle Airim. A solar van was waiting, loaded with her bags. She wore her golden Grana Gleams and carried a small backpack with her Grana Book. A castle porter swung the gates open.

She glanced into the van and saw that Janos and Castor were already inside.

"This is where we leave you," King Airos said. "Listen to your uncle and be patient with yourself. All good things will happen in time."

Pretia glanced at her mother, who wore an anxious expression.

"You mean like my grana?" Pretia asked.

Queen Helena kissed her on the cheek. "You are exceptional, Pretia," she said. But the worried look hadn't left her eyes.

Pretia hesitated. Maybe if she told her mother the truth about her grana, that anxious expression would disappear. Maybe it would be that easy. But she couldn't. If she knew the truth about her daughter's grana, it would make Queen Helena feel worse than she already did.

The queen cupped Pretia's cheek in her hand. Her worried look had turned to sadness. "First my sister and now you," she said. "One by one, they leave."

Pretia and her father locked eyes. The queen only ever mentioned Syspara in moments of extreme despair. Her sister's disappearance was too painful for her to discuss.

"Mama," Pretia said brightly, "I'm just going away for a little while. It's not permanent. It's only school!"

"I know," the queen replied. "I know. But I won't hear from you for nine months."

"I'll be with Uncle Janos," Pretia said. "It's not like I'm running away with strangers."

At the mention of her brother's name, Queen Helena smiled. "That does give me comfort. And perhaps he will break with tradition and keep me updated on how you are doing from time to time."

"Mama," Pretia urged, "I don't want to be treated differently from the other students."

"But you're not just any student," Queen Helena said.

"From tomorrow on, I am," Pretia insisted. "Please."

"Okay," her mother replied, kissing her on the head.

The driver honked his horn.

"And it's only for nine months," Pretia said. "I'll be back before you know it." She flung her arms around her mother one last time and let herself be hugged tightly. Then she walked through the gates and got into the van.

The van began the long, slow descent from the castle to the harbor. The road was twisty and on a particularly sharp turn, one of Pretia's duffel bags slid forward, knocking Castor on the head. "Packed enough, Pretia?" Castor taunted. "Or did your babysitter do it for you?"

"Anara is not just a babysitter," Pretia snapped.

"Right," Castor said, "she's a *royal nurse*. Well, when you get to Ecrof you're not going to be a princess anymore. You're just going to be normal, boring Pretia."

"Fine," Pretia said, and felt a swell of hope. That was exactly what she wanted.

The sun was a golden orb hanging in the perfect blue sky when the van reached the harbor. A group of kids was racing around the dock. When the van pulled up, the kids stopped and watched with interest as Janos, Pretia, and Castor emerged.

At the end of the dock, a ship was bobbing in the water. Instead of one of the newer hydrosolar boats that could speed around the coast of Ecrof and up to the Rhodan Islands in record time, it was an old-fashioned sailing vessel with three sails and a spinnaker flying Ecrof's green and gold colors. Each of the sails was printed with a giant image of the famous Tree of Ecrof, the oldest tree in all of Epoca, the school's cherished mascot.

Janos blew his whistle and the kids assembled in front of him, divided up by house affiliation: Dreamers to the left, Realists to the right. Pretia and Castor slipped into their ranks but kept their distance from one another. Castor stood with the Realists and Pretia hovered at the back of the group, standing between the camps, uncertain of which side to choose.

"Welcome, Ecrof recruits," Janos said. "This is perhaps the most diverse group to enter Ecrof. We have a fisherman's son, the son of a decorated gymnast, the sister of a current Epic Champion, a former Star Stealer. We have the daughter of a scientist, the son of an artist, and even two members of the royal family. But all of these differences are beside the point. Because now you are all the same. Your names were discovered on this year's Scrolls of Ecrof. You are now Ecrof recruits. The girls and boys surrounding you are going to be your best friends and your fiercest competitors for the next seven years. They will see you through hard times and glorious ones. Together you will learn, you will compete, and you will master your grana."

"And," Pretia heard Castor whisper to the Realist from the Rhodan Islands next to him, "we have my famous cousin, Pretia, who is only here because of who her parents are."

The kids all swiveled their heads, trying to get a look at their new classmates. Pretia was pretty certain when their eyes landed on her they were seeing one thing only—*princess*.

"Now," Janos continued, gesturing to the ship bobbing in the turquoise sea behind him, "this is your first taste of Ecrof tradition. You have traveled to our capital city from all over Epoca, some of you for several days. You have said goodbye to your friends and families. You will not see or hear from them for nine months. Everything that goes on in Ecrof is a secret. No news in and no news out." Janos looked at each of the recruits in turn. "Now you will get on the famous Ecrof ship. For two thousand years, since the gods graced us with grana and departed their earthly home of Corae, a ship like this one has been taking recruits to the island of Corae itself, the home of our academy. The location of the island is a secret. Only three boat captains in all of Epoca know how to get there."

Pretia heard a low groan and turned to see the small boy standing next to her clutching his stomach. "Before we board, there is one more Ecrof tradition we must honor." Janos blew the whistle that dangled from a cord around his neck, and two deckhands rushed off the ship wheeling a cart loaded with bags. "Your official Ecrof uniforms," Janos said.

A cheer burst out from the recruits. One by one, Janos summoned them forward. There were seventeen in all, eight Dreamers, eight Realists, and Pretia. Some looked nervous as they approached their imposing Head Trainer, others crossed the dock like they were already Epic Champions.

Sometimes it was easy to tell what part of the Kingdom of Epoca they came from. The kids from Phoenis, across the sea in the Sandlands region, looked not all that different from Pretia, with dark olive skin and almond-shaped eyes. The recruits from the Rhodan Islands had fair hair and dark eyes. And the children from Helios, capital of Epoca, near Castle Airim, were easily spotted by their curly red locks. There was a Dreamer girl who wore the traditional headscarf of the women of Persos, and a tall, willowy Dreamer boy who had the palest skin and most golden hair Pretia had ever seen before.

When a Realist from Alkebulan, the wild desert continent across the sea, came forward to accept her bag, Janos placed a hand on her shoulder and looked into her eyes. "We have been waiting for you at Ecrof, Vera," he said. "We expect great things." She grinned and nodded in acknowledgment, her glossy black ponytail bobbing as she did.

"That's Vera Renovo," the short Realist boy next to Pretia whispered. "Julius Renovo's sister."

Pretia's eyes widened in admiration. Julius Renovo was one of the most famous athletes in all of Epoca, and he was only seventeen. He was a three-time Epic Champion in the last games. And he was still a student at Ecrof.

"She probably thinks she's already made the Epic Elite Squad just because of her brother," the boy said. His next comment was cut off when Janos called his name, Leo Apama. Leo stumbled forward, landing on his hands and knees on the dock.

After Leo, Janos summoned a scrawny, olive-skinned boy, Rovi

Myrios, who snatched his bag from Pretia's uncle before Janos had a chance to greet him. The boy's black hair was dirty and tangled and hid his eyes so that Pretia was unable to hazard a guess at his place of origin. He tucked his duffel under his arm and darted back into the group of recruits without a word to Janos.

Next was Castor, who proudly approached his father and took his duffel and held it over his head like a trophy, which made a group of Realists, Vera Renovo included, whoop and cheer. Then came two Dreamers, Zoe and Jason, who seemed to be brother and sister.

Then it was Pretia's turn. When her uncle called her name, Pretia felt the eyes of all her fellow recruits on her at once. She took her duffel and her cheeks burned with pride. Back in the group of recruits, she unzipped the bag, digging through a stack of Ecrof school sweats, gray practice T-shirts, shorts, sweatbands, wristbands, socks, and caps all trimmed in green and gold and printed with the famous Tree of Ecrof and their class year. None of them bore any house affiliation.

She bowed her head, trying to hide her excitement from her fellow classmates. Back home at Castle Airim, Pretia had closets filled with dresses made from the finest fabrics in all of Epoca—silks from the Sandlands, traditional wax prints from Megos, water-dyed cottons from the Rhodan Islands. There was a whole room filled with royal costumes that had been passed down from generations of Realist and Dreamer women that were waiting until she was tall enough to wear them, if indeed she ever grew tall enough to wear them. But never had clothes meant so much to her as the simple gym kit she was holding in her hands.

"It's like she's never seen clothes before," Castor said. The little group of Realists gathered around him all snickered. But Pretia didn't care. She was a recruit, just like the rest of them. Nothing was going to change that.

Janos cleared his throat, summoning the students to attention.

"You will receive your official house colors and competition uniforms when you arrive in Ecrof after the Placement Ceremony. But for now, it's time to board the ship and set sail."

The recruits charged down the dock. Two kids, a Dreamer and a Realist, both clearly Rhodan Islanders, were in the lead. They scrambled up the rickety gangplank and clambered onto the deck. The rest of the recruits followed. The second the last recruit got on board, two sailors raised the gangway and two others, who were on the dock, unleashed the ropes securing the ship. The boat swayed, the sails rippled and snapped, and the ship began to sail from shore. Except for Leo Apama, who was already looking a little green, the recruits cheered.

Janos stood in front of one of the masts and blew his whistle. "Your quarters are below. This will be the only time you will share quarters as a class of recruits. When you arrive in Ecrof, you will be placed according to your house affiliation. The Dreamers will go to the Temple of Dreams and the Realists to the Thinkers Palace."

The recruits hurried below deck, jostling one another as they descended the narrow, steep stairs. The hold of the ship was one big room with round windows just above head height. Seventeen hammocks swayed from the rafters. Leo clutched his stomach.

"Choose one near a window," Pretia said.

There was a mad rush as the kids claimed their berths. Pretia was left with a hammock wedged in a narrow corner far to the aft of the ship. She flung her duffel onto the hammock and quickly pulled on her Ecrof sweats. They fit as if they'd been cut for her and her alone. She traced the Ecrof crest with her fingers, still unable to fully comprehend that the destiny that awaited her was precisely the thing she had dreamed about for years.

Pretia was the last recruit to return to deck. While she'd been below, the deckhands had laid out a breakfast feast. There were fantastic fruits from all regions of Epoca—fluorescent oranges and luminescent red pomegranates, grapes as big as tennis balls and finger-size bananas. Jars of Megos honey sparkled next to the famous golden suncakes that were the pride of the bakers in Helios. There were bowls of sweet oats and grains, and rich pitchers of creamy nut milk.

Except for Castor and Pretia, none of the recruits had experienced all of these foods before, and they marveled at the exotic tastes. Even Pretia had to conceal her wonderment that these foods, which were already familiar to her, tasted so much better when eaten on the deck of the boat carrying her to Ecrof. Pretia took a suncake and a shiny orange and carried them to the starboard side of the ship. She sat down and dangled her feet toward the turquoise water as she watched the distant coastline of mainland Epoca.

From what Pretia could tell, they were sailing northwest, leaving southern Epoca and the Dreamer-dominated cities of Helios and Mount Oly behind, and crossing into the north of the country where the Realist seats of Megos and Hydros lay. She could just make out the white salt cliffs of Limnus, where the juiciest olives were said to grow.

West of these cliffs, a jagged cluster of rocky land disrupted the pristine water. These were the Rhodan Islands, home to Epoca's finest fishermen who braved the seas far from the shore in narrow, swift boats that were built so they could pursue the largest and most dangerous catches. Epic Athletes who came from these islands were praised for their incredible endurance and usually dominated the long-distance sports in the Epic Games.

The farther into the Helian Sea they sailed, the bluer the water grew until it became the unblemished lapis lazuli hue that was the color of House Reila. The sun was reaching the midway point of its climb and now hung overhead like a great fiery ball. And just visible in the distance was the mainland that glittered gold and white.

The ship kicked up salt spray into Pretia's nose. But on the open sea, the water didn't carry the same briny, fishy scent that rose from the harbor below Castle Airim. Instead, the water smelled fresh and clean, like the sun-kissed laundry that snapped in the breeze behind the castle.

While Pretia was watching the sea and the vanishing coastline, she saw Rovi, the boy who'd snatched his bag from Janos without a word, darting back and forth between coils of rope at the prow of the ship. He moved like a cat, slipping from the prow down to the buffet table, then back to the prow. His movements were nimble, agile—and somewhat mysterious. Three times, Pretia watched as he crossed the deck to the table and returned to the coiled ropes.

And then she saw what he was doing. The boy was stealing food. If she blinked, she nearly missed it. It was like a magic trick, the way he slid an orange or a banana off the table, then hid it somewhere on his body before crossing back to the prow, where he stored his plunder in a coil of rope. Pretia couldn't keep herself from openly staring, confused as to why the boy would be stealing food, but impressed by the masterful way he was doing it.

On his fourth trip, as he was bending over the rope, he looked up and caught her eye. Pretia quickly looked away, but she knew he had seen her. The boy left the prow and was at her side in no time.

"What are you staring at, Princess?" he said.

"Don't call me Princess," Pretia replied. "My name is Pretia."

"But that's what you are, a *princess*," the boy said. "So that's what I'll call you."

"And do you want me to call you *thief*?" Pretia asked.

"What are you talking about?" the boy said, his fingers twitching and fluttering at lightning speed.

"It's free, you know," Pretia said.

The boy glanced from side to side. His eyes were lively and alert like a panther's.

"That's what the food is there for, for us to take. You don't need to steal."

“So if it’s free, I’m not stealing it then, am I?” the boy said. “And I’m not a thief.”

“Then what are you doing?”

“You wouldn’t understand.” And with that, Rovi darted across the ship and disappeared.

Pretia was about to go look for him when she heard a cry from behind. Castor and Nassos, another Realist, were standing in front of the two masts. “Race you,” Pretia heard Castor say. “First one up the rigging.”

Now all the other recruits had rushed to the action. Castor stood at the base of one mast. Nassos stood before the other. Vera stood between them. She held her arms in the air. “On your marks, get set, *go*!” She dropped her arms. The boys began to scramble. Castor was ahead at first, but then Nassos, a Rhodan Islander who was clearly used to seafaring and more comfortable on a ship, pulled into the lead. He reached the top first and let out a victorious whoop before expertly sliding down the ropes back to the deck. Castor followed, a stormy look on his face.

Next, Adira, the Dreamer in the headscarf, and Virgil, the willowy, golden-haired Dreamer boy, stepped forward. “We want to race,” they said almost in unison. Pretia watched as Virgil wound his golden locks into a knot. Adira’s headscarf whipped in the wind as she grabbed the rigging.

Once more, Vera started the race. Virgil was graceful and strong, but Adira was nimble like a gymnast or a dancer, and her quick footwork carried her up the rigging first.

Pretia watched from the deck. The excitement of the races was infectious. She heard herself cheering her classmates on. She didn’t really care who won. Just watching the kids climb—just the idea of climbing herself—was thrilling enough.

“I want to race the princess.”

Pretia looked away from the masts, where Leo had become tangled with the rigging midclimb as he raced Xenia, a Dreamer from Chaldis. Vera Renovo was standing in front of her. She had her hands on her hips. Her brown eyes were flashing and her dark skin shone like she'd been dipped in sacred oil.

"No," said Pretia, fear gripping her as she thought of her cursed grana and of what might happen if she raced Vera up the mast. But she wanted to climb. She wanted to push herself. She wanted to rise up above the deck.

"Are you afraid of heights or of losing?" Vera asked.

"Neither," Pretia said.

"So what are you waiting for?" Vera narrowed her eyes.

"Nothing," Pretia said, giving in and rushing to the base of one of the masts.

This time, Adira started the race. Pretia grabbed the ropes. "Go!" Adira said.

Pretia began to climb. At first it was difficult to balance on the ropes and pull herself up. But soon she figured out how to steady herself on the swaying ladder while reaching for the next rung. And then it became easy. Suddenly Pretia was no longer aware of the unstable rope ladder, the light wind, the group of recruits standing below her on the deck. Suddenly she could no longer feel the rope burning her palms as she climbed, or her shoes slipping on the loose rope. Suddenly she could feel herself pulling away, as if she were simply climbing a set of stairs. And suddenly she could *see* herself racing ahead, climbing faster than she thought possible. She was watching herself beating Vera.

It was her grana. Pretia glanced up at the shadow version of herself racing up the rigging and at Vera, who had momentarily lost her balance as she realized Pretia was winning. Vera hadn't just lost her balance; she was slipping down the rope ladder. Pretia's heart froze. She couldn't breathe. What if she had made Vera fall? *Stop*, she screamed silently. *Stop!* Then she felt as if she'd been punched in the stomach—like her shadow self had slammed back into her. Now Pretia was higher up on the rigging, where her shadow self had been. Except that her shadow self was gone and it was just her. And she, too, was falling, falling toward the deck. Quickly, she grasped the ropes and pulled herself to safety just in time to see Vera reach the top of the rigging and raise her arms in victory.

Pretia slid back to the deck, where the recruits were cheering Vera's win.

"What happened?" Leo asked. "You were beating her the whole way. And then it was like you let her win."

"Nothing happened," Pretia said. "She just pulled ahead in the end." She took a deep breath and looked up at the mast. But that wasn't true. Pretia had split herself—she'd revealed her evil half, if only she was aware of it. Something inside of her was bad, and she needed to hide this from everyone.

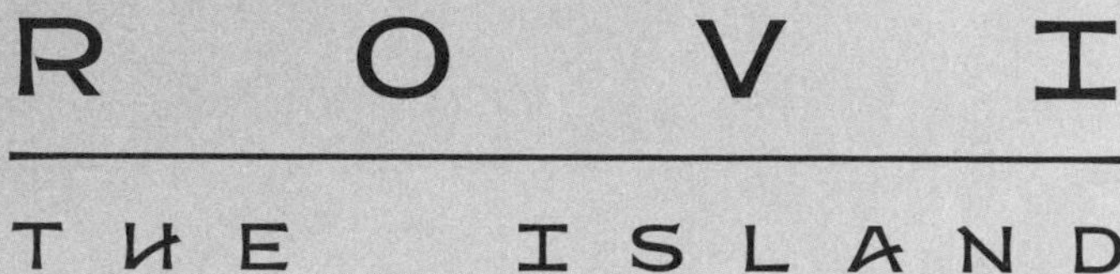

6
ROVI
THE ISLAND

ROVI STOOD ON THE DECK OF THE SHIP WATCHing the waves. The last time he'd crossed this same body of water he'd been terrified. It had been dark and he and his father were being taken away from Ecrof in the middle of the night.

Rovi had spent the voyage curled up in his bunk while Pallas Myrios raved and ranted about trees. Trees were going to kill them. He had to kill trees. Rovi shuddered at the memory of his father's last days at Ecrof and the rumor that had chased them from the island: Pallas had tried to cut down the famed Tree of Ecrof.

Rovi slammed his eyes shut to block out the memory. When he opened them again, he saw that Janos was watching him from across the deck. The Head Trainer raised his hand. Rovi offered a half-hearted wave in return and then scuttled away.

He remembered the powerful Head Trainer of Ecrof well. Janos and his father had been friends, close friends who had spent many evenings drinking Megaran wine and discussing the limits of visualization late into the night. But everything had gone wrong.

Rovi remembered the last time he'd seen Janos, raging in his father's small suite of rooms. The powerful Head Trainer had towered over Pallas Myrios as he bellowed that Pallas's behavior had brought disgrace to the academy. Janos proclaimed that Pallas's and Rovi's presence would not be tolerated on Corae for a minute longer than necessary. Pallas hadn't replied. From then on, he hadn't said much of anything that made sense. He'd just taken Rovi by the hand and led him to the awaiting ship.

Now, Rovi darted to an empty corner of this ship and sat with his back against a coil of rope. He closed his eyes. He was exhausted. The last three days had been a blur. Satis had led him from the swimming pool and out through the Upper City to a van that was waiting to drive them to the Alegian Sea. A huge picnic lunch was waiting in the van—more food than Rovi had been served at any one time since he and his father had left Ecrof three years earlier. He was so busy stuffing himself with beef pastries and honeycakes that the van had already driven far outside the limits of Phoenis before he realized he hadn't said goodbye to Issa. By then it was too late.

As Rovi felt the ship sway underneath him, he replayed the conversation he'd had with Satis in the van.

"How did you find me?" Rovi had asked.

"I'm an Ecrof scout. It's my job to find people."

"Who told you my father was dead?"

Satis had smiled kindly. "I suspected, and gossip in the market confirmed it."

"How come you held on to my Grana Book?"

"I knew you'd need it one day. Like your father, I had an idea you'd be returning to Ecrof. Your father had a sense about things. That's what made him one of the great Visualization Trainers."

Then Rovi had asked the question he most feared. "So if he was so great, why was he fired?"

A grim look had passed over Satis's face. "Your father made a mistake," he had said.

"A mistake?"

Rovi had another million questions about this mistake. But Satis had fallen silent and Rovi had drifted off to sleep. The next thing Rovi remembered, the bus had arrived at a ferry dock at the Alegian Sea. Satis had handed him a pouch of money and told Rovi that the ferry would sail overnight to the capital of Helios, where he would join the rest of the Ecrof recruits for the ceremonial boat ride to the secret island of Corae.

Rovi emerged from his resting place to eat lunch with the recruits. But he kept his distance. He didn't want to be asked questions about why he carried no luggage and how he had obtained such a fancy pair of sneakers. After lunch, when the sun was at its hottest, the Ecrof ship dropped anchor and the deckhands set up a springboard off the stern so the students could dive into the deep blue sea. Even Leo Apama, who had a Sandlander's traditional aversion to open water, allowed himself to be coaxed into the sea, where he paddled awkwardly and clung close to the ship.

Cyril and Nassos, the two Rhodan Islanders, raced each other around the boat. Adira wore a full-body swimsuit. Her aquatic head-scarf shimmered in the sun as she performed complicated flips and twists off the board, spinning her body in a seemingly impossible number of revolutions before diving into the water with barely a splash. Virgil, who was glued to Adira's side, tried to outdo each of her dives. He came close, but Adira outshone him.

Rovi watched from the sidelines. He'd just learned his lesson about competing with strange kids back at the pool in Phoenis and didn't feel like inviting criticism or making mistakes.

The less he talked to his new classmates, the less they would ever learn about him—a good thing, he figured. His father had left Ecrof in disgrace and here he was returning in stolen shoes.

After the recruits were brought back onto the ship and the springboard stored away, everyone gathered on the starboard side to watch as a pod of dolphins kept pace with the boat for several miles. Their sleek gray bodies arced over the waves as they frolicked in the wake.

Then it was time for dinner—a feast of fresh fish that the cooks grilled out on the deck. After dinner, trays of honeycakes and pistachio sweets were passed around. Janos appeared and led the students in the Ecrof fight song. Their voices carried into the air and were amplified by the waves and light wind.

"Now," Janos said when the last notes of the song had vanished into the dark night, "it's time for bed."

A chorus of groans rippled through the students. Rovi tried to stifle a laugh. It had been years since anyone had told him to go to bed. In fact, it had been years since an adult had bossed him around. While he didn't much like being ordered around, he also didn't want to attract Janos's attention.

"You may think it is early," the Head Trainer continued, "but tomorrow is your first official day at the academy and there is no telling what challenges might be in store for you. You wouldn't want to stumble on the first hurdle because of lack of sleep."

This had the recruits' attention. And without any further encouragement, they hurried downstairs and into their hammocks. But before Rovi could slip below deck, he felt Janos pulling him back from the crowd.

"You act like you don't remember me, Rovi," Janos said, smiling down at him. "But I know that's not true. My scouts tell me you're very smart, just like your father."

Rovi looked up at the imposing, bearded face of his new Head Trainer. "I remember you," he said cautiously.

"Good," Janos said, clapping a strong hand on Rovi's shoulder. "Tell me, did your father talk much about Ecrof after you two left? He was an impressive man, but he had some wild ideas."

Rovi shook his head. He was tempted to point out that he and his father hadn't exactly *left* Ecrof. They'd been evicted. But he didn't want to cross Janos.

Janos's emerald eyes bore into Rovi's. "Are you sure? Because I wouldn't have wanted him to poison you against our academy. You are honored to attend Ecrof, are you not?"

"Yes," Rovi said.

"Good," Janos replied. "Very good. Your father could have been a legend at Ecrof, you know. It's a shame how things turned out." Janos removed his hand from Rovi's shoulder, and Rovi raced below deck before he had to explain exactly how much worse things had turned out after he and his father had left Ecrof—how his father, who had supposedly been one of the most impressive Visualization Trainers in Epoca, had lost his mind and wound up a Somnium addict who ranted and raved on the streets of Phoenis. He didn't want to explain how he had watched his father drink more and more of the dark potion until Pallas became a literal shadow of his former self, a half person, an exhausted shell of a human who could barely stand. A ghost.

Below deck, Rovi climbed into his hammock and put the conversation with Janos out of his mind, focusing instead on the adventure ahead.

Despite Janos's warning, it was a long time before anyone slept. Someone had untied the strings of Leo's hammock so that when he climbed in, it crashed to the floor. After that there was much whispering between the recruits and the occasional explosion of laughter until one by one, they all drifted off.

Rovi was accustomed to sleeping in proximity to other kids. He was used to whispers, snores, and occasional fights keeping him up at night. What he wasn't used to was going to bed with a full stomach. And he certainly wasn't used to going to bed happy. On any other night the gentle rocking of the boat and the delicious food filling his belly would have immediately sent him off to sleep. But memories of Ecrof were racing around his head. He was going home.

He was finally going home. And not even his anxiety around Janos was going to change that.

He was going to see the famous Tree of Ecrof, one of the Four Marvels of Epoca, which he'd tried to climb hundreds of times. He would race across the green fields and run the obstacle course in the woods. He would find the Visualization Laboratory, where he used to hide in a secret cabinet under one of the long tables while his father designed one of his many experiments. He would explore the different temples that had originally been built by godly grana, that had been turned into classrooms and gymnasiums. Dreaming of all that lay ahead, he reclined in his hammock for hours, enjoying the gentle swaying of the ship until finally he slept.

Rovi was the first recruit to wake up. He dressed in Ecrof shorts and a T-shirt, and laced up his Grana Gleams before climbing to the top deck. He took a Cyprian orange from his hiding spot in a coil of rope and ate it, flinging the peel toward the blue water and watching as a silvery fish nosed the discarded fruit.

Two seals popped their heads out of the water and watched him curiously with their liquid brown eyes. They followed alongside the ship, then eventually arched their sleek backs and dove down out of sight.

When the seals vanished, Rovi turned his attention toward the horizon, where he thought he could make out the shape of Corae Island rising from the sea like a volcano or a mirage, the only interruption to the endless blue. Suddenly the memories came flooding in even quicker than they had last night—the white-sand beaches below the towering cliffs, the groves of fig and olive trees, the dangerous rocks on the eastern side of the island, which were off-limits to the students, the cool interior of the old temples. He felt that the island was calling to him, summoning him home.

Rovi leaned far over the railing, trying to draw the shape in the distance closer.

"Is that it?"

Rovi startled and staggered back, crashing onto the deck. He looked up and saw Pretia, Princess of Epoca, standing over him offering him her hand. He stood without taking it.

"I didn't mean to scare you," she said.

"You didn't scare me," Rovi said.

"We're wearing the same shoes," Pretia said.

Rovi looked down and saw they were both wearing gold Grana Gleams. He nodded uncertainly.

"My—uh, friend Anara got them for me," Pretia stammered.

Why did she have to mention the sneakers? "Yeah," Rovi said, "my brother Issa gave me mine."

Pretia moved to the railing. "So do you think that's Corae?"

Rovi stood and shaded his eyes. The sun had risen behind them and the shape in the distance was clearer.

"Come look," Pretia said, reaching for his arm and nearly pulling him to the railing.

The shape in the distance was unmistakable now. "It is," he said. "Definitely."

"How come you're so sure?" Rovi turned to see that Leo had appeared next to them.

"Because I grew up there," Rovi said.

Pretia's mouth dropped open. "You grew up at Ecrof?"

Rovi froze, unsure of whether he should say more. It had just slipped out. But he didn't want to explain anything else about his time at Ecrof.

"You grew up in a castle," Leo said, trying to get Pretia's attention. "That's got to be a cooler place to grow up than a school."

"Ecrof isn't just a school," Pretia said, looking at Leo. "It's a school on a secret, sacred island that was the last home of the gods. And," she added, "it's the best academy in all of Epoca."

"Everyone knows that," Leo said sheepishly.

Pretia turned her gaze to Rovi again. "So did you really grow up there?"

Rovi looked over the turquoise water at the island taking shape in the distance. "Yes," he said, "I did. It was pretty lonely," he added, hoping this dismissal would forbid any more questions. "There were no other kids."

"I know what you mean," Pretia replied.

Before Rovi could ask how in the world the Princess of Epoca could know what he meant about growing up alone on an island, Leo Apama piped up again.

"I don't believe you," Leo said. "No one grows up at Ecrof."

"You don't believe what?" Castor and his little crew of Realists—Nassos, Hector, and Vera—had arrived on deck.

"I don't believe Rovi grew up at Ecrof," Leo said.

"Why not?" Castor said. "You think he's lying?"

"Because," Leo said, "not even you grew up at Ecrof."

"That's because I had royal duties on the mainland," Castor said. "I couldn't afford to get stuck out on an island."

Pretia looked as if she was about to say something. But before she could, Castor turned and faced Rovi. "You think that I don't know who you are, Rovi Myrios?" he said. "Your father was the Visualization Trainer at Ecrof before my father fired him and sent you both away."

Rovi's eyes widened and his pulse raced.

"So, wait," Leo said. "He wasn't lying?"

"He wasn't," Castor said. "But he wasn't exactly telling the whole truth. Rovi spent a few years at Ecrof when he was younger, but why doesn't he tell us where he's been living for the last few years?"

Rovi could feel his blood beginning to boil. "Don't say another word," he hissed.

"You don't want me to tell them that you've been living on the streets? That you're a Star Stealer?" Castor said.

"You're the Star Stealer?" Leo gasped, jumping back as if Rovi was going to bite him.

Now Rovi could feel his cheeks starting to burn. He hoped his tanned skin from years of living on the streets of Phoenis hid his embarrassment. "I'm not a Star Stealer, I'm a Dreamer."

"That's not what I heard," Castor said. "I heard you were living with a band of Star Stealers under a bridge when the Ecrof scout found you. That's quite a story for an Ecrof recruit."

"At least I don't need to rely on gossip to prove I'm better than anyone," Rovi said.

Now it was Castor whose eyes opened wide. "What did you say?"

"I said, I don't need to rely on gossip I heard from my father to prove I'm superior," Rovi repeated. "I can just prove it on the field."

"Your father?" Castor laughed. "Your dad was fired after going insane. And the only gossip I heard is about how crazy your father was. He was the worst teacher ever to work at Ecrof."

"That's not true!" Rovi shouted.

Castor put a finger to his lips and cocked his head as if he were thinking deeply. "What was it I heard again?" he said.

The Realists all kept their eyes glued to his face.

"Oh yeah," Castor said finally. "Wasn't he caught trying to cut down the Tree of Ecrof?"

"What?" Leo yelped.

"No *way*," Vera said.

"No," Rovi muttered. "It's not true." His cheeks were on fire now. His heart was pounding. He squeezed his eyes shut until he could hear the blood rush in his ears, drowning out his father's delusional voice: *Kill the tree.*

"Your father tried to cut down the Tree of Ecrof?" Vera was staring at him like he'd just stolen her Grana Book. "That's one of the most holy sites in Epoca."

Rovi glared back at Vera. "He didn't. He didn't do anything to the tree."

Castor folded his arms over his chest. "I know I'm right. But if you need more proof, we can ask my dad and he can tell—"

Issa and his gang wouldn't have stood by and let some rich kid taunt them. Before Castor could finish speaking, Rovi lunged at him. He wrapped his arms around Castor and tackled him to the deck.

"Stop it!" Pretia screamed.

Castor fought back hard. The boys tumbled and rolled. Rovi was fast but Castor was stronger, and he slipped out of Rovi's grasp and pinned him to the deck. Just then the ship hit the furrow of a wave and Rovi slid out of Castor's hold and went skidding toward the railing, his feet dangling down toward the water. If the ship bucked again, he'd fall overboard.

Castor stood over him. "I think we should stop fighting," he said. "You wouldn't want to get expelled before we get there."

If he were still in Issa's gang, Rovi would have done something vulgar like spit at Castor. But Rovi had to get control of himself. He wasn't a Star Stealer and he couldn't afford to act like one. He was a Dreamer. Now and forever.

Pretia raced to Rovi's side, pushing Castor out of the way. She looped her arms through Rovi's and pulled him back on deck. Rovi was too furious to say anything. He'd lost the fight and now he was being rescued by a *princess*.

"Do I need to call Janos?" A deckhand had appeared from below and was watching the recruits.

"No," Pretia said. "It was nothing."

“Janos insists on knowing about any disturbance among the students,” the deckhand said.

“It was an accident,” Pretia said. Rovi watched as Pretia stood up as tall as she could and put on what seemed like her most regal face, looking for once like a princess, not an excited recruit. “I swear on this kingdom that it was nothing more than an accident.”

The deckhand looked doubtfully from Pretia to Castor, then disappeared.

“Gosh, Pretia,” Castor said when the deckhand was out of earshot, “maybe you really are the Child of Hope like everyone is always saying.”

Rovi saw Pretia roll her eyes at her cousin.

“Or maybe,” Castor said, snickering, “you’re a Demigen with no house affiliation.” Then he looked from Pretia to Rovi. “Actually, this is perfect. A Star Stealer and a Demigen. Two people who don’t belong anywhere. Ecrof is going to have to find a special house just for you guys.”

Demigen—half person—was a word Rovi had only ever heard used about the lowest classes in society, people who were too desperate to be loyal to either House Somni or House Reila and intermarried without thought to lineage. But he’d never in his life heard it used for anyone of royal stature, especially not the Princess of Epoca.

Before Rovi had any more time to wonder about Pretia’s heritage, a horn blasted across the ship and a different deckhand appeared in front of one of the masts. “The island Corae,” he exclaimed, pointing across the sea.

All the kids turned and stared at once. Because there it was—the towering white cliffs and the glittering plateau. Rovi had been so distracted by his fight with Castor that he’d nearly missed his first glimpse of home. Except now, it didn’t exactly feel like home anymore.

7

PRETIA

THE PATH

THERE WERE MANY TIMES THROUGHOUT THEIR childhood that Pretia had almost felt sorry for Castor, always having to watch from the sidelines while she was the center of attention at royal events. But once they boarded the boat to Corae, all sympathy for her cousin, second in line to the throne, second in all royal affairs, vanished. He'd never been particularly nice to Pretia, but she'd just thought that was how cousins were—needling each other about everything. But now that she saw him with other kids, she could see he was a bully, teasing the poor former Star Stealer for no reason other than to prove that he was from a noble family. It horrified Pretia, not least of all because the last thing she wanted to do was draw attention to the fact that she was a princess.

The fight between Rovi and Castor annoyed her for another reason—it had almost caused her to miss her first real vision of the island of Corae. What had formerly been a vague silhouette in the distance had now taken the shape of a small but impressive island. The ship approached from the east where towering cliffs rose from the sea up to a distant plateau. Pretia craned her neck, trying to see if she could make out the academy. But before she could, the boat had circled around and headed into a narrow inlet cut into the cliffs.

At first it didn't seem possible that the ship could pass between the cliffs on either side—they were so close that the kids were able to reach out and touch the white limestone walls. Only someone with great sailing expertise would be able to navigate this entry.

When the ship had passed through the narrow opening, it arrived in a hidden harbor that ended in the most pristine white-sand beach Pretia had ever seen. At the foot of the beach, just at the edge of the water, stood a giant gate—two towering columns topped by a triangular pediment. Pretia recognized it instantly from the painting in the Gods' Eye that she had spent hours staring at back at Castle Airim. Cora, the goddess of love, was lingering in this very gate, staring back over her shoulder at something in or near one of the cliffs.

As the water got shallower it turned the most extraordinary light blue—like the precious gemstones kept deep in the vaults of Castle Airim. On either side of the inlet rose craggy cliffs that were topped with scrubby trees. These cliffs reached far into the ocean and hid the harbor from view of the open water.

Pretia had traveled all over Epoca. She'd been to the Rhodan Islands and to the sacred temples on top of Mount Oly. She'd been to the Port of Hydros and the rolling hills of Megaros, where the best grapes grew. But she'd never seen anything as beautiful as Corae. It was clear why the gods had chosen it as their final home before departing the earth once and for all.

Two docks stretched out from the beach into the bay where two smaller boats were pushing off, on their way to meet the Ecrof ship, which had dropped anchor.

Janos appeared on deck and blew his whistle. The recruits assembled in front of him.

"Welcome to Corae," he bellowed. "Welcome to your new home."

A cheer rose from all the recruits at once except for Rovi, who was standing off by himself, not even bothering to look at the majestic island.

“These small rowboats will take you to shore. Your luggage will follow you to Ecrof.” Janos paused and looked down the line of recruits one at a time. “That is, if you can find Ecrof.”

Pretia winced as she thought of the dozen or so bags Anara had packed for her.

“What do you mean, if we find Ecrof?” Adira asked.

“The first challenge you will face as a student of Ecrof is finding the academy itself,” Janos explained. “I only have one hint for you. The campus is on the south side of the island. The rest is wilderness. I suggest you don’t get lost.”

“Isn’t it just on top of that hill?” Leo asked.

“Perhaps,” Janos said. “But how do you get there?”

Castor and his little crew of Realists had pulled away from the group. Vera and Castor had their heads bowed together, obviously plotting how to find the academy. Pretia had to admit those two had a leg up on the rest of them. Castor had visited Ecrof once or twice, and Vera’s brother had been a student at the academy for seven years.

The recruits scrambled down rope ladders toward the waiting boats. The Realists took one boat, the Dreamers another. Only Pretia remained on board the large ship, looking anxiously at the two boats.

“Maybe you should swim,” Castor called.

That settled it. She chose the Dreamer boat.

Virgil and Adira babbled incessantly as they were rowed to shore. Rovi sat in the stern of the boat, his back to the rest of the Dreamers, staring not at Corae, but in the direction of the open ocean.

The boats were pulled onto the beach and the recruits clambered out. Pretia surveyed her surroundings. From the beach, the looming cliffs seemed impenetrable. Several of the recruits began to tour the beach, looking for a way through. To Pretia’s annoyance, Castor found the path that led from the beach up toward the island. He led the Realists through. The Dreamers followed.

The path was steep, like it had been designed for nimble-footed goats, not people. It was rocky and slippery and dotted with small, spiky plants like sea clover. Up, up, up they climbed until the boats in the harbor were tiny specks, no larger than ants. Below, the blue sea crashed on the shore.

"Ecrof is the most magnificent place on earth," Castor boasted. "And trust me, I've been in every castle in Epoca." He raised his voice so it echoed loudly down the cliff. "Even Castle Airim has nothing like Ecrof's campus."

Pretia bit her lip. She knew Castor hadn't been in *every* castle in Epoca. But she said nothing and instead concentrated on the climb, Castor's voice grating her ears the entire way. Soon he was bragging about his visits to Ecrof, about how he was definitely going to be House Captain, how the Realists were certain to win both House Field Days that year. He also assumed that he'd get chosen for the Epic Elite Squad—a group of specially selected athletes who were taken to train in secret for most of the year in order to prepare for summer competitions with other academies.

"You think his father told him about the path?" Adira asked.

"Would Janos do that?" Virgil asked.

Both kids turned and looked at Pretia. "My uncle wouldn't cheat," she said.

Pretia could hear Castor's boastful voice up ahead. "Ecrof is the best place in all of Epoca. It has tons and tons of secrets that only some of us know."

"Like the Infinity Track," Vera chimed in.

"Yeah, that," Castor said in a tone that, at least to Pretia, indicated he had no idea what Vera was talking about. "And," he continued, "there are seven temples to the seven gods. Of course there isn't one to Hurell. Everyone knows that."

Pretia breathed an inadvertent sigh of relief, although she already knew this.

"The temples are cool and everything," Castor added, "but the absolute best place in Ecrof is Thinkers Palace. It's so much better than that cruddy Temple of Dreams."

"Where is it?" Nassos asked.

"When we get to the top of this hill, we'll be at the entrance to the Panathletic Stadium, where the Tree of Ecrof is," Castor explained loudly. "The palace is way up on the hill, looking down at everything."

"He forgot about the Decision Woods." Pretia was startled to hear Rovi's voice. He hadn't spoken since his fight with Castor on the ship. She turned and looked at him over her shoulder. "When you reach the top of the path, you don't get to the stadium. That's farther west along the cliff. You get to the Decision Woods. Maybe Castor doesn't know about that."

"What's the Decision Woods?" Adira asked.

"It's a forest," Rovi said. "Kind of like a maze. You have to figure out how to get through to reach the stadium and the rest of the campus."

"Do you know how?" Pretia asked.

"No one knows," Rovi said. "The forest changes all the time."

Adira and Virgil kept asking Rovi questions, but he remained silent until they had all reached the top of the climb.

Rovi was right. When they stopped climbing, they weren't standing at the entrance to the Panathletic Stadium as Castor had promised, but in front of a large, thick forest. Pretia snuck a look at Castor, who was now busy explaining that the stadium was just on the other side of the woods.

"But how do we get through them?" Nassos wondered.

It was a good question. Pretia shaded her eyes and peered into the trees. The forest was so dense and thick it seemed that there was no way through. Rovi didn't hesitate. Without a word to the other students, he darted into the woods. Pretia watched him circle around to the right, taking an indirect path.

"There goes the Star Stealer," Castor said.

A few of the Dreamers who had begun to follow stopped at the edge of the forest.

"He said the stadium was on the other side of the forest," Pretia said. "Which means we have to go through."

"Of course we have to go through," Castor replied. "What else would we do? I just wouldn't go the same way as Rovi Myrios." And in an instant he darted into the woods, heading in a straight line through the center.

One by one, the recruits followed. Some entered cautiously, others like Nassos and Leo plunged straight ahead like Castor had done.

Pretia was uncertain what path to take. She and Vera were the only two left at the edge of the forest. "Race you, Princess," Vera said. "One, two, three," and off she went, heading in the same direction as Rovi.

Pretia took a different path from Rovi and the others. She turned left, hoping for a way around the thick trees. It was dark in the woods, and she instantly lost sight of the other recruits. She couldn't even hear them as they made their way through the dense forest. After she'd been walking for a few minutes, it grew so dark that she kept tripping over roots, stumbling into branches, and getting tangled with swinging vines.

Pretia whirled around. She had lost her orientation. Was the cliff that led down to the beach behind her or ahead of her? Where had she started? Where was she headed? Her heart began to race. Her palms began to sweat. What if she couldn't find her way out of the woods? What if—

She raced in one direction. Then in another. Finally, at a total loss, Pretia came to a stop. The trees were so thick she couldn't see more than a few feet in any direction. All she could hear was her racing, thumping heartbeat. She closed her eyes. She took a few deep breaths, trying to calm her panic. She tried to imagine a way through the woods. She tried to imagine that strange shadow self that had appeared when she'd played tag with the castle kids and when she'd raced Vera up the rigging, appearing and leading her to Ecrof.

She counted to twenty and opened her eyes. The forest seemed a little less scary. The trees weren't as close together as she'd thought. Pretia took a few cautious steps in the direction she imagined was opposite to the cliffs. The trees grew less dense. And then a path appeared. It was narrow but clear and easily walkable. And in no time, Pretia was passing quickly through the woods with no difficulty.

She was relieved, of course. But something was nagging at her. It seemed too easy. And if not too easy, perhaps too boring. Was the challenge simply finding the path? Where was the fun in that? But then she noticed something. Off to the side was a tree with hanging vines, almost like rope swings.

Back at Castle Airim she'd spied on the castle kids swinging from ropes they'd attached to the largest of the fig trees. She'd watched them whoop and holler as they dared each other higher. They'd never once invited her to join. But this was her chance.

Before she could reconsider, Pretia left the path and climbed the tree. She grabbed hold of one of the vines and swung until she could grab the next and the next and then the next. It was exhilarating swinging through the vines. For once she felt free to use her grana. Soon she'd traveled the length of a tennis court, high above the forest. When she came to the last vine, she slid back down to the ground.

When she hit the ground, Pretia saw a long log, like a balance beam over a mossy undergrowth. She looked around but had lost the clear path she had been on earlier, so she had no choice but to climb on the log. It was round and slightly damp, which made balancing hard. But Pretia realized if she moved quickly enough, she could keep her balance.

When she jumped off the beam she came to a row of tree roots in the shape of hurdles. She needed a running start to clear them.

Over and over and over she went, picking up momentum with each leap. As she cleared the last hurdle, Pretia accelerated forward, sprinting headlong through a cluster of trees and emerging at the mouth of a tunnel.

It was a moment before she understood what had happened. The tunnel was the entrance to the stadium. Pretia stepped through an archway that led to a long, shady corridor along which busts of former Epic champions stared out at her from the cool darkness. In the distance she could hear rumbling and what sounded like the Ecrof fight song.

Pretia kept moving through the tunnel, which sloped downward gently. The closer she got to the sliver of light at the end, the louder the Ecrof fight song grew. By the time she could see the tunnel exit, the fight song was so deafening that Pretia could barely hear her own thoughts. Her heart was racing with excitement and the fight song was echoing in her chest as she stepped out into the most magnificent stadium she'd ever seen.

She was standing on a running track. The stadium rose all around her—a bowl of white marble. It was smaller than the Athletos Stadium at Castle Airim. But the setting was breathtaking. The Ecrof stadium was built at the edge of a cliff, so the open end overlooked the endless sky and the sea below.

The building was in the classical style—marble benches instead of seats. There were no monitors, no lights or megaphones or speakers. There was just the stadium, the black oval track, and in the middle of the track, the Tree of Ecrof. Pretia had seen three of the Four Marvels of Epoca—the Winter Flame in the Winterlands, the River of Sand in the desert outside Phoenis, and of course the Forgotten Palace beneath Castle Airim. But nothing was as impressive as the Tree of Ecrof. It was the largest, most majestic tree Pretia had ever seen—a massive olive tree that reached well over a hundred feet into the air. The trunk, which was nearly twenty feet around, was gnarled and twisted, as if it had been shaped by the wind. Unlike most normal olive trees in Epoca, whose bark was dark and drab, the trunk of the Tree of Ecrof was the color of buttered toast—a rich golden brown. The branches spread out in an enormous canopy thick with silvery-green leaves and dotted with small black fruits. Pretia had never seen a tree quite like it. It was almost too much to take in at once. She couldn't wait to tell Anara all about it. At the thought of her loyal, devout nurse, her heart sank a little. It was a shame that Anara would never be able to see the wonders of Corae, which she held so close to her heart.

Sitting in the first rows of the stadium's stone benches were the upperclassmen and several recruits who'd beat Pretia through the woods. They were divided according to house, the Realists in their blue silk tracksuits on one side and the Dreamers in their purple suits on the other. Most of the students were waving their house banners—brilliant purple Pegasus insignias and regal blue owls. Between them, on a long, raised dais placed on the field, was the faculty, all dressed in brilliant green silk. Each faculty member's tracksuit had a ribbon on the right arm that signaled his or her house affiliation. In front of the dais where the faculty sat was a winners' podium, the three pedestals painted gold, silver, and bronze accordingly.

Nassos had emerged from the tunnel just ahead of Pretia and was walking toward the tree, where Janos stood. When he reached the Head Trainer, the cheering from the stands momentarily stopped.

"Nassos Carthos. Welcome to Ecrof! Did you take the path or the obstacles?" Janos asked.

"The path," Nassos replied.

The Realists all stood at once and began chanting "Realists rule" as Nassos moved to join their ranks. When he'd taken his seat, a small bald man rushed over and handed him a blue silk tracksuit that Nassos slipped on over his shorts and T-shirt.

Now Pretia approached her uncle. He put a hand on her shoulder and the cheering stopped so everyone could hear him ask the same question he'd just asked Nassos. "Pretia Praxis-Onera! Welcome to Ecrof. This is the Placement Ceremony. Now, did you take the path or the obstacles?"

Pretia winced as she saw the student body realize that she was the Princess of Epoca. Now both sides of the bleachers were whispering, staring, and pointing.

"Both," Pretia said.

Confusion rippled through the stands. The teachers on the dais all started chattering at once.

"Did I make a mistake?" Pretia whispered to her uncle.

"Dreamers always take the obstacles and Realists the path," Janos said. "No one has ever combined the two before." He gave her a funny look.

"But you know who my parents are. Doesn't it make sense what I did?"

"Yes," Janos said slowly. "Yes, I guess it does."

Pretia glanced over at the Realist bleachers in time to see Castor whisper something to Nassos. She was pretty certain she knew what it was. *Demigen.* And if not that—Dreamist or Realer or any other number of terms he used to describe her mixed parentage.

The teachers had stopped conferring and were now all looking at Janos.

"This is unusual," Janos said, "but not unexpected given the unique circumstances of Pretia's birth."

Janos blew his whistle to silence the students. "Quiet," he bellowed. "Since Pretia cannot represent both houses, for the purposes of her time at Ecrof, she will have to choose whether she wants to be a Dreamer or a Realist."

"Do I really have to choose?" Pretia whispered to her uncle.

"Yes," Janos said quietly. "And this will not be the last time you will need to decide who you want to be."

Pretia glanced at the Dreamer bleachers and saw Rovi, Adira, Virgil, and Cyril sitting in the front row. Were these her friends? Were these kids her teammates? Then she looked over at the Realists. This time she saw the famous Julius Renovo sitting next to another athlete, Sintra Polis, whom she recognized from the last Epic Games. The Realists seemed to have a leg up on the Dreamers in terms of athletic talent. So it seemed foolish to Pretia to side with the Dreamers. After all, she was at Ecrof to compete.

But then her mind started to race. Competing, or at least competing well, meant using her grana. And that was something she was still determined not to do. She would let the Realists down. She would let her uncle down. She would give Castor more ammunition than he ever needed to taunt and tease her.

She felt Janos's hand on her shoulder. "Choose, Pretia."

"Dreamer," she said.

Janos gave her a curious look. "Are you sure?"

"Yes," Pretia said.

"You're certain?" That look remained in Janos's eyes, probing and questioning.

"Did I make a mistake?"

"Of course not, Pretia. It's just that you've always reminded me of the strongest woman I've ever met—my sister."

At the thought of disappointing both her uncle and her mother with her decision, Pretia felt deflated. But Janos clapped her on the shoulder. "And this just goes to prove you are strong. You followed your heart. And if you chose Dreamer, so be it."

"Sorry, Uncle," Pretia said in a quiet voice. But her apology was drowned out as the Dreamers let out a massive cheer, welcoming her to their ranks. Once more the small bald man darted forward, carrying a tracksuit. This time it was royal purple and exactly Pretia's size. She slipped it on over her Ecrof practice gear. The silk was as cool as a fast-flowing stream and as light as air. The tracksuit was the most magical garment Pretia had ever worn. She took her place on the stands between Rovi and Cyril.

She was torn away from admiring her new clothes when Vera Renovo emerged from the tunnel. She jogged over to Janos, the same cocky look on her face as always. She stared out over the bleachers, and Pretia detected a glimmer of annoyance when Vera noticed that Pretia had won their race through the obstacle course. But the look soon vanished when Janos announced her name.

"And our last but certainly not our least recruit, Vera Renovo! Welcome to the Placement Ceremony." Janos had to bellow these words over the deafening cheer from the Realist benches. All the Realists, led by Julius Renovo, were on their feet, chanting Vera's name and stomping in time.

Janos tried to quiet them. Once, twice, three times. Until at last, he blew his whistle.

"Did you take the path or the obstacles, Vera?"

Vera stood up proudly and looked him straight in the eye. "The obstacles," she replied.

The stands fell silent. Pretia craned her neck to stare over at the Realists. Julius remained standing, but the expression on his face was one of shock and horror.

"Are you sure?" Janos asked.

"I took the obstacles," Vera said. "The ropes, the hurdles, the high wire through the trees, the balance beam, the ladders. The path seemed boring."

"All right, Vera," Janos said in a strange voice.

"What happened? What did I do?"

"You only did what your nature led you to do," Janos said.

Vera was staring at him with a confused look on her face.

"Only Dreamers take the obstacles. Realists take the path," Janos explained.

"But I'm a Realist," Vera said.

"Not anymore," Janos said. "This is very unusual. You are our first Replacement in my time at Ecrof."

"A Replacement?" Vera repeated.

"Yes, Vera. Go sit with the Dreamers."

"What?" Vera cried.

"As I just explained, only Dreamers take the obstacles. True Realists always take the direct path. It's a question of nature."

"But I'm a Realist," Vera shouted. "I'm from a Realist family. My brother is—"

"The Decision Woods never give us a wrong answer," Janos said. "Now go."

Pretia turned to look at the Realist camp again. She saw Julius Renovo, who had been standing since Vera approached the Tree of Ecrof, sit down, a look of revulsion on his face.

"Please," Vera implored. "Julius!" she called over to her brother. He didn't reply. "Someone's made a mistake."

"Take your seat with the Dreamers, Vera Renovo," Janos said. "Unconventional as this may appear, with the Dreamers is where you belong."

She didn't jog to the Dreamer bench, she walked, like her feet were dipped in lead. No one cheered. When the small bald man passed Vera her Dreamer tracksuit, she didn't bother to put it on.

Pretia scooted over to make room for Vera. But Vera climbed to a high row, where she sat alone, her shoulders hunched. She hung her head and drove her fists into her thighs in anger.

Once all the recruits had been divided, Janos addressed them in his booming voice. "Now that you are no longer recruits but Ecrof's youngest class, I welcome you at last. Serve your houses well and serve your school even better." He clapped his hands. "And now on to the business of the training year."

Pretia could feel the upperclassmen shifting in their seats. She turned and saw that some of the oldest Dreamers had clenched their jaws and narrowed their eyes in tense expectation.

"I know that most of you are eagerly waiting for me to announce who the House Captains will be for this year's Field Days. But before I do that, please listen to the schedule of events and please refrain from cheers, jeers, or other commentary. Satis, the schedule, please." The bald man handed her uncle a piece of rolled paper, which Janos unfurled. "Our first Field Day will be Realist Day, held in four months. Dreamer Field Day will be held to end the school year. Of course, only the house whose day it is will know the exact date in advance. And it will be up to that house to choose the track-and-field events for the competition. As most of you already know, it is our Ecrof tradition to focus our intramural competition around track events."

Ripples of excitement and complaints passed through the students. Janos held up his hand.

"And now," Janos said, "your captains for the year." All around Pretia, students edged forward on the benches. "Athena Drago, Trainer of House Reila, who is your captain?" A tall, willowy woman with long blond hair and a face like an elegant bird stood up from the row of teachers.

"I, along with the other Trainers and students who compete for House Reila, am honored to announce that our captain this year is Julius Renovo."

Julius was on his feet before his name was fully out of Athena's mouth, as if he'd already known what was coming.

"Please come forward and accept your official sash," Athena said.

The Realist kids parted as Julius descended from his place in the stands and approached the dais, where he held out his arm for his House Trainer, who slipped a blue silk sash over his shoulder. When Athena was done, Julius held his arms up over his head in a victory salute and all the Realist kids bellowed in unison, "There's nothing realer than the real!"

Julius dropped his arms, but instead of looking at his adoring crew of Realists, his eyes drifted over to the Dreamer camp, where they landed on his sister. Vera was staring back at him, a pleading expression on her face. Pretia watched as disgust filled his eyes, and he shook his head like Vera was nothing to him. Then he returned to the Realists without another glance at the Dreamers or Vera.

Janos stood once more. "Cleopatra Volis, please stand and tell us who will be captain of the Dreamers."

A woman built like a swimmer with a long, glossy cascade of black hair stood. "On behalf of House Somni, I proudly announce Cassandra Bellus as our new captain."

Pretia heard a small gasp behind her and turned and saw a tiny girl with rich brown skin darker than Julius's and Vera's and a puff of black curls clap her hands to her mouth.

A few of the older Dreamer boys were staring at her, some with admiration and others with jealousy.

For a moment, Cassandra didn't budge.

"If she doesn't move, I'm going to take her place," one of the older boys said.

"Cassandra," Cleopatra said, "are you coming down to accept your sash?"

Then, fleet as a fox, Cassandra dashed down the stadium steps and sprinted to the dais. Janos had to bend in half in order to slip the sash over her shoulder.

Instead of raising her arms over her head as Julius had done, Cassandra waved at the Dreamers, who responded by chanting, "The world is built on dreams!" Then she dashed back to the stands and took her place.

Once she was seated, Janos stood for a final time. "For those of you who just arrived, you've already had a busy morning. You are exempt from school activities this morning while your House Captains show you around campus. The rest of you will participate in Free Play in the sport of your choice." The upperclassmen let out a cheer. "Enjoy your last day of freedom," Janos added. "Tomorrow fall training begins—for all of you."

The cheers turned to groans before Janos silenced them with his whistle one more time. Then the entire student body rose at once. The first years huddled around their House Captains while the rest of the students rushed headlong away from the field.

Cassandra led the recruits out of the stadium through an entrance opposite the tunnel that led to the Decision Woods. Pretia didn't even bother to stifle a gasp as she got her first glimpse of the Ecrof campus.

It was incredible—like she was stepping back in time while also being propelled into the future. All around her were the most magnificent buildings constructed in the old-fashioned classical style—towering temples that had been converted into stately modern buildings. Pretia had thought that Castle Airim was huge. But the scale of everything at Ecrof was mind-boggling.

The former temples rose hundreds of feet into the air with towering columns taller than any Pretia had seen before. They looked as if they had been built by the legendary giants that the stories said lived in Epoca long before man.

"As I'm sure you've heard," Cassandra said, "the legends say that the original seven buildings on campus were formerly temples to the Gods of Granity and were built by the gods' own grana. Of course, over time, the school has built many more."

"Wow," Virgil said.

"Wow," Adira repeated.

For a moment everyone fell silent, staring at the temples that surrounded them. It was almost as if they were standing in the presence of the gods, Pretia thought—or what remained of them.

◆

The minute Pretia got back to Castle Airim, the first thing she would do is find Anara and tell her all about the temples, each and every detail. She'd let her nurse know that she was right—these buildings were certainly built by divine grana, because nothing else could make something so spectacular.

"Feel free to explore any of the buildings, except for the Trainers Towers and Thinkers Palace. Those are for the teachers and the Realists alone," Cassandra said. "And if you do wander around campus, be careful. There are ruins all over. So if you go for a run, watch your step, especially if you run far away from the school. The rest of the island is empty and wild." Cassandra continued leading them to the front of an imposing building with double rows of columns. "This is the main gymnasium," she said, craning her neck to see the whole building. "Everything here is state-of-the-art. In fact, a lot of the things that we have at Ecrof don't exist on the mainland."

Pretia peered through the double row of columns. Inside she could make out three regulation basketball courts lined up next to each other. All around them were hundreds of monitors and scoreboards ready to reflect and track the students' training sessions. "This is where indoor fitness and conditioning takes place. And of course basketball practice, but not competition. That happens in the Indoor Arena, one of the only new buildings on campus. It's behind the gym and is only used for special tournaments, like when other academies visit," Cassandra continued.

Pretia could hear the sound of basketballs being dribbled coming from the Main Gym. "Can we take a look inside?" she asked.

"Of course, but don't get too excited."

"Why not?" Cyril asked.

"Because," Cassandra replied, "for your first year at Ecrof, you will only be learning track-and-field disciplines."

"What?" The entire group of Dreamer recuits had spoken at once, except for Vera.

"You didn't know that?" she said, snickering.

"Yup," Cassandra said. "Ecrof tradition. Every student needs to master sports essentials and basic conditioning before moving on to specific disciplines."

"But I hate running," Adira moaned.

"You'll learn to love it," Cassandra said.

"And I'm going to get so rusty at diving."

"That's what your grana is for," Cassandra said. "It will keep you sharp at your best skills."

At the mention of grana, Pretia felt uneasy. Luckily, Cyril and Adira were too busy launching complaints at Cassandra for anyone to notice her discomfort.

"Listen." Cassandra help up a hand. "It's not that bad. Everyone is annoyed at first but you get over it. And anyway, both the Field Day competitions between the houses are always track-and-field events to make it fair on the younger students." Then she winked. "In fact, it gives you guys a leg up on us because you guys are actually practicing track while we are busy with other things."

"I guess," Adira grumbled.

"Field Days are the best days at Ecrof," Cassandra explained. "There's nothing better than competing for your house." She opened the door to the gym. The recruits filed in.

It was unlike any place Pretia had ever been before. The main floor was dominated by the three basketball courts. Above the courts was a mezzanine with a running track that circled the gym. On a third floor, Pretia could see hundreds of different exercise machines arranged so that anyone using them could look down on the courts below.

All around were screens that flashed with endless metrics and measurements. Fountains dispensed Spirit Water, and vending machines held Power Snacks.

"Whoa," Pretia said. "I mean, *wow*!"

"Calm down for a second," Cassandra said. "You all don't get to use this stuff until next year. So it's track and field, as well as Introduction to Visualization and Granology."

"Gosh," Adira said. "That sounds . . . dull."

Cassandra smiled. "That's what everyone thinks," she said. "Luckily, it isn't. Because this is Ecrof. And," she added conspiratorially, "you get to use the Infinity Track."

"What's the Infinity Track?" Virgil asked.

"It's only the coolest thing at Ecrof," Vera muttered. "At least that's what my brother always says."

"It is pretty cool," Cassandra agreed. "It's a track that's not like any other track in the world. It moves around campus every day, and no one knows where it will appear. Sometimes it's on the ground. Sometimes it's twenty feet up in the air. And the other fun part is, the bleachers float, too. So you need to arrive on time before they lift off."

"And sometimes the track hangs over the cliff and if you're not careful you could fall off," Vera added. There was a nasty edge in her voice. But Pretia couldn't blame her. Only a few moments after arriving at Ecrof, which should have been one of the proudest moments in her life, Vera's entire world had been upended.

"Fall off!" Virgil gasped.

Cassandra gave Vera a reproachful look. "It's true you could fall off," she said. "But no one ever has. Your grana keeps you from danger."

Next Cassandra led the flock of first-year Dreamers out of the gym toward a field even more impressive than the Campos at Castle Airim. "That is the primary sports field." She pointed to the immense stretch of pristine green grass in the distance. "It's used for soccer, football, baseball, anything played outdoors. The lines can be transformed overnight to suit whatever games the coaches have planned. But you will usually train at the Panathletic Stadium, which is where you arrived this morning."

Cassandra turned away from the field and pointed to three buildings overlooking the campus from a hill. "Those," Cassandra said, "are the Thinkers Palace and the Trainers Towers, where most of the Trainers live. The Realists have their own pool, which is pretty nice. But I think you all will prefer the Temple of Dreams."

"The Trainers Towers look pretty nice," Virgil said.

"They are," Rovi replied.

Everyone turned and stared.

"Is that where you lived?" Pretia asked.

But Rovi just glared at her in response and looked sorry he'd even spoken.

Now all the kids turned and stared at the building on the hill next to the Thinkers Palace. It wasn't just a building, it was two—two towering symmetrical temples.

"Janos lives at the top of the one on the left," Cassandra explained. "Those are his quarters. No student I know has ever been in them. But they are supposed to be the most lavish in all of Epoca."

Then she glanced at Pretia and looked slightly embarrassed.

"I mean, that's what I heard," Cassandra added.

"I'm sure they are," Pretia said. She was still staring up at the towers. Was it her imagination, or were her uncle's rooms blazing with some kind of light that shone brighter than that in any other window? Before she had time to wonder about this, Cassandra led them from the field and passed a long, low building in the shape of a U. "These are the Halls of Process," Cassandra said.

"It doesn't look like a gym," Adira said. She and Virgil had been glued to Cassandra's side, hanging on her every word.

"It's not," Cassandra explained. "They're classrooms for non-physical disciplines—Visualization, Granology, and History of the Epic Games, which you will take next year or the year after."

The Dreamer recruits glanced quickly into the Halls of Process, then stepped away, eager to see the more impressive sights of Ecrof—

especially the Temple of Dreams, which would be their home. But when Pretia glanced back over her shoulder for one last look at the classrooms, she saw Rovi standing in the entry to the building.

"Come on, Rovi," she called. "Don't you want to see the Temple of Dreams?"

But it didn't look as if he'd heard her. Instead, he seemed fixated on something inside the Halls of Process, something that to him seemed more interesting than where he was going to live.

"Rovi," Pretia called again.

He still didn't turn around.

Pretia hesitated for a moment. Then she hurried to catch up with the rest of the recruits. Whatever had captured Rovi's attention couldn't hold a candle to the golden Temple of Dreams glittering on the hilltop straight ahead.

8

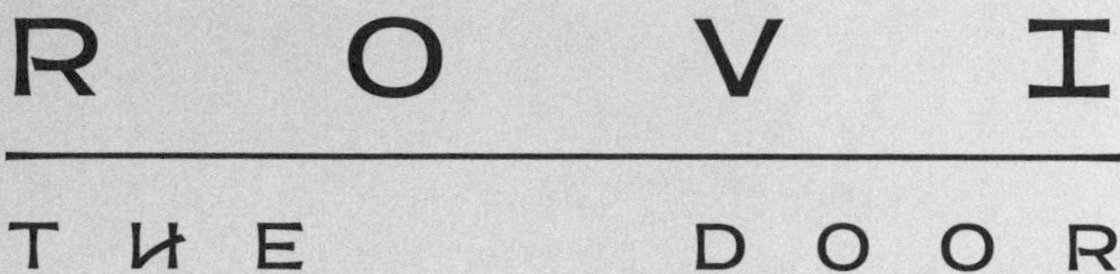

ECROF WAS BETTER THAN ROVI REMEMBERED. Maybe this was because he was going to be allowed to use all the wonderful equipment, play on the fields, run on the Infinity Track, and sleep in the Temple of Dreams instead of tagging along beside his father, a little kid always in the shadows. Maybe now he'd finally be able to try and climb the impressive Tree of Ecrof as he'd always wanted to as a little boy. He'd raced through the Decision Woods without a hitch, leaping over a set of tree root hurdles, executing a long jump over a giant mud puddle, and skirting a maze of tree stumps with no more thought than it took to evade the guards at the Alexandrine Plaza. As usual, his feet had a mind of their own. In no time he'd been on to the Dreamer bench. Then he was touring the campus he knew so well.

It wasn't until Cassandra led the recruits past the Halls of Process that reality sank in. Because the Halls of Process was where Rovi's father, Pallas, had taught and where he'd had his Visualization Laboratory. The rest of the kids had rushed on to the Temple of Dreams, bored by the classrooms where they would soon be studying. But Rovi had lingered in the doorway. He'd closed his eyes and breathed deeply. Instantly, he was able to summon the camphor, linseed oil, and jasmine scent of his father's lab. In fact, he could almost hear his father's voice.

Rovi stepped into the cool interior of the building. He remembered the precise location of the small door that led to his father's old lab that was wedged in a narrow space between two classrooms. He tried to summon the image of his father walking down the hall, his arms full of the scientific equipment, mostly his own inventions, that he used to push the art of visualization into a new realm. Rovi could almost see him as he'd been before his final experiment had gone wrong, before they'd been expelled from Corae. He could almost conjure the sight of Pallas Myrios before he'd become addicted to the powerful drug Somnium and spent his final years, drained of all energy and grana, lying on the streets of Phoenis, more ghost than human, raving about dead and dying trees.

Tears sprang to Rovi's eyes. For so long, he hadn't allowed himself to think about the past. But here, at Ecrof, he couldn't avoid it. What had really happened to his father? What had gone wrong? Why had he been raving about trees in their last days on Ecrof and for years after? Why did he mutter *Kill the tree* in his Somnium-poisoned sleep? By the time Rovi was old enough to ask, Pallas was too far gone, too lost in his Somnium madness.

Suddenly he heard voices outside the Halls of Process. Julius Renovo was approaching, leading his Realist recruits on their own tour of Ecrof. Quickly Rovi wiped away his tears and dashed from the classroom building and toward the Temple of Dreams.

He was out of breath when he reached the top of the hill where the Dreamers' golden temple stood overlooking the campus. When he was little, he and his father had lived in the Trainers Towers. The rooms had been luxurious, of course. Everything at Ecrof was. But they hadn't been designed for play or sport. The Temple of Dreams was a different story.

The rest of the Dreamer recruits had already spread out across the massive building when Rovi arrived, leaving him to explore on his own. He entered a long marble hall lined with cabinets filled with trophies won by former Ecrof Dreamers—shiny gold, silver, and bronze cups and platters, as well as towering columns topped by a tiny replica of the winning athlete. The names of all Dreamers from Ecrof who had competed in the Epic Games were etched onto one wall with gold letters. Another wall bore a list of all the Dreamer House Captains. And another had a list of all the Dreamers who had been selected for the prestigious Epic Elite Squad at Ecrof and the ever more presitigious Junior Epic Games. Hundreds and hundreds of names of the most successful athletes in the land engraved forever on the Dreamers' wall. Rovi placed a finger on the most recent one and tried to imagine seeing his own name in the ranks.

Throughout the hall, there were statues of elite athletes and pictures of teams. There were footballs, soccer balls, and basketballs cast in gold. There were running shoes from long-ago races and jerseys that had been signed and framed. Everywhere Rovi looked he was confronted by Dreamer greatness.

When he'd passed through the trophy room, he came to a large common room with huge sunken couches piled high with royal-purple pillows. Four enormous monitors on the walls showed events from past Epic Games. Beyond the common room was a cafeteria that he remembered Cassandra saying was always open and always serving a meal or a hot snack, regardless of whether it was mealtime or the middle of the night. Rovi stood in front of the buffet station, breathing deeply, drinking in the sweet and savory smells flowing from the kitchen. It was hard to believe he wouldn't have to steal a meal ever again.

In the basement, he found an entertainment room filled with every sort of game Rovi had imagined playing, from table soccer to distance darts to mini tennis. Downstairs, too, were more vending machines. Rovi approached one and cautiously pressed a button.

Down came a Choco Water. He looked around, making sure no one was watching him. Then he slipped his hand into the machine and took the water. He pressed the button again. Another Choco Water descended. He moved to the snack machine—down came Honey Crackers, Lemon Sticks, a Pistachio Brittle. He gathered all the food in his arms and raced up the stairs.

He tore into a package of Honey Crackers and shoved them into his mouth. He was chewing excitedly and trying to open the brittle when he knocked into someone. He stumbled. His snacks went flying. He looked up and saw that he'd collided with Pretia, Princess of Epoca.

"Hoarding more food?" she asked. But she was smiling.

Rovi blushed and began gathering his haul back into his arms.

"You know it's free, right? Just like on the boat," Pretia said, handing him his Choco Water.

"And you know that not everyone grew up in a castle surrounded by all the food she could ever want," Rovi said.

This seemed to make the princess pause. "I'm—I'm sorry," she stammered.

"Anyway," Rovi said, "I'm starving."

"Well, then you need to eat everything," Pretia said. "But don't let all that food slow you down," she added jokingly, then sprinted away, clearly as excited as he was to explore their new home.

The bedrooms were on the second level, off a mezzanine that looked down into the common room below. Rovi found that his name was already painted on one of the doors, alongside Cyril, the Rhodan Islander, and Virgil, the elegant, golden-haired boy who was always glued to Adira's side. Inside the room he found three single beds already made up with crisp cotton sheets and satin blankets in Dreamer purple. Rovi kicked off his Grana Gleams and shoved them under his bed so that neither Cyril nor Virgil would be tempted to steal them. Then he flopped down on the mattress.

Three years. That's how long it had been since Rovi had slept in a bed. That's how long he'd been calling his reed mat and the hard streets of Phoenis home. He'd forgotten what it was like to have a mattress and springs and a pillow and really soft blankets. He'd forgotten what it was like to have clean sheets around your feet instead of the dirty ground. Rovi closed his eyes. Suddenly he realized that in three years of sleeping on the streets, under the stars, he hadn't really *slept* at all, only dozed, always half-alert to someone coming to steal his stuff, or the Phoenician guards sweeping the Star Stealers off the streets.

Three years' worth of tired—that's how Rovi felt when he lay down on the bed that was his—*the bed that was his!* His very own bed for the next seven years. He was glad Issa's gang couldn't see how happy that made him.

He uncapped his Choco Water and drank it in one gulp. Then he tore open the Lemon Sticks and the Pistachio Brittle. When he was done eating, he lay back on his pillow—his very own pillow—and closed his eyes. It was only noon. But Rovi had sleep to catch up on, and he slept right through until morning.

The sun came up early. But Rovi was used to that. What he wasn't used to was the fact that it didn't bother him, because it didn't mean he had to get going before someone kicked him out of his sleeping place. Cyril and Virgil were still sleeping when Rovi tiptoed over to the window to watch the pink rays of dawn creep across the sky, tinting the already magical campus of Ecrof with rosy, golden color. Across the campus, Rovi could see the leaves on the majestic Tree of Ecrof glittering in the early dawn light.

Not long after the sun was fully up, a loud hunting horn blasted across campus. Cyril yawned and opened his eyes. When he saw Rovi standing by the window, he laughed. "Wow, you slept so long I was worried you were dead. You missed the rest of orientation."

Rovi shrugged. He knew the campus. He didn't need to be told anything.

"But Satis told us to let you sleep," Cyril added. "And I guess he was right."

Virgil sat up in bed. "He's awake!" he exclaimed when he saw Rovi. "We're supposed to give you your schedule and tell you to get into practice gear and head down to the main field after breakfast. We're starting with track-and-field practice."

"Which is so much better than boring classroom time," Cyril added. Then he looked apologetically at Rovi. "Well, I guess maybe Visualization could be cool."

"Maybe," Rovi said, digging through his duffel for a fresh set of clothes.

The cafeteria was swarming with Dreamers. But Rovi was too distracted by all the choices to pay attention to his housemates. He took a tray and piled it with enough food to feed five people—eggs, honeycakes, flatbreads, sausages, lavender oats, three gigantic oranges, and an entire pineapple.

"Rovi," Cassandra said as she passed by, "you have track practice first thing. Won't you be sick?"

Rovi ladled a spoon of lavender oats into his mouth and didn't reply. No one was going to tell him how much or how little to eat. No one.

He had to admit that his stomach was feeling a little sore when he and the rest of the recruits trotted down the hill from the Temple of Dreams toward the Panathletic Stadium. He could see the Realist recruits approaching from the Thinkers Palace on their hilltop. He must have looked startled.

"We train together," Adira explained. She was now wearing a royal-purple headscarf emblazoned with the Tree of Ecrof. "Apparently, it's supposed to build character or something."

When they reached the stadium that ringed the impressive Tree of Ecrof, a tall teacher with a long black ponytail and the dark, elegant features of a Sandlander blew a whistle. “Thirty seconds late, all of you,” she said. “Give me one penalty lap to start the day.”

There was a chorus of groans as the recruits, Dreamers and Realists alike, began to jog off. The pace was slow—too slow for Rovi. So he sprinted away, to get the punishment over quicker. But he was soon caught by Castor and Vera. It was a three-way race until Rovi felt his stomach cramp—an aftereffect of his enormous breakfast. He doubled over as Castor and Vera sped past. He was forced to walk the rest of the lap.

“Last place,” the teacher said when he joined the group. “I’m adding one lap for you at the end. But for now, sit down with your classmates.”

Rovi hung his head, hoping to hide the shame burning on his cheeks.

“Now, we have business to take care of. For those of you who’ve already forgotten, I’m Cleopatra Volis, the Junior Track Trainer and your Dreamer House Trainer for those of you in the Temple of Dreams. I’ll be your coach for this first year of foundational training. Running, balance, speed, and agility are the basis for almost all sports. It’s the most organic athletic discipline. Fail this class and you will not move on to the next year at Ecrof. It’s that simple.”

A ripple of chatter ran through the recruits.

The small Realist boy, Leo Apama, raised his hand. “You mean we’d have to leave school?”

“That’s exactly what I mean,” Cleopatra said. “If you can’t run, how can you play basketball? How can you play tennis?”

Now Adira had a question. “What if I want to dive?”

Then Virgil. “And what if my sport is gymnastics?”

Cleopatra gave the students a tolerant smile. “That approach to the end of the diving board, that three steps and a skip, is that not about balance and footwork? And do you not run to the vault when you approach it?"

Virgil and Adira nodded in unison.

"In this class and in others, you will learn to master your grana. Maybe your grana makes you run faster, maybe your grana makes you jump higher or find pathways that other players can't see. Whatever your talent is, this is the place to start to let it shine."

Castor raised his hand. "What if your grana is the kind that makes you a Replacement?"

In an instant Vera was on her feet. "Shut up, Castor," she shouted.

Cleopatra blasted her whistle. "Three penalty laps," she said.

Castor slapped hands with Nassos, who was sitting next to him.

"Both of you," Cleopatra said, pointing at Castor. Castor reluctantly got to his feet and followed Vera to the edge of the field. Rovi watched them go, his stomach still knotted from earlier. He would have loved to have challenged them, but the thought made the pain in his gut even worse.

When Vera and Castor took off for their first lap, it was at a breakneck pace—so fast that it didn't seem they would be able to keep it up for one entire lap, let alone three. The remaining recruits all jumped to their feet, watching what had turned into a race. The Realists were cheering loudly for Castor, the Dreamers somewhat more quietly for Vera. After two laps, both runners looked on the verge of collapse. Castor's gait had grown unsteady while Vera's eyes showed the strain of her effort. Now it looked like it would be a competition not between who came in first, but who finished at all.

Castor had nearly slowed to a walk. But at the last turn, Vera set her jaw and stood up straighter. With one final burst of energy, she sprinted away from Castor and returned to the group of recruits, where she fell to the ground, panting and straining.

“Now, that wasn’t the most intelligent use of your training time,” Cleopatra said. “In fact, it was pretty stupid.”

“But . . . I . . . won,” Vera said, gasping for air.

“You won’t be getting a pass on today’s training,” Cleopatra said. “Let’s hope you haven’t used up all of your energy.”

“Of . . . course . . . not,” Vera said, still breathing heavily. “It . . . was . . . just . . . three . . . laps.” Then her breathing slowed. “At least I’m not some lazy Realist who had to walk the final leg,” she added, pointing to Castor, who had just barely dragged himself back to the group. With that, she stood up. “And I’m ready for whatever.”

“Good,” Cleopatra said. “Now, in this class we will learn the basics of running,” she continued, “and we will learn—”

But Rovi was tuning her out. He already knew the basics of running. He’d been running his whole life. And he was good at it. He was pretty sure whatever form his grana took, it was what allowed his feet to lead him wherever he needed to go. He didn’t need additional training. He’d do the exercises, of course. But as for instruction, there wasn’t much to it.

Suddenly the whole class was on their feet. They had spread out across the field in the center of the track where the Tree of Ecrof grew. Each of the recruits was standing on a large rubber square. Rovi scrambled to join them. He had no idea what was going on.

Cleopatra blew her whistle. The other sixteen recruits began doing exercises, each one different. Rovi looked around wildly, trying to figure out what to do. Pretia was doing push-ups. Castor, situps. Vera, jumping jacks. Leo was hopping like a frog. Nassos was sprinting in place. Virgil was doing squat jumps.

“Squat thrust,” Adira hissed.

“What?” Rovi asked.

“You’re on squat thrusts. Hurry.”

Rovi wasn’t entirely sure what a squat thrust was. He squatted down uncertainly.

Suddenly Castor appeared at Rovi's station. "Still not done?" Then he squatted down, put his hands on the ground, and kicked his legs out behind him, over and over until he reached twenty. Then he moved on to the next station.

"Rovi!" Cleopatra blasted her whistle. "Rovi Myrios, how come you're not doing your circuits?"

"I—I—" Rovi stammered. "Because I don't need to. I already know how to run."

"Oh, really," Cleopatra said. "Then you will run. Penalty laps for the rest of practice."

"Fine," Rovi said. "No problem." And he took off for the track. He'd rather run any day than do dumb exercises in the middle of the field.

It was hot on the track. Unlike the field, which was shaded by the massive tree, there was no relief from the sun. As he ran around the stadium, he watched the recruits do their circuits. Vera was the fastest. She finished each of her exercises first, then moved on to the next station, nearly pushing whoever was occupying it out of the way. Castor seemed to be the next best, powering through his exercises but still clearly exhausted from his run. Virgil and Adira were the most agile, fast-footed, and flexible. Rovi was also surprised to see Pretia the Princess hanging in there, doing her circuits just like a regular recruit. Of all the kids, Leo was struggling the most, usually being passed by three other first years before he finished at a particular station.

Rovi had completed two laps when he heard Cleopatra blow her whistle and order the recruits to stand on the starting line, where she had set up blocks at the end of a straightaway. "The one hundred meters is competition at its simplest and purest," Rovi heard her say as he jogged past. "Today we will be doing basic head-to-head races to determine your individual baselines."

Vera was first into the starting blocks. She looked over her head at

Castor. But this time it was Nassos who rose to the challenge. Cleopatra blew her whistle and the runners took off. It was Vera's race from the start. She crossed the finish line a whole stride ahead of Nassos. When she returned to the recruits, the Dreamers surrounded her, trying to give her high fives. But Vera just jogged in place, ready for the next race.

Rovi picked up his pace, hoping that if Cleopatra noticed his dedication, she might let him run. He could beat Vera and the rest. That, he was sure of. They might be royalty or the children of famous sports families—but he was Swiftfoot, the fastest Star Stealer ever to terrorize the streets of Phoenis.

As he jogged, he kept an eye on the races. Adira beat Cyril. Virgil beat Hector. Castor destroyed Leo. Nassos beat Xenia.

From across the field, Rovi watched Pretia take the starting blocks for the first time. She was paired with Adira. Cleopatra blew her whistle. At first it looked as if Pretia didn't hear her. When Adira took off, Pretia remained crouched in the blocks for a few seconds. And when she did run, finally, her pace was halfhearted. Adira crossed the finish line before Pretia hit the fifty-meter mark.

By the time Rovi had finished two more laps, Pretia had lost four more times. She hadn't simply been beaten, she looked as if she was losing on purpose—like she wasn't trying at all. The next time Rovi passed the starting blocks, Pretia was matched with Leo. Like Pretia, Leo also hadn't won a race. Cleopatra blew her whistle. Once more, Pretia looked as if her feet were glued to the blocks. She started slowly, then barely accelerated down the track. Leo's start wasn't much better than Pretia's. But it was clear that he was trying. His face showed strain as his arms pumped frantically, as if he were *pulling* himself down the track.

At the end of the race, Cleopatra blew her whistle repeatedly, summoning Pretia over. Rovi slowed to listen.

"You're not trying," Cleopatra said. "Do you think because you're a princess, you don't need to try?"

"Because she's a princess is the only reason she's here. We all know that." Castor laughed. "It's not like anyone expects her to win."

"I expect her to try," Cleopatra said.

"I am trying," Pretia said.

"You just lost to *Leo*," Castor said.

"Hey," Leo said, "we're on the same team, Castor."

"Barely," Castor replied.

Cleopatra blew her whistle again. "Silence," she barked. "Pretia, penalty laps. Five for not trying. And five for being dishonest about it."

In an instant, Pretia bolted to the outside lane of the track, where Rovi was jogging in place. She looked relieved.

"You look happy to get penalty laps," Rovi said as they set off together, their gold Grana Gleams striking the track in sync with one another.

"I was getting sick of racing," Pretia said.

"You know," Rovi said, "it really didn't look like you were trying. I mean, there's no way you'd really lose a race to Leo."

"How do you know?" Pretia said.

Rovi shrugged.

"Maybe I don't like racing," Pretia said. "Maybe I'd rather run laps."

Rovi laughed. "No one wants to run laps."

"You don't seem to mind."

Rovi thought about this for a moment. "Well, I guess running laps is better than being bossed around by some coach on the field."

"So you don't like being coached and I don't like racing," Pretia concluded.

"But that doesn't make sense," Rovi said. "Your name wouldn't have appeared on the scrolls if deep down you didn't *really* like competing."

"Who knows," Pretia said. "Maybe my name is just on the scrolls because of my parents."

“There’s got to be more to it than that,” Rovi said.

“Or not.” Pretia picked up the pace. “I’m telling you, I don’t like competing. You don’t have to believe me.”

“Well,” Rovi replied, “I *don’t* believe you. There’s something you’re not telling me.” How could someone prefer running around the boring field to racing?

“Do you tell everyone everything about you?” Pretia asked.

Definitely not. There was too much Star Stealer in him for that. He didn’t do what people told him and he didn’t talk about the past. When he didn’t reply, Pretia said, “See, I guess we both have secrets.”

Rovi glanced across the field. While they’d been talking, practice had ended and the recruits had left for their next class.

“Well, if we both have secrets, Princess, I’m going to find out yours,” he said.

“Oh yeah?” Pretia said. “Maybe I’ll find out yours first.”

Rovi stopped and stretched his calves. There were some things he hoped he’d never have to tell.

9

PRETIA

THE CROWNS

IT HAD TAKEN ALL OF HER CONCENTRATION not to use her cursed grana during the first track practice. She could feel it tingling in her fingers and toes, urging her to run faster, unleash her new inner strength and talent. But Pretia couldn't shake the memory of Davos falling from the cliff and Vera slipping down the rigging on the two occasions she'd used her grana. So she'd have to be on the bottom. And if that meant she'd be assigned penalty laps, she'd do them. Anything was better than accidentally hurting someone.

By the time the horn sounded to end foundational training, Pretia's legs were aching from running laps. As she left the track, she watched a group of older Realists arrive and begin to set up hurdles.

"We need to hurry," Pretia said, tugging on Rovi's arm. "We don't want to be late again."

"I don't think the Viz Trainer is going to assign us penalty laps, do you?" Rovi said.

"I don't want to risk it," Pretia said, hurrying on ahead and leaving Rovi to bring up the rear.

The cool interior of the Halls of Process was a welcome relief after running around the field in the hot sun. Pretia hurried down the main corridor, peeking into classrooms until she found her class of recruits. The closest seat was next to Castor, which she took to avoid attracting attention for tardiness.

The minute she sat down, her cousin tapped her on the shoulder. "Hey, Pretia," he said. "I have a question."

"What?" Pretia asked, intrigued by the unusually pleasant tone in Castor's voice.

Castor waited a beat. "I'm wondering if the people of Epoca should be informed that you lost a race to Leo Apama."

Pretia rolled her eyes and shoved his shoulder. "Quit it," she said.

"I bet the Dreamers are super-excited to have you on their team," Castor said. "I bet—" But he was cut off as a teacher entered the room.

It was Satis, the small bald man who had handed out the tracksuits the day before.

"Quiet," Satis said, clapping his hands.

Before he could say anything more, Rovi made it into the classroom. "Nice of you to join us, Mr. Myrios. I didn't imagine that you of all people would be late to your first Visualization class."

"Sorry," Rovi grumbled, and found a seat at the back of the class.

"I'm surprised he's allowed here at all," Castor said, "especially after what his father did."

"Castor Praxis," Satis warned, "your father might be the Head Trainer of Ecrof, but I am in charge of this class, and you will not speak out of turn."

Pretia glanced over at her cousin and saw him whisper something under his breath to Nassos.

"Now that everyone's paying attention," Satis said, "welcome to your first Visualization lesson. I'm sure many of you would rather be out on the field playing sports, but without being able to visualize your success, you will never achieve your potential. The work you do in here is as important as the work you do in the gym or on the court. Because if you cannot visualize what it is you need to do when you compete, how are you going to do it when the time comes on the field?"

Pretia heard a few groans from her fellow students. Satis rubbed his bald head and ignored them.

"Students," he said, "visualization is the marriage of belief, concentration, and imagination. Once you are able to do these three things at once, for a sustained period of time, you will have mastered the art." He held up one finger. "Belief—the unwavering conviction in your own abilities." He held up a second finger. "Concentration—the ability to think about a single thing with no external or internal interruptions for five minutes or more. And finally," he said, holding up a third finger, "imagination—the creativity to see yourself in a wide range of situations. Sounds easy, right?"

"No," Rovi said. "It doesn't."

"You're right, Mr. Myrios," Satis said.

"But it doesn't sound very interesting," Leo offered.

Satis looked over. "Leo Apama, right?"

Leo nodded.

"What if I told you the ultimate goal of visualization was to be able to literally step outside yourself?"

"Like leave your body?" Leo asked.

Satis clapped his hands together. "Exactly."

"Wow," Adira said. "Can you do that?"

"No one can actually do it," Rovi said.

"So what's the point of the class?" Leo asked.

A question was buzzing in Pretia's head—*literally step outside yourself*—but before she could raise her hand, Satis had continued speaking.

"When an athlete or an artist or an actor or anyone in any profession is performing at the peak of his or her abilities, a place opens up in his or her mind called the Selfless Zone. If you work hard enough, you will be able to enter this zone."

"And what happens when you enter it?" Leo asked.

"You will be able to do whatever it is you're doing, like play tennis, for instance, without even thinking about it. Your body will act without your mind telling it what to do. You will not be aware of the outside world or your opponent. You will not even be aware of yourself."

"But that's not stepping outside yourself," Leo said.

"Because it's impossible," Rovi muttered again. "It's a theory, not something anyone can do."

"Your dad sure tried," Castor said. "Your dad—"

"This is your final warning, Mr. Praxis," Satis cautioned. "Rovi is right. Literally stepping outside yourself and watching yourself from a distance is impossible. But it still is the ultimate goal of visualization."

"Are you sure it's impossible?" Pretia asked. She remembered watching herself playing tag on cliffs and climbing the rigging.

"So far," Satis said, sitting down on the desk at the front of the room. "It would take exceptional grana to do so. Even so, we need to try."

Exceptional grana. The phrase worried Pretia. She was certain her grana was exceptional, all right—exceptionally cursed.

Before she could dwell on this, Satis continued. "The ultimate goal of visualization is teaching yourself to envision the impossible so that you can make it possible. And the ultimate impossibility is to step outside yourself so you can simply watch yourself perform without nerves, without awareness of the world around you. To allow your shadow self to do the work. Only then can you truly perform without fear."

"Shadow self?" The phrase was out of Pretia's mouth before she even knew she had spoken.

"Yes," Satis explained. "When you compete, you are not just competing against your opponent, you are competing against your shadow self. Before you can beat anyone, you must first make peace with your shadow self. That's what holds you back."

Pretia heard a snort from the back of the room. "I don't have a shadow self," Vera said. "I just beat my opponent."

“Well, Vera, we will see about that,” Satis said.

Pretia raised her hand but started to speak even before Satis had called on her. “What does your shadow self do?”

“Your shadow self is something you need to learn to control,” Satis said. “It can either bring you down or lead you to greatness.”

“What do you mean control—” Pretia began. But Satis was already passing out metal circles the size of crowns. Her shadow self was certainly out of control. Or worse, her shadow self was under the control of Hurell.

“Let’s save the questions for later,” he said. “Soon you will understand more. Now, these are Mensa Crowns,” Satis explained. “They are a simple device with which we can see your thoughts projected on the screen over my head.”

All around the room, the kids were examining the crowns. But Pretia didn’t pick hers up. She had no interest in seeing her shadow self. She suspected she’d already seen it . . . and didn’t like what she’d seen.

Rovi, on the other hand, was staring at his crown with a strange expression on his face, half-delighted, half-sad.

“Yes, Rovi,” Satis said. “These are the ones your father designed.”

Pretia watched Rovi turn the crown over and over, as if he were staring into the past.

“Why don’t you go first,” Satis continued. “Stand up and place the crown on your head. Now, what I want you to do is hold on to a sustained image of yourself running a race or competing in an event of some sort. Anything in which you hope to excel.”

“Be careful, Satis,” Castor said. “We wouldn’t want Rovi to go insane like his father after a visualization experiment.”

Pretia kicked her cousin under the table. Why was he harassing Rovi so much? “Lay off,” she whispered.

Castor leaned closer to her. “You don’t know anything about your new friend, do you, Pretia?”

Pretia looked up to see Satis standing in front of her and Castor. "I see that obedience doesn't seem to be a royal trait," he said, putting a finger to his lips.

Pretia blushed. But Castor looked Satis squarely in the eye and smiled. "I only mentioned anything for Rovi's safety," he said.

"Thank you for your concern," Satis said. "But I think Rovi will be all right."

Pretia looked over at Rovi and he seemed anything but all right. His cheeks were quivering and his lips were trembling. He looked as if he were about to explode with rage.

"All right, Rovi, put the crown on your head and concentrate."

Rovi did as he was told, or at least pretended to. In a few moments, a white light appeared on the screen over Satis's head. Soon, a blurry image of Rovi running on a track emerged. It flickered and flashed. Pretia could just make out the shape of Rovi in the starting blocks beside a shape that looked like Castor. The image wobbled, disappeared, then reappeared with Rovi crossing the finish line in first place.

"In your dreams, Rovi." Castor snickered.

Rovi took off the Mensa Crown.

"Not bad," Satis said, "but not particularly focused, either. True visualization requires holding a sustained and clear image in your head for a consistent period of time."

"Did I visualize or not?" Rovi asked, sitting down.

"You did, Rovi. But I believe that you can certainly do better."

The rest of the class took turns coming to the front of the room with their Mensa Crowns. Virgil, Nassos, and Cyril couldn't get theirs to project an image at all. Leo, Adira, and Hector managed to get theirs to show an image, but it was one that had zero relationship to sports. The entire class laughed as the clear and perfectly sustained image of a bunny hopping around a flower garden appeared over Leo's head. When it was Castor's turn, he tried to conjure the same image as Rovi had, but with him coming in first. But he failed to sustain the visual long enough to see the race across the finish line.

When Vera took the crown, she jammed it so forcefully on her head and pressed her fingers so hard into her temples that Pretia worried she was going to bruise herself. The white light instantly sparked to life, and an image of Vera playing tennis against her brother appeared. She was zinging balls at his head and driving them full force into his body. The visual was clearer and steadier than any that had been conjured by the rest of the class. But it didn't last. After one minute, the projection of Vera and her brother faded, and no matter how hard Vera drove her fingers into her head, she couldn't pull it back.

She ripped the crown from her head and nearly flung it across the room.

"Good job," Satis said.

"It was terrible," Vera said, slamming her body down in her chair and kicking the empty seat in front of her. "I totally sucked."

Finally, it was Pretia's turn.

"All right, Pretia," Satis said.

Pretia didn't pick up her crown. She wouldn't pick up her crown. She couldn't. She didn't want the class to see her shadow self. She couldn't control her shadow self. And she didn't want to see what would happen if her shadow self appeared.

"I can't," Pretia said.

"Why?" Castor asked. "Is the crown not fancy enough for you?"

Pretia shook her head. "I just can't."

"Nothing bad happens," Adira whispered. "Just do it."

Pretia flipped the crown over in her hands. What if it showed her shadow self—her cursed self—pushing another student off the cliffs of Corae? What if it showed her pulling Vera off the mast? What if it showed the flame she'd lit for Hurell? She couldn't think about all the possibilities.

"I just can't," she repeated.

"Can't or won't?" Satis said.

Pretia thought about this for a split second. "Can't," she said.

"And why not?" There was an edge in Satis's voice. He was clearly getting impatient.

"Yeah, Pretia," Castor said. "Why not?"

Pretia could feel her cheeks burning. "Because I don't have grana," she said finally.

The room fell silent. Castor was staring at her in amazement. Then a satisfied smile—a smile of actual happiness, not sneaky malice—appeared on his lips. She knew exactly what he was thinking. But she didn't care. Let him think he was going to be King of Epoca. Let him be king for all she cared.

"But, but—" Satis stammered.

"I don't have grana," she said again.

"That's impossible," Satis said.

"I *don't*," Pretia said for a final time. Then, without another word, she fled the class. She rushed back to the Temple of Dreams and climbed into bed, hiding under the covers and wishing for all the world that Anara was there to comfort her.

10

ALL NIGHT CYRIL AND VIRGIL HAD WHISPERED back and forth from their beds about Pretia—the princess who didn't have grana. Of course she was only here because of her parentage. How unfair was it that the heir to the throne just got to go to Ecrof for no reason? Her spot should have gone to a real athlete with real grana.

Eventually Rovi had to tell them to be quiet. He knew what it felt like to be the outsider. He didn't need to hear people running Pretia down, even if she was a princess. *A spoiled princess*, Virgil had insisted. But Rovi hadn't really seen too much evidence of that. When she'd been given penalty laps, she'd run them, just like Rovi had. And she'd had to find her own way through the Decision Woods, the same as all the other kids.

When he woke up, both Cyril and Virgil were already out of the room. Rovi dressed quickly in his training gear and rushed down to the cafeteria. Even after his mistake overfilling his tray on the first day, he still couldn't resist taking way more food than he should have. The cafeteria was mostly empty. Most kids had already finished eating and left.

Carrying his tray, he found a seat at a table where Adira and Virgil were still sitting over their breakfasts. They didn't notice when Rovi joined them. They had their heads bowed together, whispering animatedly. He could guess what, or rather whom they were talking about.

"Are you still talking about Pretia?" he said.

Adira glanced up and gave him a funny look.

"Don't you have anything better to do than gossip?" Rovi asked.

"Who's gossiping?" Adira said.

"Oh," Rovi said, "I just assumed—" Then he looked at the table in front of them and saw that they were huddled over their Grana Books.

"Assumed what?" Virgil asked.

"Why are you dressed like that?" Adira added.

"To go to track training," Rovi said. "Wait, why aren't you in your exercise clothes?"

"We don't have track training," Adira said. "Don't you ever look at your schedule? Or is that why you're always late?"

Rovi had hardly looked at his schedule. He just followed others' lead about where he needed to be and when.

The first hunting horn blared across campus. Adira and Virgil bolted from the table. "We have Granology, of course," Adira said, clutching her book to her chest. Her eyes were wide with excitement.

"Granology?" Rovi repeated.

"How could you forget?" Virgil called over his shoulder. "Today we're going to learn how to use our books!"

Rovi had totally forgotten. Yet again, he was going to be late.

The Temple of Dreams had already emptied out. Rovi dashed up the stairs to his room. He'd been too afraid of anything happening to his Grana Book to ever take it out of his Ecrof duffel. It was his only connection to his parents and he dreaded anything harming it. So he'd carefully wrapped it in his old Star Stealer clothes and stashed it away. Now, for the first time since boarding the ship, he removed his book from its hiding place and sprinted as fast as he could to the Halls of Process.

When Rovi was halfway there, he heard the next horn blast. He wondered what the punishment was for being late to Granology.

Rovi picked up his pace. He was closing in on the Halls of Process. He could see the Panathletic Stadium in the background with the magnificent Tree of Ecrof towering above even the highest level of seats. Without thinking, Rovi passed the Halls of Process and entered the stadium. He had the place to himself, exactly what he'd hoped for. When he'd been little, he'd spent the hours while his father was teaching dreaming of scrambling up the wide trunk and reaching the branches thirty feet overhead.

He'd been dying to try since he'd arrived at Ecrof. And now, with the rest of the school already in class, he had his chance. The marble stadium was silent. Rovi approached the tree. He placed his book on the grass, then grabbed the trunk. He looked for a foothold and a handhold. He gripped the tree and pulled himself up. He climbed higher and higher, shinnying farther than he'd imagined possible. His heart soared as his feet found the necessary footholds. Then he looked up—the branches were still too far out of reach.

He pulled himself higher. His arms were burning. Higher. Higher. Now the first branch was only a few feet from his grasp. Just a little more. Just a little more. Rovi reached up. He almost had it. Almost. But then his hand slipped. He felt the bark cut his palms. He clawed for the tree, trying to keep ahold of it. But it was too late. Soon he was sliding down the massive trunk, scraping his knees and elbows on the bark before crashing to the ground with a painful thud. He felt the wind get knocked out of his chest.

He lay at the base of the tree gasping for air, staring into the towering canopy of leaves. When Rovi got his breath back, he rolled over. His face was pressed against one of the enormous tree roots that rose from the earth and ran toward the surrounding track. From where Rovi was lying, the roots seemed oddly black. He sat up and rubbed his eyes. No, he wasn't imagining things—the roots were black. Dark, inky black. It wasn't just the roots in front of him, either—all the tree's roots were the same unnatural color. They crawled from the earth like sick black tentacles.

Rovi rubbed his eyes one more time. Was he hallucinating? Was he—?

No. The tree roots were black. There was no mistaking it.

Rovi jumped to his feet and raced out of the stadium. He dashed past the Visualization class and headed for the Granology classroom. As he was about to enter, the narrow door between the two classrooms caught Rovi's eye for the second time—his father's lab. He reached out for the doorknob. But he stopped. He couldn't risk being even later than he already was to Granology.

The classroom was dark and cool. The rest of the first-year recruits were sitting with their Grana Books in front of them when Rovi burst in, interrupting the teacher, who was standing at the front of the room.

"Sorry," Rovi muttered. "I couldn't find my book."

"You misplaced your Grana Book?" The teacher was a slender Realist with pale, almost silver hair tied back with a blue silk scarf.

"No," Rovi said. "It was just buried somewhere."

"Take a seat . . ."

"Rovi. Rovi Myrios."

A curious look passed across the teacher's face. "Rovi Myrios," she said. "Rovi Myrios. I'm Saana Theradon. Please take your seat and keep your Grana Book closed in front of you."

She consulted a chart on her desk. "Your chair is next to Castor Praxis."

Rovi hesitated.

"Take your seat, Rovi," Saana said again.

Reluctantly, Rovi sat down next to Castor. The minute he took his seat, Castor leaned over. "Hey, Rovi. How come you were running out of the stadium?"

Rovi stared at the cover of his book. "I wasn't."

"Come on," Castor continued. "I saw you."

Rovi took a quick glance out the window. To his horror, the entrance to the Panathletic Stadium directly faced the Granology classroom.

"You weren't messing with the Tree of Ecrof, were you?" Castor said.

Rovi looked back at his book and refused to acknowledge Castor.

Castor tipped sideways in his chair and leaned over toward Rovi. "I can't remember," Castor said. "Wasn't your father fired because of something to do with that tree?"

Rovi could feel the blood rush to his cheeks.

Their exchange had attracted the instructor's attention. "Excuse me, Castor," Saana said in her soft but forceful voice. "Is there something you want to share with us?"

"No, I was just catching Rovi up on what he's missed." Castor gave Rovi a wicked smile, then turned his attention to the large, stately Grana Book lying on his desk.

Rovi dragged his desk as far away from Castor as he could. Then he craned his neck and looked out the window, trying to get a clearer look at the Tree of Ecrof rising out of the stadium. Maybe he had imagined it. Maybe the fall had made him see things. But the tree hadn't seemed as majestic as usual. In fact, it had seemed sick.

"All right," Saana said, "now that we are all settled, let's return to the principles of Granology. As you know, your books are made on the island of Docen. There are many theories as to how the Guardians of the Book select the images. What is known, however, is that the images are said to be a combination of the way your parents see the world and the way they hope you will see it. What we will learn here is how to interpret your books. Interpretation is a personal process. To each of you it will come differently. The only thing that is universal is that you will know when you have arrived at the right interpretation."

"How?" Virgil asked.

"You will feel it," Saana said. "It will be different for each of you. But soon you will come to recognize that sensation of realization that arrives from properly interpreting your images."

"But the images don't say anything," Leo said.

"Is that so?" Saana said. "Now, what's a question that all of you want answered?"

Vera raised her hand. "I want to know why I became a Replacement."

"Unfortunately the books only provide a key to your future, not your past. But I'm sure if you look through the book, you will see it with the eyes of a Dreamer, not a Realist."

"What does that mean?" Vera asked.

"A Realist sees what is on the page, a Dreamer sees what is behind the page."

Vera rolled her eyes. "But I see what's on the page," she said.

"All that means is that you haven't really looked yet. At least not with open eyes."

"My eyes are open," Vera grumbled.

"No one is saying the Dreamer method is better than the Realist one," Saana explained. "That is the most important lesson that I can teach you. There are no wrong ways to approach your books. There are only lazy interpretations," Saana said. "Now let's think up a question that's universal to all of you."

Leo's hand shot into the air. "How about, *What will our first year at Ecrof be like?*"

"Well, you're not going to be chosen for Epic Elite," Nassos teased.

"How do you know?" Leo said.

"All right," Saana said. "Let's see what the books say. Who would like to go first?"

Adira and Virgil were out of their chairs in an instant.

"One at a time," Saana said, beckoning Adira forward. While

Adira was approaching the front of the room, Saana switched on a projector. "Now think hard about the question, Adira. And when you are ready, open your book to the page that you believe will give you the answer."

"How do I know what page to choose?" Adira asked.

"You don't," Saana said.

Adira looked nervous. "But what if I pick the wrong one?"

"The page you pick becomes the right page."

"But what if it's a bad page?" Adira asked.

"There are no good or bad pages," Saana said. "The only thing that matters is how focused your interpretation is."

Adira opened her book, peering carefully at the pages. The whole room was silent as they watched her flip through her book. Finally, Adira chose her page. She put the book facedown on the projector, and the image of a golden turret rising from a stormy sea toward a puff of white clouds appeared. On one side was a capsized ship, on the other a giant, glimmering leaping fish. At the bottom of the page, below the stormy waters, were the skeletons of large sea animals.

"All right," Saana said. "What do you see?"

"A tower," Adira said.

"And what does that mean?"

"It means . . . diving. Like a high diving board. And that means it's going to be difficult at first. That's what the stormy water means. But it will get better."

"Okay," Saana said slowly. "Fair enough. But what about the fish? What about the capsized boat? What about the whale or dolphin skeletons? Do those forecast good things or bad things?"

Adira bit her lip nervously.

"You must interpret the whole picture, not just the parts that jump out at you," Saana said. "You chose the page. This entire page is your Ecrof story. Now go back to your seat and think quietly."

Adira screwed up her face in irritation as she returned to her chair.

"Now," Saana said in her distant manner, "I'm not here to make examples of anyone. But let that be a lesson to you not to look for a picture to match the image of the answer you want to your question. As I said before, none of the pictures in your book are good or bad. Just like your entire time at Ecrof will neither be all good or all bad. There are elements of both on every page. You need to be open to everything you see in front of you."

One by one the students stepped forward. Some of them, mostly Realists, opened their books quickly and randomly to whatever page. Their interpretations were quick and literal. *I will run many races. At first I will lose. Then I will win.* The Dreamers took more time finding their pages and when they did, they took a roundabout way of explaining what they saw. But none of the interpretations were precise. *Success is possible but slippery. My friends will be like waves, my sports will be like mountains.*

Rovi's hands trembled as he opened his book. He had yet to look inside it. He was worried about what he would find. After all, his father had lost his mind. What if that was reflected in the pages? What if the book prophesied his own madness?

"Rovi?" Saana said. "Are you joining us for this assignment?"

Reluctantly, he opened the book. The page Rovi turned to had an image of two snowy mountains and a smaller green hill. A bouquet of dead flowers was on one side of the page and a trio of birds stood opposite. He wasn't sure why he'd chosen this page except that something inside of him told Rovi that it contained the answer to Leo's question.

"And what do you see, Rovi?" Saana asked.

"I don't know," Rovi said.

"Is that it?" Saana asked.

He didn't really think too much of the picture. Why did he need a book to tell his future? Wasn't his future just going to *happen*? What was the point in knowing about it?

"Rovi," Saana said. "I'm waiting on your interpretation."

Rovi stared down at the image, thinking how strange it was that this one incomprehensible thing was the only object he had that his parents had held, that they'd meant for him to have. It was the last remaining connection to his father and mother.

His father! His mother!

"Maybe the big mountains are my parents and I'm the little one," he said.

Saana was looking at him with interest. "And?"

"And that's it," Rovi said.

"Rovi," Saana said, "that's an impressive start. Can you take it any further?"

Rovi glanced up and saw Castor whispering to Hector. Suddenly he wished he hadn't mentioned his father. But it had just come to him. The idea had flown into his mind unbidden. He snatched his book from the projector and returned to his seat. When he sat down, he saw that Saana was still looking at him as if he'd done something impressive. "You know, Rovi, I believe your mother was a Granologist, am I right?"

Rovi nodded.

"I think I've come across her name in some professional books on the study of grana. Perhaps you have inherited her talents."

"Maybe," Rovi muttered. He stared down at his book, trying to hide his pride that he'd impressed the teacher.

Now it was Pretia's turn.

"Can she do it if she doesn't have grana?" Castor asked as his cousin came forward.

Saana ignored the question.

Pretia flipped through the pages blindly, like one of the card magicians in the plaza at Phoenis. Then, without looking, she placed the book on the projector. Up came a dark picture. It took Rovi a moment to see what he was looking at. The image showed a forest in the moonlight at the edge of a large lake at night. The trees were reflected in the water, except their reflection made them look sickly, like firewood or something that had been burned. The moon was also reflected in the water, but it was dull, almost muddy.

"Is that the Decision Woods?" Pretia asked.

"It is if that's what you see," Saana said.

Pretia was squinting up at the projection, a baffled look on her face. "I have no idea what I'm seeing," she said. "Trees. Upside-down ones. Sticks. Maybe it's all one tree with a lot of roots. I really don't know."

"What else?" Saana asked.

"Everything is doubled. Maybe I'll have to do everything twice," Pretia said.

"Since she'll fail the first time," Rovi heard Castor whisper to Hector.

"Perhaps you should forget about what you see and think about how you feel," Saana said.

A queasy look crossed Pretia's face. "I don't feel anything. Just confused."

"Relax into the image," Saana urged.

Pretia contorted her face and stared down at the book. "There will be a hard side and an easy side to everything. Everything I do will have two sides to it—easy and hard?" She didn't sound too certain. In fact, it sounded to Rovi as if Pretia was simply making something up.

Her answer, however, seemed to satisfy Saana, who told her to return to her seat.

For the rest of the class, Saana told the recruits to sit quietly with their books and contemplate their chosen image. Then she asked them to write out their interpretations—because some things are better not spoken aloud, she added.

When Rovi turned in his paper at the end of class, he noticed that Pretia's was blank.

"Hey," he said, grabbing her arm on the way out of the room. "How come you didn't write anything?"

"Because my page made no sense." Then Pretia lowered her voice. "And it made me a little bit sick to look at it. What do you think that means?"

"Probably nothing," Rovi said. But he wasn't so sure.

11

PRETIA

THE BRANCH

AFTER A FEW MONTHS IT BECAME EASY FOR Pretia to pretend that she didn't have grana. It was sort of like making your mind go blank so it felt as if you didn't know the answer even when you did. When she was asked to run faster or jump higher or throw farther, Pretia made her body and mind go numb, so she did whatever she was asked to do mindlessly, halfheartedly, with no effort or grana. It didn't matter that she was always on the bottom. It didn't matter that she was usually assigned penalty laps. At least she had hidden her cursed grana.

All day, every day, Pretia was aware of all her grana building up inside her. It was like her body was full of electricity. She felt jumpy, twitchy, and sometimes unable to sleep at night. She had to restrain the urge to go for a run, to explore the Decision Woods, to sprint along the Infinity Track or around the Panathletic Stadium.

One day, Saana let the recruits out of Granology early to study their books in the field behind the three residential temples. Pretia was happy for the early dismissal because she could be alone with her book instead of being forced to explain it to her classmates. She loved turning the pages, trying to figure out why the Guardians of the Book had chosen the images that they did and which images, if any, reflected her parents' worldview. But mostly she returned to the image that she had opened to the first day in class—the page that showed the trees reflected in the water. Where had this come from? Which of her parents had chosen it? And what in the world did it have to do with her time at Ecrof?

She wondered if the mirror images had to do with her heritage—half Dreamer and half Realist. But how was that specific to her time at Ecrof in particular as opposed to her life anywhere else? Or maybe it had to do with her cursed grana. Maybe that's why the trees in the water looked sick or burned—half of her was poisoned. Maybe the image was yet another warning not to use her grana.

While she was staring at the image for the hundredth time, the rest of the recruits had put down their books and split into teams—Dreamers and Realists, of course—for a game of capture the flag. She looked up in time to see her classmates heading to opposite sides of the small woods at the edge of the field behind two of the residential temples.

"Wait up," Rovi said, calling to Cyril. "What about Pretia?"

"I mean, if she wants to play," Cyril said. "But it's not like she'll add anything."

"Come on, Pretia," Rovi called. "You don't want to stare at a book all day, do you?"

Pretia hesitated. Of course she wanted to play. More than anything. And what could the harm be in a game of capture the flag? She could hover on the sidelines, protecting her team's flag while mostly staying out of the way.

"Okay," she said, leaping to her feet.

"Show us what you got, Star Stealer," Castor taunted from his side of the woods.

"I'm going to steal your flag before you know what's happened," Rovi said.

Cyril quickly appointed himself Dreamer captain. "Okay," he

said. “Adira and Virgil, you are the guards. You protect the flag. Rovi, Vera, and I will be the runners. Zoe, you protect our jail so that no captured Realists can be tagged by their teammates and escape. Xenia and Jason are on general offense—distract the Realist guards while Rovi and I try to get their flag.”

“I don’t need anyone to run interference for me,” Rovi said. “I’m just getting the flag.”

“Not if I get it first,” Vera said.

Cyril gave both of them a funny look. “Listen, this is a team sport. We are going to work together.”

“What should I do?” Pretia asked.

“Just help out,” Cyril said. “I mean, do whatever you can.”

Hector clapped his hands to signal the start of the game.

“Race you to the flag,” Vera called to Rovi. And the two of them sprinted away into Realist territory.

The game was underway. Quickly, Leo made a pointless dash into the Dreamers’ defense and was tagged by Zoe and put in jail. Then Cyril got captured on the Realists’ side. Jason and Virgil managed to lure the Realist guards away from their base so Vera could grab the flag. But just as she was about to cross to the Dreamers’ side, Nassos tagged her and sent her to jail.

Hector made it through the Dreamers’ defense and grabbed the flag. He slipped past Adira and Virgil and passed close to Pretia.

“Pretia, tag him!” Zoe cried.

She took a few steps toward Hector. She could almost touch him. But then Pretia stopped. She couldn’t—she wouldn’t. “Pretia,” Vera screamed, “catch him!” Pretia didn’t move.

Then, just as Hector was about to cross to safety, Rovi dashed from behind and tagged him, sending him to the Dreamers’ jail. But in all the commotion, no one had been watching the jail on the Dreamers’ side where the captured Realists waited and Castor had snuck through, freeing his teammates.

"Thanks a lot, Pretia," Virgil called, tugging his blond curls into a tighter topknot.

Pretia turned away to hide her anger. What would have happened if she'd touched Hector, if she'd run toward him? Maybe nothing? Maybe something terrible. She couldn't risk it. For the millionth time, she cursed herself for lighting that silly ceremonial flame to Hurell. No grana would have been better than this gnawing fear that she'd hurt someone.

"Okay, okay," Cyril said. "Let's regroup." After a time-out, the game started again.

Now Rovi was off on his own. He dashed across into the Realists' side, sidestepping most of the defenders, but couldn't get through to the flag and, without getting tagged, made it back to safety. Three more times he tried, each time getting closer and closer to the flag, and each time just barely making it back.

"Come on, Rovi," Vera called. "Get me out."

But Rovi clearly only had eyes for the flag.

"I guess no one wants you on their team," Castor called to Vera.

"At least I almost got your flag," Vera taunted in return.

"Quiet," Nassos called, "we're trying to play here."

Pretia was losing focus. Without being able to tag anyone—or rather because she was restraining herself from tagging anyone or chasing anyone—she lost interest in the specifics of the game. She watched her teammates race past. She watched Rovi and Vera, whom Jason had freed, running back to their side. But mostly she stared at the fig trees overhead and the lush green grass below. She looked for shapes in the few clouds in the azure sky.

The trees were casting intricate shadows on the grass. Pretia hopscotched between them, challenging herself to step only on the green.

The game proceeded without her. Now Castor was on the Dreamers' side, darting between defenders. But Adira tagged him and put him in jail. It wasn't long before Nassos freed his captain.

Once more, Vera attempted to get the Realists' flag, but when Alexis and Tassos closed in on her, she ran back empty-handed.

Suddenly Castor had the Dreamers' flag. Somehow he'd snuck past all the defenders and snatched it. He was threading his way past Pretia's teammates. He ran straight for Vera, who was dashing in the other direction from the Realists' side to stop him. Castor was running with his elbows out. Pretia had no doubt that he was going to charge straight through Vera. He was aiming to run her down.

"Tag him! Tag him!" the Dreamers were chanting. "Someone tag him."

Vera was running full tilt toward Castor. And Castor was barreling toward her.

Pretia didn't think. She just ran. Ran as fast as she could. Ran so fast she saw herself break away from herself. She watched herself sprint. Instantly, her shadow self was within arm's reach of her cousin. She tagged him.

And as she did, there was a horrible crack overhead. The kids looked up, almost in unison, to see one of the branches from a nearby fig tree breaking off and plummeting to earth. Castor froze in his tracks, startled to have been tagged by Pretia of all people. His hesitation cost him. The branch swirled down and hit Castor on the head, knocking him to the ground.

Immediately, the Realists and even some of the Dreamers left their posts and rushed to Castor's side. No one seemed to notice or care that Rovi had sneaked across to the Dreamers' side with the Realists' flag. No one cared that the Dreamers had won.

A whistle blast sounded across the small field. Janos had appeared from the Trainers Towers and was now rushing to Castor. Pretia stared at her cousin in horror. She had done that. She had made that branch fall. It had to have been her. She'd tagged Castor. She'd used her grana. She was right—her grana had been poisoned by lighting that flame to Hurell.

The kids made way for the Head Trainer. By the time Janos reached his son, Castor's eyes were fluttering open. A nasty bruise was starting to appear on his forehead.

"Everyone, stand back," Janos bellowed. He squatted down next to his son, his green eyes clouded with concern.

Castor was groaning and rubbing his forehead.

Pretia stared up at the tree. How had she done it? How had she made that branch fall? What was her grana capable of? She didn't want to know. She wanted to run and hide and keep away from her classmates.

Janos tried to pick up Castor. But Castor rolled away. "I'm okay," he said groggily.

"Recruits," Janos said, "let this be a lesson. No unsupervised games at Ecrof."

"But it was just a freak accident," Nassos said.

"Yeah," Vera said. "It's not like we made that tree branch fall."

Pretia glanced up at the tree. The branches *were* rotten. Still, she couldn't shake the feeling that maybe her shadow self had something to do with it. Yet again, when she used her grana, something dangerous had happened. Surely this wasn't a coincidence.

"But if you got injured when there were no teachers around, things could have been very dangerous," Janos said. "Be more careful in the future."

Pretia didn't wait for Janos to tell her to head back to her dorm. She grabbed her Grana Book and hurried to the common room. Rovi was already there. He had two Choco Waters and several snacks from one of the vending machines open in front of him.

"That dash you made across the field was epic," Rovi said when he saw Pretia, standing up to give her a high five. Pretia held out her hand without much enthusiasm. "You saved the day! If you hadn't tagged Castor, he would have got their flag over to their side before I crossed with ours."

If only Rovi had known what she had done, he certainly wouldn't be congratulating her. And if her uncle Janos found out, she'd be done for. Once he learned she had used her grana and it might have hurt Castor, her time at Ecrof would be over. There was no doubting it.

"Come on, Pretia, lighten up," Rovi said. "You helped us win. You should be proud."

Pretia stared at him blankly. It didn't really feel like a victory.

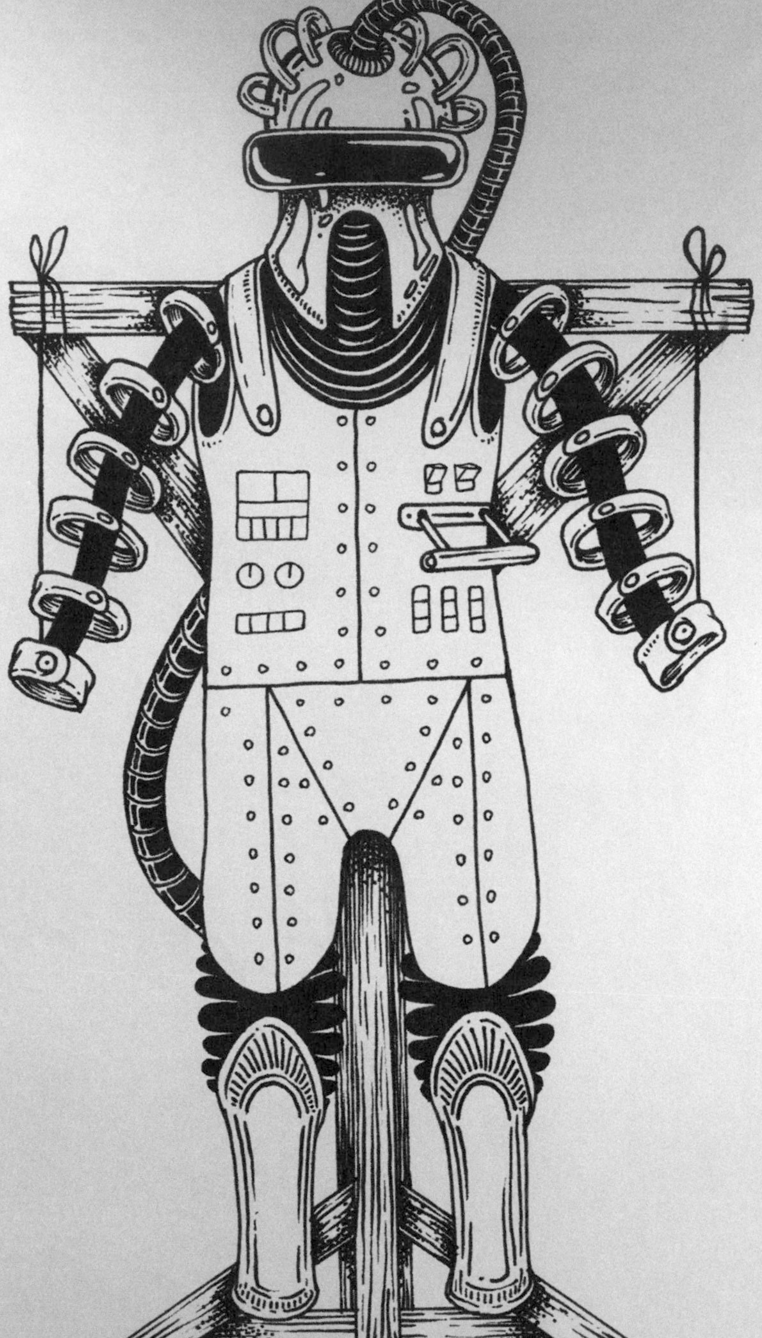

12

ROVI

THE MACHINE

ISSA AND HIS CREW WOULD HAVE SAID BOOKS were boring. Especially Grana Books. Why read about the world when you could be in it? And why look at a bunch of silly pictures to figure out what your future held instead of just living your life? Books didn't play games. They didn't help you steal. They didn't give you that thrilling rush of escaping the Phoenician guards. All of this was true. So why did Rovi keep returning to his Grana Book? Why was he always pulling it out in secret, flipping through the pages? Why, in particular, even after several months at Ecrof, did he return to that very first page he'd opened to in his first Granology class—the picture that showed the two snowy mountains and the green hill? Because he did—late at night after Cyril and Virgil were asleep. Between classes. Whenever he could.

Rovi couldn't forget the look on Saana's face when he had interpreted his picture as having something to do with his parents. No one had looked at him like that since his father died—as if what he had said was worthwhile. As if he had said something intelligent.

At dinnertime, he walked into the cafeteria, his book clutched under his arm. He scanned the room for an empty seat. The room was packed. More than that, it was noisy with Dreamers shouting and cheering from table to table.

It took a moment for Rovi to understand that the Dreamers were all revved up because someone had heard a rumor that the first of the two Ecrof Field Days—Realist Field Day—was happening in a few days This would be the first chance the houses would get to compete with each other directly. The Dreamers were busy making plans, figuring out teams and trying to guess the events the Realists would choose. Normally Rovi would have stuck around, trying to eavesdrop on the action and see if there was even a slim chance he'd be chosen. But he wanted to spend some time alone with his book.

He ate speedily and took a few snacks from one of the vending machines. Then he left the Temple of Dreams and headed for the main campus. He couldn't resist the urge to check on the Tree of Ecrof. It had been on his mind since he'd seen its odd-looking roots, black and sickly. He darted into the Panathletic Stadium. At night the marble steps that rose on all sides, except the one that opened to the sea and sky, glowed like the moon.

From a distance, the tree looked fine. Its silver leaves glimmered in the moonlight. Rovi took a glance at the roots. Even at night he could tell they were still black. And was it his imagination, or was the base of the trunk now black as well? He was tempted to take a closer look. But he didn't dare. He couldn't risk being caught next to the tree—not after what Castor had insinuated about his father in Granology. He didn't want anyone thinking he had bad intentions toward the majestic tree.

People, thanks to Castor, were starting to learn that Pallas Myrios had left the school under a cloud of disgrace. Rovi wasn't sure Castor knew the whole story about what had happened with his father, but he certainly knew enough to drop hints and start rumors.

He hurried back out of the stadium and approached the Halls of Process. He passed under the arch where Prosi, the God of Process's name, was carved and ducked into the cool interior of the building. Between the Granology and the Visualization classrooms was the small door Rovi had wanted to open since he'd returned to Corae. And now with everyone distracted by the upcoming Field Day, he had his chance. Behind the door was his father's old laboratory—or it used to be.

Clutching his Grana Book in one hand, Rovi tried the handle. It rattled but didn't budge. He tried again. Then he took a deep breath and jammed his hip against the door with all his force. It didn't move.

Rovi glanced over his shoulder and then out the doorway toward the field outside. He didn't see anyone. There were tricks you learned as a Star Stealer, tricks you probably shouldn't show off at Ecrof. Quickly, he darted outside the Halls of Process and gathered two sticks perfect for picking locks. With his nails he scraped the tips of both into fine points. Then, working quickly, he wedged them into the lock on the door to his father's old lab. He didn't quite possess the talent Issa did for opening doors. But after fiddling for a few minutes, he heard the satisfying click. The lock opened. Rovi turned the doorknob. And with a mighty, rusty creak, the door opened to his father's old lab.

The room was narrow, just like he remembered. At the far end was a large window through which the glowing moon was shining, illuminating the room. Rovi righted himself, caught his breath. Tears sprang to his eyes. All of his father's old inventions were there. The lab looked untouched since the day Pallas Myrios had been exiled from Ecrof.

Rovi spun around, taking stock of his father's many machines and inventions—the little whirring devices that were supposed to help you empty your mind to make it possible to visualize clearer; the muscle memory suits you wore when you trained that recorded your movements so if you did something perfectly all you had to do was put the suit back on in order to re-create it; and the Mensa Crowns.

He tiptoed across the lab. Suddenly it was as if he'd traveled back in time. Rovi could instantly remember sitting in his hiding spot under the long table that ran the entire length of the lab, watching his father tinker. How many days, weeks, months had he spent wedged into the little cabinet, listening to his father while he worked? How many times had he heard his father let out a delighted gasp after testing one of his inventions? "Rovi," he'd exclaim, "don't let anyone tell you there isn't a science to sport. One day, we will be able to create perfect performance through technology."

"But wouldn't it be better to just practice and improve?" Rovi had asked.

"Of course," his father had replied, breaking off from his work. "But only the blessed few are graced with grana good enough for true perfection. Why not level the playing field? Why not give everyone the chance to be his or her best self? I'm sure that the old Gods of Granity would have wished it this way."

Rovi closed his eyes. He could almost see his father standing in front of him banging, fiddling, winding, and unwinding. He could summon his old impatience to be allowed to go play outside, to run on the field, or try to climb the tree. Rovi moved toward the window where the moonlight was strongest and took a seat. He opened his book to the page that he'd chosen to represent his time at Ecrof.

He stared at the two mountains and the little hill beneath them. What if those mountains really were his parents? His mother had died right after they'd come to Ecrof. She had been expected to teach Granology, but her health hadn't allowed it. Rovi's memories of her had always been vague, but now they were fading into nothing.

So, his parents were the big snowy mountains and he was the small hill. Why was he green? And what did the birds to the right of the mountains mean? Flight? Air? Could he choose their meaning? Could he decide?

And more important—what about the dead flowers? Did they

have something to do with his mother, who had died at Ecrof? Was she a key to what would happen next? Or was it something else? Was it something to do with what had happened to his father? Rovi closed his eyes and shook his head, driving away the thought of his father's last days at Ecrof. He didn't want to remember. He couldn't let himself. He always stopped his memory before it unfolded.

But now, in the lab, it came flooding back. In his last months at Ecrof, Rovi's father had been trying to build a machine that mimicked perfect grana—that replicated the end goal of visualization—the ability to stand outside yourself.

They had been standing in this very room when Pallas had shown Rovi his final invention. The warm sunlight was streaming through the window behind his father so it looked as if his father were glowing with magic energy. "This, Rovi," Pallas had said, "is going to be the invention of a lifetime. The Self-Splitter. If it works, anyone will be able to achieve the nearly impossible. We will all be able to separate ourselves from ourselves. We will be able to leave our conscious bodies behind and perform unburdened by anxiety and the demands of the real world. We will all have exceptional—no, not just exceptional, but perfect—grana. And that means we will play without fear."

"Come on, Dad," Rovi remembered saying. "No one can actually step outside themselves. I've heard you teach that a thousand times."

"Rovi, no one can do it by themselves. But with my machine, they can." And at that, his father had lifted up a strange metal suit that looked like a cross between a skeleton and a suit of armor. "This, my son, will make the impossible possible."

That suit—was it here? Rovi bolted to his feet. He began to pick his way through the various old machines and contraptions.

Rovi made one entire tour of the narrow room, and then another. But he didn't find it. Perhaps it was for the best that it wasn't here. He was about to return to the window to collect his book when he knocked over a large cardboard box that was hanging over the edge of a shelf. Thankfully, the box turned out to be empty. He put it back on the shelf, but it teetered and slipped off again. He looked around for a place to stash the box. There was a freestanding mirror blocking a corner of the room. He'd chuck the box behind that. But when he did, the box hit something that clattered and groaned. Rovi peeked behind the mirror. There was the Self-Splitter, hanging on the frame his father had made for it.

The brass had rusted and some of the bolts looked corroded. But otherwise, the contraption looked the same as the day his father had unveiled it in the main field under the Tree of Ecrof. The memory rushed in before he could stop it.

The entire school had been there. Rovi had sat with Janos and stared at his father with pride. "This is the wildest thing your father has attempted yet," Janos had whispered. "But if he succeeds, he will be the most famous man in Epoca. Even more famous than yours truly," he'd added with a wink, squeezing Rovi's shoulder.

Pallas Myrios had started a long introduction about how he was preparing to stand outside himself—perform the ultimate act of visualization. And how if he was successful, this would usher in a new era in sports history—an era without nerves and anxiety, an era of peak performance.

Rovi's father had stepped into the machine—legs, then arms—then clipped the skeletal helmet and visor over his head. He'd pressed the lever. There had been an odd whirring noise. Then a crackle. Then Pallas had started shaking. Suddenly a white cloud seemed to fly off his body. As it rose to the sky, it took the shape of Rovi's dad.

"By the gods," Janos had gasped, "he's done it!"

But Rovi hadn't been interested in the cloud. Instead, he'd been staring at the strange version of his father left behind in the Self-Splitter. He had been pale. No, pale was the wrong word—he'd

been more like a shadow, featureless and gray. Rovi's dad had left his shadow behind.

Five minutes had passed. Then ten. Then half an hour. The kids grew restless. Finally, Janos dismissed them. Something was wrong. Something everyone tried hard to hide from Rovi. "Come on," Janos had said, leading Rovi back to his own opulent rooms in the Trainers Towers.

Rovi had followed in stunned silence. He'd looked over his shoulder once to see a few other Trainers carrying the shadow version of his father to the TheraCenter. At that point, he didn't know that his father was never coming back, at least not in any way Rovi would recognize.

Now, Rovi reached out and placed his hand on the Self-Splitter. This was the last thing his father had touched before everything changed forever. How could a machine have done that?

Before Rovi knew what he was doing, he lifted the contraption off its hook. It was designed for a bigger person—for his father, of course. He stepped into the legs. Then the arms. The Self-Splitter was too loose on him. He couldn't walk in it.

But why would he want to? The machine had turned his father into someone unrecognizable—"a crazy person." That's what everyone else had said. "A crazy person who had tried to cut down the Tree of Ecrof." It was an accusation Rovi did everything in his power not to believe.

It was hard to say whether Pallas's selves had ever come back together properly. He sure never looked the same. He seemed like half a person. That much was clear. The minute his father could talk again after the experiment, it was clear to Rovi that Pallas was not the same. He immediately started raving about trees. Ranting about them. It was all he talked about from the moment he returned to his and Rovi's rooms. All he talked about until the rumor spread across Ecrof about what he had done—how he was found trying to destroy the most famous tree in Epoca—was killing trees. How trees were the enemy. How they were coming to destroy the students. The school. The world. Even when he became poisoned by all the hallucinatory Somnium potion he drank that made him seem even less like the brilliant inventor he had been before his final experiment went wrong, he still babbled about trees. But Rovi never told anyone this. And he never would.

Rovi had now fully stepped into the Self-Splitter. Of course he couldn't make it work. He didn't know how. It required some kind of power. And Rovi had no idea what that was. But he wanted to know what his father had felt like in the last moments he was himself.

He pulled the visor down over his face. He felt trapped. He couldn't move his arms or legs. He wobbled to the left and then to the right. And then—with a deafening clatter, the whole contraption was on the ground. Rovi lay still.

"Who's there?"

Someone was outside the window.

"Who is in there?"

He held his breath. The last thing—the very last thing—Rovi needed above all else was anyone in Ecrof finding him trying out his father's old equipment. Especially the Self-Splitter.

13

PRETIA

THE TOWERS

PRETIA WAS RELIEVED WHEN CASSANDRA TAPPED her on the shoulder on her way into the cafeteria to let her know her uncle Janos had invited her to eat in his rooms. She'd been looking around for Rovi, the only person who didn't seem to care whether or not she had grana, the only person she enjoyed eating with. But he was missing . . . which was weird. Rovi never skipped a meal. He usually got there early and kept eating long after all the other students had bused their trays.

Pretia noticed the looks she was getting from the rest of the Dreamers as word quickly spread that she'd received a coveted invitation to eat at the Trainers Towers, but she ignored them. What did it matter? They already thought she didn't have grana and that the only reason she'd been invited to Ecrof was on account of her parents. So she might as well go.

In fact, Pretia kind of missed being a princess. She missed her childhood bedroom and she missed her nightly chats with Anara, who always managed to soothe Pretia's anxieties.

She hoped this didn't mean she was spoiled. She knew the accommodations at the Temple of Dreams were luxurious. But there was no privacy. Pretia shared a room with Adira and Xenia, who were always whispering together late into the night, poring over their Grana Books and making silly predictions about everything from what would happen the next day to who would win the first House Field Day. They weren't unkind, but they didn't include her, either.

And while the food in the cafeteria was terrific and plentiful, she wouldn't have minded her favorite simple meal—honey chicken and flatbread—prepared by Castle Airim's cooks and delivered to her room so she could eat in peace.

She dashed down the marble steps that led from the Temple of Dreams to the hill that descended to the main campus. Instead of cutting across the campus, she climbed another hill, where the imposing Trainers Towers looked down on Ecrof. The towers were tall, twin temples to Metus, the God of Fear, who had taught the people of Epoca the importance of embracing and transcending their fears to be their best selves. Both temples had eight columns supporting a narrow triangular roof.

The interior was pleasantly cool, as if the warmth of the sun knew exactly when to disappear in the evening. The sight of a Flamekeeper tending a ceremonial fire when Pretia entered made her miss Anara more than usual. The man looked up from the flames and directed her to the very top floor, where she would find her uncle.

The stairs zigzagged up the temple, cutting back and forth over the atrium below. Pretia was out of breath when she reached the top floor. She knocked and in no time Janos had flung the door open. Without even thinking, Pretia rushed into his arms. His strong hands drew her close, filling her with happiness.

And suddenly she wasn't in Ecrof anymore. She was momentarily back in Castle Airim or the Ponsit Palace—her mother's ancestral home.

"Favorite niece!" Janos said.

"I'm your only niece," Pretia reminded him.

Janos let her go. "It's so good to see you, Pretia," he said.

“You see me every day,” she replied.

“But it’s not the same. Out there you are only a recruit. Here, you are family.”

Pretia looked away to hide the tears that had sprung to her eyes.

“Come,” Janos said, leading her away from the door.

As Cassandra had mentioned, Janos’s rooms were magnificent and luxurious. They stretched across the whole top floor of the tower. The front was a double sitting room, as opulent as the king and queen’s quarters at Castle Airim. Behind the sitting rooms, Pretia could see a large kitchen and what she imagined was a bedroom that seemed to be glowing with a flickering light.

Everything in Janos’s chambers was done up in Realist blue—drapes, cushions, couches. The fabrics were luxurious—the finest Chaldean silks. Pretia recognized all the finery. It was exactly how she’d grown up. Without having to be told, Pretia flopped down on one of the large floor cushions.

“Aaah,” she exclaimed without thinking.

Janos laughed. “You don’t find Ecrof up to your standards?”

Pretia bolted from the cushion. “Oh, no— Everything is perfect. Everything—” she stammered.

“I’m only joking, Pretia,” Janos said, his green eyes shining under his heavy brow. “I invited you here so you could feel at home.”

Pretia breathed a relieved sigh and fell back again on the cushion.

“Now,” Janos said. “I seem to remember you liking honey chicken, and what was it?”

“Buttered flatbread!” Pretia exclaimed.

“The girl who could have anything wants chicken and buttered flatbread.” Janos laughed.

Pretia tried to hide her excitement. “Is that what we’re having?”

“Of course!” Janos clapped his powerful hands together. “My cook trained under the best at Ponsit Palace. Even I need a break from all the variety of food in the cafeteria! Sometimes simple is best.”

As if on cue, Pretia could smell the sweet caramelizing scent of her favorite food. She closed her eyes in anticipation.

"Honey chicken? For real? I climbed all the way up here to have peasant food?"

Pretia's eyes snapped open at the sound of her cousin Castor's voice. He was standing in the doorway to Janos's chambers, an irritated look on his face.

"If I'd known, I'd have stayed back at the Thinkers Palace."

"Castor, aren't you going to say hello to your cousin?" Janos said.

"Oh, hey, Pretia," Castor said. "Make yourself at home."

Pretia rolled her eyes. "I already have."

"All right, you two," Janos said. "I thought Ecrof might teach you to put aside this childish rivalry."

"What rivalry?" Castor snorted. "How could I ever even compare myself to the Child of Hope?"

"Quit it, Castor," Pretia said. "That's just a dumb name my parents use to impress people."

She was cut off by the cook bringing a heaping tray of honey chicken and buttered flatbread to the table.

"Child of Hope," Castor teased, "I *hope* you're hungry."

Pretia ignored him, went to the table, and started helping herself to the enticing food. Janos and Castor followed. For a few moments, all Pretia could think about was how every bite of chicken reminded her of Castle Airim and her parents. Life had been so much simpler then. She didn't have to decide between Dreamer and Realist—her parents celebrated her as both. Even with her cursed grana, she could have easily hidden away in her room in the castle. She wouldn't have been tempted to use it in races, in Granology, and in Visualization. She could have kept on playing her pretend games alone and waiting until she had to become queen. That is—if she would be allowed to be queen.

Despite his earlier complaints, Castor was eating furiously, shoving chicken into his mouth as if he hadn't had a proper meal in months.

“Guess honey chicken isn’t that bad,” Pretia said. In her uncle’s chambers, she was feeling more like her old self—like she could stand up to Castor.

Castor finished chewing. Then he looked from his father to Pretia. There was a devious gleam in his eye. “Father,” Castor said, “is it true that if Pretia doesn’t have grana, I get to rule?”

A grave look crossed Janos’s brow. “Castor, that is a very serious question. Probably not one that I should be discussing with you.”

“Why not?” Castor asked. “Who else should you be discussing it with?”

Janos sighed and rubbed his muscular hands together. “Well,” Janos said, “if it were *really* true that Pretia didn’t have grana, I suppose that when the time came, the rule would eventually pass to you—rule of House Reila, that is. Of course, rule of Epoca itself is decided by the Epic Games every four years. So the Realists would have to win the Epic Games for you to be ruler. And if the Realists lost, I believe Moira, Pretia’s second cousin on King Airos’s side, would rule.”

“Well,” Castor said, “judging from the way things look around here, I don’t think I’m going to have to worry about my distant cousin Moira. Our Realist players are amazing. Julius Renovo alone could—”

Janos held up his hand before Castor could say any more. “Hold on, Castor,” he said. “All of this talk is nonsense unless Pretia really doesn’t have grana. I’m not sure I believe it. Pretia, is it true?”

Pretia stared at her uncle. For as long as she could remember, he’d believed in her. He’d told her that she was good enough, strong enough, that she would one day be an Epic Athlete even if no one else in all of Epoca believed it. He’d always told her she reminded him of the strongest woman he knew, and she’d basked in this comparision to her mother. The truth was on the tip of her tongue.

Castor’s eyes were wide with anticipation.

“Pretia,” Janos said quietly, “is it true?”

Pretia looked from her cousin to her uncle. Her mind was

ping-ponging between telling the truth and maintaining the lie that she didn't have grana. If there was anyone she could tell, it was Janos. But then she'd have to explain why she'd been hiding it. And the minute Castor got hold of the fact that she had done something dangerous—not just one thing, but several things—he'd never let it go. He'd make her life even more miserable than he already had.

"It's true," she said finally.

Janos looked at her quizzically. "Pretia," he said, "grana comes at different times for everyone."

Pretia shrugged.

Castor's eyes lit up with delight. "She doesn't have grana, Father. Remember."

"Castor," Janos warned.

"But that means I—"

Janos banged his fist on the table. "Castor, I'm warning you, as the Head Trainer of Ecrof, to hold your tongue. Or there will consequences for the Realists."

Castor clenched his fist just as the cook emerged from the kitchen carrying a tray of pistachio cakes. "You know what," Castor said, "I don't need dessert." And he dashed from the table.

Janos watched him for a moment, then shook his head. "Come on, Pretia," he said, placing a hand on her shoulder, "have a pistachio cake. They came via ship from the mainland for you."

Reluctantly, she reached out and took one of her favorite pastries.

"Grana is different for everyone," Janos said. "Sometimes it comes on strong and early but never gets stronger. Sometimes it's weak and only gains strength as you mature. In fact, my sister's grana came very late. Very, very late."

"My mother?" Pretia asked.

A strange look crossed Janos's face. "Not Helena. Syspara."

"Syspara?" Pretia said. She rarely heard anyone mention her aunt.

"Yes," Janos said, "her grana was different."

Pretia bit her lip. It probably wasn't as different as her grana. It probably wasn't cursed. She shoved the rest of the pistachio cake in her mouth.

"But you know what?" Janos said. "Sometimes challenging events have a way of drawing out your grana. So perhaps yours will come on Realist Field Day. Castor is right about one thing. From all the reports from the Trainers, your house is going to need all the help it can get to beat the Realists. So I'm counting on you! It's time for your grana to emerge."

Pretia nodded, her mouth full of food. She was glad the sticky pastry was preventing her from speaking, from lying once more to her uncle about her grana.

When she'd eaten her fill of pastries, Janos put the rest in a small bag for her and showed her to the door. "I love my son, Pretia, but I see him with open eyes. You know enough to understand that Castor teases you because he's so insecure. After all, he's spent his life second to the marvelous Pretia."

"I guess," Pretia said.

Janos opened the door to his chambers. Then he wrapped his arms around Pretia. "You are always welcome here. Ecrof is magical, but it's not perfect. I want you to know that my rooms are your second home if you ever need it."

"Thank you, Uncle," she said.

"But a word of caution. Tomorrow, I'm not your uncle. I'm back to being the mean Head Trainer who expects great things." And with that, Janos pinched her cheek and sent her on her way.

Pretia took the steps quickly and in no time she was out of the Trainers Towers and down on the main field. She was in no hurry to get back to the Temple of Dreams. The moon was full. The campus was quiet. For once she could enjoy it without the snickers and stares of the other students. The Infinity Track was hovering over the cliffs—half of it dangling over the sheer drop. The leaves of the Tree of Ecrof were glowing like mercury. She could smell the eucalyptus vapor wafting from the TheraCenter.

She passed the Halls of Process, the low temple of classrooms. Suddenly she heard a bang, like crashing metal. Pretia froze. She was standing in front of a large window that looked into the storage area between the Visualization classroom and the room for Granology.

"Who's there?" she called.

Someone was behind the window. She could hear a sharp intake of breath.

"Who is in there?" she repeated.

There was no answer.

Pretia tiptoed toward the window and, holding her breath, peered inside. In the silver moonlight she saw Rovi on the floor, trapped inside some kind of strange cage that looked like the skeleton of a diver's suit.

"Rovi!" she exclaimed. "What are you doing?"

"N-nothing," Rovi stammered.

"It doesn't look like nothing." Pretia laughed. "What is that thing?"

Rovi looked from side to side, like he might avoid answering the question.

"And what is this place?" The room seemed to be filled with all sorts of wild machines of different sizes, forged out of all the metals mined from different areas of Epoca. It was a mess and looked long abandoned.

Rovi took a deep breath. "It's my father's old lab," he said.

"A lab for what?"

"His visualization machines. So are you going to help me or not?"

"With what?" Pretia asked.

"I'm stuck in this thing."

Pretia covered her mouth to avoid laughing. He looked so ridiculous, toppled over in the weird cage suit.

“Are you going to stand there and laugh at me, or are you going to help?” Rovi asked.

Pretia held her laughter and rushed around the Halls of Process to the entrance. Between the doors to the two classrooms was a narrower doorway, which she found unlocked. Inside, Rovi waited in his strange contraption.

“So your dad invented all this stuff?” Pretia asked when she’d helped Rovi out of the machine.

“Yes,” Rovi said.

“And what does it all do?”

“Different things. Some allow you to re-create a perfect motion. Some allow you to experience what another player is feeling. Some help you visualize better, like those Mensa Crowns we used on the first day of Visualization class.”

“And it all works,” Pretia gasped.

“Kind of,” Rovi said with an unusual look in his eye.

Pretia was about to ask another question, but Rovi quickly changed the subject. “What are you doing out of the Temple of Dreams?” he asked.

“I could ask you the same thing,” Pretia said. “I was having dinner with my uncle in his rooms.”

“Oh,” Rovi said, turning away.

“You don’t like my uncle, do you?” Pretia asked. She had seen the dark, defiant look that crossed Rovi’s face every time Janos addressed him.

“That’s not it,” Rovi replied. He glanced around the room. “We should go.” He headed for the door. Pretia followed.

“So, what is it, then? Is it just because he fired your father? He must have had a reason.”

“Why do you think that?” Rovi said.

“Because Janos is—”

Rovi picked up his pace.

"Hold up," Pretia said.

"He's your uncle, Pretia, but I don't trust him."

Pretia stopped dead in her tracks. "You don't trust Janos? He's the most decorated Epocan athlete of all time. And he's the Head Trainer of Ecrof."

Rovi shrugged, then hurried on. "I just don't trust him, that's all."

"That's ridiculous!" Pretia snapped. "Just because you used to be a Star Stealer doesn't mean you have to mistrust people from powerful families."

"I trust you," Rovi said. "It's your uncle I have a problem with."

"Why?" she called after him.

But Rovi didn't stop. And Pretia watched him climb the hill to the Temple of Dreams without her. "It's just a feeling," he shouted over his shoulder.

Well, if it was a feeling, it was *Rovi's* feeling, Pretia told herself. And she didn't have to worry about it.

14

ROVI

THE TORNADO

ROVI HAD BARELY TAKEN A BITE OF HIS EGGS when three Realists appeared in the Dreamers' cafeteria. They jumped up on one of the tables, cupped their hands over their mouths, and shouted, "It's Realist Field Day!"

Immediately the entire room exploded with shouts and cheers. Realist Field Day meant no class. No Visualization. No Granology. No foundational training. It meant a day of eating and competition—an entire day of fun. It also meant that Rovi's first year at Ecrof was nearly halfway over.

It didn't take long for the Dreamers to begin booing their rivals and chasing them out of the Temple of Dreams.

The atmosphere was electric. Rovi watched as older Dreamers rushed to their rooms and returned dressed in head-to-toe purple. Already, someone was offering to paint everyone's face purple.

In all the excitement, Rovi forgot about his argument with Pretia the other day and immediately moved over to make room for her at his table when she passed by with her tray.

"So," Rovi said, digging into his second mound of fluffy eggs, "who do you think is going to be chosen to compete?"

"Not me," Pretia said.

As usual, she seemed oddly relieved to have nothing to do with competition.

He looked around the cafeteria. Cassandra and the rest of the seventh years were gathered around a table, clearly plotting the best teams to put forward to challenge the Realists. He watched Vera Renovo approach the table and start a heated conversation with the House Captain.

"I'm not sure there's anyone here who can beat Julius," Rovi said.

"Maybe you, if you tried harder," Pretia said.

"I like running," Rovi replied, "if there's a point." Which was true. Racing through the market away from the guards and the merchants was fun. Racing the other Star Stealers along the narrow walls high above Phoenis was exciting. But running around a track or a field while someone timed you was just boring.

"Isn't winning the point?" Pretia asked.

Before Rovi could answer, Vera appeared at the table and slammed her tray down next to theirs. Rovi and Pretia exchanged a surprised look. Vera always ate alone. "I'm racing Julius," she announced.

"Really?" Rovi asked.

"You don't believe me?" Vera challenged.

"It's not that," Rovi said. "You just don't seem really happy about it."

"I'm not," Vera said. "If I'd known before today, I could have started training. This system of the other house getting to know the events in advance is stupid."

"Well, we get that same advantage next time," Pretia said.

"Can you beat your brother?" Rovi asked. He knew Vera was fast, but Julius was an Epic Champion and a Junior Epic Champion, as well as an Epic Elite at Ecrof.

"Yes," Vera said, sitting down.

Rovi returned to his food, taking down five sausages and a stack of honeycakes. As he finished draining his second mug of Choco

Water, Cassandra stood up from her table and clapped her hands.

"Dreamers!" she called. "Today is Realist Field Day. It may seem like they're stronger than us, but we'll challenge them with everything we've got. They've chosen a 4x100 relay, the 100-meter dash, the 100-meter hurdles, the 200, the 400, the 800, and the mile, all run on the Infinity Track instead of in the Panathletic Stadium." When the chatter had died down, Cassandra announced the squad.

All the students stopped eating to listen to the roll call of athletes. The whole room started buzzing at once when Vera was announced for the 800.

Instead of beaming, as Rovi had expected she would, Vera crossed her arms over her chest. "This whole system is dumb," she grumbled.

But Rovi ingored her, more interested in who else would be chosen.

"And, finally," Cassandra said, "Daria Nestor and Rovi Myrios will run the mile."

"Wh-what?" Rovi stammered. "Me?" He was blushing and he knew it. Suddenly his entire breakfast was sitting heavy in his stomach, but he felt his chest expand with a curious, elated feeling.

The cafeteria burst into applause and started chanting, "Dreams never die! Dreams never die!"

"For those of you competing, spend the morning getting some rest," Cassandra shouted over the ruckus. "Then you will meet for warm-ups down at the main field. The rest of you will be needed for supporting your teammates, joining in the pregame feast, and rallying as much Dreamer spirit as you can." Once more, there was thunderous applause as Rovi and the rest of that day's competitors rose to their feet.

When it was quiet, Pretia pulled on Rovi's arm. "So, do you still think racing is pointless?"

"It's just the mile," Rovi said. But he knew the smile on his face told an entirely different story.

Rovi had to admit that he felt pretty great dressed in his official Dreamers racing kit—a slick running singlet that was the nicest and fanciest piece of clothing that he had ever worn. But the real surprise that afternoon was that all selected athletes were taken into the Ecrof gear room and told to select a new pair of running shoes in official Dreamer purple.

Rovi's heart leaped when he saw the rows and rows of Grana Graces, Grana Sparks, Grana Glows, Grana Bolts, Grana Epics, and Grana Golds.

"Take one in your size," Cassandra urged. "And don't worry. They'll mold to your feet instantly. No need to break them in."

Rovi reached for a pair of Grana Epics. They were royal purple, of course, and shiny, so shiny that it looked as if they produced their own light. "I'll take these."

"Good choice for the mile," Cassandra said.

"But why am I running the mile?" Rovi asked.

"Well, since you've been assigned so many penalty laps, I figured you'd be in pretty good shape for distance," Cassandra replied.

Rovi's heart sank. "I was chosen because of my penalty laps?"

Cassandra smiled. "Well, that and something else. You know Iskander Dracos?"

Rovi did. He was an Epic Elite, a fourth-year Dreamer from Phoenis.

"Well, he knows all about Star Stealers."

Before Rovi could feel ashamed, Cassandra continued. "He told me exactly how fast you have to be to avoid the guards and the merchants in the market. And he figured you had to be sprinting at least a mile to safety on a daily basis."

Rovi had never considered the distance he'd been running away from the market. He'd never considered that there was a direct relationship between the kind of running he'd been doing in Phoenis and here at Ecrof.

"So just pretend you're running from someone at the Alexandrine Plaza," Cassandra said. "That's what Iskander suggested."

"Done," Rovi said.

After the Dreamer athletes had gathered to warm up, plan their strategies, and do run-throughs of their events on the track, they went to join the rest of the school at the Panathletic Stadium, where the Realist feast was going to be held.

Eight long tables had been set up on the grass surrounding the Tree of Ecrof. As was Ecrof tradition, during the meals before Field Day, students were not allowed to segregate themselves according to house affiliation, so Dreamers and Realists sat together. This only made the noise at the tables louder as friends called to friends several seats away.

Every inch of the field was festooned with banners and signs celebrating the Dreamer or Realist teams. Two marching bands circled the tables, playing the various anthems and fight songs of the two camps. The sound echoed off the bowl of the stadium. Fireworks exploded, sending shooting stars of Realist blue into the air. And every once in a while, a group of Dreamers or Realists would leap to their feet, commanding the rest of their house to do the same, and chant, "Dreamers dominate" or "Realists rule," before the teachers waved them back into their seats.

Since it was Realist Day, giant blue streamers and banners hung from the Tree of Ecrof. The Spirit Water was dyed blue. All the cakes were frosted blue. The cushions on the seats of the benches were blue. So much blue, in fact, that it made Rovi a little sick seeing it.

The Realists got to pick the menu. Since so many of the Realist-dominated cities were near the water, there were dozens of varieties of fish—small and large, red and silver. There were mussels, clams, shrimp, and lobster. Rovi was pretty excited about the prospect of eating lobster. That was something he'd never have dreamed of as a Star Stealer.

Most of the first-year recruits had gathered at a table at the edge of the festivities. Rovi sat opposite Pretia. They had to shout to be heard over the cheering and the music on the field. Servers circled, refilling glasses of blue Spirit Water and loading trays with piles of crisp meat, golden breads, and bowls and bowls of creamy shrimp pasta. Everyone ate as if they hadn't seen food in weeks while fireworks popped and banners flew overhead.

Pretia was talking excitedly about the upcoming race. Normally, her chatter would have been making Rovi nervous. But he was distracted by something going on over her shoulder. A third-year Realist was trying to climb the Tree of Ecrof to hang more Realist streamers.

Rovi watched him get a boost and scramble up the wide trunk.

"Are you even listening?" Pretia asked.

"What?" Rovi asked.

"I was talking about the race. I heard—" she said.

But Rovi's focus was on the boy in the tree. He'd made it up to the first branches, which was farther than Rovi had.

"Rovi!" Pretia said. "Pay attention."

But Rovi couldn't take his eyes off the tree. He'd done his best to keep his distance from it. He didn't want anyone to associate him with the black roots he'd seen. He'd heard enough of Castor's comments about what his father had been rumored to have tried to do—killing the Tree of Ecrof.

"What are you looking at?" Pretia asked.

She turned to follow Rovi's gaze. At that instant, there was a sickening crack. The limb that the Realist boy had climbed out on split from the tree, sending the boy plummeting to the ground.

“It’s going to land on top of him,” somone cried, pointing at the falling tree limb.

But instead of falling straight down, the branch began to disintegrate, crumbling as if it were made of ash.

Rovi’s mouth hung open.

A few kids leaped to their feet to help the fallen boy.

“What just happened?” Pretia exclaimed. “Did the tree just— Did it just—crumble?”

Rovi took a big gulp of Spirit Water.

“Do you think he’s okay? Rovi, do you?” Pretia sounded panicked. “I can’t believe the branch just snapped like that,” Pretia added. “It’s supposed to be the strongest tree in Epoca. But it just fell apart like burned paper. Do you think it’s rotting?” she asked. “That’s not possible? Is it?”

“Excuse me,” Rovi said, standing up. He wanted to get as far away from the tree as possible.

He could see medics crossing the field. Janos blew his whistle to clear the students away from the tree so the fallen kid could get treatment.

“He’s having trouble breathing,” an older Dreamer called. “He’s having trouble—”

Janos blew his whistle even louder. “Stay away from the tree,” he ordered.

The benches fell silent as the medics lifted the injured boy onto a stretcher. Rovi watched Janos confer with them before they hurried away to the TheraCenter.

When the medics had disappeared, Janos called the students to attention. “Now, you all know that sports do come with a risk. Students will be injured. But there is no point in endangering yourself with foolish activities. Let this be a lesson to you all not to engage in pointless risks.”

"But is he okay?" a voice called.

"He's fine," Janos assured them. "Just stunned. We'll check him for a concussion and then get him back on his feet."

Rovi looked at the tree uncertainly. He waited for someone to ask about why the branch had crumbled the way it did. But everyone seemed more interested in the fallen student than the Tree of Ecrof.

"All right," Janos continued. "Now that we have feasted, let us all join together in the Ecrof fight song—a symbol of our unified devotion to the art of sport and the perfection of grana. May our song reach Petros at the TheraCenter and grant him a speedy recovery. And with our voices singing as one, we will send our chosen competitors off to the Infinity Track for their final warm-ups." He blew his whistle, summoning the entire student body to its feet.

The two marching bands came together. As the song began, Rovi felt his heart swell in his chest and unexpected tears fill his eyes as the students' voices and the sound of the instruments rose from the field into the evening sky.

The song ended. Rovi stood, ready to file out. But before he could leave the benches, he heard his name.

"Hey, Rovi."

Rovi turned and was dismayed to see Castor and his clique of Realists standing in a semicircle behind him.

"What did you do to the tree?" Castor asked.

Rovi's cheeks burned.

"Are you finishing what your father started?" Castor continued.

"Is it *really* true your father tried to cut down the Tree of Ecrof?" Nassos asked.

"No," Rovi said.

"That's not what I heard," said Sophia, one of the Realists.

"Seems kind of strange that your father was fired for trying to kill the tree and now that you're here, a branch just snaps off," Castor said. "Don't you think?"

“I—I don’t,” Rovi said quietly.

“What’s that?” Castor said. “I couldn’t hear you. I couldn’t hear you, Tree Killer.”

“I said, I don’t think that’s strange,” Rovi repeated, louder this time. But he didn’t sound convincing, even to himself. In all honesty, it did seem a little strange.

“Tree Killer.” Nassos laughed. “That’s a good one.”

Tree Killer. Tree Killer. Tree Killer. The name rippled from one Realist to another.

Rovi felt anger coursing through his body. If he were back on the streets of Phoenis, he knew what he’d do. He’d fight back. But he had to remember he wasn’t a Star Stealer anymore. He was a Dreamer, and he was competing for his house.

He felt a hand on his back. “Ignore them.” He turned and saw Vera standing next to him.

A hunting horn blared, signaling that the Field Day athletes were meant to start parading out of the stadium.

“Ignore them,” Vera repeated. “Rovi didn’t do anything to that tree,” she told the others.

“Well, his father did,” Castor said.

“You don’t know that,” Rovi said. He’d balled his hands into fists. He was ready to strike. But he felt Vera’s grip on his arm, restraining him.

“Castor,” Vera said, “maybe you should stop focusing so much on trees and start worrying about why you weren’t chosen for Field Day and Rovi and I were.”

“Be quiet, Replacement,” Castor snapped. “You wouldn’t have been chosen either if you were a Realist. But then again, you’re *not*.”

“That’s right,” Vera said. “I’m something better. I’m a Dreamer.”

Before the fight could escalate, Janos blew his whistle, urging the athletes onward.

The Infinity Track was hovering between the Decision Woods

and the cliff up which Rovi and the rest of the recruits had climbed on their first day at Ecrof. It was about ten feet off the ground. A quarter of it dangled over the cliff, and a small section was tangled with a few trees that stuck out from the woods.

A large set of bleachers had been assembled on the ground underneath the track. Rovi, Vera, and the rest of the Field Day athletes stood to the side, watching the rest of the school approach through the woods. The Realists came right down the middle through the path that was now clearly visible, and the Dreamers approached from either side through the many obstacles. The students raced to the bleachers, eager to get there before they lifted off the ground.

Rovi watched as Pretia took a seat in the front row. Suddenly the bleachers began to rise. If Rovi's stomach weren't fluttering so badly, he would have been able to admire the floating bleachers. But it was doing flips. Were those nerves? He couldn't actually be *nervous* at the prospect of running around a track, could he? He'd never been nervous running from the plaza in Phoenis before, and back then, guards had been chasing him. Back then, the stakes had been real—if he'd been caught, he could have been sent to make sand bricks. This was just a race. This was just a race around a track.

Vera was doing complicated stretches as she stared at the Realist runners, an angry look on her face. "Everyone is just too in awe of my brother to actually challenge him," she said. "They get distracted and can't run their best. That's what happens at Ecrof. That's why no one can challenge the great Julius Renovo."

"Really?" Rovi asked. From what he'd heard when he was a Star Stealer, there was no one in all of Epoca, from the capital of Helios to the distant Sandlands to the remote region of Alkebulan, who was as fast as Julius Renovo.

Vera was bouncing in place. "But I'm not in awe of him. I'm not afraid of him. He's just my dumb, conceited older brother. And," she added, "he's a Realist."

"All right," Rovi said. "Whatever motivates you . . ."

Janos put his whistle to his lips and blew. The stands fell silent. "Today is Realist Day," Janos bellowed. "But that doesn't mean they are guaranteed victory. They have chosen their events. They have selected their runners. But they still have to defeat the Dreamers, who I'm sure are planning to rise to the challenge."

Rovi felt a tap on his back. He turned and saw Satis behind him. "Your father would be proud of you," Satis said. But before Rovi could respond, the mysterious Visualization Trainer had slipped away to join the rest of the faculty in the stands.

Cassandra gathered the Dreamer runners around her. "All right," she said. "The Realists are expecting to win this. For every first-place finish, a team gets three points. Second place, two points, and third, one point. We don't need to win everything. We just need to make it onto the podium as much as possible."

"No," Vera said, "we need to win."

"Well, we can try," Cassandra continued. "But what we need to focus on is chipping away at them. Let's get on that podium."

First up was the 100-meter dash—the marquee event. No matter what Vera had said, Rovi figured this was something the Realists had on lockdown. After all, Julius had won the 100 meters in the actual Epic Games.

Julius took the starting blocks to raucous applause. There were only six entrants in the race. For this short-distance event, the competitors would race over the track hovering above land, not over the cliff, something Rovi would not be spared.

The cheers were deafening. The starter's pistol went off. Julius immediately took the lead. His feet flew faster than the other runners'. Rovi couldn't believe his eyes—Julius's feet actually *flew*. They never touched the track at all. Instead, his sneakers raced above it, gliding faster than Rovi would have thought possible. And it was over even before it started, with Julius flying across the finish line, upright and graceful, like it had taken no effort at all. For a moment, Rovi didn't care about Dreamers and Realists. For a moment, he was able to enjoy sports at their finest and most pure. Because that's what Julius was in this race—elegant perfection. Rovi had never seen anything like it. Nothing in his entire life. He barely noticed that Iskander Dracos, who had suggested he run the mile, had finished in third place.

"It's like I said." Vera snorted. "I'm sure everyone was just too in awe of him to actually run their best. That's why he won so easily."

"Probably," Rovi said, snapping back to reality. He didn't want to destroy whatever competitive zone Vera was in by telling her the truth.

Next up were the hurdles. All six of the runners were girls. This was Cassandra's event, and she hopped on the track to wild cheers from the Dreamer camp. The Realists in the bleachers were keyed up after their initial victory and didn't sit down, even when the hurdlers got into their starting blocks. Nor did they sit when the pistol went off.

But it didn't matter. Cassandra was out at front right from the start. As she sprang over each hurdle, she remained in the air longer than the rest of the runners, flying between each jump, which took her farther and farther into the lead. She crossed the finish line a good six seconds before her closest opponent. Now the Dreamers were on their feet, cheering wildly.

In the 200, Julius was up again. *How many races will he run?* Rovi wondered. Vera was hopping from foot to foot, eager for her chance to race her brother. But that wouldn't come until the 800—Cassandra hoped that the slightly longer distance might remove some of Julius's edge. Once more, Julius glided across the finish line. But this time the Dreamers took second and third place.

Rovi knew his race was next. He was up on the track even before the race was announced, looking over the other seven runners. He could beat them all, he figured. Easy-peasy. "Just focus on yourself,"

Cassandra said. "Don't worry about the competition. Don't look over your shoulder. Just run."

"This is your race to win," Iskander added. "The other runners don't matter. Just worry about your own feet, your own speed. The other racers aren't there."

Rovi barely heard them. All he had to do was run around the track four times. That's it. As fast as he could.

He lined up. The pistol went off. And Rovi dashed away. Running on the Infinity Track was exhilarating. Here he was, ten feet above the ground, racing for House Somni. His feet were doing their thing, leading him on, figuring out a path between the runners ahead of him. They didn't falter when the track led him over the cliff, a terrifying drop to the beach below. He didn't care about the height, or about the plunge to the rocks and water hundreds of feet down.

His feet were certain, every step perfectly timed and perfectly placed. They figured out the best way to dodge the trees that blocked the small section of the track that reached into the Decision Woods. While some of the other runners slowed as they neared this section, Rovi didn't skip a beat. His feet led the way, doing all the work for him. He felt no strain. He was sure it showed to the spectators watching from the floating bleachers.

For two laps he was in the lead group of four, two Dreamers and two Realists who'd broken away from the start. By the third lap, the second-year Dreamer girl who'd been keeping pace with him fell away. Now it was Rovi and two older Realists. And he was winning. He was winning easily.

On the fourth lap, he darted through the trees blocking the course. He sprinted over the field. And then he hit the section dangling over the cliff. He still felt no strain. How amazing was this? *How amazing was this!* He could just imagine the looks on the faces of the two Realists behind him when they watched Rovi Myrios, the first-year recruit and former Star Stealer, cross the finish line ahead of them. He wanted to see them see him win.

As he was closing in on the finish line, he turned. The Realists were behind him, but they weren't looking at him. They were staring straight ahead, their eyes fixed on the goal.

And before Rovi knew what had happened, the two other runners had passed him, finishing first and second while he stumbled to third.

Rovi's cheeks burned. His heart sank. He climbed off the track feeling furious and ashamed. Cassandra and Iskander patted him on the back and congratulated him. But their words sounded half-hearted. Rovi should have won, and he knew it. His stupidity had cost House Somni two points. He should never have looked back.

"Good work, Tree Killer," Castor called from the Realist camp.

Rovi moved away from the other runners and sat alone. Before long, Cassandra came over. "Don't worry about it. It's your first race. Everyone makes mistakes. Everyone."

Rovi just shrugged.

"Rovi," Cassandra said sternly. "You need to support your teammates."

"Fine," Rovi said, getting to his feet and pushing his shame away. "Fine."

It was time for the 800—Vera's event. Rovi watched her climb onto the track. She was in the starting blocks next to Julius. She turned and gave him a nasty scowl. "You're going down, Realist," she said.

The Realists were on their feet chanting. Some called Julius's name. Others urged him to destroy the Replacement. None of it seemed to bother Vera. Her face was cool and professional now, as if she wasn't even listening.

She'd never make the same sort of mistake he did, Rovi thought. Never. But there was no time to dwell on his missteps. The starter's gun went off. And the race began.

The bleachers went wild.

The runners started off, a steady jog that would turn into an all-out sprint at the end of the second lap. For the first lap, all the runners stuck together as a pack. At the start of the second, a small group pulled away: Julius and two Dreamers, including Iskander. Vera was stuck in the middle of the remaining group, all of whom seemed edgy, trying to jockey for position and jostle each other. Half-way through the second lap, Julius was still in the lead. One Dreamer girl had dropped back and a Realist girl had taken her place.

Now Julius, Iskander, and the Realist girl were out front, with Vera right on their heels. The other four runners had fallen behind. Vera could catch them, Rovi was sure of it. There was so much noise from the bleachers it was thumping in Rovi's chest.

They were on to the last 200 meters. Vera would have to make her move soon to get onto the podium. Julius, Iskander, and the Realist girl were keeping a steady pace, but Vera was closing in. The three leaders sprinted over the track that dangled over the cliffs with Vera at their heels. They passed back over land. Now all that remained was to run through the branches one more time and sprint the final 150 meters.

"Go, Vera!" Rovi shouted. "*Go!*"

She made her move. A few feet before the trees, she had nearly closed the gap. It was clear she would catch them, either before the trees or emerging from them. The three lead runners were in the branches, navigating them easily. But then something changed. The leaves shifted. They began to swirl. The branches all bent forward and a wild tornado of leaves gusted from the trees, chasing the lead runners.

The students in the bleachers gasped as they watched the leaves charge down the track. In an instant, the leaf funnel had swallowed the first three runners so that all that was visible of them was a green mass moving down the track at an alarming rate. It was like the wild sandstorms that swept through Phoenis from the desert, but made out of leaves.

Vera had been a step behind when the tornado of leaves erupted, and she remained outside of it. She was chasing it. Rovi wanted to scream at her to keep back. Everyone knows you don't run into the eye of a sandstorm! But she was determined. And Rovi was too stunned to find the words to call out to her.

Right before the finish, the tornado ceased. The swirling leaves fell to the track and the ground below. And the three front-runners emerged, choking and sputtering. The older Realist girl staggered to one side and fell off the track, landing on the hard-packed earth.

Iskander and Julius were stumbling forward, Vera between them. She crossed second, just behind her brother, who doubled over at the finish line gasping for breath. Iskander came third, just. By the time he crossed, he was unable to stand and fell on the track, a terrifying choking sound emerging from his throat.

Chaos erupted in the stands. Both teams had stopped cheering. A few older students rushed to their fallen teammates. But they were pushed aside by medic techs. Rovi rushed to Vera's side.

Janos was blowing his whistle. "Quiet, everyone. Quiet."

He rushed into their midst, scattering the competitors so that he could approach the fallen students.

Vera stood a few feet from Julius, who was clutching his throat, gasping and gasping as if he couldn't breathe. "What happened?" she shouted, frantic. "What happened to my brother? Why can't he breathe?"

No one was listening to her. She grabbed Janos's arm. "What is going on?" she screamed. "What's wrong with Julius?"

"Vera, let go of me. I need to see for myself."

"What happened—" Vera began.

"Vera, you need to step back," Janos warned. He squatted down, a concerned look on his face. Two other Trainers joined him. "I need to examine your brother."

"What were those leaves?" Vera asked.

“A sea gust,” Janos explained. “A wild gust of wind. It happens when the salty air rises from the cliffs.”

The three gasping students were struggling to stand. Janos and the other Trainers urged them to rest so the medics could attend to them.

Julius was coughing and sputtering like he was trying to clear something from his lungs.

“Did he inhale something?” Vera asked.

“I told you, Vera, it’s the salt air. Now, if you don’t stop asking questions, your brother won’t get the help he needs. You don’t want to cost us our star athlete.”

“What did those leaves do to him?” Vera demanded.

Janos took Vera by the arm and pulled her away from the track. “Enough,” he said.

The medics began helping the runners to their feet.

Vera went to follow, but Rovi put out an arm to stop her. “There’s nothing you can do,” he said.

Vera glowered at him.

“Vera,” Rovi said, “Julius is going to be okay.”

“How do you know?”

The truth was, Rovi didn’t. “Because they can fix anything at the TheraCenter.”

“I guess,” she said. “And Julius is basically invincible.” But she didn’t sound too certain.

Together, Rovi and Vera watched Julius being led away by the medics. He looked exhausted, like he’d worn himself out in the race. He needed both medics for support just to walk away from the Infinity Track.

Janos blew his whistle once more. “All right,” he bellowed. “That was not the ending we’d hoped for. But Corae Island is full of surprises. Tomorrow you will see our runners are as good as new.” Then he took a piece of paper that Satis had handed him. “Now,” he said, “the results.” Students from both houses fell silent as Janos consulted the paper. “Victory to the Realists. But only by a single point!”

A deafening cheer rose from the Realists’ camp.

Rovi’s stomach twisted. A single point. If he hadn’t looked over his shoulder, the Dreamers would have won.

Rovi sat off to the side, watching the Realists’ celebration. The Dreamers were filing back into the woods. He had no intention of joining them.

“Hey!”

He looked up and saw that Pretia had squatted down next to him.

“You were great,” she said.

Rovi shrugged. “I wasn’t. I lost.”

“But those leaves,” she continued. “That was intense. I’ve never seen anything like that. Why do you think that happened?”

Rovi sighed. He didn’t care about the leaves.

“It was like a tornado,” Pretia said. “They were so fast, it was like they were part of the race.”

“Huh,” Rovi said. He could barely get the word out. He had failed. It would have been better if he’d been the one swallowed by leaves instead of Julius and the others.

He stood up and walked away, leaving Pretia by the track.

15

PRETIA

THE LESSON

IT WAS COOL IN THE GRANOLOGY CLASSROOM, as usual. Cool and dim. Pretia found this to be a welcome relief from the constant sunshine on Corae Island. Saana, the quiet Grana Trainer, claimed that the dark room allowed the students to channel their inner thoughts and bring themselves into a more organic understanding of their Grana Books. Whatever that meant. Pretia had been concerned about her book from the day she'd received it back under the Gods' Eye at Castle Airim. She worried that it contained the same sort of uncontrollable darkness as her grana itself. But so far, she hadn't been able to make heads or tails of any of the images. If she'd been home, she could have asked Anara about the book. The Flamekeeper seemed to understand so many of the mysteries of the world. But those questions would have to wait for the summer.

Most of the kids thought Granology was boring. There were days that Saana didn't even allow them to open their books at all. Instead she would give them tables of various images to guide their interpretations. She made them categorize natural elements—water, flowers, plants. Then she quizzed them on what an empty glass meant, a portrait, a still life, a metal spoon. She made them look for the negative and the positive in each image. A spoon could mean hunger or need, but it could also be nourishment. A bouquet of dried flowers could be longevity or death. An ocean could mean adventure or disaster.

There were two sides to everything. There were no right answers. There were no wrong answers. It made Pretia's head spin. But she enjoyed it. At least in Granology, she didn't have to worry about losing control. In Granology, she worked alone and didn't worry about hurting anyone with her cursed grana.

The best days, as far as Pretia was concerned, were those when Saana instructed them to sit quietly with their books. As much as Pretia loved Granology, she hated sharing her intepretations with the class in case some hint of her poisoned grana came out.

On these quiet days, Saana wanted the students to develop their powers of concentration so they could be comfortable looking at an image for a long period of time, finding meaning in every corner of the picture.

But today, none of the students were focused on Saana's lesson. Instead, they were all talking about Realist Field Day, which was all anyone had been able to talk about for the last three weeks. How close the Dreamers had come to winning. How the Realists had won. How Rovi should have clinched it for the Dreamers, but that he'd looked over his shoulder at the last second. How Vera might have overtaken her brother. But mostly what everyone was talking about was the mysterious leaf tornado that had swallowed Julius, Iskander, and the Realist runner, who Pretia had learned was named Livia. Three of Ecrof's best brought down by leaves. And not just any leaves—a literal leaf tornado that had swept out of nowhere.

"All right," Saana said at the front of the Granology classroom, "let's get going with our books."

But before she could begin the class, a loud blast of horns shook the campus. It went on for five full minutes, playing the Ecrof fight song over and over. The entire class looked at one another, confused by the disruption. When the music fell silent, a dark shape appeared in the doorway, casting a long shadow into the room. It took a moment for Pretia to realize that it was her uncle, Janos.

"Recruits," he said, stepping into the room and to the front of the class. "That noise represents one of our proudest Ecrof moments. Just now the Epic Elite Squad departed to the far side of the island for intensive training. They will remain there until close to the end of term. As you know, these athletes are the ones who have already represented their houses in the Epic Games, and a few others who have shown exceptional promise."

Adira's hand shot into the air. "How can we get classified Epic Elite?"

"You will all get your chance in our yearly tryout," Janos said, "which is exactly why I'm here. This tryout will be held in just over a month—"

Before he could finish, Adira's hand was back in the air. "But what are we trying out for if the team has already been selected?"

"Well," Janos said, an irritated flicker in his eye, "you are trying out for the chance to join next year. And perhaps even this year, if you show exceptional ability."

Now Vera's hand was in the air. She didn't wait for Janos to call on her. "Did my brother go?"

For a moment, the Head Trainer looked confused.

"Did my brother go with the squad?"

"Yes," Janos said. "Yes, of course. He's always on the squad."

"But wasn't he in the TheraCenter?" Vera asked.

"He was. But he isn't anymore. Both he and Iskander Dracos left directly from the TheraCenter for secret training."

"I didn't see him go," Vera said.

"There's a reason it's called *secret training*," Janos replied.

"Is he okay?" Vera persisted.

"He's better than okay," Janos said. "He's leading the squad. As always."

Vera crossed her arms over her chest. "I'm going to make Epic Elite," she said, "and I'm going to join him."

"Very well," Janos said gravely. "Then you will have your work cut out for you in the coming weeks."

"And beat him," Vera added.

Janos gave her a half smile. "Very well, Vera. Only two recruits have ever made the squad before."

"So that means it can be done," Vera said.

"I admire your spirit, Vera Renovo, in the face of everything," Janos said, fixing her with a dark stare. Then he turned to the rest of the class. "So, you all have been warned. You'll be competing against your classmates and the rest of the school to make the squad. My suggestion is to up your dedication to training. Practice as much as you can. Never rest. And never take anything for granted."

Adira's hand shot up once more.

"Yes, Adira," Janos said, a tense note in his voice.

"You didn't tell us what the event is."

"My apologies," Janos said. "Long jump." And with that, he strode out of the room.

"Long jump," Rovi whispered to Pretia. "Seems pretty unfair to the younger students with shorter legs."

Pretia chose not to reply. She didn't want to get into another tiff with Rovi about her uncle's fairness.

"All right, all right," Saana said, trying to settle the class once more. "I think that today is a good day for quiet contemplation of your books. Now, who would like to think of a question?"

Castor's hand shot into the air. "I can."

"Careful, Mr. Praxis," Saana cautioned. "I won't have any bullying questions in my class."

"I wouldn't dream of it," Castor said. "I think we should ask,

What is the hardest challenge I will face this year?"

Virgil raised his hand. "Can't we ask something less serious?"

"Are you scared?" Castor asked.

"Of course not," Virgil replied.

"That is a rather big question," Saana said, considering.

"I thought we were at Ecrof to challenge ourselves," Castor said.

Pretia recognized the simpering tone in his voice from a hundred family occasions where she'd had to endure him kissing up to their relatives.

"Well, if that's how you see it, Mr. Praxis, I hope you rise to the challenge with a profound interpretation," Saana said. Then she clapped her elegant hands together. "Everyone, open your books." She wrote Castor's question on the board. "Now, don't rush into knowledge. Take your time."

There was the sound of rustling as the recruits began to leaf through their Grana Books. Pretia closed her eyes and flipped through the pages until one just *felt* right. She couldn't say why it did, why she stopped flipping when she did, only that she knew she had come to the right page.

She'd tried different methods before. She'd tried opening the book at random and sticking with whatever picture she'd come to. That's how many of the Realist kids did it. *Bam.* Open. There's your page. This didn't work for Pretia. It seemed too slapdash, too reliant on luck instead of focus. She'd also tried selecting her pages like Adira and Virgil and the other Dreamers, carefully turning through the book, page by page, slowly, slowly, looking at everything until something spoke to her. But this intense concentration took too much effort and made the practice of learning anything from the Grana Book seem unnatural. Deliberately selecting a page seemed to be forcing her into an interpretation instead of letting one come naturally.

Pretia had her thumb wedged in her book. She could feel that same eager electricity coursing through her body as it had the few times she'd let her grana loose on the playing field. She was about to open the book and see what page she'd chosen as an answer to Castor's question about the hardest challenge she would face when a cry erupted in the silent Granology classroom. The cry was followed by a crash.

Pretia looked up and saw Leo standing up at his desk. His mouth was wide open in shock. And his Grana Book was now lying on the opposite side of the room. Had he . . . *thrown* it?

"Leo," Saana said, her quiet voice filled with concern. "What did you see?"

Leo clapped a hand over his mouth and was shaking his head.

"There's no need to fear your book," Saana said. "It's not a fortune-teller or a crystal ball. As I've told you before, there is good and bad in every image."

Leo was still shaking his head.

"Something has clearly spoken to you," Saana continued, now sounding impressed more than concerned. "Something powerful."

Adira and Virgil exchanged annoyed looks that something strong hadn't spoken to them.

"I—I—I . . ." Leo stammered.

"Trust yourself," Saana urged. "Trust your book."

"I—I—I . . ." Leo stammered again. Then he took a deep breath. "I saw my grana vanishing."

For a moment, the room fell into an even deeper silence than usual.

Saana looked confused. Then she brushed her confusion off with a smile. "All right, Leo. That certainly qualifies as a strong and interesting interpretation. Can you take us through it?"

Timidly, Leo walked to the front of the room. He put his book facedown on the projector so the image he'd chosen could be seen by the rest of the class. The picture was bright and sunny, which took Pretia by surprise. The page was divided in half by a vertical river. On one shore was a bunch of flowers—dandelions. The opposite shore was empty except for the dry, baked earth common to much of Epoca.

"If that tells you your grana's disappearing," Nassos said, "I can't wait to see what you make of something that's really scary."

"I didn't say the *picture* was scary," Leo said in a small voice. "I just said how I interpreted it."

"And how do you see a picture of flowers and water and sunshine as meaning that your grana vanishes?" Adira asked in a concerned voice.

Leo looked at her, his mouth opening and closing as if he couldn't find the words.

"It's all right," Saana said. "There are no wrong interpretations. An interpretation can be something you feel or fear. It's not necessarily something that is actually going to happen. For instance, what you are sensing could be a moment in the future when you might perform terribly and it might feel to you as if your grana is gone, even though that's not what's really happening."

A tidal wave of relief seemed to crash over Leo's face. And he started to speak. "Well, okay," he said. "I'm guessing this picture represents Epic Elite trials. See those flowers on the left? Well, there are seventeen. So that's seventeen recruits, right? That's us. Now, one of the flowers is smaller than the rest. I guess that's me." Leo took a deep breath. "Now, the river represents Epic Elite trials. Because what do rivers do? They run. And how do you cross them? You jump. So that's the long jump."

"All right," Saana said so slowly that Pretia couldn't tell whether she approved of Leo's interpretation.

"But see what's happening on the left?" Leo said, pointing at the flowers. "See?" He tapped his finger on the smallest flower, the one he seemed to think was him. "It's being blown by some kind of wind."

Pretia peered at the picture. It did seem that the flower was bending forward.

"In fact," Leo said, "some of the petals are being blown off the flower. But the flower hasn't turned to seed yet. It's not ready. It's being forced."

Pretia glanced at Saana, who had cupped her chin in her hand and was nodding as Leo spoke.

"So that's my grana disappearing," Leo added in a whisper. "You can tell it's gone, because the opposite side of the river is totally dry. It's empty. And that's what it would feel like to miss your grana."

When Leo finished speaking, Saana continued staring at the picture for a moment without saying anything. "Very nice, Leo," she said eventually. "Very nice usage of what you see on the entire page. So it seems, at least as far as you are concerned, there is something to fear on Epic Elite trial day. But remember, your interpretations are not literal. They are not real. They are only suggestions."

Leo closed his book and returned to his seat. A few seconds after he sat down, Nassos snuck up behind him and pinched him on the neck. "Poof, there goes your grana!" he said.

Leo shrieked and fell out of his chair.

"Recruits!" Saana said softly but sternly. "Until you all can come up with as complete and complex an interpretation as Leo just did, I suggest you refrain from joking around."

"Even if our interpretations don't make any sense?" Castor said.

"Even if they sound as if they don't make any sense," Saana said. "Now, those of you who haven't opened your books, please do so."

Pretia was sick of listening to Nassos and Castor tease Leo. She dragged her desk closer to his. "Don't worry about them," she said. "And don't worry about your grana."

Leo looked at her. "What do you know about grana?"

Pretia flushed and opened to the page she'd selected. "Sorry," Pretia snapped, "I was just trying to be nice."

"Leave me alone," Leo said. He was staring at the closed cover of his book like it might bite.

Pretia dragged her chair back to its original place and looked down at her page. And to her surprise, she was staring at the same image she'd opened to on the first day of Granology—the forest reflected in the lake with the bright moon above and the muddy one below. And just like the first time she'd opened it, the initial sight of the image made her slightly sick to her stomach. Pretia furrowed her brow. If she looked at it one way, it seemed as if there were a lot of trees in the water. If she squinted her eyes, it looked like a single tree. She cocked her head from side to side, hoping an interpretation would come. But the picture still meant nothing to her, unless it was cautioning her not to use her grana. Perhaps the healthy tree was Pretia herself as she had been before lighting Hurell's flame.

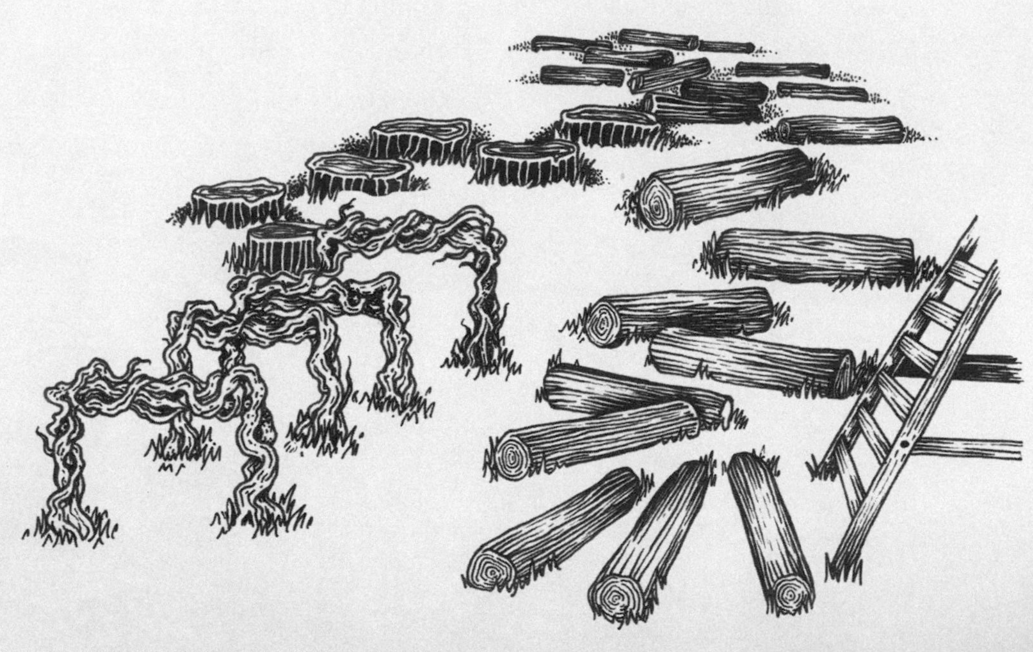

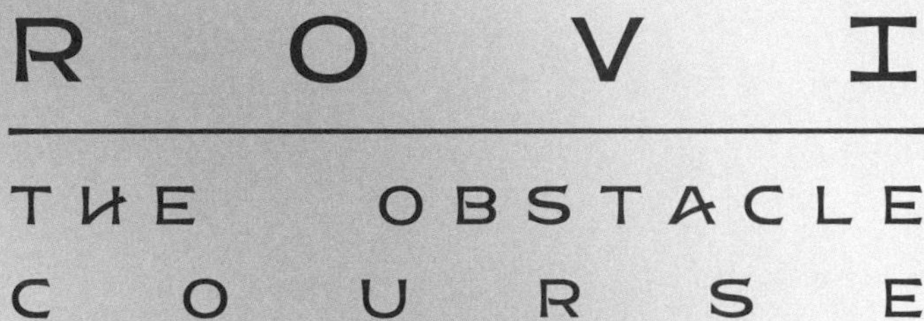

16

ROVI

THE OBSTACLE COURSE

SOMETIMES IT SEEMED TO ROVI THAT THE recruits spent their time at Ecrof doing everything but training. This was especially frustrating because they were supposed to be training for Epic Elite trials. But between Granology and Visualization, Rovi was pretty sick of sitting still in a classroom. Sitting still wasn't really part of his personality. He was made to run, to escape, to dodge and evade. Luckily, with Epic Elite trials a few weeks away, all students were assigned extra training sessions, which meant less time in the classroom and more time running around. And that suited Rovi just fine.

Cleopatra met the recruits at the Panathletic Stadium, as usual. For once, Rovi was early. But he was not the first to arrive. Vera was already running around the track, and from the looks of it, she'd been at it a long time. Rovi began to warm up, something he never did. He desperately wanted to make Epic Elite. He wanted to do anything to distract from the nasty nickname "Tree Killer."

What made things worse for Rovi was that something definitely was wrong with the Tree of Ecrof. There was no denying it anymore. The bottommost branches were completely black. Rovi took a quick glance up at the tree, then moved away and started jogging and stretching on a far outside lane of the track.

Cleopatra blew her whistle, summoning the recruits to attention. Vera sprinted over from the track. She was already drenched in sweat.

"I hope you saved enough energy for training," Cleopatra said.

"I've only been here an hour," Vera said.

"Show-off," Virgil hissed.

Vera tossed her ponytail defiantly. "I guess you don't want to make Epic Elite."

Cleopatra blew her whistle again. "All right, let's get going. Off to the Decision Woods. Last recruit there gets a penalty lap after practice."

Rovi was off like a shot, but not before hearing Vera complain, "The Decision Woods! Aren't we supposed to be training for long jump?"

Rovi didn't stick around for the rest. In no time he was at the Decision Woods, ahead of the other recruits. As usual, Pretia brought up the rear, moving no quicker than a leisurely jog. Rovi suspected she could run faster. She easily kept pace with him and never tired when they were assigned penalty laps, so he guessed she was holding herself back. But he couldn't figure out why. And he couldn't figure out why she so easily accepted her penalty punishments day after day. Even if she didn't have grana, there was no explanation, no excuse for her performance.

However, there was no time to worry about these questions before Cleopatra started explaining the day's training.

"Today we are having a relay race," she said. "The race will take you through the woods. But these will not be the same woods you came through last time you were here. The obstacles are never the same. So be prepared. In fact," she added, "they might even change as you move through the course."

"We got this."

Rovi turned and saw that it was Vera, whispering in his ear.

"We got this for sure," she said again. "After all, Realists take the path, but Dreamers take the obstacles."

Rovi gave her a low five. She was right. This was a Dreamer day.

But before they could plan their victory, Cleopatra was talking again. "Okay, recruits. There's a wrinkle. Today, we are not teaming up by house. This won't be Dreamers versus Realists, for once."

"What?" Virgil cried with a desperate look at Adira. "We're *always* on the same team."

"Sports are filled with uncertainty, and teams are not always who you want them to be," Cleopatra explained. "One of the most important things, as an athlete, is to learn to work with anyone at any time. You need to be your best under any circumstances."

"But when would I have to team with a Realist?" Virgil grumbled.

"Listen," Cleopatra said sternly, fixing Virgil with her fierce almond eyes, "just because you consider your Dreamer recruits friends doesn't mean every Dreamer in Epoca will be someone you want to team up with. You came to Ecrof to challenge yourself. I'm hoping you rise to it."

Virgil looked down at his sneakers and didn't reply.

Although he hadn't spoken up—for once—Rovi pretty much felt the same way. He wasn't much into teaming up in general. As a Star Stealer, he'd usually worked alone.

Cleopatra assigned the teams. Vera was with Tassos, Nassos, Cyril, Alexis, Myra, Adira, and Jason, which left Rovi with Leo, Pretia, Virgil, Hector, Zoe, Sophia, and Castor. He rolled his eyes and shuffled off to join his group. Xenia, a Dreamer, agreed to sit out to keep the teams even.

"Before anyone says anything, I'm captain," Castor said. "We're at a disadvantage already," he added with a meaningful glance at Pretia, "so I'm taking charge."

"Why?" Rovi grumbled.

"Because I'm a natural leader, that's why," Castor said. "It's how I grew up."

"Isn't Pretia a natural leader?" Rovi asked. "I mean, she's going to rule Epoca one day."

"Maybe she will and maybe she won't," Castor said, giving his cousin a strange look. "You don't mind if I take charge, Pretia, do you?"

"Whatever," Pretia said.

Man, Rovi thought. *There's no denying it—sometimes Pretia acts like a total pushover.*

"Are there any more complaints?" Castor asked.

Rovi shrugged. He wasn't complaining. He just wasn't saying anything.

"Okay," Castor continued. "I'm going to lead off. We need a strong start."

"But we don't even know what the race is," Leo said.

"It doesn't matter what the race is, it's a race," Castor snapped. "So I'm leading off to give us a good head start. Then we'll need a strong finish." Rovi felt Castor's eyes land on him. "So I guess, for lack of anyone else, that will have to be Rovi."

"Wow," Rovi said. "I'm honored."

Castor arranged the rest of the team in order. "We'll do our best with what we have."

"But," Leo repeated, "we don't even know what we're doing."

Rovi glared at him. Didn't he know better than to antagonize Castor?

"Didn't I just say it doesn't matter?" Castor snapped.

Cleopatra blew her whistle. "Now that your team order is settled, let's go to the course." She headed into the woods.

The woods were totally different from the last time Rovi had run through them, on his first day at Ecrof. Right in the middle where the Realist's path had been, there was now a large clearing about the size of a basketball court. It was surrounded by a wall of olive trees on either side. Down the middle was a set of obstacles, all of which, like the last obstacles Rovi had encountered in the woods, were made of trees and branches. There were four hurdles shaped from tree roots, tree stumps arranged in a zigzag pattern, and twenty loose logs lined up like a raft, all of which led up to a tall wooden ladder with the rungs three feet apart that the recruits would have to scale to reach a large tower that was made from an enormous tree. Once they reached the top of the tower, they would have to cross a long log, twenty feet up in the air, hanging from loose ropes, to another tower. When they reached the final tower, they'd have to slide down a thick vine, touch the ground, then climb back up the vine and repeat the course until they reached the beginning.

"All right," Cleopatra said. "Well, like any other relay, the purpose is for each of your teammates to complete the obstacle course from start to finish and then back again, and tag the next runner. The team whose members finish first is the winner. Simple."

"Too simple," Vera said.

"Well, looks can be deceiving," Cleopatra said. "Confidence, too. Now, on your marks."

Vera and Castor took their places.

"Get set. *Go!*"

And they were off. Vera and Castor cleared the first hurdle. As they approached the second, it grew higher off the ground. They both stutter-stepped but made it across. The next hurdle grew even higher. This time they were ready and cleared it. The fourth hurdle, however, was impossibly high at first. It took both runners several turns to clear it.

The Realists on Rovi's team were cheering for Castor. The Dreamers on Vera's team urged her on with slightly less enthusiasm.

Now the runners had moved on to the tree stumps, jumping between them without hitting the ground. Each time they landed on a new one, the stump descended into the earth like it had been hit by a hammer. Castor fell and had to start over again. Vera was in the lead.

Vera sprinted across the logs lined up next to each other on the grass. The logs rolled wildly beneath her feet as if they were covered in grease, causing her to lose ground. Castor caught up. Neck and neck, they climbed the treacherous ladder that led to the swinging beam twenty feet off the ground. The log swayed violently as they crossed.

Without thinking, Rovi cupped his hand over his mouth. "Don't look down, Vera," he called.

"I'm delaying ten seconds from your start for cheering for the wrong team," Cleopatra said.

"Keep quiet," Hector snapped, shoving Rovi.

Vera and Castor made it across the log. They descended the vine. They touched the ground, then began to climb back up.

How badly did Rovi want to see Castor struggle on those vines, maybe lose his grip? That would be epic. What did he care if his team lost? But Castor didn't fall; he and Vera finished at the same time and each tagged the next runner.

Leo cost Rovi's team some time, but Hector made up for it. Virgil's gymnastic agility on the obstacles pulled them far into the lead. In fact, his performance was so impressive that even Castor slapped his hand when Virgil crossed the finish line a full two minutes before Nassos.

Then it was Pretia's turn. She had a two-minute head start on Cyril. And she began well. Rovi watched her closely. Her movements were technically sound. She cleared the hurdles easily, even as they got higher. But there was a lack of inspiration in the way she moved. Once more, it looked as if she wasn't really trying. Halfway through the course, Cyril was gaining on her.

Pretia had no trouble on the swinging log. She didn't look panicked like Leo and Hector had, but she also didn't look motivated.

Rovi cupped his hands over his mouth. "Come on, Pretia," he cried.

"I thought Cleopatra warned you about cheering," Castor said.

"Um, not for our own team. Come on, Pretia," he called again.

Then Hector copied him. "Let's go, Pretia. Looking good."

Without warning, Castor pulled Hector's hands away from his mouth. "Don't encourage her," he snapped.

"What?" Hector stared at him, amazed. "Don't you want to win?"

Castor pulled him slightly away from the group, but they were still within Rovi's earshot. "Don't encourage her."

"Why not?"

"Because," Castor hissed, "the worse Pretia is, the better it is for me. If it's clear she doesn't have grana, I get to rule."

Rovi didn't hear the rest. He'd cupped his hands over his mouth and started cheering for Pretia so loudly, he thought his lungs would burst. He wasn't going to do what Castor said, not now. Not ever. Not even if Castor became the King of Epoca. And that thought made Rovi's blood run cold. He cheered even louder. But it didn't do any good. When Pretia crossed the finish line, their team was now three minutes behind.

Cleopatra watched Pretia's finish with her hands on her hips. Pretia didn't wait for the Trainer to speak. She simply trotted off to start the penalty laps for her lack of effort.

Finally, it was Rovi's turn. Sophia had made up a little time when she tagged Rovi. But Rovi still had to wait out his ten-second penalty before taking off. When he did, he heard Pretia cheering for him with all her might. He took the first hurdle. Then the next. Pretia's voice was in his ear, urging him on. But then he heard another voice—Castor's. It stopped Rovi dead in his tracks. What had he just promised himself? He would never do anything Castor asked. Never.

"Rovi, what are you doing?" Pretia shouted. "Run!"

But Rovi couldn't run. His feet wouldn't let him do it.

"Get a move on," Castor shouted. "Go!"

Rovi walked. He took the hurdles easily, but with no speed. He skipped from tree stump to tree stump. He walked over the rolling logs, moseyed up the ladder, ambled down the swinging log, took his time sliding down the vine. By the time he was halfway through, Tassos had already finished. The other team had won.

Rovi didn't even bother to finish. He just walked back to the group. He knew exactly what the dark look on Cleopatra's face meant.

"What were you doing out there?" Castor yelled. "Did you hear us shouting for you?"

"Nope," Rovi said. "I didn't hear a thing."

"You're as crazy as your crazy father," Castor snapped.

Rovi didn't even bother to reply. "Pretia," he called as she passed on a penalty lap. "Wait up. I'm joining you."

17

PRETIA

THE LEAVES

IT WAS GETTING HARDER AND HARDER TO restrain her grana. She could feel it almost bursting out of her. It was like her veins, muscles, tendons, even her blood, were filled with some kind of untamed energy, like there was a wild animal running around inside of her. One careless step and Pretia was certain her grana would reveal itself in some horrible way. She'd hurt someone, or worse. Her body wanted to compete. But Pretia wouldn't let it. So she moved slower than ever. She worked harder than ever to hold it back. And if that meant losing even worse than usual, so be it. There was less than three months to go before she left Ecrof for the summer—less than three months to keep her secret.

She was dreading Epic Elite trials, not just because she knew the pitying looks her fellow recruits would give her when it was her turn to perform the long jump. This was the first time she would demonstrate for the whole school how pathetic she was—or how pathetic she was pretending to be. And that would be humiliating enough if she didn't have to worry about trying to hide her dangerous grana at the same time.

The night before the trials, she could barely sleep. The vision of Hurell's flame danced in front of her eyes. And when she finally fell asleep, she dreamed of the Hall of the Gods back in Castle Airim, except that in her dream the hall was dark and the only light came from the altar to the Fallen God—a bright blue light that filled the entire room. And from inside the flame, Pretia could hear her name. Hurell was calling her.

At breakfast on the day of the trials, Pretia picked at her food while she listened to Rovi chattering manically between huge bites of sausage and lavender oats. She was exhausted from a poor night of sleep and her bad dreams.

"I'm going to be furious if Castor gets Epic Elite," he said. "The only way he'd get chosen is if the school made an exception."

"My uncle wouldn't do that," Pretia muttered. The way things were going, there was a good chance Castor was going to be king. He surely didn't need to be Epic Elite as well.

"Maybe he'll make it a few years down the road," Rovi said. "But not this year. I'm not even sure that any recruits are going to make it."

"What about you?" Pretia asked.

Rovi put down his fork and looked at Pretia. "What about you?"

His stare was making Pretia uncomfortable. "Don't be ridiculous," she said. "Everyone knows I'm the last person in Epoca who's an elite anything."

Rovi frowned. "Actually, Pretia, no one knows that, because no one has ever seen you try."

"I am trying," Pretia insisted. "You're the one who never tries."

Rovi shrugged. "Whatever," he said.

The horn to end the meal blasted across the campus. The remaining Dreamers in the cafeteria rushed to clear their trays. On their way out the door, Rovi doubled back for some Power Snacks from a vending machine in the common room.

"Do you ever stop eating?" Pretia asked.

"Never when it's free," Rovi replied.

The entire school had assembled down by the track on the main field. Kids were warming up, racing each other, practicing their jumps and leaps. Pretia and Rovi joined the rest of the recruits, gathered by the Tree of Ecrof. A huge pile of leaves had fallen at the base of the trunk.

Virgil picked one up. It crumbled in his hands. "It's like they've been burned."

"Maybe it's cursed," Adira said.

Virgil's eyes widened. "Maybe. There was a woman back in Mount Oly who could do curses."

"Curses aren't real," Castor said. "Everyone knows that."

"I don't know that," Virgil said. "Do you know that, Adira?"

Adira looked from Virgil to Castor. "No, I don't," she said finally.

Pretia looked down at the leaves. There definitely seemed to be something off about them. She'd traveled to the Winterlands and seen fallen leaves, lots and lots of them during the seasonal change. Those leaves had been colorful and still bore a resemblance to the way they'd looked when they'd been on their tree. These leaves were a different story. They were a sooty black and they'd curled inward so they looked more like insects than leaves.

The pile was almost as tall as Pretia and surrounded the entire base of the tree.

"The farmers in my region pile leaves and burn them," Xenia said. "But before they do, we like to sneak in the fields and jump in them."

"Don't," Rovi said.

"Don't what?" Castor asked.

"Don't jump in the leaves."

"Why? Did you *do* something to them, Tree Killer?" Castor taunted.

Pretia didn't like the tone in her cousin's voice.

"No," Rovi snapped.

"So are you *scared*?" Castor asked.

"No," Rovi said. "I just wouldn't jump in them. Why don't you do it?"

Castor shrugged. "Fine," he said. "I'll race you. See who can reach the leaves first."

"Forget it," Rovi said. "I'm saving myself for the trials."

"Okay," Castor said. "Who else? Or are you all scared of a pile of leaves?" He looked at the recruits one by one. His eyes passed over Pretia quickly.

"Not me," she said.

"I want a challenger, not a princess."

Then his gaze stopped on Leo. "Leo, you're it."

"Me?" Leo said in a small voice.

"At least you're better than Pretia," Castor said.

"Fine," Leo said a bit uncertainly.

"So, here's the deal," Castor ordered. "We line up to race. First one to the leaves gets the benefit of jumping into the fresh pile. Got it?"

"Sure," Leo replied.

They lined up. Hector counted down. At "go," they both took off. But Castor only went a few steps before he stopped. Leo, oblivious, raced on ahead. At the edge of the leaf pile, he shouted, "I won," and then leaped as high as Pretia had ever seen him jump, and disappeared into the leaf pile.

There was a moment of silence as the recruits looked from Castor to the leaf pile. Castor was doubled over with laughter. There was no movement from the leaves.

"Is he okay?" Pretia asked.

No one answered.

"Where is he?" Pretia asked. Then, without waiting for help, she raced toward the leaves, digging frantically until she found Leo. It sounded like he was choking. She dragged him away from the tree.

Leo lay flat on the ground. His jaw hung slack, his mouth open. He was gasping for air.

"He must have gotten the wind knocked out of him," Virgil said.

"That was some jump," Adira replied.

"Leo," Pretia said, *"Leo."*

Leo was still struggling to breathe.

"Leo?" she repeated. Pretia looked over her shoulder and saw that two medics and Satis were making their way through the crowd of students to get to Leo's side.

Satis pulled Castor aside. "I didn't *do* anything," Pretia heard her cousin protest. "It was just a stupid joke."

Instantly, Nassos and the rest of Castor's crew were at his side, defending their leader.

"Castor," Satis said. "Leo is badly hurt. Tell me what you did."

"Nothing," Castor insisted. "I can't help it if he knocked the wind out of himself jumping in a pile of leaves." Then Castor looked over Satis's shoulder to where Pretia and Rovi were standing. "Why don't you ask the Tree Killer what *he* did to the tree to make it look like that?"

"The who?" Satis asked.

"The Tree Killer," Castor replied, pointing at Rovi.

"Castor Praxis, I suggest you refrain from talking about things you don't understand and making up names that are both hurtful and nonsensical."

Castor met the Visualization Trainer's eye. "His father *was* a Tree Killer."

"Now, what makes you say that?"

"Everyone knows," Castor said.

"No," Satis said. "They don't. There are some things that no one knows."

"Like what?" Castor asked.

"Yeah, like what?" Rovi repeated.

"Now is not the time," Satis said.

Pretia could feel Rovi tense at her side. But before Castor could get another word in, the familiar sound of Janos's voice filled the air. "All right!" her uncle bellowed. "All right!"

The group of students parted and Janos walked between them, a solemn look on his face. "From now on, please keep away from the Tree of Ecrof. As you can all see, it's quite sick. A botanist from the mainland will be sailing over to examine it. The tree is fragile enough without you messing around with it."

"No one was messing with the tree," Pretia whispered to Rovi.

"Right," Rovi muttered.

"The leaves were just on the ground."

"I don't want to talk about that tree," Rovi said.

Pretia gave him a look. "I hope you're not taking this Tree Killer stuff seriously," she said.

"Of course not," Rovi replied.

"Rovi? Pretia? Are you joining us?"

Pretia startled at the sound of her uncle's voice. "I believe tryouts are over that way," he said, pointing at the track.

Pretia saw that the rest of the students were already heading for the track, where a long jump had been set up along one of the straightaways. "This is one of the more important Epic Elite trials because next year is the selection for the Junior Epic Games, and those already on the Epic Elite squad are guaranteed a spot. Now, we have room for two athletes to join Epic Elite this year," Janos said when the students had gathered, "and two reserves who will join them next year. The selection will be simple. The jumpers with the best distances will be selected. That's it."

Cleopatra Volis stood next to Janos with a clipboard and a whistle. "The format is easy. One jump. That's it," she said. "If you overstep the line on the takeoff board before you jump, it's a foul. No do-overs. No second chances."

Vera's hand shot in the air. "In the Epic Games, you get three attempts."

“This isn’t the Epic Games,” Janos said. “The Epic Games are a product of years of training. What we are testing here is your focus and your potential. Not your skill.” Vera looked chastised.

“Okay,” Cleopatra said. “We’ll be jumping oldest to youngest. So, seventh years, line up first.”

“Ugh,” Vera groaned. “I might as well have not even warmed up. I’m going to visualize my jump to sharpen my focus. Pretia, come get me when the second years are jumping.” And with that, she stormed off to the opposite side of the field, where she flopped down on her stomach and seemed to be concentrating furiously.

The seventh years started jumping. “Well, this is going to be boring,” Rovi muttered to Pretia. She had to agree. It was boring watching something that she had no part in. Without using grana, there was no way she’d be Epic Elite.

Pretia sat with her fellow recruits as they critiqued each of the jumps of the seventh years. She knew nothing about long jump. In fact, when Janos had announced the trial event for Epic Elite, she’d done everything in her power not to even think about anything to do with jumping. So she had zero idea what a good jump was or how to execute one.

From what the kids around her were saying, a seventh-year boy named Marcus jumped extraordinarily well. “But what’s the point?” Nassos said to Castor. “He’ll only be Epic Elite for a few months before he leaves Ecrof.”

No one in the sixth year came close to Marcus’s score. A fifth-year girl named Hera executed well, her feet bouncing down the track as if they had springs in them, each step sending her higher and higher, until she took off for her jump, which came in short of the current leader by half an inch. Then, to everyone’s surprise, a fourth-year girl named Leda from the Rhodan Islands passed Marcus by an extraordinary two inches, using her arms like wings to literally fly through the air. Then another fourth year, Daria, beat Leda, putting her in first place.

None of the third years posted any scores of note. When the second years lined up to jump, Pretia scurried over to tell Vera. She found Vera on her feet with her eyes closed. She was clearly lost in some vision of jumping. She was swinging her arms in a steady rhythm as if she were approaching the board. Then she nodded and bent her knees slightly. The movement of her arms changed, as if she were now flying through the air, trying to pull herself as far as possible from her takeoff.

"Vera," Pretia said, anxious about breaking into her concentration.

Vera's eyes snapped open. She was looking at Pretia, but it didn't seem that she was actually seeing her.

"Vera," Pretia said again. But Vera was marching off toward the track. She was on a mission.

When it was Rovi's turn, he jumped well but fell just short of fourth place overall. Then it was Vera's chance.

She stood at the starting line. She tossed her head once. Then she took off. She glided down the track, her arms smooth, her feet graceful. She hit the takeoff board perfectly. Then she flew. She really flew. Her arms and legs cut through the air with none of the violent churning the other students had used to jump as far as they could. Her grana didn't have any wild manifestations. Her jump was perfect. She landed and the entire Dreamer camp rose to their feet, cheering wildly. Vera was in the lead. With a defiant glance at Janos, she stood up and jogged back to the first years.

There were only three runners left.

Castor slipped on the running board and fouled out.

Zoe barely jumped four feet.

Then it was Pretia's turn.

She hadn't warmed up. She had barely been watching. She didn't want any of the previous jumpers' techniques to work its way into her subconscious. She could feel her grana pumping in her veins. It wanted to be turned loose. Pretia moved as slowly as possible. She couldn't be careless.

She stepped up to the starting line. How badly did she want to explode down the track? How badly did she want to sprint, then pound the takeoff board, then soar as far as possible? Her body wanted her to fly like Vera. So maybe—

She closed her eyes. And instead of seeing the track in front of her, she saw the cliff back behind the Royal Woods at Castle Airim, and Davos flying over the edge after she'd pushed him—after her cursed grana had made her push him. "No," Pretia told herself. "Go slow."

Cleopatra clapped her hands. Pretia took off down the track at a leisurely jog. She couldn't allow herself to try. She couldn't allow her shadow self to emerge. She couldn't reveal to the school that she was cursed. Halfway toward the takeoff board, she picked up the pace. Well—she didn't, her legs did. They were moving of their own accord. And then it happened. Before she knew it, she could feel herself pulling away from herself. She knew she was going to watch herself hit the takeoff board and soar into the air. She didn't want to know what would happen after.

It happened in an instant. One moment Pretia was jogging down the track, watching herself sprint toward the board. The next, she'd caught up to herself at the very moment she was supposed to lift off from the board. She hit her split self with a terrible impact, as if she'd crashed into a wall. And then, instead of flying forward as the other jumpers had, Pretia rose up. Up, up, up, and up. She jumped well over ten feet into the air. She was towering over the students on the ground. For a moment, time stopped, or it seemed to stop as she hovered, marveling at how high she was.

And then it was over and with a painful thud, she crashed back onto the track.

There was a moment of silence. Then a collective gasp rose from all the students. "Whoa," Pretia heard Cassandra say. "That was intense."

She glanced over at her House Captain, who was staring at her with a curious look on her face.

"Yeah, totally intense," another Dreamer echoed. "I've never seen anyone jump that high."

"Especially someone without grana," Castor snapped. "I mean, someone with grana would have done the correct jump, right? Right?" Suddenly Castor didn't sound too sure.

"Yeah, someone without grana couldn't have done that," Cassandra said. "No way."

"Too bad it's not the high jump," Adira said.

"If it were, she would have won," Rovi said.

Pretia could feel Rovi looking at her with curiosity. She could almost hear the question hanging on his lips: *Do you really not have grana?* She wouldn't tell him. No way.

She staggered to her feet. What had just happened? What had her grana made her do? She'd controlled it, but just barely. She looked around at the rest of the students. "It was a mistake," Pretia said. "I didn't mean to."

"But it was awesome," Rovi said.

"Is everyone okay?" she asked him.

"Except for Castor's ego," Rovi said.

"You're sure?" Pretia whispered. "No one got hurt or anything?"

"Why would someone have been hurt?" Rovi said.

Pretia sighed with relief. She'd used her grana, but she'd hurt only herself.

"How did you do that?" Rovi asked. "Do you—"

Here it was. "I slipped," Pretia said. "I slipped as I approached the board. Weird timing, I guess."

Cleopatra placed a hand on Pretia's shoulder. "Interesting, Pretia. Very interesting. That's one of the best attempts at anything I've seen you do. Too bad it was the wrong thing."

"It was nothing," Pretia grumbled. "A total accident. There's no way I could do it again."

"Whatever you say," Cleopatra replied. Then she clapped her

hands to get the kids' attention. "All right. Our top four finishers are Vera Renovo, Daria Osso, Leda Signa, and Marcus Velo."

Thunderous applause rocked the track as the winners rose to their feet. Vera looked so proud that it seemed her chest was going to explode.

Janos stood with Cleopatra to address the group. "Now joining the Epic Elites," he announced, "at a secret camp on the eastern side of Corae will be Leda and Marcus. Vera and Daria will stay as reserves and move up to Epic Elite next year."

"WHAT?" Vera's voice tore through the assembled students. "I won," she cried. "I won. I'm going to join them."

"Not this year, I'm afraid," Janos said. "You'll have to wait until next year."

"But I came in first," Vera said. "Those were the rules. The top two join the Epic Elite. I'm joining the Epic Elite." She was screaming so loudly, her words echoed off the marble seats of the Panathletic Stadium.

"I'm sorry," Janos said. "But that's how it will be."

Vera remained on her feet. She put her hands on her hips. "It's because I'm a Replacement, right?"

"No," Janos said.

"So why can't I go?" Vera sounded close to tears.

"I don't have to explain myself to you or to any student," Janos said, narrowing his eyes at her. Pretia had never seen such a stormy look on her uncle's face.

"I want to join my brother," Vera insisted. "I want to see him."

"Your temper is the problem," Janos said. "It's holding you back. It's why you can't be Epic Elite this year."

"I won," Vera wailed. "This isn't fair."

"Even with all the work we put into rules and regulations, sports are often not fair. Sometimes outcomes are dependent on a judgment call. And not everything will go your way. I'm sorry, Vera. This is my decision. It's your job to learn from it, and when you do, you will have the maturity to be Epic Elite like your brother."

Vera looked like she was going to cry. But instead, she sprinted away into the Decision Woods as fast as her legs would go.

"Now, Leda and Marcus," Janos said, "go back to your rooms and get your gear. You'll be headed to the far side of the island immediately. The rest of you, get ready for whatever is next on your schedules."

The students got to their feet. Pretia's entire left leg was sore from where she had crashed into the ground from her towering jump.

As they left the field, Rovi took her arm. "That was some jump," he said. "How did you do that?"

"I didn't do anything," Pretia said. "It was an accident."

"It was amazing," Rovi said. "I didn't know you—or anyone—could jump so high."

"Don't get used to it," Pretia said. "I'm never doing it again."

Rovi grabbed her by the wrist. "Why not?" he said.

She shook him off. She'd already said enough.

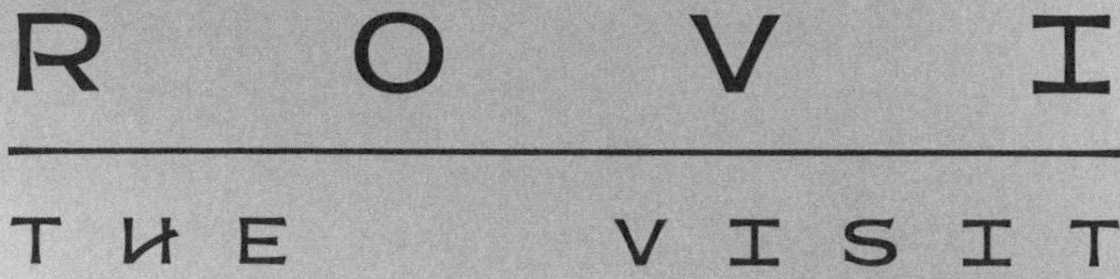

18 ROVI

THE VISIT

THERE ARE SOME THINGS THAT NO ONE KNOWS. Satis's words rang in Rovi's head long after Epic Elite trials had ended. They kept him up at night. He couldn't stop wondering what the Visualization Trainer meant. Did he know something about Rovi's dad that he wasn't telling? Was there more to the story than he was letting on?

For two nights, Rovi barely slept, taunted by Satis's words. He knew he needed to find out more.

It didn't take long for Rovi to learn in which of the Trainers Towers Satis lived. He put his old scouting skills to work, lurking outside the building, watching the Trainers come and go like he was keeping tabs on a vendor at the Alexandrine Plaza from whom he wanted to steal.

Before dawn broke on the second morning after the trials, Rovi was dressed. He grabbed a Choco Water and a couple of snacks from the vending machine in the common room, then left the Temple of Dreams before anyone else was awake. It was a cool, damp morning. Soon enough, the sun would rise and dry the dew.

Aside from Janos, Satis was the only teacher at Ecrof who had ever mentioned Rovi's father to him directly, and Rovi was burning with questions he wanted to ask. He didn't want to wait until class, when Satis might be less willing to speak freely.

Rovi's Grana Gleams were already soaked through when he arrived at the Trainers Towers. He stood staring up at the buildings. For a moment he thought he saw something glowing or burning on the top floor of the eastern tower where Janos had his quarters. Rovi shaded his eyes and squinted. Then he realized—the sun was rising. Since the temples were originally built by the gods' own grana, it seemed that Metus, whose temple this had been, had found a way to harness the first light. Rovi stared at the warm glow for a few more minutes.

Of course Janos would have picked the best rooms with the most magical light for himself.

Thankfully, Satis lived in the western tower, which meant less chance of encountering Janos. Still, Rovi needed to avoid being seen by any other Trainers, since the towers were strictly off-limits to students.

Just as his grana had helped him as a Star Stealer, allowing him to do things like dash through the market without being caught and figure out how to escape notice, now it led him into the western tower, past the chefs who were up early preparing breakfast, to a set of stairs at the back of the temple. It was his grana that told him to hide behind a column when one of the chefs climbed the stairs carrying a tray.

Satis's room was off a mezzanine on the fourth floor of the temple. Rovi stopped in front of the door. Now he was uncertain. Would the Visualization Trainer be angry if he woke him up? Would he tell him to go home? He raised his hand to knock at the heavy wooden door. But then he hesitated. He was sneaking around like a Star Stealer, not a recruit. He should go back to the Temple of Dreams and wait until after class to talk to Satis.

But before he could turn back, the door swung open.

"Rovi," Satis said. "I was waiting for you."

"You knew I was coming?" Rovi asked.

“Well,” Satis said with a wink, “I happened to see you cross the campus.” He held the door wide so Rovi could enter.

His quarters were small and cozy—a simple wooden bed with linen sheets, a table for two, two armchairs, and a set of bookshelves so crammed with books that Rovi worried they would collapse. “Make yourself at home,” Satis said, pointing at the chairs. Then he moved to the small kitchen and started slicing bread. “So, Rovi, what can I do for you?”

Rovi glanced around the room. Suddenly he felt like a baby, coming to a teacher for help because another student had called him names. But it was too late to change his mind. “You heard what Castor said at the trials, right?”

Satis sighed. “Castor says a lot of things. But I have a feeling I know what you mean.”

“He called me Tree Killer,” Rovi said.

Satis shook his head sadly. “The things kids say.”

“You don’t think it’s my fault, do you?” Rovi asked.

Now Satis put down the knife, turned, and gave Rovi a look that was both irritated and concerned. “Think what is your fault?” he said.

Rovi lowered his voice to a whisper. “The rot affecting the Tree of Ecrof. Do you think *that* is my fault?”

Satis shook his head in disbelief. “Well, Rovi,” he said as if he were lecturing a very young child, “are you doing anything to the tree?”

“I don’t think so.”

“You don’t think so or you’re not?”

“I’m not,” Rovi said.

Satis finished filling the breadbasket and brought it to the table. “Of course I don’t think it’s your fault,” he said. “Why would it be your fault that the Tree of Ecrof is sick?”

Rovi took a piece of bread but didn’t take a bite. He flipped it over once, twice, three times, as if it might give him the courage to continue.

"Is there something you're not telling me?" Satis said kindly.

Rovi took a deep breath. "I think my father really did try to kill the Tree of Ecrof." It was one thing to say the words in his head. But it was a whole other challenge to utter them aloud.

Satis placed two pots of honey and two different jams, as well as a crock of butter, on the table. "That's what people say. Now eat."

Rovi looked at him. Perhaps the Visualization Trainer hadn't understood. The secret that Rovi had never uttered to another soul flew out of his mouth before he knew it. "I know that's what they say. But I actually *heard* him talking about it."

Satis took the bread from Rovi's hand, slathered it with butter and honey, then motioned for him to eat and continue.

"It started the night after he got out of the TheraCenter," Rovi said between mouthfuls. "After the disaster with the Self-Splitter. He came back to the room and he was totally changed. That night he started talking about killing the tree. I thought he was talking in his sleep at first. In fact, he almost seemed half-asleep sometimes. Like he was in a dream."

"What did he say?" Satis asked.

Rovi took a deep breath. The memory was crystal clear. "Kill the tree." The same words his father would utter over and over again until his death.

"Kill the tree," Satis repeated.

Rovi nodded. He'd lost count of how many times he'd heard his father utter those words.

"I've always wondered exactly what happened to your father when he performed his experiment," Satis said.

"He lost his mind," Rovi said. "He stepped outside himself and couldn't get back. It exhausted him. Every day that passed after the experiment, my dad got more and more tired."

Satis sighed. "I've always thought there was more to it than that.

Much more. I don't think the experiment made him lose his mind. I think something happened when he stepped outside himself."

"Like what?" Rovi asked.

"I don't know," Satis replied. "I've been trying to figure it out for years. Maybe he saw something terrible. Maybe he accidentally sent himself somewhere frightening. But you and I know that he was never the same."

Rovi took a big bite of bread to hide the tears that had sprung to his eyes. "Or maybe he just lost his mind and tried to cut down the Tree of Ecrof."

"Rovi," Satis cautioned, "that is a story that you've been told, but I knew your father. I don't believe he'd have done such a thing."

"But people saw him on campus with an ax."

Satis looked out the window where the sky was turning from gray to pink. "*Kill the tree.* I wonder what tree he meant." Before Rovi had time to think about this, the Visualization Trainer continued. "What do you remember about those last days before you left Corae?"

Rovi paused. "Let's see. We were here for three days before Janos sent us away. My father didn't teach. He wasn't well enough. But I don't remember being in our rooms the whole time. We were somewhere else." He screwed up his face and tried to think. He hadn't wanted to let his father out of his sight. He'd followed him everywhere, clinging to his father even more than usual. Suddenly it hit Rovi. "We were in his lab," he said. Rovi had gone with his father, of course. He remembered now. He'd hidden in his spot under the long worktable—his secret cabinet. He'd almost outgrown it and his knees had knocked against the metal door.

"What was he doing?" Satis asked.

"I don't know," Rovi said. "I never really knew what he was doing. I think he was writing. Writing and muttering about trees."

"Do you remember if he took the writings when you left?"

Rovi thought for a moment. "I don't think so. We only had one small bag. Janos made him leave most of his stuff here."

Satis was rubbing his bald head as if it were a crystal ball. "The only thing I found after he left was your Grana Book. There weren't any writings. And I've checked the lab."

Me too, Rovi almost said. But he stopped himself. He didn't want to admit that he'd been in the lab. And the truth was, he hadn't looked for any writings. He'd just marveled at his father's old equipment.

"Rovi," Satis said, "the easy way out is to believe what other people say without thinking about it. And since you're not a Tree Killer, don't you think it's possible that your father wasn't, either?"

Rovi sighed. "I don't know what to believe," he said. "My dad lost his mind, that's all I'm certain of."

"That is true," Satis said sadly. "But the question is why."

Suddenly the breakfast horn blasted across campus.

"You need to get back to your own temple," Satis said. "But we can continue this conversation later."

Rovi took a piece of bread and stood. "I have one more question," he said. "Why did my father leave my Grana Book? Do you think it was a mistake?"

"I've often wondered about that," Satis said. "He wasn't very lucid when you left, so it's possible that he simply forgot it. But part of me thinks it was intentional. Maybe he feared he wasn't going to live to see your tenth birthday and he worried about what would happen to the book if he died. I think he knew that he was changed for good." Satis lowered his voice. "I think he knew something bad had happened to him."

"Something besides the experiment?"

"I believe so, yes," Satis said. "I think he sensed he was never coming back. Ever."

Rovi opened his mouth to ask another question, but Satis put his hand on Rovi's shoulder. "I don't have the answers, Rovi. All I know is that your father was an exceptional man and something terrible and tragic befell him. I don't fully understand it myself. Maybe one day."

Satis held the door open for Rovi.

"Rovi, the best way to honor your father's legacy is by being the best student and athlete you can be. Apply yourself. Don't give up. He believed in you."

And before Satis could see the tears in Rovi's eyes, Rovi darted down the steps and out of the Trainers Towers.

The sky was the color of rose petals when Rovi got outside. He took the long way back to the Temple of Dreams, behind the Halls of Process and the TheraCenter, where it was less likely to seem as if he'd been anywhere near the Panathletic Stadium and tree. Even though Satis had told him to ignore Castor and his taunts, Rovi didn't want to give him any more ammunition.

As he approached the TheraCenter, he heard footsteps ahead of him. But he didn't stop. At dawn it wasn't unusual to see overly eager students out for additional training.

He had crossed from the TheraCenter toward the entrance to the Halls of Process when the person in front of him stopped walking. Rovi quickly overtook him and was surprised to see Iskander Dracos, the fourth-year Dreamer who Janos had said had gone to Epic Elite intensive training.

"Hey," Rovi said, "are the Epic Elites back on campus?"

Iskander stared as if he were looking straight through Rovi.

"Iskander?"

Maybe it was the strange dawn light, but Iskander looked pale. Not just pale but transparent.

"Are you okay?" Rovi asked.

Finally, Iskander nodded. He was breathing strangely, like he had something caught in his throat.

"So are you guys back from secret training?"

Iskander nodded again.

"Weird," Rovi said. "The new Epic Elites were just sent to join you."

"Yes," Iskander said. His voice was hoarse, like one of the old men in Phoenis who spent all day smoking sweet fruit vapor.

"Well, it'll be cool to have you back on campus for Dreamer Field Day." Rovi meant it. After all, Iskander was the one who had suggested Cassandra choose Rovi for the Dreamers' squad.

"Field Day," Iskander said, like he couldn't quite place what the words meant.

"Yeah, Field Day," Rovi said. He stared at Iskander before asking, "Are you sure you're okay?"

Iskander nodded again, slowly. It looked like it took a great deal of effort to move his head up and down.

"Man," Rovi said. "They must really work you hard at secret training." If this was how students emerged after months on the eastern side of Corae, he wanted none of it.

"Yes," Iskander said. Then, still in a daze, he wandered away, leaving Rovi standing by the Halls of Process.

Rovi watched him go. Except for his father in his final days, he had never seen anyone look so exhausted in his entire life.

19

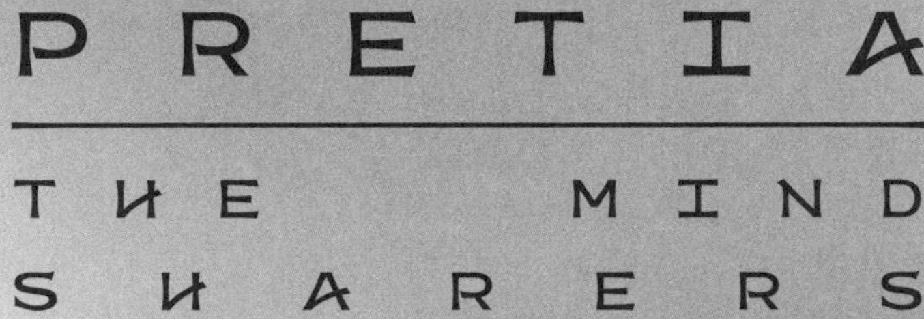

PRETIA

THE MIND SHARERS

ROVI HAD SHOVELED HIS BREAKFAST DOWN faster than usual and raced back to his room, clearly distracted by something, which left Pretia to eat with Vera. Vera was still steaming after what had happened at Epic Elite trials. She shoved food into her mouth like it was the food's fault she was still stuck on this part of the island and not training with the rest of the Epic Elite. She pierced sausages and buttered toast like she wanted to hurt them. When she bused her tray, it seemed like she was trying to break everything on it. It didn't matter to her that she'd be chosen next year and that she'd be guaranteed a spot on the Junior Epic Team. She'd been cheated out of her place this year—and she couldn't stop talking about it.

Pretia took a final look around the Temple of Dreams for Rovi before heading down to Visualization. She found him already seated in the class, early for a change.

When the recruits were settled in the classroom, Satis broke them into pairs and handed each pair a set of short batons, like the ones used in track relays. "These are Mind Sharers," he explained. "When you master them, you can share visualizations with a partner. You can even enter each other's visualization."

Hector had his hand in the air instantly. "What's the point of that?"

"Well, first of all, if you are able to let someone into your visualization, it shows the strength of your own concentration. But more than that, it's an important tool for various partner sports: ice-skating, synchronized diving, doubles tennis, beach volleyball."

"So, girls' sports," Hector grumbled.

"That will be three penalty laps after class, Hector," Satis said. "As you know, there are no girls' or boys' sports. There are only sports."

"Yeah, Hector," Adira said. "I'd like to see you try diving."

"Or ice-skating," Virgil added.

"All right," Satis said, waving a hand to settle the class. "Now, these look like the batons in a track relay for a reason. The handoff in a relay is the hardest part of the race. It requires both runners to be in perfect sync. As you know, hold on too long, you're disqualified. Race ahead of the pass, you're also done. Just like in the relay, you will use the batons to work together, almost as a single organism."

Virgil and Adira pulled their chairs closer together, obviously eager to get going.

"Now, I don't expect any of you to master this right off the bat," Satis continued. "In fact, there's no shame in never being able to share visualization with a partner. All I can ask is that you try, and in trying, produce the best visualization you can, regardless of whether your partner can see it." He held up two batons. "The process is deceptively simple. You hold one in each hand and your partner takes the other end. Use a loose grip. You don't want to suffocate the mental transmission. Then let your mind go."

"Sounds easy," Adira said.

"Totally," Virgil replied, slapping her hand. "Synchronized diving, here we come!"

"We're going to nail that," Adira said.

Satis clapped his hands for quiet. "One more thing—choose something simple, something you can easily see yourself doing. Perhaps even something you've done before. That way you will be able to hold on to the image longer and more clearly. And remember, the Mind Sharers are only a tool. When you are truly in sync with one another, you will be able to share your visualizations without using any sort of device. All you will need to do is hold hands. Now you may scatter around the room as you wish."

Pretia and Rovi hurried to a cool corner in the back of the room where the light was dimmest.

Rovi was staring at the batons with fascination.

"What?" Pretia asked.

"My father invented these," he whispered.

"Don't let Castor know," Pretia teased.

Rovi hid a small smile. "I've always wanted to try them," he said.

"What are you going to visualize?" Pretia asked Rovi.

"Hurdles," Rovi said. "You?"

Pretia shrugged.

"Come on," Rovi said, "don't tell me you're not going to try today."

Pretia gritted her teeth. "I do try," she said. "It's complicated." She thought for a moment. She was able to visualize strong, clear images of herself doing all the sports and games that she didn't allow herself to do on the playing field. "Satis said choose something simple, so maybe, I don't know, the hundred-meter dash."

"Sounds simple enough," Rovi said.

Pretia glanced around the room. Adira and Virgil were holding their batons between them, a shared look of concentration on their faces. Vera was frowning furiously as she gripped the batons with Satis. Castor and Nassos were playing tug-of-war.

"You want to go first?" Pretia asked Rovi.

"Sure," he said. "I don't quite understand what to do. But here goes."

He gripped one side of each baton and Pretia took the other sides. They both closed their eyes as they held on in silence. Nothing.

Through the batons, Pretia could feel the tension in Rovi's hands. After a few minutes, he let go. They both opened their eyes.

"Did you see it?" Rovi asked.

Pretia shook her head. "Maybe you should relax a little."

"How can I relax at the same time I'm trying to force a vision into your head?" Rovi asked.

"I think you're not supposed to *force* it," Pretia suggested.

"Fine," Rovi said, slamming his eyes shut again.

After ten minutes of feeling Rovi's tension through the other end of the batons, Pretia let go. She opened her eyes and saw that Rovi was sweating. "Let's switch," she suggested.

"Phew," Rovi said. He wiped his brow.

Pretia grabbed her end of the batons and closed her eyes. Bringing up the image of running along the track was simple. In no time, Pretia was imagining herself running the 100-meter dash. Three, four, five times she crossed the finish line. Then she started adding in competitors. First Vera, then Rovi. After a while, she was able to perfectly imagine a race with six other runners. She could conjure each of her competitors precisely—every detail of their face, hair, clothes, and running style. But she never allowed herself to win. Finally, she opened her eyes.

Rovi was staring at her with an exasperated look on his face. "So you don't push yourself in your mind, either?"

"You could see my visualization?" Pretia gasped.

"Clearly," Rovi said. "But you weren't *trying*."

"I was," she said.

"Race me," Rovi said. "Race me and win."

Pretia rolled her eyes. "Fine," she said. She closed her eyes. If Rovi wanted her to try, she'd try. She'd show him. It was only a visualization. She couldn't injure him—it wasn't real.

She saw herself get into the starting blocks. She imagined Rovi next to her. She heard the starter's gun explode. And then she watched herself take off. But wait—she *watched* herself take off in her visualization. Pretia remained in the starting blocks while a shadow Pretia sprinted toward the finish faster than she had ever thought possible.

This other Pretia charged down the track, knocking the imaginary Rovi over on her way to the finish.

Pretia was snapped out of her visualization by Rovi dropping the batons. She opened her eyes and saw him lying on the floor.

"I'm sorry," she cried, dropping to her knees. "What did I do?"

Rovi was staring at her, wide-eyed.

Pretia's heart was racing. She wanted to cry. "I hurt you," she said.

"You split yourself," Rovi gasped. He was staring at her as if she were one of the Gods of Granity returned to earth.

"Are—are you okay?" she stammered.

"Me?" Rovi said. "Yeah, I'm fine. But you . . . you . . . can you really do that?"

"Shh." Pretia put her finger to her lips. "It was just in my head."

Rovi was nodding slowly. He looked as if he was in shock. "No. It was more than that." He lowered his voice. "You can do it for real, can't you?"

"No," Pretia snapped. "I can't."

"Come on," Rovi said. Now his eyes were flooded with something like knowledge or recognition. "You have grana," he gasped.

Pretia reached out and clamped a hand over Rovi's mouth. "Be quiet," she said.

"That's your secret," Rovi said through the muzzle of her hand. "You have grana."

"Please, Rovi. Shh."

"Okay, okay," Rovi said. "Just move your hand."

"Hey," Vera called from across the room, "it's hard enough to concentrate without you guys making a lot of noise."

Rovi raised his hand. "Satis, can Pretia and I go outside to work? I think the sunlight will help me focus."

Before Pretia could object, Satis had granted permission and Rovi was dragging her out the door. Overhead was the Infinity Track, higher than Pretia had ever seen it.

"Do it again," Rovi said.

"Do what?"

"Step outside yourself."

Pretia shook her head.

"But you've done it before?" Rovi asked. "For real, not just in a visualization exercise?"

Pretia nodded reluctantly. She didn't want to tell him any more. She couldn't.

"Can I see?"

"No," Pretia said. "No way."

"Why not?" Rovi urged.

Pretia bit her lip. "Because my grana is bad." Her stomach flipped and she clapped a hand over her mouth. Her pulse was racing. Her stomach felt knotted. Her palms started to sweat. She couldn't believe she had actually said it aloud. She glanced around, panicked that someone besides Rovi might have heard her. But they were alone. Now that the truth was out in the world, it made her feel even more sick.

"What do you mean, bad?"

"It's cursed."

Rovi rolled his eyes and laughed. "It's not cursed. It's powerful. Self-splitting is supposed to be impossible," Rovi said. "Only someone with perfect grana can do it. That's what my dad always said. Please, can I see you do it again?"

From the stadium, Pretia could hear older students playing a game, soccer or football. "No," she said firmly.

"Please." There was a desperate note in Rovi's voice.

"Why does it matter so much?"

Rovi took a deep breath. "The last thing my father did before he started raving was an experiment to step out of himself. He invented a machine called the Self-Splitter. He made it work, but something went wrong."

"Because it's not something you are supposed to do," Pretia said. "It's not normal."

"But you can do it," Rovi said. "And you haven't lost your mind. I want to see you do it. Maybe it will help me realize what went wrong with my dad."

"Sorry," Pretia said. "You saw what happened. I knocked you over."

"You only visualized that."

"But you fell!"

"Pretia, you're the best at visualization in the entire class. If you can visualize knocking me over, you can also visualize running without knocking me over. All you have to do is try."

Rovi didn't know. He didn't understand—he couldn't understand—what she was capable of. She'd nearly killed Davos back at Castle Airim. Then she'd almost made Vera fall from the rigging. And then Castor during the game of capture the flag—she'd injured him, too. Rovi didn't know about any of that. And he didn't know that she'd lit the flame to Hurell.

"I'm never, ever doing it," Pretia said. "Never. It's dangerous. And your father was foolish to even try."

"What?" Rovi said.

"Look what happened to him. It cost him his sanity. I'm not going to let that happen to me. Sorry." There were tears in her eyes, but she didn't care. She'd hurt Rovi unintentionally in her visualization. *In her visualization.* Even in her mind she was dangerous.

"Please," Rovi said. "Please, just once."

"No, Rovi, never. I'm never doing it. And you have to promise never to tell anyone." She tugged on his arm. "Rovi, you have to promise."

"Come on, Pretia. If you have grana, you should use it."

"There are things about my grana you can't understand," Pretia insisted. "Terrible things. So promise you won't tell anyone."

"Fine," Rovi said. "Fine, I promise. But I still think—"

His last appeal was drowned out by the hunting horn to end class, and Pretia hurried off without a backward glance.

20

ROVI

THE NOTEBOOK

THE MOMENT HE SAW PRETIA STEP OUTSIDE herself—actually, sprint outside herself—Rovi had an idea. It built on something Satis had suggested when Rovi had visited him in the Trainers Towers. Maybe it wasn't stepping outside himself that had made his father lose his mind. Maybe it was something that Pallas Myrios had seen when he'd been outside himself that had changed him for good.

Pretia had stepped outside herself, more than once. She'd admitted it to Rovi. And it hadn't harmed her. She was a little weird, for sure, but nothing like Rovi's dad.

The second hunting horn sounded to start track training. Rovi watched the rest of the first-year recruits leave the Halls of Process and head toward the obstacle woods, where they were supposed to meet Cleopatra Volis for their practice session. What would it matter if he skipped practice?

Rovi waited until the classroom building was empty, then he dashed back inside. He made sure no one was looking, then he slipped into the door to his father's old lab. Dust was swirling in the rays of sunlight that were pouring in through the window. Everything was just as he'd left it. But suddenly Rovi was struck by something.

Everything was not as his *father* had left it. The last time he'd been with his father in the lab, the day they left Ecrof, the place had been delightfully disorganized as always.

When he'd first visited the lab earlier in the year, he'd figured the additional disarray was something that had just happened over the three years that he'd been away from Corae. But now, in the light of day, he could tell that someone had been in the lab—someone who seemed to be looking for something. All the cabinet doors and drawers were open. He'd been too distracted by finding the Self-Splitter to notice.

Rovi peered into one of the large flat drawers where he remembered his father storing his drawings and sketches of his many inventions. It was empty. So were the three drawers above it and three below. Then he checked the bookcase where books on visualization once sat. They were all gone.

Also gone were his father's ledgers and class plans—his study guides and attendance books and exam papers. Weird. In fact, all evidence of his father's writing, drawing, planning, doodling, noting, recording—every single scrap of his father's handwriting—was gone. Someone had taken it all. Hundreds—no, thousands—of pieces of paper.

As far as Rovi knew, his father hadn't kept any secrets. Everything he drew, he either built or tried to build or discarded as too ridiculous. He shared all his drawings with anyone who wanted to take a look. Rovi was certain of that. He remembered his father and Janos debating them late at night in the Trainers Towers over rich cups of Megaran wine. Any student who wanted to come into his father's lab was welcome, invited even. Rovi would hide in his special spot, wedged in the small cupboard underneath the long worktable, and listen to his father explain his weird inventions to Ecrof students.

Rovi's last memory of Corae before he'd left with his father was of hiding in that cupboard. For their last three days at Ecrof, Rovi had glued himself to his father's side as he tried to ignore his dad's increasingly strange behavior—the way his dad kept ranting and raving about trees, especially about killing them. When he wasn't ranting about trees, he was drawing. As for what he was drawing, Rovi had no idea. He didn't even look. He'd just jammed himself into the little cupboard, happy to be near his father, even if it meant that he was in that tight space for hours, long after dinner, long after bedtime.

Rovi moved away from the drawers and cabinets along the wall and went to his father's long worktable in the middle of the room. He squatted down and looked for the door he'd hidden behind while his father worked above him. He almost missed it—just a tiny handle in the smooth metal. He opened it and looked inside. The space was small. Really small. He marveled that he'd fit in there at all.

His father never stored anything in the cupboard beneath the worktable, knowing it was Rovi's special spot. Still, Rovi put his hand inside, expecting to feel nothing but the cool metal interior. But something was there—a book.

Rovi's heart skipped. He looked over his shoulder as if someone might be watching him. Then, slowly, he pulled out the book.

He recognized it instantly as one of the large leather-bound notebooks his father had filled with sketches. It was thick, at least two hundred pages or more. Carefully, as if it might fall apart in his hands, Rovi opened the cover.

His father's style of drawing was unmistakable. So were the images. Trees. Trees. Trees. And not any trees—the same tree over and over and over. Rovi turned the pages. More trees. More of the same tree.

It wasn't a tree he'd ever seen before. It was massive, with a trunk that looked more like tentacles than a solid mass—like it was a tree growing over another tree. The base of the tree was made up of hundreds of strange tentacles that wound up and around, twisting and turning into a knotted whole before eventually spreading out into gnarled branches that were as tangled as the trunk.

Rovi turned the pages. He'd never seen anything like it. Over and over, the same tree—the same twisted wood—from different angles. Sometimes the tentacle-like branches looked like arms strangling something hidden inside. Sometimes they looked like a body clinging to the tree itself.

Hundreds of times his father had drawn this same tree. Each image was terrifying—the tree was sinister.

And there was something else weird about the tree. It didn't have leaves. The branches reached up and out like a dead thing—a tangle of skeleton arms. The top of the tree was strange, too. At the highest point, the twisted branches almost flattened out, like they had reached some kind of ceiling and they were growing against it, spreading horizontally, not vertically.

Rovi kept turning the pages. How many times had his father drawn this tree? It seemed impossible that he'd had the time or the energy to draw it so many times. But each drawing was perfectly detailed—each dark crevice in the twisted branches, each burl in the wood, each knot and twist.

A tree like this clearly didn't exist in the real world, only in Pallas Myrios's imagination—his fractured and fragmented mind. Perhaps it wasn't a tree at all. Maybe it was an invention, a killer tree or something used to kill a tree.

Rovi flipped through the hundreds of drawings again. They were drawn with the same precision his father had used when he sketched his inventions. So that's what this tree must be. A tree-killing device. Was this what he was planning to use to kill the Tree of Ecrof?

Rovi slammed the book shut with a cry. He'd been trying to deny this fact for years. His father had been out of his mind when they'd left Corae. He hadn't known what he was doing. That's all

Rovi would ever allow himself to admit. But now the evidence was in front of him. Pallas had wanted to build a machine to kill the tree.

He tucked the book in his gym bag and rushed to track training. The penalty laps wouldn't be so bad. They would distract him from what he'd found—the evidence that his father had not just lost his mind but had wanted to destroy one of the Four Marvels of Epoca.

21 PRETIA THE SELECTION

THE LAST MONTHS HAD BEEN LONELIER THAN usual for Pretia. She was so afraid of the rest of the school guessing her secret after her accidental jump at Epic Elite trials that she started to find excuses to skip training. She was worried she'd revealed too much. She was worried she'd let the school glance her shadow self. So she pretended to be sick or injured. She got herself assigned penalty laps immediately so she could go off on her own.

At mealtimes she ate quickly and alone, often huddled around her Grana Book. She always returned to the image of the reflected forest that she'd opened to the first day in Granology, the image that was supposed to represent her time at Ecrof and her biggest challenge while she was there. Since the start of school, she had been staring at this page, but she'd come no closer to an interpretation. The picture still gave her an unsettled feeling, like there was something bad or evil in it somewhere. And Pretia couldn't shake the feeling that this had to do with her cursed grana.

Two months after the trials, Pretia came down to breakfast to find the Dreamers' cafeteria buzzing with excitement. For once, her fellow Dreamers weren't devouring the delicious breakfast that came pouring out of the kitchen like it was their last meal of all time. In fact, many of them hadn't even filled their trays. Most of the students were gathered around Cassandra, who was holding court in the middle of the room.

"What's going on?" Pretia asked Virgil, who was trying to find a seat in the center of the crowd of students.

"They announced Dreamer Field Day," Virgil said. "It's next week. Cassandra is choosing the events."

"Then she's picking the athletes," Adira added, tugging Virgil toward a free spot on one of the benches.

Pretia had no interest in Dreamer Field Day beyond sitting on the sidelines and cheering her fellow Dreamers on. So she filled her tray with honeycakes and found a seat on the outskirts of the group. The only upside to the Field Day was that it meant the year was nearly over. A few weeks after the competition, she'd be sailing home to Castle Airim.

"Okay," Cassandra was saying. "As usual, the focus of Field Days is track events. That way the entire school, not just the older kids who have moved on to different sports, can participate."

This drew cheers from the youngest students and groans from the upperclassmen.

"I was really encouraged by how well so many of you guys did at Epic Elite trials."

Pretia watched the entire crew of Dreamers turn and look at Vera, who was staring moodily at Cassandra.

"So I decided the focus of our Field Day will be jumping. Long jump, high jump, triple jump, pole vault, and one race—steeplechase. I think we have a pretty good chance to win this one," Cassandra added, "especially since I heard the Epic Elites won't be back from secret training in time to compete."

Pretia saw Rovi open his mouth to say something. But before

he could, he was cut off by Virgil. "But if they don't have their best athletes, we don't have ours," he said.

Cassandra gave Vera a meaningful look. "We have both Epic reserves," she said. "And I was keeping track of the scores during trials. Four of the remaining top-ten finishers were Dreamers. So, as I said, I think we're in good shape."

Pretia looked at Vera again. The deep scowl was still on her face. "I want to compete against Julius," she said.

"I can't control that," Cassandra said. "But I want you to compete because you're you, not because you're Julius's sister and have an advantage others don't have when racing him."

"If Julius doesn't compete, the Realists will always say they would have won if he'd been there," Vera continued. "We should postpone until the Epic Elites are back so we can beat House Reila fair and square."

"No way," Adira said.

"I understand your point, Vera," Cassandra said, "but, unfortunately, those aren't the rules."

Vera rolled her eyes. "Isn't it a little weird to schedule a Field Day when the Epic Elites are gone?"

Cassandra tilted her head to one side and thought for a moment. "It's a little unusual. But I guess Janos wants them prepared for the summer interschool meets."

Vera opened her mouth again. Pretia knew what she was going to say without her saying it—some complaint about how she should be competing in the summer interschool meets. But before she could get this out, Cassandra told all the athletes who'd competed in the last Field Day to meet in the common room for a strategy session and to help her round out their teams.

Pretia finished her breakfast listening to Adira and Virgil speculate endlessly about which first years, besides Vera and Rovi, might be chosen for the Field Day. Pretia got up and helped herself to a plate of eggs. When she returned to the table, she saw Cassandra approaching. Adira and Virgil exchanged excited looks. But their faces instantly fell when Cassandra tapped Pretia on the shoulder.

Pretia froze.

"Pretia?"

Slowly Pretia turned her head and looked at her House Captain.

"I'm picking you for the high jump," Cassandra said.

Pretia's eyes widened. "Me? No," she said. "No way."

"If you can do what you did at Epic Elite trials, you'll be awesome," Cassandra said.

"But she was supposed to be doing the *long* jump," Adira said.

Cassandra ignored her.

"Adira's right," Pretia said. "I did the wrong jump. I'll be terrible."

"Pretia," Cassandra said, "this is a huge honor. Everyone wants to represent her house."

Pretia shook her head. There was no way she was going to let this happen. "Not me."

"Why not?" Casssandra asked.

"You know why. *Everyone* knows why. I don't have grana."

"That's not what I think," Cassandra said. "And I'm sure I'm right. I've been watching you."

Pretia's stomach flipped. This was her worst nightmare. She inclined her body so that she blocked Adira and Virgil from listening in.

"I don't know what you think, but you're wrong."

"You do have grana," Cassandra said.

"I have no idea what you're talking about," Pretia said. She glanced across the table and saw that Adira and Virgil had stopped whispering and were straining to hear what she and Cassandra were saying.

"You're just hiding it for some reason," Cassandra insisted.

"No," Pretia said. "I'm not. I don't have it. And if anyone said that, he's lying."

“Who would know about your grana?”

Pretia frowned. Had she given herself away?

“So there is someone else out there who knows about your grana?” Cassandra continued.

“No,” Pretia said, “there isn’t. No one knows anything.”

“I don’t believe that,” Cassandra replied.

“Believe whatever you want. It’s not changing anything. And I’m not competing for the Dreamers. That’s final.”

She stood up. She wanted to get as far away from the Temple of Dreams as she could.

She rushed out of the cafeteria without busing her tray. She raced through the common room and into the Hall of Victory, where she was instantly surrounded by the glory of all the best Dreamer athletes.

“Pretia!”

She didn’t stop when she heard Rovi’s voice echoing through the marble halls.

“Pretia!”

Pretia raced on, out of the Temple of Dreams, down the steps, down the hill. Before she hit the main field, Rovi had caught up to her.

“Go away,” she said.

“If you’d used your grana, you could have escaped,” he said.

Pretia turned and faced him, her eyes full of fury and her heart racing. “You of all people should know that I’m never using my grana.”

“So you’re not going to compete for the Dreamers?”

Pretia narrowed her eyes. Her cheeks were burning. “No.”

“Pretia, we’re here to win. We could use you to win. If you hadn’t noticed, the Realists won the last Field Day.”

Pretia placed her hands on her hips and glowered at him. “I can’t use my grana. It’s cursed.”

Rovi tried to grab her wrist. “That’s ridiculous.” Pretia stepped back. “The Dreamers need you. I need you,” he said.

"And I'm the last person the Dreamers need."

"Look," Rovi said, pointing across the Panathletic Stadium at the top of the leafless Tree of Ecrof. "Look at the tree."

Pretia looked. The formerly beautiful tree was a collection of withering black sticks.

"Everyone thinks that's my fault. Everyone," Rovi said. "Maybe if I'm on a team that helps the Dreamers win, that will change. And we need you to win. Do this for me."

Pretia pursed her lips, trying to bite back her anger.

"My dad was fired for supposedly trying to cut down the Tree of Ecrof, and the minute I got to Corae Island, the tree began to die. So it doesn't matter whether or not it's my fault. What matters is that everyone—or at least every Realist and even some Dreamers—think it is. Excelling at Ecrof is my only chance to clear my name and my father's name."

"Then you should have tried harder in track training instead of butting heads with Cleopatra."

"I know," Rovi said. "But help me out. Help me be more than the kid who killed the Tree of Ecrof."

Pretia stared at Rovi, then at the tree. "Sorry," she said. "You guys will have to do it without me."

"You're going to let us all down," Rovi pleaded. "What kind of ruler does that?"

"I'm not a ruler," Pretia said. "And I am not competing, I'm doing my duty. I'm keeping you all safe. From *me*."

"That is the most ridiculous thing I've ever heard," Rovi said.

The two friends stared at each other. Rovi blinked first. "Fine," he said. "Have it your way. Be a disappointment." And he went off to join the other Dreamer athletes, leaving Pretia to stand staring over the campus toward the Tree of Ecrof. A disappointment? Well, that was true. But revealing her dangerous grana would be worse. Then her parents would know. *Everyone* would know.

Pretia bit her lip. She hated thinking about her parents and what the revelation of her bad grana would do to them. Instead, she focused on the tree. It was ridiculous that anyone thought Rovi was hurting the tree. How could he be? What would he be doing? She shaded her eyes and squinted at the spindly black branches that were visible over the top of the Panathletic Stadium. Sure, they looked terrible, but that was certainly not Rovi's fault. It was simply absurd for anyone to think so, that he had somehow poisoned the tree, turned it black, made it look like—

Pretia's mouth fell open. It looked just like the image in her Grana Book. She raced up the stairs to her bedroom and grabbed the book. She found the picture that she'd chosen to explain her time at Ecrof on her first day in Granology and stared at the familiar images of the mirrored forests—the green one growing right side up and the reflected black copy. She closed her eyes. Two forests. Two sides to her. Dreamer. Realist. Dark and light. Two ways to do everything. Two sides to everything. It still didn't make sense.

She sighed. And just like Saana had suggested, she relaxed into the image almost involuntarily. She needed to try an alternative method of interpretation. She needed to rethink her thinking.

She had thought the trees represented her. But what if that was wrong? Pretia tried to reconfigure her thoughts. What else could they be?

She tried to make her mind blank. That didn't work. She tried to narrow her focus to different elements of the image: the water, the moon, the trees.

The trees!

What if the trees didn't actually represent her? What if the trees were Ecrof, instead? Now, that made sense. The school's mascot was a tree.

Pretia shifted her focus from the healthy trees to their dark reflection in the water.

What if there was something dark in the trees?

She opened her eyes. Of course! First, the branch that hit Castor. Then the leaf tornado. Then Leo, who was smothered by leaves. It wasn't just the Tree of Ecrof—all the trees were sick. The trees were harming the students.

Pretia placed a hand on her book. She closed her eyes. She could see the image perfectly in her mind. She knew what it meant. For the first time, she *knew*. And for a moment, she forgot that her secret was no longer a secret. She forgot about her cursed grana.

She was as sure of her interpretation of the image in her book as she was of anything else in her life. And that realization felt incredible. She felt as if she was on the verge of something important. She let her mind relax into the remembered picture as the certainty washed over her. The trees were harming the students. There was no doubt. She wished more than anything in the world that Anara was there so she could share her interpretation. She had a feeling her nurse would have been extremely proud of her.

She opened the book one more time and looked at the image. Only two small questions remained. What did the moons in the picture mean and what did any of this have to do with her?

22

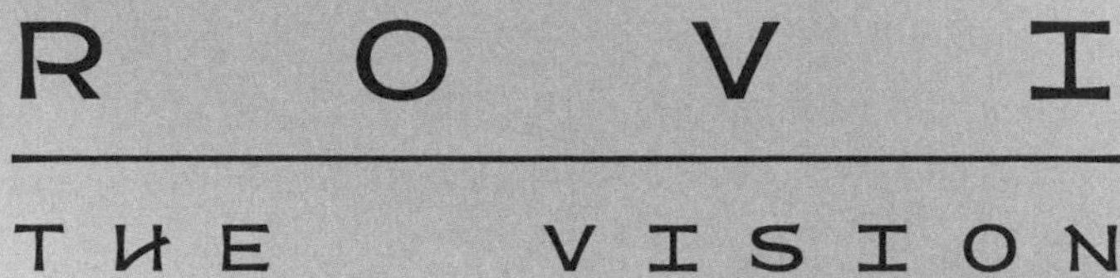

ROVI RACED AROUND THE TRACK AS FAST AS he could, then pulled up short and limped across the finish line, a stitch in his side. He had taken to putting in extra practice before breakfast so that he would excel on Field Day.

Cassandra had selected a team of fifteen athletes, including Vera and Rovi, for Dreamer Field Day. Pretia's spot had gone to a fourth-year boy from Helios who had finished eleventh at Epic Elite trials. The House Captain worked them hard. Every morning for the week leading up to Field Day, Cassandra had her team meet behind the Temple of Dreams before dawn to train in secret. She didn't want the Realists getting word of the events they had chosen until the last possible minute.

Cassandra had assigned Rovi to run the steeplechase. It was a strange event—a sort of obstacle course with twenty-eight barrier jumps and seven water jumps, something Rovi had never practiced before. Of course, he knew the reason he'd been chosen for steeplechase—his time as a Star Stealer, when he'd dodged obstacle after obstacle from the Alexandrine Market, through the Upper City, and finally into the mazelike Lower City of Phoenis, had prepared him well.

By the time the breakfast horn sounded, he had already put in two hard hours in the woods behind the Temple of Dreams and in the temple's private gym. He raced to the cafeteria, almost too exhausted to fill his tray and lift his fork before the next horn sounded, telling the students to get to their first class.

Rovi shoved two sausages in his mouth before the horn to start class sounded, telling him he was late to Visualization. Then, with heavy legs, he hurried down the hill to the Halls of Process. As usual, he took the long way around, staying as far as he could from the entrance to the stadium. Even so, Castor was already leaning out the window of the classroom, watching him.

"You're late, Tree Killer," Castor taunted. "You were trying to finish the tree off once and for all, huh? If that tree dies, I don't think you'll be coming to Ecrof next year."

"That's enough," Satis cautioned.

Castor shrugged, then lowered his voice so only Rovi could hear as he passed: *Tree Killer.*

"All right," Satis said. "Today we are going to work on sustained visualization. As you know, concentration is the ability to think about a single thing for a prolonged period of time. The average person can only concentrate for ten minutes before the outside world breaks in."

"I can do twenty," Vera called.

"Show-off," Castor hissed.

Satis waved an arm at both of them to settle down. "Now," he said, "what you are going to do is spend the first half of class thinking about a single thing. Every time you break concentration, your timer will reset to zero and you'll start over again."

"What are we supposed to think about?" Virgil asked.

"Well, anything you can hold in your mind comfortably," Satis said.

Virgil had his hand in the air again. "That's it? Just concentrate?"

"Well," Satis said, "there is more. The true test of focus is to be able to stay in the zone while outside forces are trying to distract you. So everyone will need a partner." He held up the Mind Sharers.

Adira and Virgil slapped hands, as did Nassos and Castor.

"Not so fast," Satis said. "It's easy to concentrate when your partner is on your side. What we need to do is test your strength when someone is trying to distract you. So everyone team up with someone from the opposite house."

A chorus of groans rippled through the room. Begrudgingly, Cyril and Virgil formed a team. Nassos went with Adira. Eventually, everyone had paired up but Pretia, Castor, and Rovi.

"Castor, you go with Rovi," Satis said. "I'll work with Pretia."

Rovi's heart sank. But he didn't have time to object before Satis was giving them further instruction. "Choose who will go first. Then both partners must take hold of the batons with both hands. Once you are able to see your partner's vision, your timer will start. When that vision breaks, hit the timer, and the next person is up. Every time the visualization breaks, you switch. The timer will record who lasts the longest."

Castor took a set of sticks from Satis and joined Rovi at his table. Rovi hesitated before taking the sticks. "Come on," Castor said. "I'm not getting penalty laps because you're lazy."

Rovi rolled his eyes.

"It's not like I *actually* want to see what's inside the mind of a Star Stealer."

"I'm not a Star Stealer," Rovi said.

"Tree Killer, then," Castor said.

Rovi tensed his jaw, then grabbed his end of the sticks so hard he nearly pulled Castor out of his chair.

"Watch it," Castor said. "I'm going first."

Vibrating with anger, Rovi held the sticks until he felt Castor's vision being transmitted into his mind. It was a podium in a large stadium, a more impressive stadium than Rovi had ever seen before.

Rovi recognized it from pictures—the stadium at Castle Airim where the Epic Games were held. In fact, Castor was visualizing the Epic Games. Rovi laughed. The vision flickered. Rovi laughed again. Once more, Castor's vision flickered, but it didn't disappear.

Then Rovi watched as Castor approached the podium. What was that on his head? Was it a crown? Rovi heard Castor's name announced as the winner. He watched Castor mount the podium and bow so an Epic Medal could be placed around his neck.

"In your dreams," Rovi snickered.

The vision broke. The timer buzzed. Four minutes. Not bad.

"Okay, Tree Killer," Castor said. "Let's see what nonsense you imagine yourself doing."

Rovi knew he had to keep it simple. A race. A simple race. A 100-meter race around the track at Ecrof.

Rovi took a deep breath and cleared his mind. He saw himself get in the starting blocks. *On your mark, get set*— Immediately he realized his mistake. The track wasn't just any track—it circled the ailing Tree of Ecrof, the last thing Rovi wanted to visualize. Now his mind wasn't clear. *Tree Killer.* He could hear Castor whispering under his breath. Rovi fought to ignore his partner's voice. *Go.*

He took off. It was a field of one, just him racing around the track. He was running well.

Tree Killer. Tree Killer.

And then, instead of the track, something else flashed into Rovi's mind—his father's drawings. His father's thousands of drawings. Pages and pages flashing before his eyes. A dead tree. He broke concentration and the timer went off. Two minutes.

"Not so good, Tree Killer," Castor said.

Now it was Castor's turn again. Once more, Rovi saw the same podium. He heard Castor's name called as the winner. He saw Castor approach the podium. Rovi thought hard of some way to distract him. "Nice crown," he said. "But shouldn't that be Pretia's?"

Castor's vision didn't flicker. One, two, three, four, five times Rovi watched him mount the podium and receive his medal. No matter what Rovi did to distract him, nothing had any effect.

Finally, Castor broke. The timer went off. Twelve minutes. A class record.

When Rovi opened his eyes, Castor had a nasty smile on his face. "I wouldn't expect a Star Stealer to understand the way the royal family works," he said. "But your friend Pretia will never wear the crown, because she doesn't have grana. She'll never rule Epoca."

Rovi opened his mouth, then snapped it shut. As much as he wanted to defend her, he wouldn't betray Pretia. "What are you waiting for?" Castor said. "Let's see your dumb vision again."

Rovi closed his eyes. He cleared his mind. Or he tried to.

"What's the holdup, Tree Killer?" Castor said.

Rovi could see the starting blocks. He could almost see himself in them. He tried to imagine himself taking off.

"Let's go, Tree Killer."

He made his imaginary self take off. He tried to watch himself run down the track. But his father's drawings kept flying into his mind. Over and over. And instead of seeing the track, he was seeing the Tree of Ecrof. He was hearing his father's voice. He was seeing himself leave the track, running toward the tree. What was happening? Suddenly the tree burst into flames. He tried to stop the vision, but it was too late. It was perfectly clear. And Castor had seen.

He opened his eyes and dropped the sticks.

Castor was staring at him, goggle-eyed. "It's true," he gasped. "You really are trying to kill the Tree of Ecrof. I knew it."

"No," Rovi said. "Let me go again." He grabbed the sticks and slammed his eyes shut. He concentrated so hard he could hear the blood rushing in his ears. He tried to bring the track into view. But there he was again, approaching the Tree of Ecrof with a burning torch. He was burning the tree. He was destroying it. He opened his eyes and dropped the sticks. The harder he tried not to think about killing the Tree of Ecrof, the more clearly he thought about it.

Three more times when he tried to visualize the track, all he could see was himself doing horrible things to the tree. Finally, Castor dropped the sticks. "Satis," he said, raising his hands, "I'm uncomfortable with Rovi's visions. Can I have another partner?"

"No," Satis said. "You will continue to work in the groups you are assigned."

"But, Satis," Castor said, "Rovi's visions are violent."

At that, the entire class looked up.

"Violent?" Satis asked.

"He's visualizing burning the Tree of Ecrof," Castor said. "And he's getting good at it. His last vision went for nearly fifteen minutes."

Rovi hadn't even thought to check the timer. He'd been working too hard to clear the vision from his mind. He'd let it go on for fifteen minutes!

"Rovi, is that true?" Satis asked, a distressed look on his face.

"Yes," Rovi said quietly. "But it was an accident. I was trying not to think about the tree, but it didn't work. I was—"

"Do you think you got your visualization talent from your father?" Castor interrupted. "You're definitely as unstable as him."

Rovi couldn't help himself anymore. He picked up one of the batons and hurled it at Castor, hitting him squarely on the forehead. The stick clattered to the ground, and immediately, a trickle of blood blossomed on Castor's forehead.

"Satis," Castor cried.

Rovi didn't hang around to hear the rest. He was on his feet and running as fast as he could to the Temple of Dreams. Was he as unstable as his father? Did he want to kill the Tree of Ecrof, so deep down he didn't even know it?

The drawings in his father's book flashed in front of his eyes: the sickly tree. The tree that looked like it wanted to strangle anyone who came near. The tree of death.

Maybe just looking at drawings of this tree was enough to make you lose your mind. Rovi certainly *felt* unstable. His mind was deserting him. He couldn't get the image of both his father's tree and himself killing the Tree of Ecrof out of his head. The harder he tried to banish the thought of either, the stronger they both grew.

Rovi got into bed and pulled the covers over his head, trying to drown out the thought of any tree at all.

His thoughts were racing. They were sprinting. They were making him sick to his stomach.

"Stop it!" Rovi screamed at the top of his lungs. "Stop!" He covered his eyes and squeezed them shut, but still he saw himself harming the beautiful tree, the symbol of all the good and strength in Ecrof. Had his father made him a monster? Or had he been born one?

All he knew was he was never going near that tree again. Never.

Rovi heard the hunting horns blaring, signaling the passing of the school day. He'd missed foundational training. He'd missed lunch. Just before dinner, there was a tap at his door.

"Go away!" Rovi shouted.

The knocking persisted.

"Go *away*," Rovi insisted.

Before he could say it again, Pretia let herself in.

"I thought you were mad at me," Rovi said.

"I am."

"I'm sorry," Rovi said. "I should never have asked you to use your grana if you didn't want to. Especially for something as stupid as a Field Day."

"When did you start thinking Field Day is stupid?"

Rovi shrugged. "I just did, that's all. What are you doing here, anyway?"

"I wanted to see if you're okay."

"Because I threw a Mind Sharer?"

Pretia shook her head. "Well, there's something else. Castor told Satis and Janos that you shouldn't be allowed to compete in Dreamer Field Day because you're a danger to the school. I see what you're up against."

Rovi tossed his pillow across the room. How much worse could things get?

"Don't worry," Pretia said. "I heard Cassandra talking to Cleopatra Volis. As far as the Dreamers are concerned, you're on the team."

Rovi sat up in bed. "Pretia," he said. "What if I'm actually doing something to the tree?"

"But you're not."

"How can you be so sure?" Rovi asked.

Pretia took a deep breath. "I don't think anyone's harming the tree," she said. "I think the tree is harming us."

"That's ridiculous," Rovi said.

"Is it?" Pretia opened her Grana Book. "Look," she said. She turned to the image she'd revealed on the first day of Granology. Rovi looked down at the page, instantly remembering the mirror-image forest—the green one growing straight up and its black reflection in the water. "I've been trying to figure this out since we came to Ecrof," Pretia said. "We were supposed to be looking for an answer to what our first year at Ecrof would be like, right? Well, I couldn't make sense of it. I kept thinking that the two forests were my heritage; you know, half Dreamer and half Realist."

"And that's not right?" Rovi said.

"Maybe," Pretia said. "But it didn't feel right. Maybe it's more literal than that."

"You sound like a Realist."

Pretia shrugged. "I'm half Realist, Rovi, even if I live in the Temple of Dreams. So listen. Maybe there's something bad happening here. Just think of what happened to the kids on the first Field Day, and then to Leo."

"And you think that has something to do with the tree?"

"I don't know," Pretia said. "But look at those trees in the water. What do they remind you of?"

Rovi didn't answer.

"The Tree of Ecrof, right?"

"Maybe," Rovi said. "What about those moons, though? What do they have to do with anything?"

"I'm not sure. I can't figure them out yet. But that's not important. The trees are dangerous. Something bad is going to happen at Field Day. Just like every time we've all competed together. Maybe you shouldn't compete, after all."

"I don't think it's the trees," Rovi said. "It's me."

Pretia tugged his arm. "That's ridiculous. Now get out of bed and come down to dinner."

"Fine," Rovi said. He'd go to dinner. But there was no way he was going near that tree. He didn't trust himself. Maybe Castor was right all along and Rovi was killing the Tree of Ecrof. Maybe Pretia was right, too, and grana could be dangerous. Or maybe it was something else—maybe he was just like his father. Maybe he was going to lose his mind. One thing was for certain. He was not allowing the entire school the chance to witness him doing something dangerous like his father did. There would be no Dreamer Field Day for him.

After dinner, when Rovi was sure everyone was in bed, he slipped out of the temple and went looking for the Infinity Track. Earlier that day it had been hovering fifteen feet off the ground near the Thinkers Palace, and it was still there. He didn't think. He just found the stairs to the track. Ten feet. Exactly the right height.

It took two laps of the track to build his courage. And then one more. Rovi ramped up speed—fast, fast, and faster. All it would take was one misstep, that's it. On his fourth lap he sprinted into the turn and then let his mind relax—took his mind off his feet—did what he imagined Pretia did. He blocked his grana. And that's all it took. Rovi went flying off the track, spinning top over tail toward the ground. And just before he hit the grass, he put out his hands. His right arm broke his fall. He heard a *crack*.

The pain in Rovi's wrist was as horrible as it was relieving. It took his mind off the episode with Castor and the Mind Sharers. It allowed him to momentarily forget the sickly Tree of Ecrof. And even better, the pain in his wrist assured him that he wouldn't be competing in Dreamer Field Day. Now he would have no reason to go near the Tree of Ecrof again, which is exactly what he wanted.

23

PRETIA

THE ROOTS

IN ALL THE COMMOTION IN THE TEMPLE OF Dreams the morning of Field Day, Pretia didn't notice Rovi was missing. When she woke up it looked like a factory of purple paint, purple glitter, and purple silk and satin had exploded inside the temple. Purple streamers hung from the ceilings. The walls were plastered with purple banners urging Dreamer victory. Purple confetti was strewn along the halls.

In the cafeteria, Pretia found that most of her fellow Dreamers had already painted their faces purple. Some had even sprayed purple in their hair. And, of course, everyone was dressed in head-to-toe purple. She moved through her housemates in a fog. They all looked so happy and excited. They couldn't wait for Field Day. Their energy was almost infectious. Almost.

But Pretia wasn't excited. She was anxious.

What if she was right? What if someone wasn't harming the tree? What if the tree was harming the students? It sounded impossible. But she couldn't shake the notion.

What had Saana told them on their first day in Granology? *You will know when you have arrived at the right interpretation. You will feel it.*

Well, Pretia had been staring at the image she'd chosen to represent her time at Ecrof for eight months. And for eight months, it had puzzled her. But now it was starting to make sense. She didn't understand everything yet, but still—she could feel that she was close, just like Saana had said she would be. There was something bad in the trees: the leaf tornado, the branch that hit Castor, Petros's fall, and the leaves that had suffocated Leo. She knew they were connected.

If the trees were trying to harm all the students, though, why was the image in Pretia's Grana Book and not in anyone else's? And what was she supposed to do about it? That's what she needed to figure out.

Her anxiety mounted throughout the day, adding to the ever-present uneasiness that had plagued her ever since she lit Hurell's flame. She was increasingly certain that something terrible was in store for the students at the Dreamer Field Day. There was something dark in the trees that came out during competition. Today would be no exception.

She joined a few other Dreamers in decorating the Tree of Ecrof. The tree's condition didn't seem to bother the other kids. But it made Pretia anxious, especially when she saw the dark patch of grass encircling the sickly Tree of Ecrof. Now the majority of the tree was black—black and dry. The branches looked like the limbs of skeletons, all bone and no life. She allowed a fifth-year boy to hoist her on his shoulders so she could throw streamers up into the tree, and when her hands touched the bark, they came away smudged with black ash that took a long time to wash off.

Pretia felt as if she were in a trance when she followed the rest of the students back to the Panathletic Stadium, where both the feast and the Field Day would be held. Despite the incredible spread of food, she had no appetite.

The Dreamers had managed to get even more of their streamers into the tree, but they didn't look as vibrant or as lively as they had on Realist Day. They just hung limply from the crumbling branches. Just like the previous Field Day, the marching bands circled the students, trying to outdo each other with rival fight songs.

From where Pretia sat at the feast, she could already see where the high jump, the long jump, the triple jump, and the steeplechase had been set up. The jumping events took place on the track itself, while the steeplechase obstacles were both on the track and in the field at the center.

Halfway through the meal, hundreds of purple lanterns rose into the air, carried upward by small flames. When the lanterns had disappeared, Janos rose and blew his whistle. "Students of Ecrof, our tree might be sick, but our school spirit is not. Today is the Dreamer Field Day. They have chosen their events and their squad, and they have prepared for a hearty challenge from House Reila."

He paused while both houses cheered raucously.

"Tonight we dine as friends," Janos said. "But shortly, we will meet on the track as competitors. May the gods grant both houses exceptional grana, and may you meet in the spirit of respectful competition. And perhaps your spirits will raise the spirit of our treasured tree so it may thrive once more."

Again, a chorus of cheers erupted.

Pretia was wedged between Hector and Adira, who were having a lively argument about which of their houses was going to destroy the other house in the impending competition.

"We're going to beat you even without Julius and the rest of our Epic Elites," Hector insisted. "We don't need them to win."

"Even if you had them, you wouldn't beat us," Adira countered, listing the Dreamer athletes who'd excelled at Epic Elite trials. "We are jumpers," Adira continued. "That's our thing."

"Well," Hector said, "we're not just *jumpers*. We're good at everything."

Adira smoothed her headscarf. "We're good at everything, too.

Anyway, you don't need to be good at everything to win this Field Day. Only jumping. Right, Pretia?"

It took Pretia a moment to tune in to the conversation.

"Right, Pretia?"

Pretia looked up and saw Adira staring at her meaningfully.

"Oh, right," Pretia said. "We're really good at jumping. There were so many athletes to choose from, we could have fielded two teams."

"See?" Adira said, putting a nail in her argument.

But Hector wouldn't let it drop, and the two continued bickering and ribbing each other. Pretia tried to join in, but the image in her Grana Book kept returning to her. The reflected forest. The good trees and the bad ones.

Despite all the entertainment and distractions, the music and fireworks and lanterns, the banners and streamers and colorful signs, Pretia could not take her eyes off the sickly tree. How could it be hurting the students? What was it doing?

She was so distracted that at first she didn't realize Rovi's name hadn't been announced as part of the Dreamer squad. It was only when the entire team had left the banquet that Pretia realized she'd slapped every athlete's hand but Rovi's.

She bolted from her seat and rushed to find Xandra, another seventh year, who had taken over as House Captain for the day while Cassandra was off with the Dreamer squad. "Where's Rovi?" Pretia demanded.

Xandra looked at her, confused.

"Rovi," Pretia insisted. "He was supposed to be on the team."

"You didn't hear?" Xandra said. "You must really be in another world."

Pretia's stomach started to churn. She felt as if she might pass out. "What happened?"

"He had an accident while training. Apparently, he fell off the

Infinity Track and broke a bone in his wrist," Xandra said. "Pretty stupid if you ask me."

"He fell off the Infinity Track?" Pretia repeated.

"Gosh, Pretia, you sound relieved," Xandra said.

"No," Pretia snapped. "No, I'm not."

But she realized that she was. Rovi wouldn't be competing in the Field Day. He was safe in the TheraCenter. The minute she could slip away, she'd go visit him. But right now, with the entire staff in the stadium, there was no way to escape.

Pretia joined the group of students making their way to the bleachers. She watched the marching bands circle the track, entertaining the students while the competitors warmed up. She found a spot high up in the stands where she would have a decent view of the events but an even better one of the tree. She took a poster that read DREAM BIG and held it aloft as the competitors and the events were announced.

The bleachers were in an uproar by the time the competition started. The first event was high jump— which should have been Pretia's event. The scoring system was the same: three points for first place, two for second, and one for third. Pretia watched the twelve competitors—six from each house—take three turns each. She barely noticed who won.

Virgil had been a last-minute addition to triple jump. His skill as a diver granted him the necessary footwork to execute the complicated approach to the takeoff board, a hop, then a skip, then a jump. When he took his first turn, Pretia joined all the other first years in getting to her feet and cheering. He approached the jump like a dancer, a graceful execution that saw him soaring like a bird, his legs pedaling through the air like he was riding an invisible bicycle that propelled him farther than he'd ever jumped before. Virgil made it onto the podium and finished in third place.

Next was long jump, then pole vault. Then steeplechase, Rovi's event, was last. Only three more events and Field Day would be over.

Pretia realized she didn't care whether the Dreamers won. All she wanted was for the events to conclude without anything horrible happening. Perhaps she really was imagining things, she told herself. Maybe the day would end without incident.

The Realists eked out a win on the long jump, snagging two out of three spots on the podium. The Dreamers, much to everyone's surprise and delight, swept the podium at the pole vault. Cassandra, who'd also competed in this event, won by executing an enormous backflip that took her over the bar.

Now it was time for the steeplechase. While the Junior Trainers began to set up the obstacles, Cleopatra Volis came and stood in front of the bleachers. "We have a substitution today," she announced. "Vera Renovo will be taking the place of Rovi Myrios for the Dreamers in the steeplechase."

Pretia let out an involuntary cry that was swallowed by her fellow Dreamers chanting Vera's name.

The runners lined up on the track, eight in total. A series of obstacles lay in front of them—long puddles, high hurdles, and other sorts of barriers that they would have to negotiate as they sprinted along the track. Pretia could immediately see why Rovi, with his nimble feet, would have been a force to be reckoned with at steeplechase.

Janos blew his whistle and the runners took off at a restrained pace. They splashed through the first puddle. They skirted the first hurdle. It was a pretty cool event, Pretia had to admit, all these tricky obstacles that had to be negotiated in totally different ways. You could never release fully into a sprint because you had to prepare for the next obstacle, but you also couldn't afford to be overly cautious on the obstacles and lose ground to your competitors.

The course ran halfway around the track and veered into the field for the water obstacles. Then it cut across the field and finished on the far side of the track where the students and faculty sat in the bleachers.

Vera was in a breakaway pack of three. She and two Realists had dashed away at the start and were the first runners to finish on the track and turn into the field. Pretia joined the rest of the student body in leaping to her feet, cheering them on. She wasn't just cheering for Vera and the Dreamers, she was cheering the end of the race—the impending end of Field Day.

As the runners were cutting through the field, though, passing to the left of the tree, the ground began to shift. At first Pretia thought she was imagining it. But no—it was happening. The ground was moving and black roots were rising from the green grass. They weren't just rising, they were chasing the lead runners.

Pretia cupped her hands over her mouth. "Run, Vera!" she shouted.

All around her in the stands, the rest of the students were staring openmouthed as the large black roots rose from the ground like the tentacles of a huge sea creature. The roots had fully broken free of the ground and were lashing at Vera and the leaders.

Only Pretia seemed to have found her voice. The other students were too stunned to say anything. "Run!" she cried again. "*Run!*"

The roots were grabbing for the lead runners. And then, in a horrible instant, a black root curled around the ankle of one of the Realists next to Vera and pulled him back. As it did, there was a terrifying cracking sound and the ground around the tree caved downward like it was rotting. It swallowed the runners who'd been following Vera and the other leaders.

At the sound, Vera stopped. She turned and grabbed for the Realist boy who'd been yanked back by the root. She caught his arm and pulled, yanking him from side to side, trying to break him free from the root.

"Vera, let go!" Pretia called.

But Vera was, as always, determined. She was not going to let the root beat her. With a massive effort, she pulled her Realist competitor as hard as she could, breaking him out of the root's grasp, sending the two of them flying backward onto the ground.

All the faculty were on their feet at once, rushing to the field. "Stay back!" Cleopatra shouted. "Everyone keep away."

"Nobody move," Satis called. "Nobody move."

But there were too many students to hold back. Everyone was desperate to check on their friends. Pretia pushed past the throng of kids to the hole in the ground.

It wasn't deep—which was good—no more than three feet. But it stank like rot, like the earth was sour and festering. The five students who'd been at the back of the pack lay tumbled where they'd fallen in a dank pit of wet earth and tangled roots. All of them seemed to have the wind knocked out of them, and all of them seemed to be struggling to get their breath back.

Everyone was talking at once. Some students were hysterical. Some were trying to pull the fallen runners from the pit. Pretia moved to the side to let the medics through. Her heart pounded; her mind raced. She had known something like this would happen. She'd seen it in her Grana Book. But she'd had no idea how she was supposed to prevent it.

She watched as the fallen runners were lifted one by one onto stretchers. Several of them had breathing masks placed over their mouths.

"Did we win?" Vera had appeared at Pretia's side.

"What?" Pretia asked.

"I guess I got second, and that Realist came first, and the kid I pulled from the root got third, so that's two points for us and four for them, right?"

"Who cares?" Pretia asked. "You just saved that kid's life."

Vera looked dazed. "I guess that was a dumb thing to do," she said. "I mean, from the Dreamers' standpoint."

“No,” Pretia said. “It was brave. That tree could have pulled you into the pit.”

“Brave, huh?”

“Absolutely,” Pretia said.

Vera shrugged. But she couldn’t hide her smile. “Brave and stupid,” she said.

“You’re a hero, Vera.”

“Do you think he’s okay?” Vera asked.

“I don’t know,” Pretia said. She feared that everyone involved in the Field Day disaster was pretty far from okay.

“We should check,” Vera said.

Janos was blowing his whistle for the students’ attention.

“Let’s go to the TheraCenter after this,” Pretia said. “I want to see Rovi.”

“I want to go now,” Vera said. Then she cast a sideways look at Janos. “I really don’t care what *he* has to say.” And before Pretia could stop her, Vera raced off.

Janos’s powerful voice echoed through the stadium. “Students, to the bleachers.”

When the students had assembled, Janos stood in front of them. “It seems that whatever has infected our tree has caused the ground to be unsafe. From now on, this field and any other outdoor arena will be off-limits. All training will continue indoors. And the result of the steeplechase will be scrubbed from Field Day. As it stands now, the Realists are ahead by two points. When things settle down, we will hold an indoor event in place of the steeplechase to determine the Field Day winner. And if they don’t improve by the end of term next week, victory will go to the Realists, who are currently in the lead.”

A chorus of groans rose from the slighted Dreamers. But these were drowned out by a volley of questions.

“What happened to the kids who fell?” Virgil called. “Are they all right?”

Castor cupped his hands over his mouth. “Shouldn’t the Realists just be declared winners?”

Pretia shot a look at her cousin, then added her own suggestion. “Shouldn’t Vera get the Dreamers extra points for saving someone?”

Janos blew his whistle loudly, but he couldn’t quiet the students.

Pretia took advantage of this moment to slip away. She needed to find Rovi and tell him what had happened. She had to tell him that it wasn’t his fault.

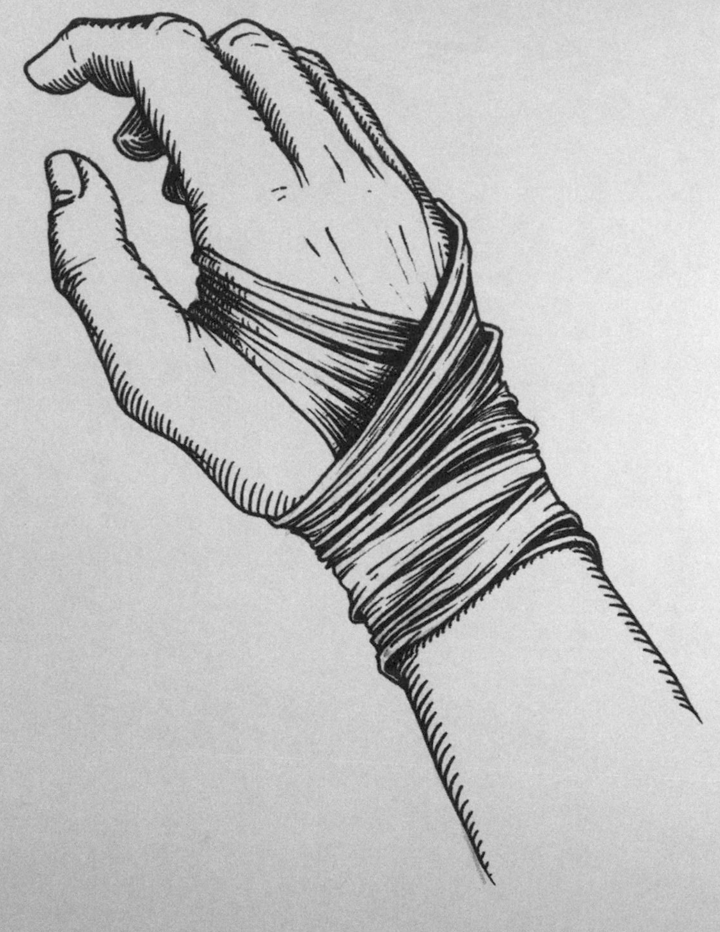

24

ROVI

THE THERACENTER

IF ROVI WERE HONEST, HE WOULD HAVE TO ADMIT that his wrist wasn't that bad. The medic had told him he had a hairline fracture. And the Mineral Sleeves at the TheraCenter had done their job, healing Rovi's broken wrist overnight. But Rovi didn't want to risk being around if something terrible happened at Field Day—something that Castor would claim was his fault. So he'd faked it, telling the medics that his hand ached whenever he walked around.

It was boring in the TheraCenter. There was nothing to do but stare at the ceiling while he "healed." At least the place smelled great—steamy, eucalyptus-scented air that wafted up from the stone baths on the lower level. Rovi had pestered the medics for a chance to soak in the large tubs, but no matter how many times he'd asked, they told him no.

He could hear the festivities from Dreamer Field Day underway—the fireworks and singing. Soon, the events would start. Then it would be over and then he could stop pretending to be hurt.

Rovi rang the bell and asked the medic on duty to bring him a second dinner. If he had nothing else to do, he might as well eat. After he'd finished that dinner, he rang for dessert. And then seconds on dessert. Full and bored, what else did Rovi have to do but sleep? Which he did.

"Rovi!"

Rovi rolled his head from side to side. His stomach was full. The bed was comfortable. He had nowhere to be.

"Rovi!"

Why was someone shaking him awake?

He cracked his eyelids. In the dim light of the TheraCenter room, he could just make out Pretia standing next to his bed.

"Come on, Pretia. This is my one chance to rest without worrying about oversleeping," Rovi grumbled.

"Rovi, wake up!" Pretia grabbed his shoulder and yanked him into a sitting position.

"Wha . . ." Rovi groaned. "Wha . . ."

"Rovi, you're not going to believe what happened. You're so lucky you weren't there."

"Slow down," Rovi said. "Pretia, slow down."

"The ground around the Tree of Ecrof just sort of . . . opened up during the steeplechase. It swallowed some of the students and there were these big black roots, like tentacles, that tried to grab the runners."

A smile had broken out on Rovi's face.

"Why are you smiling?" Pretia snapped. "It was terrifying."

"Because I wasn't there."

"So what?"

"I wasn't there," Rovi repeated. "I was here. So whatever the tree did, it wasn't my fault. Now no one can blame me." He was beaming so widely that his cheeks hurt.

"Rovi, concentrate on what's important here!" Pretia said. "I think the tree is hurting the students. I think it's attacking us."

"Why?"

"I don't know," Pretia said. "The tree seemed to be chasing the kids with its roots. And when the ground opened up and the runners fell in, it seemed like they couldn't breathe. Vera saved one of them by pulling him out of the root's grasp. Then the medics came and brought everyone to the TheraCenter."

Rovi must have been fast asleep to have missed the arrival of the injured athletes.

"How's your wrist, by the way?"

Rovi looked at his bandaged hand guiltily. "Okay, I guess."

"So how long are you going to have to stay in here?"

"I can leave tonight," Rovi said. Now that it was clear he wasn't responsible for whatever was going on with the tree, he wanted to get out.

"Tonight," Pretia said. "They'll just let you leave whenever you want?"

Rovi shrugged. "Sure. In fact, I think I'll leave now." He swung his legs out of bed and looked around for his Grana Gleams. "You coming?"

"Rovi, you can't just sneak out."

"Why not?" Rovi said. "I'm feeling much better."

They headed down the dim hallway. From somewhere in the TheraCenter they could hear voices. "They're probably too busy with the Field Day athletes to care much about me," Rovi said as they approached a corner.

Suddenly they heard footsteps. Someone was running down the hallway they were about to turn in to. Rovi stopped walking, unsure of whether he should head back to his room or keep going. But before he had time to decide, Vera came racing down the hall. She skidded to a stop when she saw them. Her eyes were wild.

"What's wrong?" Rovi asked.

"It's Julius," Vera gasped.

"What's Julius?" Rovi said.

"He's here."

"Isn't he at training?" Pretia asked.

"That's what Janos said," Vera whispered. "That's what everyone keeps telling me. But I saw him. I think they've been lying this whole time."

"Why would they be lying about that?" Rovi asked.

"Because they didn't want me to know," Vera said. She was nearly panting.

"Know what?" Pretia asked.

"That he's really sick." Vera looked about her frantically.

"Where is he?" Rovi asked.

"Downstairs," Vera replied. "I wanted to see if the kid I rescued was okay. So I followed the medics downstairs behind the baths. I lost them in all the steam. I tried opening a few doors. And that's where I saw Julius. He's—he's—he's . . ." Tears sprang to Vera's eyes. She was breathing so fast it seemed she was about to hyperventilate.

"Vera," Rovi said, "calm down."

"Calm down! Calm down? You haven't seen my brother. Or what's left of him."

Pretia took Vera's hands to try to calm her. "What do you mean, what's left of him?"

Vera tried to take a deep breath. "I've known Julius my whole life. I've seen him tired. I've seen him sick and injured. But I have never seen him like this. I've never seen anyone like this. It's like, it's like—"

Vera stopped talking, searching for the words.

"It's like what?" Rovi said.

"It's like he's not there. It's like he's beyond exhausted. He can barely move. He can barely talk. But it's more than that. It's like part of him is missing. Let me show you," Vera said. "You need to see him. Otherwise, you can't understand."

Pretia tried to object, but Vera was already hurrying down the hall. Rovi didn't hesitate. He followed close on her heels, descending the circular stairs to the bottom level of the TheraCenter. Downstairs, the halls were filled with thick eucalyptus steam that cleared Rovi's lungs and nose. It was hard to see, but Vera seemed to know the way.

She led them past the warm, bubbling baths. All around them they could hear water dripping down the walls.

"Here," Vera said, pushing open a wooden door.

Rovi had to stoop to get into the room. Pretia followed behind him, trying to muffle a cough.

The room was illuminated by a small lamp in a far corner that caught the thick, steamy air. On one side was a small cot, on the other all sorts of equipment that on closer inspection turned out to be breathing tubes and oxygen masks.

It took Rovi's eyes a moment to adjust to the dim, foggy room. It took him a few seconds to make out a person on the bed.

"Julius," Vera said, crouching down near the pillow. "Julius!"

The person on the bed rolled over.

"Julius, come on. Stand up."

There was no reply. Rovi waved the steam away. And when the air in front of him cleared, he gasped. It was definitely Julius, but also not Julius—more like a shadow or the shape of the track star. There was no solidity to him. He looked like a ghost.

Julius was withered. His face was slack, as if it had lost all its muscle. Rovi had seen only one other person look like this before—his father, in the months before his death. Like Pallas, Julius's lips were purple. But it was his eyes that terrified Rovi. They were vacant. Totally empty. Hollow. It was as if he were dead. He was breathing, but it sounded labored.

"Can you at least sit up?" Vera asked, shaking his shoulder. "What happened to you?"

Finally, Julius moved. He lifted his head slightly. "Tired," he whispered.

The effort—the effort to say that single word—seemed to have exhausted him. He closed his eyes. "I'm so tired," he whispered.

"Come on, Julius! Sit up."

"I can't," Vera's brother said. His voice was so far away. "I can't. It's too hard. I just want to sleep."

"Please," Vera said.

Julius sighed. Then he put his hands on the mattress and pushed himself to a sitting position.

"Are you sick?" Vera cried.

"The medics tell me I need to rest," Julius said. His breathing was raspy, like the air was choking him.

Vera tugged on his arm, as if she could bring him back to his normal self. "Are you sick?"

Slowly, and with great difficulty, Julius shook his head. "I don't think so. No. I'm just tired." And then, without warning, he collapsed back on the bed.

Vera whirled around so she was facing Rovi and Pretia. "See?" she said.

Rovi was staring at Julius. He'd seen this before. He knew what was wrong. But still, it didn't seem possible.

"Vera," Rovi said slowly. "Vera, I know what's wrong with him."

"What? How?" Vera cried.

"I've seen this before. My father was a Somnium addict—" Rovi began.

Vera whirled around, a furious look in her eyes. "Rovi! Julius is not a Somnium addict."

"I'm not saying he is. But listen. Do you know what Somnium does to your body over time? It drains your grana."

"*What?*" Pretia and Vera exclaimed in unison.

"That's how my father died. He lost all his grana. He looked exactly like Julius. Exactly. He was exhausted and pale. He could barely stand. He just . . . wasn't there."

Now Vera was staring at her brother. "His grana? He's lost his grana?"

Rovi couldn't take his eyes off Julius. It wasn't what was there in front of him—the deflated superstar athlete—but what wasn't. Something was missing. Some sense or essence.

"Julius!" She held her face inches from her brother's. "There's nothing in there," she said. "Nothing."

This time when she whirled around to face Rovi, her eyes weren't filled with anger but with tears. "How can this be happening?" she said.

"I don't think it's just Julius," Rovi said slowly. "I ran into Iskander a while ago when he was supposed to be at Epic Elite training. I didn't think much of it. I just thought he was really worn out. But he was like this—sort of vacant and not aware."

"Iskander was also hurt in the leaf tornado," Vera said. "I bet," she began, unable for a moment to finish her thought. "I bet he and Julius never went to Epic Elite training at all. I bet they've been sick this whole time. And that's why Janos kept me off the squad. He didn't want me to know. He knew I'd be suspicious if I went to train and my brother wasn't there. So he kept me off on purpose."

Pretia looked around uncertainly. "Do you think Iskander is down here? Do you think there are more kids down here?"

"Let's see," Rovi said, heading for the door.

"I don't want to leave him," Vera cried.

"Vera," Pretia said. "He's not going anywhere."

"That's not the point; he's my brother, even if I'm a Replacement. You guys wouldn't understand. You don't have siblings."

"Rovi," Pretia said, "don't you have a brother?"

"What?" Rovi asked.

"When we were on the boat to Ecrof, you told me your brother gave you your Grana Gleams."

"I what—" Rovi said. It took him a moment to remember that he'd told Pretia that his brother Issa had given him the shoes. But now wasn't the time to explain. "It's a long story," he said. Then he turned to Vera. "Vera, I know you're worried about Julius. But if we learn more about what's going on here, maybe we'll find a way to help him."

Vera looked from her brother to Rovi and Pretia. "Okay," she said. "I'm coming."

Rovi led the way through the damp hallways, pushing away the steam and trying not to slip on the wet stones. He traced the wall with his hand, hoping for another door. After a few minutes, he found one. He pressed his shoulder against it and it opened.

It was identical to Julius's room—small, steamy, with a lamp at the back that barely cut through the chest-clearing eucalyptus-scented air. Together, Rovi, Pretia, and Vera waved their arms until they could make out a figure lying on the bed.

"Iskander?" Rovi whispered.

He tiptoed closer.

"Iskander?"

A noise filled the air in this room—a wheezing, whirring sound. The person on the bed was hooked up to a breathing machine. Vera stayed in the doorway. She clearly didn't want to enter the room.

"Iskander," Pretia said, kneeling next to the bed. Rovi watched her reach out and touch the patient. Suddenly she recoiled. "Leo!" she cried, crashing into Rovi. "It's Leo."

Rovi rushed to the bed, waving his arms so he could see through the steam. It was indeed Leo. He looked just as Julius had, but worse. There were strange black marks around his neck.

"What are those?" Rovi asked.

"I don't know," Pretia said.

Leo lay still, pale and limp on the bed. He looked as if he was missing blood and muscle. Rovi bent over him, still waving away the steam. "Pretia, look." He pointed at Leo's discolored skin. "Do those look like—"

"Leaves," Pretia said. "They look like leaves."

"Maybe you're right about the tree," Rovi said. "Maybe—"

But before he could finish the thought, Pretia interrupted with another question. "Since this is Leo, where's Iskander?"

"I don't know," Rovi said. Then he bent close to Leo's ear. "Leo, can you hear me?"

Slowly, Leo opened his eyes. His eyelids moved as if they were attached to heavy weights. It seemed as if it was taking every ounce of his strength to keep them open. He moved his lips.

"What's he saying?" Pretia asked.

"I can't hear through the oxygen mask," Rovi said. Carefully, he reached out and lifted the mask. Then he bent over Leo. "It's like my book," Leo said. "It's like my book."

"What did he say?" Pretia asked.

"His book," Rovi whispered. "He said it's like his book."

"Grana." Rovi and Pretia turned to see Vera still standing in the doorway. "That's what Leo saw in his book. That his grana was going to be stolen. Rovi, you're right." Vera leaned against the wall and sank to the floor. "What's going on?" she said, sounding dazed. "Ecrof was supposed to be a dream come true. But this school is a nightmare." Tears were streaming down her face. "First I turn out to be a Replacement, and now my brother has lost his grana." Her voice was reaching hysteria. "I hate this place. I hate it, hate it, hate it. And I won't spend one more minute here."

"Hold on," Pretia said, reaching out to comfort Vera.

"If no one at Ecrof will help my brother," Vera said as she stood up, "I'm going to find someone back home who will."

"Wait," Rovi said, rushing to the door. But he was too late.

Before Rovi or Pretia could do anything, Vera sprinted away, her feet slapping the condensation on the damp floor.

25

PRETIA

THE TEMPLE

IN AN INSTANT, PRETIA AND ROVI WERE CHASing Vera. Pretia's thoughts were racing as she ran through the damp corridors of the TheraCenter. Leo was right. How could Leo have been right? It sounded impossible: How could you lose your grana? But he'd predicted it. And it had happened.

Vera was right to be scared. She was right to want to find help for Julius. But running away from Ecrof was not the solution. How was she even planning to get off the island? They had to find her.

The circular basement of the TheraCenter was like a labyrinth. Vera's footsteps faded into the distance, and Rovi and Pretia lost her. They stumbled, slipped, and tripped. In searching for the exit, they found more doors. Behind each one was another one of the students who'd been injured.

Pretia couldn't believe it. They were all there, and they were all just like Julius and Leo: pale, drained, exhausted. They had all lost their grana. It was obvious now.

Just the thought of losing grana made her shiver. Pretia had become so used to her grana, even though she never used it, that the idea of it missing—well, it made her feel a little faint, like she might pass out if she thought too much about it. What would it feel like?

Pretia couldn't imagine. She didn't want to imagine. Would it be like losing a limb? Would it be like losing your mind? Would it—

Stop, she told herself. *Stop*.

Finally, she found the stairs that led up and out a back entrance. In the fresh air, she put her hands on her knees to clear the sharp eucalyptus air from her lungs.

"Which way do you think she went?" Rovi asked.

"I don't know." Pretia looked left and right. It was dark, and the only light came from the moon, which cast a silver glow across the campus. She didn't see Vera.

"How would you run away from Ecrof?" Rovi asked.

"It's impossible without a boat," Pretia said. "But I'd probably try the beach."

They locked eyes. "The Decision Woods!" they chorused.

They circled to the front of the TheraCenter. Pretia and Rovi sprinted for the woods, their feet in sync. They passed through the stadium, raced through the tunnel, and reached the edge of the woods. They raced through the obstacles—swinging from vines, running across branches, clearing hurdles until they reached the cliff.

As they emerged at the cliff, Rovi stopped. He put a finger to his lips. "Shhhhhh," he said. "Do you hear her?"

Pretia tried to listen. She thought she heard something, but she wasn't sure. She and Rovi spun around, looking up and down the cliff. Suddenly Rovi pointed. "What is that down there?"

Something was hovering in the air near the cliff.

Pretia squinted. The moon was full, but still it was hard to make out. "I think it's the Infinity Track," she said. "Do you think Vera might be there?"

"Worth a try," Rovi said.

They dashed toward the track.

Pretia cupped her hands over her mouth. "Vera," she called. "Vera, where are you?"

There was no answer.

"Vera!" Rovi tried.

Then they heard footsteps, followed by a burst of movement as someone darted along the cliffs farther ahead. "That's her," she said. "Vera, wait!" The track was slightly ahead of them. Half of it was dangling over the cliff, half over a pile of rocky rubble.

Vera ran on ahead. Pretia and Rovi followed. "Go away," Vera called back to them. "I'm leaving to get Julius the help he needs."

"That's impossible," Rovi shouted. "There's no way off the island."

Pretia watched Vera race underneath the track. "She's not getting on it," she said.

Now Pretia and Rovi were beneath the track. "Where is she going?" Rovi asked.

"Vera, stop, please," Pretia shouted.

They had all left the track behind and were racing along the rocky cliffs, trying to avoid the scraggly bushes and small trees that sprang from the ground. The land over here was untamed. It was wild. It had none of the polished landscaping of the Ecrof campus.

Pretia was having trouble seeing in the dark. She had to trust her feet to find their own placement and not slip on the smooth quartz rocks. She looked over her shoulder. The track was disappearing in the distance.

"Leave me alone," Vera shouted. "Stop chasing me."

"Vera—" Rovi called after her.

"I said, leave me *alone*," Vera yelled again. But as she did, she stumbled and went skidding along the ground. She picked herself up, but not before Pretia and Rovi were able to catch her.

They had come to a clearing along the cliff—a flat area without many trees. Pretia could see the crumbled remains of a long-forgotten building strewn on the ground, the tops of some fallen columns sunken into the earth. Chunks of marble—the remains of statuary and other decorations—were scattered on the ground.

"Vera." Pretia was panting as she tried to talk. "Are you okay?"

Vera took a deep breath. "What do you think? I'm going to be disowned by my family. My brother is sick. And the school is lying to me about what's going on." She placed her hands on her knees and leaned against the stubby remains of an old column. "I need to sit down."

"Me too," Pretia said. Together they collapsed onto the ground. Only Rovi remained standing. Pretia leaned her head on the flat top of one of the columns that had sunk into the earth. "What is this place?" she asked, looking around. "I've never seen it before."

"Some old pile of rocks," Vera said. "A ruin, or whatever."

"It looks like the remains of an old building," Pretia said.

"So it's an old building," Vera said.

"You know you can't really run away, right?" Pretia asked.

Vera bit her lip. In the moon's silvery glow, Pretia could see the defiant look in her eyes.

"Vera," Pretia began again.

"I know," Vera muttered. "But I don't want to stay."

"Me neither," Pretia said. And the minute the words were out of her mouth, she realized they were true. She had no interest in staying at Ecrof if she couldn't use her grana. She wanted to go home, be with people she felt safe around, like Anara and her parents.

Suddenly Vera bolted up. "Where's Rovi?"

Pretia looked around. She didn't see him.

"Rovi?" Pretia called. "Rovi," she called again. She leaped to her feet.

"There he is," Vera said, pointing toward the far side of the clearing from where they'd entered.

"Rovi!" Pretia called. "Rovi!"

Rovi seemed too entranced by whatever had caught his attention to turn. "Come here," he said. His voice was odd, as if it were coming from very far away.

When Pretia and Vera joined him, he was staring openmouthed at the strangest-looking tree Pretia had ever seen. It wasn't much taller than she was. And it didn't have a trunk. Instead, it was an odd tangle of dozens—or maybe even hundreds—of vines that were wound around each other in an extremely thick braid. The top of the tree was strange, too. Instead of reaching for the sky as most tree branches did, the branches on the tree in front of Rovi all flattened out and grew parallel to the ground, almost as if they were forming a tabletop.

"Well, that's a weird tree," Pretia said.

"It's a strangler fig," Vera said.

Rovi turned away from the tree for the first time. The expression on his face was something between panic and recognition. "A what?"

"A strangler fig," Vera repeated. "You see them in southern Alkebulan."

"Is that its real name?" Rovi gasped.

"Yeah, it's a tree that devours other trees. They mostly grow in the tropics, but I guess they can pop up anywhere."

"So it strangles trees?" Rovi asked.

"Yeah," Vera said. "What's the big deal?"

Rovi was shaking his head from side to side as if what Vera had just said couldn't have been further from the truth. "No," he said, "no. It's not just a tree. It's not. I've seen this tree before. Except that I didn't think it was a tree. I thought it was one of my dad's wild inventions."

"You've been here before?" Pretia asked.

"No. I saw it in my father's lab. In his notebooks. He drew this tree hundreds of times. Maybe thousands. I thought—I thought it was a machine that he was designing to kill the Tree of Ecrof. But it wasn't. It's an actual tree. This very tree."

"Why would he draw this tree?" Pretia asked.

"I don't know," Rovi said. "But he did. In the days before we left

Ecrof, he filled notebooks with endless drawings of it." He paused. "He must have seen it right before we left. He must have seen it when—" His breath caught on a gasp. "He must have seen it when he used the Self-Splitter."

"What's a Self-Splitter?" Vera asked.

Quickly, Rovi filled her in on his father's disastrous experiment. "He figured out a way to step outside himself, and afterward he was never the same. His two halves never rejoined. That's what made him a Somnium addict." He paused. "And that's how he lost his grana," he added in a quiet voice. Rovi looked at the tree once more, then shook his head from side to side as if he couldn't process what he was seeing. "It's incredible," he said. "It's exactly like all of my father's drawings. Exactly. Except . . ." His voice trailed off.

"Except what?" Pretia said.

"The tree he drew was much bigger. This was just the top. It had huge roots. Like a whole forest of roots."

"I still don't get what's so special about this tree," Vera said.

Rovi turned away from Pretia and Vera and stared at the strange tree and the flat treetop. "Kill the tree," he said.

"What are you talking about?" Pretia said.

"Kill the tree!" Rovi was shouting now.

"Is he okay?" Vera whispered.

Rovi wheeled around and grabbed both girls by the arms. "Don't you get it? Kill the tree? This tree. Not the Tree of Ecrof. *This* is the tree my dad was talking about."

"I don't understand," Vera said.

Pretia put her hands on Rovi's shoulders. "Start from the beginning."

"Okay," Rovi said. "Okay." He took a deep breath. "So, you know how everyone thinks I'm doing something to the Tree of Ecrof because there was a rumor that my dad tried to kill the tree?"

"And that's why he was fired, right?" Vera said.

"Sort of," Rovi said. "I'm not sure exactly why he was fired. No one told me. I was just a little kid. All I know is that he lost his mind after a failed visualization experiment. And he started saying *Kill the tree.* Over and over. Of course everyone who heard him must have thought he was talking about the Tree of Ecrof. But—"

"But what if it was this tree?" Pretia said.

"Why would he want to kill this tree?" Vera asked.

"I don't know," Rovi said. "But I know he became obsessed with it. He filled notebooks with thousands of drawings of it."

"How do you kill a tree?" Vera wondered.

"I don't know," Rovi said.

"You destroy its roots," Pretia suggested.

Rovi spun around. "Where are the roots?"

"Probably underground like on any other tree," Pretia said.

"My dad saw them," Rovi said. "He drew them as often as he drew the top of the tree. We need to find them."

"So we're going to kill the tree?" Vera said. "Why?"

"I'm not killing anything," Rovi snapped. "I just want to see what my dad saw."

He left the flat treetop and moved toward the cliff's edge.

"No way," Vera said. "I'm not going down there. I don't want to ruin my Epic Elite career by, you know, plunging into the sea."

"Pretia, are you coming?" Rovi asked.

"Coming where?" Something was nagging at the back of Pretia's mind, but she couldn't quite put her finger on what.

"I think I see a path," Rovi said.

"A path down the side of a cliff?" Vera asked.

"It's no worse than what we climbed up to get to Ecrof that first day," Rovi said. Then he paused. "Well, maybe it's a little worse."

Pretia followed him to the edge of the cliff. Rovi had already started down the treacherous path. It was only a sneaker-width wide.

Rovi was darting down the cliffside, nimble as a cat.

"You're really just going to let him go alone?" Vera said.

"Aren't you going?" Pretia asked.

Vera hesitated. She peeked over the edge. "Yeah," she said finally. "I am. What if something bad happens to him?" Vera took a step down the path. And then another. Soon the angle from the top made it impossible for Pretia to see her or Rovi on their descent.

"You guys okay?" Pretia called.

"Are you coming or not?" Vera called from the darkness below.

"I'm coming," Pretia said. But still, she didn't move. She felt stuck, like her grana had frozen her in place. It was almost as if it was telling her not to go, as if it was keeping her away from the tree roots or whatever else Rovi and Vera were about to encounter.

Then it hit her: The trees in her Grana Book! The healthy aboveground trees and the scary underwater ones. The image she'd been puzzling over for months. What if it wasn't the trees that were hurting the students? What if it was a single tree? This tree? If she closed her eyes and thought about the image, the trees in the picture blended into a single tree, especially the ones reflected in the water. In fact, the first time she'd seen the picture, she'd been unsure whether she was looking at a large tree or a group of smaller ones. Now she was sure.

The tree that had poisoned the Tree of Ecrof and done so much other damage *was* this very strangler fig? Even the name was perfect. And Rovi and Vera were heading right for it.

"Rovi! Vera! Come back," Pretia called. "Come back!"

She waited, her heart thumping in her ears.

"Rovi! Vera!" she tried again.

But they didn't reply. Either they couldn't hear her or— Pretia didn't want to think about this possibility. She had to go after them. She had no choice. The image was in her Grana Book. It was destined for her. She paused, thinking for a moment about those moons in the picture. The one above the trees and its weak reflection in the water. What did they mean? But there was no time to worry about that now. She had to stop Rovi and Vera.

She rushed down the path, hoping her feet would guide her. She willed her mind not to think about the sheer drop down to the crashing ocean and rocks below. She could feel the path crumbling beneath her sneakers. She heard the gravel and rocks clattering against the cliffs as they fell.

Pretia slipped and caught herself. Her hands scraped the cliff face. She continued down. Down. Down. The path grew steeper and narrower. Soon she had to turn her back to the cliff and edge down, facing out over the terrifying drop.

And then—her left foot went over. The path ended. There was only the treacherous drop in front of her and the sheer cliff to her side.

Pretia's heart began to race. She was stuck. It would be nearly impossible to climb back up in the dark. But she would have to unless—

Then she heard voices: Rovi's and Vera's. They seemed to be coming from inside the cliff. She reached out with her left hand and fumbled for an opening. And there it was—a space just big enough for her to crawl through.

In one swift motion, Pretia turned and dove into the interior of the cliff. She tumbled head over heels, falling ten feet to the ground.

"Nice entrance!" Rovi said.

She picked herself up and dusted herself off.

She and her friends were standing in a cavernous room—sort of like a cave but more structured. There were columns running along all four sides as if it was actually some sort of underground building. At the front was a tree—the strangest and scariest tree Pretia had ever seen before. The trunk, if you could even call it a trunk, was made up of hundreds of vines wrapping around each other in an impossible tangle. They looked like the limbs of skeletons, like the Tree of Ecrof's branches had looked earlier. The vines spread from the core of the tree up and out, pushing through the roof of the cave where Pretia knew they emerged in the shape of the strange tabletop they'd seen above. In the center of the tree, something was glowing with a creepy, eerie light, like oil burning on water.

"It looks like a temple or something," Pretia said. She looked at the columns and now understood that what she had assumed were ruins aboveground were their tops. "Has it fallen through the ground somehow?" she asked.

"But whose temple is it?" Rovi asked. "And what is that glowing in the middle of the tree?"

They all stared over the wide expanse of the temple—about the length of two tennis courts—to the tree.

"Exactly where on the island are we?" Pretia asked.

"We're down by the beach," Vera said. "Look. You can see the harbor and the stone archway we saw on our first day." She pointed through a dark opening that Pretia hadn't noticed before. Outside it, Pretia could make out the dark water lapping at the shore and beyond it, the towering gate that greeted ships arriving at the island.

"Hold on," Pretia said.

"Where are you going?" Rovi asked.

But Pretia had already dashed out of the cave.

She was standing on a beach, of course, about half a mile farther down from where the ship had left them when they'd arrived at the academy. She'd never been here before—not exactly. But for some reason, it was familiar. She glanced back over her shoulder at the cave, then back at the water.

Pretia closed her eyes. She knew this place—this exact place. She was certain.

And then she understood.

The mural in the Gods' Eye. She was standing exactly where the goddess Cora stood as she took her one last backward glance at her island.

Pretia opened her eyes. She followed the path of Cora's gaze from memory. Her eyes landed right in the center of the tree—right at the glowing object.

When she'd stared at the mural, she'd always thought Cora was taking a final, longing backward glance at her island, her gaze landing on a tree root that had broken through the roof of the cave. But now she could tell that the object in Cora's sight line was too straight, too uniform. Like something man-made. But how could it be man-made when only the gods had ever been on the island?

Pretia squinted. She put herself in Cora's place, staring back into the cave. She knew her eyes were traveling the exact path of the goddess's. But what was she looking at? What was that object?

It looked as if it had been driven through the roof of the cave. Driven straight into the ground with enormous force. Only a god could have done something like that. Only a god—

"Hurell."

The name was out of Pretia's mouth before she could stop herself.

Suddenly the story Anara had told her the morning she departed for Ecrof came flooding back. What had her nurse said? In a final attempt to call the people of Epoca back to him, Hurell had gone to his temple on the cliff's edge and called out across the ocean. When there was no answer, he'd driven his Staff of Suffering into the ground with such force, he'd broken the cliff. Driven his staff!

Pretia knew exactly what that glowing rod was: the Staff of Suffering. And she knew where they were—the Temple of Hurell.

For years under the Gods' Eye, Pretia had imagined that Cora was looking longingly at her island—taking one last look before she departed forever. But now Pretia was sure that she had been looking back anxiously at the staff, a reminder of Hurell. An earthly remnant of the Fallen God. Something that had stayed behind and might allow him to return.

26

ROVI

THE STRANGLER FIG

ROVI WAS IN A STATE OF SHOCK. FIRST THEY'D stumbled upon the strange flat treetop identical to his father's drawings, and now they stood before the entire tangled tree itself—every detail, every branch, every terrifying dark space between the vine-like branches. Rovi's father had perfectly re-created every single inch of the massive strangler fig except for one thing—the strange glowing light at the center. That was missing from his drawings.

But Rovi had too much to think about to worry about this one difference. How had his father wound up here, in this strange cave-temple? What was this place? And what had happened to him here? Suddenly Rovi's heart filled with dread. What if whatever happened to his father in this place happened to him? Rovi shuddered.

He looked around. Vera was still standing at his side, but Pretia had disappeared through a hole in the cave wall that led out to the beach.

"Pretia!" Vera called. She turned to Rovi. "Should we follow her?"

"If she doesn't come back soon," Rovi replied. He hoped she did. He was too interested in the enormous, terrifying tree to waste time retrieving Pretia from the beach.

He looked across the expanse of the cave floor to the base of the tree. How had his father planned to kill it?

Rovi took a step toward the tree but had to put out his arms to steady himself as the floor shifted beneath him. "Did you see that?" Rovi asked.

"What?"

"Look." He pointed at the ground in front of them. "It's moving."

He took another step. There was a horrible creaking noise as the ground moved again. Rovi looked around the cave to see what was making the sound. He didn't see anything, so he took another step toward the tree.

This time the sound was deafening. And this time the floor didn't just move beneath his feet, it fell away. Rovi felt Vera's hand grab his arm, yanking him back just before he dropped into a cavern that had opened in front of him.

Rovi glanced down. He and Vera were standing on a ledge with a wide-open space between them and the tree.

"What just happened?" Vera gasped.

"It's like the tree doesn't want us to get near it," Rovi said.

"So maybe we shouldn't get near it," Vera said. "Maybe we should just go back."

Before Rovi could reply, Pretia burst through the opening from the beach. "We need to kill the tree," she shouted. "We need to kill the tree." She was running full tilt toward Rovi and Vera.

Rovi reached out and caught her so she wouldn't plunge into the cavern.

"Whoa," Pretia said, reeling back from the newly formed ledge. "Where'd the ground go?"

"I don't know," Rovi said. "I took a few steps toward the tree and then the ground disappeared. I don't think the tree wants us near it."

"So I guess we can't kill it, then," Vera said.

Pretia was looking around the room in disbelief. "But we have to," she said. "I know what this place is." She looked from Rovi to Vera. Then she lowered her voice. "It's the Temple of Hurell."

"What?" Rovi gasped.

"The Temple of Hurell," Pretia whispered. "The woman who took care of me back at Castle Airim is a Flamekeeper, a guardian of the old stories. She told me about this place when I was little. I thought it was just a myth. But it's true."

"Come on," Vera said. "The myths are just exaggerations to explain how we became the way we are."

Pretia shook her head. "No," she said. "When the people turned away from Hurell, he drove his Staff of Suffering into the cliff so forcefully that his entire temple crumbled."

"Or not," Rovi said, staring at the columns that ringed the cavern.

"Exactly," Pretia replied. "Or not. But there's more," she said. "There's this painting in the castle of the beach right outside." She pointed through the opening toward the sea. "It shows the gods departing the island when they left Epoca for good. All of them except Hurell are getting in the ship, but Cora is looking back over her shoulder right at this cave. She must have been looking at the Staff of Suffering."

The three kids looked at each other in horror.

"And the top of the tree," Rovi said. "It's not just the top of a tree. It's an altar."

"Hurell's altar," Pretia said.

Now Vera pointed at the tree, at the glowing shaft of light that sat right in the center of the tangled trunk. "Is that—"

"Yes," Pretia said. "I think that's the staff. I always thought Cora was looking at it with longing, but now I think she was worried."

"Maybe the staff is made from a strangler fig," Vera suggested, "and she knew if it was planted, it might grow. That's how they work. At least the ones I've seen. They take over other trees."

"Wait," Pretia said, "they take over other trees? Do you think this one could be doing that to the trees on Corae?"

"What do you mean?" Vera asked.

"What if this one is poisoning them, corrupting them, whatever you want to call it. Maybe this tree is why everything has gone wrong this year. Maybe it's destroying all the healthy trees aboveground. Remember the first Field Day?"

"The leaf tornado," Vera said.

"Right," Pretia continued, "and the leaves that smothered Leo, and the branch that hit Castor, and then the Tree of Ecrof looking black and withered, not to mention what happened to Petros, who fell while hanging streamers. The trees are attacking the students because of *this* tree. It's making them do it."

"Why?" Rovi asked.

"Something to do with the temple?" Vera asked.

It looked as if a horrible realization had dawned on Pretia. "What did Cassandra tell us the day we arrived?"

"That we'd have to do foundational training instead of real sports," Rovi said.

"Come on," Pretia snapped. "Not that. What did she tell us about the temples? What does *everyone* say about how they were built?"

Vera rolled her eyes. "The gods' own grana made the temples rise? You believe that?"

"Yes," Pretia said. "The evidence is right here."

Rovi and Vera looked at her, confused.

"Grana made the temples rise. Grana built the temples. And what's happened to Julius, Leo, and the rest of the students?"

"They've lost their grana," Rovi said slowly.

"Somehow, someone or something is stealing their grana," Pretia said.

Now all three of them looked at the staff glowing in the center of the tree.

"Is that why it's glowing?" Rovi asked. "Because of the students' grana?"

“Pretia!” Vera exclaimed. “Do you think that’s what’s happening to Julius? Do you think his grana is making the temple rise?”

“It sounds impossible, but I do. And we have to stop it.”

“You’re right,” Rovi said quietly. “We know at least one other person saw this evil tree—my dad. This is where he wound up after he went into the Self-Splitter. This tree must have tried to steal his grana. It must have *succeeded* in stealing his grana. That’s why he was never the same.” Then he paused. “And that’s why he wanted to kill it.” Relief coursed through Rovi’s body. His father hadn’t been out of his mind. He’d been trying to save everyone. He looked from Vera to Pretia. “Let’s finish what he started.”

“How?” Vera asked.

“We need to get the staff,” Rovi said.

“And destroy it,” Pretia added.

All three kids looked over the gaping cavern to the tree. “The question is,” Rovi said, “how do we get there?” The tree was the length of a basketball court away. And in between was a deep cavern.

“There has to be a way,” Pretia said.

“I don’t know,” Vera said. “It looks impossible.”

“Impossible?” Rovi said. The word had given him an idea. “Well, there’s one way to deal with that.”

Vera laughed. “The fact that something is impossible means there is no way to do it.”

“I guess you weren’t paying attention to Satis,” Rovi said. “On the first day of his class, he told us that visualization makes the impossible possible.”

“So what are you saying?” Vera asked. “You think if we can visualize being able to cross this enormous hole, we’ll be able to do it?”

“Yes,” Rovi said. “That’s exactly what I’m saying. Are you saying you’re too scared to try?”

Vera didn’t reply.

"Or maybe you're worried that you're not good enough at visualization," Rovi added.

Vera's eyes flashed with competitive fire. "I'm good enough. So what's your plan?"

Rovi's mind started churning. "Well, first of all, we're going to need to work together. And we're going to have to believe we can do this."

"Why?" Pretia asked.

"Because," Rovi explained, "we're going to do a linked visualization, just like Satis taught us. We are going to be a team."

He saw Pretia's jaw tense and fear creep into her eyes. "Pretia," Rovi said, placing a hand on her shoulder. "You can do this."

Pretia shook her head. Rovi knew what she was thinking. "You're not going to hurt anyone," he said. "This is not a competition. This is teamwork." He looked straight into her eyes. "Pretia, you have to do this."

"Since when did you become Mr. Teamwork?" she said. "I thought you were a solo operator."

"Since it started to matter," Rovi said. "You said it yourself: We need to kill the tree. And . . ." He paused. There was something else. Something even more important. "And," Rovi began again, "if we do this, we can clear my father's name."

Pretia hesitated. "I can't," she said. "I can't use—"

"Pretia, this is not the time to worry about what you can and can't do. You need to help. For me. And for the school."

Pretia glanced around the cavern. For a moment, Rovi thought she was going to object. Then she took a deep breath. "Okay," Pretia said. "I'm in."

Rovi did not break eye contact with Pretia. "And," he said, "you have to try your hardest. Promise?"

"Promise," Pretia said.

"Now what?" Vera said.

Rovi's heart sank. He was all out of ideas. He knew they needed to work together. He knew they needed to do a shared visualization, but as to what they should visualize, he was totally lost.

A loud groan echoed through the cavern. "What's that?" Pretia said.

Vera was staring out over the gaping space toward the tree. "It's glowing brighter than before," she said.

The same groan echoed again. Then dirt began to rain down from the ceiling of the cavern as the columns rose higher.

The whole room shook as more dirt and debris fell. Then, as quickly as it had started, the noise and movement stopped and the cavern was still. "How are we going to get across to the tree?" Rovi asked. "We've got to do it soon so we can get out of here."

Vera was staring at the roof. "Look!" she said. "Vines."

Rovi followed her gaze. Dozens of vines were now dangling down between the columns. "The columns must break them loose," Rovi said.

"We can swing," Vera said.

"But those are the tree's vines," Pretia said, sounding horrified.

"And they're totally out of reach," Rovi said.

"If I stand on one of your shoulders, I think I can jump to the closest one, then I can grab one of you and swing you over to the next vine," Vera said.

Rovi looked up. The closest vine looked out of reach, even if Vera were to stand on his shoulders and execute a decent jump. Then he looked down. And if she managed that somehow and then somehow was able to grab his hand, he would be swinging over an unknowable plunge, supported only by Vera's grip on his arm. "I don't know," he said.

"I thought the idea was to visualize the impossible," Vera said. Her face was determined. "That's what we're going to do."

She held out her hands. "And we don't need any tools or props or dumb sticks to do this. Satis said it was possible to do this just by holding hands. So that's what has to happen."

Rovi took one of Vera's hands and one of Pretia's. He closed his eyes. He was Pallas Myrios's son. He could do this! It took him a moment to conjure a perfect image of the cavern, the columns, the vines, and the distant tree. And when he did, he discovered that Pretia was already there, perfectly poised. Vera was the last to arrive in their shared imagination. She appeared several times, then faded away. Rovi could feel her hand sweating in his.

"It's only practice," he whispered. "Deep breath."

Then Vera was with them.

"Okay," she said. "Let's do this." She climbed onto Rovi's shoulders. Even though they were really still standing next to each other on the ledge, he could feel the weight of her feet. "One, two, three—" He felt more pressure as Vera bent her knees, preparing to jump. She took off, her arms flailing for the vine. She missed. She began to fall. All three opened their eyes.

Vera was furious. "Again," she said. She squeezed Rovi's hand hard as she shut her eyes. Just like last time, Vera was the final one to arrive in their shared visualization. Once more, she climbed onto Rovi's shoulders. Once more, she jumped. And once more, she missed the vine.

She broke out of the visualization. Sweat was beading down her forehead. "Again," she insisted.

Once more, the same thing happened.

"Let's take a break," Rovi suggested when they all opened their eyes.

"Maybe I should jump first," Pretia suggested. "Maybe that would work better."

"No way," Vera snapped. "This was my idea. I'm not going to fail."

"I really think we should take a break," Rovi said.

"No," Vera barked, slamming her eyes shut and squeezing

Rovi's hand so hard it felt as if she might break his fingers. This time, when Vera finally entered the visualization, her image flickered in and out of focus like a bad projection.

She got onto Rovi's shoulders. But she couldn't make herself jump. She opened her eyes, dropped Rovi's and Pretia's hands, and stormed away in the direction of the beach.

"She's making it harder and harder for herself," Pretia said. "The more frustrated she gets, the worse she does. Let me talk to her and see if I can get her to calm down and focus."

"How?" Rovi asked.

"I'm going to tell her I have grana and that I'm going to use it to cross this cave."

"Why's that going to work?"

"Because Vera is motivated by competition. And if she wants to measure up to me, she is going to have to figure out a way to relax and do so."

"Whoa," Rovi said. "That's wild enough to work."

Pretia crossed to where Vera stood and put a hand on her friend's shoulder. He watched them conferring. After a moment, the girls returned. Pretia was smiling. Vera had a determined look on her face.

"Did you know?" she asked Rovi.

"Yes," he said. "I've seen her grana. It's amazing."

"We'll see," Vera said. She took a deep breath. Then she did something Rovi realized he'd never seen her do before a competition. She smiled. "I got this," she replied.

She took his hand. They closed their eyes. And in no time, they were in the shared visualization. Vera stood on Rovi's shoulders. She jumped off and caught the closest vine. She built momentum and swung back. Then she grabbed for Rovi's hand at the same moment that he jumped to reach hers. Their hands connected. She lifted him, swinging him out over the ledge and up until he could catch the next vine. Soon Rovi was swinging vine to vine ahead of Vera.

Then Vera went back for Pretia and did the same, grabbing her as she jumped and swinging her up to catch the vine next to her. Now Pretia was following Rovi, swinging over the cavern. Finally, Vera followed.

Once they had all arrived safely at the tree, they opened their eyes.

"Wow," Rovi said, "we did it."

"We need to visualize it again before we attempt it for real," Pretia said. "And then again and again, so everything is perfect."

Five more times, they executed the visualization perfectly—Vera leaping from Rovi's shoulders, swinging out and back, and grabbing first Rovi, then Pretia, so they could grab a vine of their own. And each of the five times, all three of them made it.

"Okay," Vera said after the fifth successful run-through. "Are you guys ready?"

Rovi and Pretia nodded in unison.

"Let's do this!" Vera said.

She and Rovi moved to the edge of the ledge, and just like every other time in their mental run-throughs, she vaulted onto his shoulders and leaped for the closest vine. Rovi did his best to ignore that his pulse was suddenly racing. He reached up and felt Vera grasp his wrist. Her grip was much stronger than it had been in his mind. She swung him forward and he caught the next vine before she let him go to swing on his own. Then she went back for Pretia.

Using all his power, he swung to the next, and the next. Then he did something he hadn't done during their mental practice. He looked down. All he saw was an unknowable blackness, a certainly deadly plunge. For a split second, it felt as if his heart had stopped. He felt his grip slip on the vine he was holding.

"Rovi!" Pretia called from where she was hanging a vine behind Vera. "Careful."

I can't do this. The words were out of his mouth before he knew what he was saying.

“Yes, you can!” Pretia cried. “You got this!”

I can’t. “I can’t,” Rovi said. The doubt had taken over. He was frozen. He wasn’t going to be able to hold on much longer. His hands were aching. His palms were sweating. It would be so easy to let go.

“You have to push yourself,” Pretia called.

“I am,” Rovi said. What did she know? What did anyone know about how hard Rovi tried? Why did they assume he wasn’t doing his best?

“You can do better,” Pretia said. “I know you can.”

Rovi looked down into the blackness below. How far would it be to fall? What would happen when he couldn’t hold on anymore? How long would it take?

“Rovi, please!” This time it was Vera, not Pretia, who was speaking.

He could see Vera’s arms starting to tremble. She’d been hanging longer than him or Pretia, and she’d done all the hard work in hoisting them both up. But he couldn’t move. His body wouldn’t let him.

“Rovi, you have to try,” Vera urged. “If we do this, we clear your dad’s name.”

“I can’t—” he began.

“And we save Julius,” Pretia added. “And Leo and Iskander and all the rest.”

Rovi took a deep breath. He gripped the vine with all the strength that he had left. He pumped his legs and swung forward. He grabbed the next vine. He kept his eyes on where he was going, never allowing them to stray downward. And soon he was swinging freely between the columns on his way to the base of the tree.

When he landed on the ground in the tangle of roots, he looked back across the impossible distance he had crossed. “Wow,” he whispered.

Vera had already swung Pretia up onto a vine and the girls were now making their way across the cavern, side by side. Neither of them looked panicked or anxious. In fact, they both seemed to be enjoying the adventure.

Vera landed first, letting go of the final vine and landing right next to Rovi.

"I can't believe we did it," Rovi said. And then he realized how close he'd come to ruining the whole endeavor. "I'm sorry," he said.

"For what?" Vera asked.

"I almost let you down."

"It was a team effort," Vera said. "We did it together."

Pretia had now grabbed the final vine and had pumped her legs forcefully for the last push. When she was safely over the cavern she let go, landing closer to the tree than either Rovi or Vera.

But before Rovi or Vera could make their way over to her, the tree moved. The branches trembled and creaked. They reached out like tentacles and wrapped around Pretia.

"What's going on?" Vera cried.

There was an empty space where Pretia had just been standing.

Rovi's jaw was quivering. "The tree got Pretia," he said. "She's inside the tree."

27

PRETIA

THE STAFF

EVERYTHING WAS A BLUR. IN FACT, EVERYTHING was actually blurry. Pretia was having trouble seeing a few feet in front of her. It was hard to tell what was happening.

One moment she'd been swinging from the vines, working her way across the cavern before alighting on the ground in front of the tree. And the next—well, she wasn't exactly sure what the next was.

She couldn't see the tree. But no . . . that wasn't precisely true. She could see the branches all around her—but she couldn't see the whole thing. It was like . . . It was like . . . It was like she was inside the tree. But how? What had happened?

Pretia wriggled from side to side with no luck. She tried to take a step forward, but she was stuck. Indeed, every time she tried to move, it was as if the tree gripped her tighter. It was as if the tree was holding her. It was as if she was the tree's prisoner.

She looked up. She could see the staff glowing overhead. In fact, everything around her seemed to be glowing. If she could only grab the staff, she could destroy it.

Pretia dipped her chin. Now she could see that the tree had wound itself around her wrists, holding her like handcuffs. But even stranger, her hands seemed to be glowing. Not just her hands—the glow seemed to be coming from within her.

"Pretia!"

She could hear Rovi's voice but she couldn't see him.

Once more, she looked up. There again was the Staff of Suffering, glowing overhead. She attempted to stretch out her arms. The tree tightened its grip.

"Pretia!" This time it was Vera's voice.

Pretia squinted through the cage of vines that imprisoned her. She could barely see the cave. She could barely see anything at all. The mysterious glow surrounding her had obscured her vision.

She could hear her friends. But their voices sounded distant. Her head felt fuzzy, like she'd drank too much of Anara's lavender tea. "She's inside the tree," Rovi said.

"I can see her," Vera replied.

"What is that all around her?" Rovi said.

"Pretia, can you hear us?" Vera called.

Pretia tried to reply. But opening her mouth was so hard.

"Can you reach the staff?" Rovi called out.

Again, Pretia tried to respond. But her head felt so heavy. It just seemed simpler to close her eyes.

"It looks like she's fallen asleep." Vera's voice was so distant now, like something out of a dream.

"Why would she be sleeping?" His voice, too, seemed very far away. "Pretia! Pretia! Can you hear me?"

Yes, Pretia said. Or perhaps she only thought she'd said it. Because talking seemed too difficult.

"She's nodding off," Vera said. "What's happening to her?"

"Wake up," Rovi said. "Pretia!" But his cries were interrupted by a terrible shaking. The whole room around Pretia seemed to be moving and groaning. She didn't care. All she wanted to do was keep her eyes closed.

“The temple is rising faster!” Vera cried.

“It must be Pretia’s grana. It’s stealing her grana and it’s using it to grow more quickly,” Rovi said.

The urgency in his voice exhausted Pretia. Why couldn’t her friends be quiet? Couldn’t they tell she just wanted to rest?

Pretia felt a weird tingle, like liquid was trickling out of her hands and head. The staff glowed brighter. Then there was another loud groan. The cavern shook again.

“Pretia!” Vera screamed. “You need to get out!”

Pretia opened her eyes. For a moment, her friends were quiet. She could see Rovi through the maze of vines.

“Pretia,” he called, “you have to stay awake. There’s something you need to do.”

Didn’t he understand that *doing* anything was impossible? *Doing* was the last thing on earth that Pretia was going to *do*.

But Rovi was still talking like a coach at track practice. “Pretia, I know what you’re capable of. I know what you can do. Now is the time. I believe in you, Pretia.”

Pretia’s eyes were so heavy. She was trying to listen. Trying.

“Pretia, you have to use your grana. You have to use everything you’ve got. It’s now or never,” Rovi continued.

The glowing light was so nice, all purple and blue. Pretia wouldn’t have minded staring at it forever, watching it flow out of her toward that staff overhead. And wasn’t that staff pretty, too?

“Pretia, listen,” Rovi’s distant voice insisted, “you’ve got this. All you need to do is reach up and grab the staff. All you need to do is reach. I know you think your grana is cursed, but it’s not. It’s strong, stronger than anyone else’s. And it doesn’t control you. *You’re* good, so *it’s* good.”

But she couldn’t. There was no moving. No reaching.

“Step outside yourself,” Rovi called. “You need to access your shadow self.”

"What does that mean?" Pretia heard Vera ask. "That's impossible."

Pretia closed her eyes. Yes. It was impossible. And she was so exhausted.

"Pretia! Listen!" Rovi was screaming now. "Your grana is making the temple rise. If you don't use it now, you'll *lose* it! Your grana is going to bring Hurell and his temple back to Epoca."

And for a split second, the hazy fog cleared. The purple-and-blue glow turned angry.

"Her eyes are open," Vera exclaimed. "Look."

"The tree is using you to bring Hurell back," Rovi said. "You need to use your grana. You need to do the thing that only you can do. Pretia, now!"

There was a great shuddering again.

"The columns are moving fast," Vera screamed. "Hurry before it breaks all the way through."

"Only you can stop this, Pretia," Rovi said. "Only you can stop Hurell."

And suddenly Pretia wasn't in the tree anymore. She was standing back in the Hall of the Gods in Castle Airim. She was in front of Hurell's shrouded bust. She was watching in horror as a flame leaped to life in his ceremonial bowl. She was watching herself try to blow it out.

"Pretia!" Both her friends were screaming her name. But why were they here in the Hall of the Gods?

Pretia watched herself try to extinguish the flame. But her breath only made it blaze brighter. Like she was the one making it bigger. And she knew that, somehow, she had to put it out. Somehow, she would need to extinguish the fire she'd started.

If only she could reach up and grab the staff. If only she weren't held prisoner by the tree. If only she had the strength. If only she could do the impossible.

"Use your grana," Rovi shouted. "Use it!"

It took all the effort in the world, but Pretia craned her neck upward so she could see the staff. She would need to jump—and it would have to be the most powerful jump she'd ever done, higher than the one that had misfired at Epic Elite trials when she had tried to restrain her grana.

"Pretia, please," Vera cried.

One.

It was too much, but she would try.

Two.

Pretia closed her eyes, not to rest this time, but to find whatever shred of strength remained in herself.

Three.

She bent her knees just slightly. She coiled her body incrementally. She tensed. And she leaped.

From where the tree held her, Pretia watched her shadow self leap. This other Pretia burst through the branches like they were made out of twigs.

"Is she—is she—" she heard Vera stammer. "Is she stepping outside herself?"

Pretia watched as this other Pretia, the Pretia who was her but also wasn't, grabbed the staff. She felt the whole tree shaking around her, pulling her this way and that. And then, with a deafening noise, like a thousand branches breaking at once, the tree opened. And Pretia fell out on the ground at Rovi's and Vera's feet, now holding the staff in her hands.

Pretia felt the staff radiating energy. With all her might, she focused her grana and cracked the staff in two over her knee. There followed an explosion of purple-and-blue light that rose from the two halves of the staff toward the top of the cave.

The entire cave seemed to be vibrating. But it didn't shake. It hummed. It thrummed with an enormous blast of energy—a life force that rushed around the stone walls.

Pretia could feel some sort of electricity coursing through her as beams of light shot from the staff and disappeared overhead. The current of energy died out. The light extinguished. And she was holding nothing more than two large pieces of wood.

"You did it!" Rovi exclaimed. But before anyone had a chance to ask any questions, there was a terrific groan and the temple began to sink again. The three friends huddled near the base of the tree as the columns sank from the roof of the cave, plummeting into the cavern until all sign of Hurell's temple was lost belowground.

Where there once had been a cavern, now there was a solid cave floor.

Pretia stepped away from the tree, and no sooner had she done so than the tree itself began to crumble, turning to dust all around them. The branches were disintegrating as if they were made of nothing. The dust rained down on Pretia and her friends—mountains of dust. And then, in a giant gust of wind, the dust blew out through the opening of the cave to the sea, where it disappeared.

Vera was staring at Pretia, her mouth hanging open. "How did you—how did you—"

"Step outside myself?" Pretia finished. "I don't know. It's just what happens when I use my grana."

"What was all that—that energy?" Rovi asked.

"Grana," Pretia said. "That was grana."

"Yours?" Vera asked, wide-eyed.

Pretia laughed. "I might be able to step outside myself. But I'm not all-powerful or anything. I think that was the grana that was stolen from the students. I think we just expelled it from the tree."

"Where did it go?" Vera asked.

"Let's find out," Pretia said. "But first, there's one more thing we have to do." She turned toward the mouth of the cave. "Come on."

A pink dawn was rippling on the horizon, dyeing the distant water, as Pretia quickly climbed the narrow footpath she had descended hours ago, in the dark. It was easier to find her footing in the weak sunlight. In no time, she, Rovi, and Vera were up on top of the cliff.

Pretia toed up to the edge and held both halves of the staff over her shoulders like javelins. She pulled her arms back and concentrated as hard as she could. Her arms sprang forward like a catapult and the split staff flew. The pieces rose upward, arcing over the beach, out to sea. And then they fell, plummeting downward with the swiftness of an arrow, where they collided with a distant rock, shattering into a thousand pieces.

"Good throw," Rovi said.

"Thanks," Pretia replied.

"So?" Rovi asked. "What did it feel like?"

"Feel?" Pretia said.

"To really use your grana."

Pretia could feel a broad smile break across her face. She stretched her arms wide. She felt the most relaxed she had since before she'd accidentally pushed Davos off the cliff. She felt as if a great weight had been lifted from her shoulders. "Amazing," she said. "But—" She broke off.

"What?" Vera asked. "Is something wrong?"

"No," Pretia replied. "It's just that my grana was only a small part of our adventure. What really mattered was that we did this together. You know, this probably sounds unbelievable, but I've never really had friends before."

"I guess there are downsides to being a princess," Rovi said.

"I'm serious," Pretia insisted. "This is the first time I've actually worked together on anything with kids my own age. And that was better than using grana."

Rovi held up his hand. Vera did, too. And Pretia high-fived them in turn. Then she yawned. "I'm exhausted."

"Me too," Vera said. "But I need to find Julius. I need to see if he's okay. He's never going to believe what we just did. And," she added, "he would never have been able to do that kind of linked visualization himself, I bet."

"Why not?" Rovi asked.

"Because he's a Realist," Vera said. "No imagination. But he's still my brother, no matter what."

"Even though he's been so mean to you?" Rovi asked.

"I told you before, you don't understand siblings," Vera explained.

"Which reminds me, Rovi," Pretia said. "What was that long story you were going to tell me about your brother?"

"Brother?"

"The one you said gave you your Grana Gleams?"

Rovi looked down at his sneakers. "I don't have a brother," he said. "I stole these shoes."

"For real?" Pretia said.

"I really did." He looked at Pretia anxiously.

"Well," she said. "That's a way more interesting story than getting them as a birthday present from my nurse. So you win."

Now it was Rovi's turn to yawn. "I don't know about you guys, but I need to sleep."

"Go ahead," Pretia said. She was exhausted but exhilarated. She had used her grana—for something *good*. She felt her grana rooted in her in a new way, no longer held at bay but part of every piece of her. She couldn't wait to tell her uncle that she wouldn't be a disappointment to the royal family anymore.

They walked away from the cliff in silence and crossed through the Decision Woods. Pretia's feet felt heavy and she could sense how exhausted her friends were beside her. At the stadium they parted ways.

Pretia pushed on and climbed the hill to the Trainers Towers, hurrying past two Junior Trainers who tried to stop her. Adrenaline was pumping in her veins and she easily evaded them. She sprinted up the stairs and pounded on her uncle's door. She pounded again. And when he didn't answer, she opened the door and stepped inside.

"Uncle Janos," she called with the last of her strength. "Uncle Janos?"

There was movement in the back of the quarters. A door opened, briefly showing Pretia a roaring fire lighting up what must be Janos's bedroom. Her uncle stepped out, shut the door behind him, and rushed to Pretia's side.

She fell into his arms, pressing her face into his rich blue dressing gown.

Janos pressed his powerful hands on her shoulders and pulled her away from him. "What is wrong, favorite niece? It's very early. What are you doing awake?"

"The tree—the temple. My grana!" The story came tumbling out so erratically that Pretia had to start over several times before any of it made sense to her or to Janos. And once she had told it clearly, Janos made her start over from the beginning and repeat everything.

When she was done, he looked at her with a terrified expression. "What if something had happened to you?" he said. "What if you had completely lost your grana, or worse?"

"But I didn't," Pretia said. "I used my grana."

"Which means you had it all along," Janos said. "Why were you hiding it?"

Pretia took a deep breath. Suddenly the adrenaline that had been driving her since she'd destroyed the tree seemed to abandon her. "That's a complicated story, Uncle. But I thought my grana was cursed. The first time I used it I—" She stopped. It was difficult to admit what she'd done.

"You what?"

Pretia looked down at her lap. "I stepped out of myself and I accidentally pushed one of the castle kids. He broke his arm. I hurt him, so I thought my grana was bad. Wrong, somehow."

Janos looked stunned. "The first time you used your grana you stepped out of yourself?"

Pretia nodded. "It's supposed to be impossible, right?"

Her uncle took a deep breath. "That's what most people say. But I've seen it done once before."

"By Rovi's dad?"

"No, Pretia, not through the use of some silly machine. For real."

"Who—" Pretia began.

Janos placed his hands on her shoulders. "By your aunt Syspara," he said. "But that is a story for another time. All I can tell you now is that your grana is not cursed, but it's very powerful. And you will have to work very hard to learn to control it."

Pretia couldn't stop the smile that erupted on her face.

Janos gave her shoulders a squeeze. "And what's more, you saved the school. You're not just a champion, Niece, you're a hero. You are a truly exceptional child." But then Janos's face clouded. "Although what you did was brave, it was also foolish," he said. "You put yourself in grave danger. And I would never be able to forgive myself if something had happened to you." He kissed the top of her head.

"I'm so tired," she said, staggering to her feet. "I'm so—"

Janos led her to a pile of blue velvet cushions. "Sleep," he said. "You've earned it. You, Pretia, will be the greatest leader Epoca has ever had. You . . ."

But Pretia didn't hear the rest. Her eyes were closed. And just before she fell asleep, she finally fully understood the image in her Grana Book. The moons had continued to trouble her. But now she knew—they were her grana, in the two different directions it could have gone. One powerful and luminescent, the other on the verge of being snuffed out forever.

◆

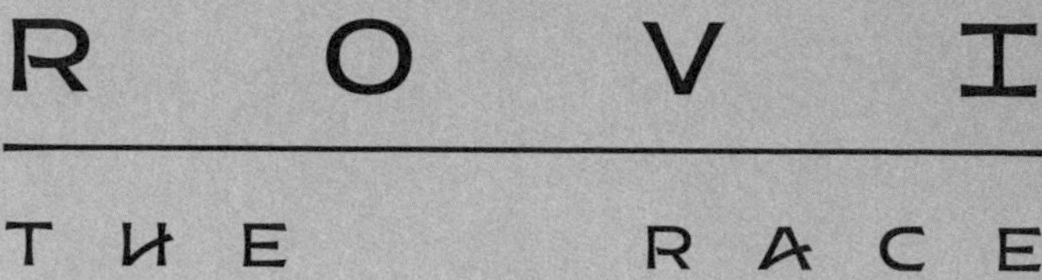

28 ROVI

THE RACE

ROVI WAS BACK IN PHOENIS, UNDER THE BRIDGE. He could hear the muddy river slipping by and the first horn announcing the market was open.

"Rovi!"

Rovi rolled over, swatting away Issa's arm.

"Rovi!"

"Go away," he moaned. It was a sacred code among Star Stealers never to wake each other up except in the case of grave danger. They all knew how precious sleep was, especially in their living conditions. If someone was managing to sleep despite the heat and noise, he should be left to do so.

"Rovi!" Issa had grabbed Rovi by the arms and was pulling him upright.

"Issa, stop!" Rovi said, shaking free. He opened his eyes. He was face-to-face not with Issa, leader of the Star Stealers, but Vera. He was in his room in Ecrof. The sun was shining through the window. The room was cool. The sheets and pillows were clean and fresh.

"Rovi," Vera said, "you've been asleep all day."

"What time is it?"

"Dinner just finished," she said.

At the word *dinner*, Rovi's stomach grumbled. "I need food," he said, swinging his legs out of bed.

"Wait," Vera said, pulling him back. "There's something I need to show you. We can eat later. Get dressed."

"But I'm hungry," Rovi said.

"Trust me," Vera said.

The excited edge in her voice made Rovi willing to do what she said. He pulled on his Grana Gleams and followed Vera out of the Temple of Dreams. She set a brisk pace so he didn't even have time to give the vending machines a longing glance before they were out the door, heading down the hill, in the direction of the Panathletic Stadium.

When Rovi figured out where they were headed, he stopped. "Wait, Vera, no." He didn't want to go anywhere near the Tree of Ecrof.

"Come *on*," Vera said, yanking his arm.

Reluctantly, he followed. Vera was sprinting now, dragging Rovi along with her. Together they raced through the entrance to the stadium. Without warning, Vera stopped. Rovi stumbled, tripped, and hit the ground. "Vera! What—" But the words caught in his mouth. Because right in front of him was the Tree of Ecrof in all its colorful glory.

"The tree," Rovi gasped.

It was healthy. In fact, it looked even more radiant than it had when they'd arrived at Ecrof many months ago. The leaves were glittering green, reflecting the bright sun overhead. The branches looked strong and solid—a rich golden-brown color.

"I can't believe it," Rovi said. The overnight transformation was miraculous.

"We did that," Vera said proudly.

Rovi rushed to the base of the tree. He stomped on the ground, trying to find any sign of the black rot. The ground was solid, perfect, as if it had never been sick in the first place.

“We did this,” Vera repeated. “And there’s more. I saw Julius last night. He recognized me. He’s getting better.”

“Really?” Rovi said.

“He stood up and walked around. His grana is returning.”

“That purple-and-blue explosion,” Rovi said. “Pretia was right.”

“Exactly,” Vera said. “That *was* the grana returning from the tree.”

“Wow, we need to tell her.” Rovi looked around. “Where is she, anyway?”

“Satis told me she spent the night in her uncle’s quarters,” Vera said.

“She’s probably exhausted,” Rovi said. “I mean, she almost lost her grana.” An involuntary shudder passed through him as he remembered Pretia trapped in the tree, fading in and out of consciousness. And then he remembered the painful realization that had hit him in front of the underground tree in the cavern. His father hadn’t lost his mind. The strangler fig had stolen part of his grana. That was the change. That’s why Pallas Myrios had never been the same.

“There you are!”

Rovi and Vera turned, startled by another voice in the stadium. “We’ve been looking everywhere for you.” Cassandra was rushing toward them. She was dressed as she had been the day before, in her head-to-toe Dreamers competition kit.

“Where have you two been?” Cassandra asked. She sounded exasperated.

“Nowhere,” Rovi and Vera said in unison.

“I was starting to panic.”

“Why?” Rovi asked.

Their House Captain gave them a funny look. “Well, anyway,” she said. “As you can see, the Tree of Ecrof somehow got better overnight, which means we are going to finish yesterday’s Field Day this evening.”

“Tonight?” Rovi said.

“Janos’s orders. He says we need to redo the steeplechase.” She looked at Rovi. "I went to the TheraCenter to check on you last night, but you were gone."

"Yeah," Rovi said, "sorry about that. I feel better."

Cassandra narrowed her eyes. "How much better?"

"I'm fine," Rovi said, holding up the wrist that the Mineral Sleeve had healed. "See?"

His House Captain stepped forward and examined his wrist. "So your wrist was like this yesterday?" she asked. "And you stayed in the TheraCenter?"

"I didn't want to risk it," Rovi said.

"Rovi—" Cassandra began in an annoyed tone.

"It doesn't matter now, does it?" Vera said. "The steeplechase was basically canceled."

Cassandra looked from one of them to the other. "I'm not sure what's up with you two, but listen up. We are two points behind the Realists. If we get first and second place, we can win. I want you both to run. Are you up for it?"

"Yes," Rovi said eagerly. "Totally."

"Okay," Cassandra said. "And I expect you both to make that podium. Now get prepared." And without another word, she left them in the stadium.

"So, Vera," Rovi said, "now can I eat something? Since I'm going to beat you on the podium and all."

"In your dreams," Vera said. "But since I want to win fair and square, we can't have you passing out. Let's get you some food."

They raced back to the Temple of Dreams and headed straight for the cafeteria. In no time, Rovi was seated in front of a plate of honey chicken, fennel sausage, and pistachio cakes. He finished three entire plates before he felt the familiar ache in his stomach that told him he'd eaten enough.

All around him, the temple was buzzing with Dreamers getting ready for the final event. A few kids patted Rovi on the back and wished him luck. Others left him alone, clearly worried that they might jinx him.

Adira and Virgil both gave him hugs and chanted, "You can do it, Star Stealer!"

"Hey," Rovi said.

"Sorry," Adira muttered.

"That's okay. I guess I'll always be part Star Stealer." Rovi beamed, suddenly proud of his old life back in Phoenis. It had given him the skills he knew he would need to win the steeplechase. He was going to win the Field Day for the Dreamers. No more was he the son of the Tree Killer. He knew his father was a hero, and that's all that mattered. And even better, he was a hero, too. He'd saved the Tree of Ecrof. If only Pallas Myrios could have known.

Now he knew what the image in his Grana Book meant—the picture of the two snow-covered mountains and the smaller, greener hill. His parents had expected him to do something great. They guessed that even before he was born. They'd made him this book and they let him know that they were always watching over him. They were here, somewhere, on Corae, even if it was only in his heart. He understood the entire picture now. The dead flowers were the past and the trio of birds—that was him, Vera, and Pretia. The three of them were bonded together, embarking on a new start.

He ran his fingers over the two snowy mountains. Today, he would race for his parents.

A special hunting horn blared across campus, summoning the students down to the track. Since there was only one event, there would be no feast, just a race, plain and simple.

Rovi joined the throng of Dreamers heading for the stadium. He wore his original Grana Gleams, the ones he had stolen at the market, the ones that reminded him of who he was and where he came from. They would bring him victory.

Vera was at his side. They walked in silence, trying not to address the fact that although they both wanted to win for the Dreamers, they also wanted to beat each other.

But their silence was interrupted at the entrance to the stadium, where Pretia was waiting. The minute she saw Rovi and Vera, she rushed over to them and flung her arms around them both at once.

"Careful, Pretia," Adira said, who was walking right behind them. "You don't want to hurt our runners."

"Pretia!" Rovi exclaimed. "How are you?" He knew he was staring at her. But he couldn't help himself.

"I'm fine," she said. "I slept forever."

"And your grana . . ." Rovi began.

"The same," Pretia said. "Or maybe better. Now that I used it, it seems stronger."

Vera was giving her a curious look. "Stronger?"

"I can't describe it," Pretia said. "It's just a feeling I have."

"Hey, look, it's the princess and her misfit crew." Rovi turned at the sound of Castor's voice. "Don't block the entrance."

"Shut up, Castor," Pretia said. "My friends are going to win the day for the Dreamers."

"I'm not holding my breath," he said, barreling past with his Realist buddies. Then he turned. "It's not like you can even hope to win against Julius."

"I don't know about that," Vera said. "I think you'll be surprised."

"Go on," Castor said. "Surprise me."

They stepped into the stadium. The bleachers were already packed.

"There's Julius," Vera exclaimed. "He looks even stronger than last night."

"And Iskander," Pretia added.

"They're all here," Rovi said. "All the sick students." He slapped Pretia on the back. "What does it feel like to be both a princess and a hero?"

He heard Pretia take a deep breath. "I'm not a hero," she said. "It's all of us. You, me, and Vera are all heroes."

Cassandra appeared and clamped her hands over Rovi's and Vera's wrists. "You two need to warm up. You can all chat later."

Vera hesitated.

"Come on," Cassandra said. "We need the best prep we can get."

"Hold on," Vera said. She looked down at Pretia's shoes. Like Rovi, she was also wearing her gold Grana Gleams. "Can you run in those?"

"Of course," Pretia said.

"Pretia's taking my place," Vera declared.

"What?" Pretia and Cassandra said in unison.

"Pretia is taking my place," Vera said. "She's going to run for me."

"But Pretia isn't a runner," Cassandra said. "And, according to her, Pretia doesn't even have grana."

Vera whirled around so she was face-to-face with the House Captain. "She has the strongest grana of anyone I know. And what's more—she's the only person I know who can actually step outside herself. And trust me, that's what it's going to take to beat Julius."

"I thought *you* wanted to beat your brother," Cassandra said.

"I do," Vera replied. "But I also believe in Dreamers. I want us to win. Come on, Pretia," she said, "I'll lend you my racing kit. But first, you have to tell me something."

They waited until Cassandra moved out of earshot.

"Why were you afraid to use your grana?"

Pretia glanced at Rovi.

"Tell her," Rovi said.

"I was afraid of it," Pretia said. "I thought if I used it I would hurt someone."

"Why?" Vera asked.

"Yeah, why?" Rovi echoed. "You never told me."

"I did something stupid back at the castle. The first day I got my grana, I couldn't control it and accidentally pushed someone off a cliff playing tag. I figured my grana was cursed." That was all she was going to tell them. There was no way, especially after what they'd just been through, that she was going to mention Hurell's flame. "What I didn't understand," she continued, "was that my grana is powerful and I needed to learn to control it."

"Well, you better let it loose right now," Vera said. "Don't hold back."

"For sure," Pretia said. "One hundred percent."

As the girls dashed into a corridor of the stadium to change, Rovi followed Cassandra to the area near the track where the other two Dreamers were warming up. "I hope Vera knows what she's doing," Cassandra said.

"I think she does," Rovi replied.

A tidal wave of whispers and gasps crashed over the stadium when Pretia emerged dressed to race. The noise and speculation only got louder when she joined Rovi and began to warm up on the track. When they were warm, they walked the obstacle course together, familiarizing themselves with the water jumps and barriers.

On their way to the starting line, they walked past the bleachers. "Did your parents force the school to let you race?" Castor called.

"Ignore him," Rovi said.

"A Demigen and a Star Stealer," Castor taunted. "What a pair!"

This, Rovi couldn't let slide. He took a deep breath, then, as calmly as he could, approached Castor. "Castor," he said, "I have bad news." Rovi raised his voice so as many of the students as possible in the bleachers could hear. "You know how you think you're going to be king because your cousin doesn't have grana? Well, Pretia's got the most amazing grana in the entire land. So, sorry. I guess the throne isn't your destiny, no matter how often you visualize it."

"I—I—I . . ." Castor stammered. "I never said I wanted to rule Epoca."

“You did. I saw it in our shared visualization,” Rovi said.

“That’s not true,” Castor said.

“Keep it up, Castor,” Pretia said. “Satis told us we should practice visualizing the impossible. And if there’s one thing that I’m sure of, it’s that you aren’t going to rule Epoca.”

“Ruling is boring, anyway,” Castor said. “Kings and queens don’t compete in the Epic Games. They’re too busy with other stuff to train.”

“Well,” Rovi said, “I think that’s about to change. I think Pretia is going to be an Epic Athlete, for sure.”

“Pretia.” Castor snickered. “Don’t make me laugh.”

“Just wait and watch from the sidelines,” Rovi said. “I think after the race you won’t have much to laugh about.”

He walked off, Pretia at his side. “So, that should shut your cousin up.”

“What should what?” Pretia replied. She’d barely heard a word of what he’d said to Castor. She was in a zone Rovi had never seen before, a place of focus and concentration. He realized that for the first time, he was going to see Pretia try at sports—try hard.

The Dreamers’ chant rose from the stands. Rovi’s adrenaline started to pump. His heart accelerated. He glanced at the bleachers and saw the ocean of purple banners, the sea of purple faces and purple tracksuits. He only had ears for the cheers of his teammates. He was ready.

The stands fell momentarily silent as Janos blew his whistle.

“First of all, let us welcome back all of our students to Ecrof,” he boomed. “We have missed you.” There was an explosion of cheering from all the students. “And now, I’m sure that you can all see our magnificent tree has made a remarkable turnaround overnight and is back to its former glory. It’s an Ecrof miracle.” Rovi watched as Janos caught Pretia’s eye and winked. “I’m sure there is a hero somewhere who knows exactly what happened. But for now, let us all simply enjoy the splendor of our mascot.” A loud cheer burst from all the students at once. Janos silenced them with another blast of his whistle.

"And," he bellowed, "the revitalization of our tree means that we can conclude this year's final Field Day with the steeplechase that was interrupted yesterday by extraordinary events. As you know, the standings have House Reila leading by two points. Good luck to all. Runners, take your places."

Rovi and Pretia lined up next to each other at the start. Julius was farther down, towering over the rest of the field. Rovi could feel an electric current coursing from the stands down to the track and up through his shoes into his legs and to his heart.

Janos stepped onto the field, preparing to start the race.

"On your marks," he said. "Get set. Go."

They took off. Rovi's feet felt as sure as ever. They guided him over the first water barrier. They didn't touch down on the other side. Instead, they carried him through the air so that he flew between obstacles. He soared.

Rovi knew that he had never run better. He passed over obstacles and barriers like he was jogging on flat ground. He glanced down once and saw that his sneakers were a gold blur. He could sense the entire field at his back chasing him.

There were four obstacles left. He made a turn and headed for the Tree of Ecrof. And then Pretia caught up to him. She was pacing him evenly, in lockstep as they leaped over a water barrier. Rovi could sense what was about to happen before it did. Pretia was at his side, and then she was ahead of him—*at the same time*. If he hadn't been racing, he would have stopped short to watch as the Princess of Epoca stepped outside herself for the last three obstacles.

Rovi stumbled slightly. But it didn't matter, Pretia was too far ahead to catch. She finished the race three obstacles ahead of him. At the finish line her two sides collided, reuniting.

When Rovi finished the race, Pretia was waiting for him, an ecstatic smile on her face.

"You did it," he said, between breaths.

"And so did you," she said, beaming. "We both beat Julius. We won Field Day."

Rovi took Pretia's hand and raised it over her head in a victory salute. The minute he did so, a group of Dreamers raced from the stands and rushed her. Along with Rovi, they hoisted Pretia onto their shoulders and paraded her around the track for a victory lap. When they passed Castor and his crew, Rovi slowed the procession.

"What did I tell you?" Rovi shouted over the cheers.

For once Castor didn't have a reply. He was stupefied, staring at his cousin with a look of awe on his face.

29

PRETIA

THE SECRET

SOMETIMES THE LAST WEEKS AT ECROF FELT like a dream. First the adventure with the strangler fig, and then the steeplechase. It all seemed too fantastical to be true. Pretia had destroyed the Staff of Suffering . . . and she'd won the steeplechase.

She, Rovi, and Julius had been neck and neck going into the final three obstacles when it happened—Pretia stepped out of herself. She'd watched herself race away, leap over a water pit, clear a hurdle, and nagivate the final barrier to cross the finish line first.

The second she'd done so, she found herself under a pile of Dreamers who'd rushed from the stands to congratulate her. Pretia had helped clinch the Field Day for her house—and she'd used her grana without anyone getting hurt.

Now her name was engraved in gold letters in the trophy hall of the Temple of Dreams. There was even a little star next to it, indicating that not only had Pretia won her event at Field Day, she'd done it as a recruit, a feat so remarkable it received its own separate commendation.

For the last week, Ecrof had been emptying out. The ship that brought the recruits to the island was making journeys back and forth to mainland Epoca, transporting one class at a time. The recruits, the last to arrive, would also be the last to leave.

Pretia liked the empty campus. It allowed her to truly enjoy herself for the first time, letting loose on the Infinity Track and sprinting full tilt around the Panathletic Stadium. It was as if she hadn't really been at Ecrof at all during her first year. She'd only been pretending.

Pretia stood in her bedroom and looked out over the campus. The ship had returned the night before from bringing the second years back to the mainland. Today, she and her fellow recruits would set sail.

Her bags were packed. Her Ecrof gear was stored for the upcoming term. Part of her wanted to stay longer and get to experience all the magic of the academy she'd forbidden herself because she'd feared her grana. But mostly, Pretia was ready to go back to Castle Airim. She couldn't wait to tell Anara about the island and about Hurell's temple.

More than anything, Pretia was longing to get back to her parents, to see the look on her mother's face when she admitted that she actually had grana, and not just any grana, but grana that people thought was exceptional. Maybe this news would erase those worried glances and sad expressions that often filled the queen's eyes.

Pretia took a last glance around the room. How strange that not too long ago, she'd been anxious to leave Ecrof forever. Now she was already excited to get back.

Carrying a small backpack, she descended the stairs to the cafeteria, where she found Rovi loading up his Ecrof backpack from one of the vending machines. "You know there's food on the boat," she said.

"Just in case," Rovi replied.

"Maybe it's the fancy castle food he's worried about." Pretia turned and saw that Vera had appeared behind them at the machines. "Maybe he's worried he won't find a single thing to eat in the entire royal kitchen."

"Impossible!" Rovi laughed.

Pretia had been delighted when Rovi had accepted her invitation to spend the summer at Castle Airim. How could he return to sleeping on the streets of Phoenis after nine months at Ecrof? She wouldn't let it happen.

Once Rovi had stuffed his backpack with snacks, Pretia and her friends headed out of the temple for the last time that year. As they passed through the trophy hall, she took a final look at her name on the wall.

"Pretty cool," Vera said, then gave Pretia a little nudge. "I'll get mine next year."

"And next year, you'll already be Epic Elite," Pretia reminded her, which made Vera beam. "Rovi, you have some catching up to do."

"Don't worry," Rovi said. "Next year, you two are in trouble. Next year I'm actually going to *try*."

"Bring it on," Pretia replied.

They descended the hill, crossed the main field, passed by the Halls of Process, and headed into the Panathletic Stadium, where the rest of the recruits had already assembled. Cleopatra Volis stood at the head of the group, ready to lead them around the Decision Woods and down to the awaiting ship.

"Later, Ecrof," Castor said, waving at the campus.

Pretia grabbed her cousin's arm. "Where's your father? Is he at the ship?"

"He's in his rooms," Castor said. "I already said goodbye."

"But I didn't," Pretia said. She couldn't leave the island without saying goodbye to her favorite uncle.

"You'll see him back at the castle over the summer," Castor said. "I'm sure we'll be dragged to visit the amazing Pretia."

"I want to say goodbye," Pretia replied. "Cleopatra, do I have time to run to the Trainers Towers?"

"Hurry," Cleopatra said. "You have ten minutes. When the second horn blasts, you need to be back here or we'll head to the ship without you."

Pretia rushed off. But not before she heard Castor mutter, "Now that she won a Field Day event, everyone has to do whatever Pretia wants."

Her cousin's gripe didn't dampen her spirits. She flew back across campus, letting the full force of her grana carry her toward the Trainers Towers. At the entrance, she glanced up to the top of the eastern tower and saw the familiar warm glow in her uncle's chambers. She raced up the stairs, hurrying as fast as she could.

She opened the door without knocking, calling her uncle's name.

Janos wasn't in his living room or the well-appointed kitchen. The door to the bedroom was slightly ajar. Pretia could see shadows flickering on the floor. She guessed three minutes had passed since she'd left the recruits.

"Uncle Janos!"

Behind the door she could hear her uncle's voice. She drew near and peeked through the slight opening.

It took her a moment to figure out what she was seeing. Her uncle Janos stood with his back to her in front of a ghostly silver ceremonial flame. He was deep in prayer, so deep he didn't hear her enter.

Behind the flame was a bust of a male god like those in the Hall of the Gods back at Castle Airim. Except that this was a god Pretia didn't recognize. It wasn't Metus, Somni, or Prosi. Which meant only one thing. Hurell.

His bust was always kept under a shroud, so Pretia had no idea what he looked like. But she had no doubt now what she was seeing. The Fallen God. A wild torrent of hair. A broad brow and deep-set eyes.

She clapped a hand over her mouth to stifle a cry. But she was too late. The sound that had escaped her lips broke her uncle's trance.

He turned and pulled the door wide. It took a moment for him to process her presence.

"Well, Pretia," Janos said in a calm voice. "Now you know."

"But, but, but . . ." was all Pretia could manage.

How could her uncle, of all people, be praying to Hurell? Why would anyone pray to Hurell?

"Uncle Janos, what are you doing?"

"Pretia, there are things about this world that you don't understand."

"But this is forbidden. It's dangerous!"

"Nothing in this world is black and white. There are not simply good gods and fallen ones. Everything is much more complex and interesting than that."

Pretia stared at the ceremonial flame. "So you knew about the temple all along."

"I did."

"And the tree?"

"That, too. You see, this is one of the beautiful quirks of our world. Who would have known that Hurell's staff was made of a strangler fig? That when Hurell received strength from prayers, the staff would grow into the miracle you saw?"

"And you made all of this happen?"

Janos let out a warm laugh. "Pretia, you imagine I have more power than I do. I'm just a man. This is the work of the gods. I made nothing happen. I only . . . allowed certain things to. In the service of divine power."

Pretia turned away so she didn't have to face Hurell's bust. "So none of this is my fault," she said. The question had been weighing on her since she'd first seen Hurell's temple. "The temple didn't return because I stupidly lit the flame to the Fallen God back at Castle Airim?"

A fresh smile broke across Janos's face. "You did that? You are a surprising young lady." Then he placed a hand on Pretia's shoulder. "I can't imagine that you lighting that flame had much to do with anything. This story has been developing since long before you were born. And one day you will understand everything."

"Understand what?"

"There's more to our world than just Dreamers and Realists."

"B-but that tree," Pretia stammered. "It was stealing students' grana to make the temple rise."

The first horn blast sounded across campus.

"And we would have found a way to return it to them when the temple rose. But you prevented that. I'm disappointed, Pretia, but also proud of you. There are amazing things in store for you. Things you can't possibly understand right now."

"Things to do with Hurell." Pretia dropped her voice to a whisper.

"Things to do with a destiny greater than simply being the Crown Princess of Epoca." He firmed up his grip on her shoulder.

Pretia's mouth opened and closed, and she struggled for a reply.

"Great and marvelous things. Things you wouldn't believe even if I told you." Janos smiled. "Now, you don't want to miss the boat and be stuck here, do you?"

He pulled her into a powerful embrace. Pretia's arms hung limp at her sides, pinned in her uncle's clutches.

"I love you more than you will ever understand, favorite niece. That much is all that's important for now."

Pretia stumbled out of the room, then out of her uncle's chambers. Her mind was racing. Too many thoughts were occurring at the same time. Her uncle—her beloved uncle—was praying to Hurell. He had tried to raise the temple. He had allowed the strangler fig to steal her fellow students' grana. And, somehow, all of this had to do with her.

It was all too much to process at once. First the adventure in the tree, then what she'd witnessed her uncle doing. Luckily, she had all summer to think things through. Maybe by the time she returned to Ecrof everything would make sense to her, just like the puzzling image in her Grana Book.

"What's wrong?" Vera said when Pretia rejoined the group in the stadium.

Pretia could only shake her head. There were no words. Not yet.

She followed the recruits the long way through the Decision Woods and down the steep cliff to the beach. The small boats had been pulled up on shore, ready to transport the recruits out to the stately ship that was bobbing out in the harbor.

Pretia watched her classmates board the rowboats.

"Pretia?" Rovi called from the stern of the boat filled with Dreamers.

She hesitated. There was one last thing she needed to do.

"Pretia!" Vera called.

"Now what?" Castor griped.

But Pretia had already darted a little way down the beach. It didn't take her long to reach the exact spot she'd stood upon a little over a week earlier—the exact spot where Cora had stood on her final departure from Corae Island. Pretia looked into the cave a final time. It was empty. She shaded her eyes. The sun was directly overhead and shone right into the opening of the cave, illuminating the place where the strangler fig had stood. That, too, was gone.

There was no tree, no temple, no staff to summon Hurell. There was only Janos in his room with his flame.

Pretia took one final look. And then, satisfied, she joined the others in the boat.

KOBE BRYANT is an Academy Award winner, a *New York Times* best-selling author, and the CEO of Granity Studios, a multimedia content creation company. He spends every day focused on creating stories that inspire the next generation of athletes to be the best versions of themselves. In a previous life, Kobe was a five-time NBA champion, two-time NBA Finals MVP, NBA MVP, and two-time Olympic gold medalist. He hopes to share what he's learned with young athletes around the world.

IVY CLAIRE is a former world-ranked athlete and a national and collegiate squash champion. She spent a decade competing internationally before turning full-time to writing. She holds a degree in classics and in a parallel life is a literary novelist. She lives in Los Angeles with her family.

GRANITY STUDIOS, LLC
GRANITYSTUDIOS.COM

Library of Congress Control Number: 2019945521
ISBN (hardcover): 9781949520071
ISBN (eBook): 9781949520088

Printed in the United States of America
1 3 5 7 9 10 8 6 4 2

Book design by Karina Granda
Cover illustration by Simone Noronha
Interior and spine illustrations by Simona Bunardzhieva
Type design by Typozon
Art direction by Sharanya Durvasula